ORWELL ON WHEELS

By
Bertrand Cote

Copyright © 2023 by Bertrand Cote

All rights reserved. No part of this publication may be reproduced, stored or transmitted in any form or by any means, electronic, mechanical, photocopying, recording, scanning, or otherwise without written per-mission from the publisher. It is illegal to copy this book, post it to a website, or distribute it by any other means without permission.

Published by: Book Writing Founders
www.bookwritingfounders.com

DEDICATION

To My Dear Wife

I write fiction because it's a way of making statements I can disown, and I write plays because dialogue is the most respectable way of contradicting myself
Tom Stoppard

Thank Jo for bearing with me for so many years

PROLOGUE

It is a black and white universe of flying saucer made of chromed car hubcaps hooked on invisible fishing wire and satin-clad extra terrestrial. A world as suspended in the ether. Right off the sci-fi imagination of Ed Wood. You, earthlings, are idiots! You are Stupid, stupid, stupid: said the martian leader. (Eros). Plan 9 from Outer Space. Eros was a transgender 50s Hollywood B Movies, martian type of deal.

This affirmation: an appeal to something higher. A more creative and funny way to grasp the universe. Some code of creative discipline I could abide by. This: hey, don't worry, it's a freak show. Life is a freak show. Live with it. It will last from day one to your last one if you are still aware of getting it.

My first thoughts are of a little boy sitting on the staircase of a suburban bungalow on Carswell st, in the suburbs of Quebec City. A gray wooden staircase. Somehow, I always felt comforted seated on a staircase. It has that subconscious; Mom will be home soon to pick you up. I've always found comfort in sitting on a staircase. It already felt strange.

Came the quest for negotiable truth and sane living arrangement. Live the show without losing it or becoming one of them. Them ! The idiot whose humanity and souls have been kidnapped by a form of progress, just as in the invasion of the Body Snatchers.

It went on, from elementary, High school, army cadets, army reserve, regular forces, to college, technical college to local, national, and international tourism, sales, from tours to IT, to stocks brokerage to finances, banking, and IT banking and all schemes to finally end up driving a city bus. In every field of endeavor, I questioned, took notes on pieces of paper, analyzed, and tried to understand: where this whole existence was going. Making sense of this so ever moving and multidimensional puzzle.

I wish it could have been a more straightforward. Simple life like my 5 brothers and sisters, but it is a cruel world that could not have been this easy. Every single day is a new challenge.

I've had those deep conversations about the universe with the other soulmate Earthling met by coincidence (as if there were such a thing as coincidences) as she was managing sales at a posh Washington DC hotel decades ago. We have kept in touch ever since as we share that love for words, concepts, and a strange form of contemporary beauty. A robust resistance to fundamental change. Our own way.

Contemporary nonconformity. Or is it a form of aesthetic nostalgia?

From her moon and June and ferries wheel world.

She said you should write a novel. Writing is this gift God gave you. Write about your bus. Write about your army experience. Tell us about this dip in the IT world and banking sales. Tell us about all ordinary anodyne stuff; you see things because you see life in an uplifting and funny light. Share with us this wisdom by which you turn cerebral darkness into hope and light.

Tell them about the angels you met and the reflections on life and architecture crossing your mind while driving the big-city bus. Tell them about your takes on your mentors and heroes, the 3 Georges: Orwell, Carlin, and Patton. Tell them how this tragic world could, in fact, be so funny. Tell them: All the things you are. So, here I am. It's a telltale.

It's an erratic novel. A nouveau genre.

Tell them !

It's Jazzy, it's lively, it's sexy, and it has all really happened to me for real. Yes, For real.

SYNOPSIS

A short, coffee induced, erratic novel on a life detour in a busy festival weekend.

A detour into closure. A detour in multiples types of vehicles: physical, mental and coincidental. A detour by definite road, memories, history, building, monuments and views of the world. The detour of an observed society though many lenses and angle. A detour inspired by the vision of the Georges: Orwell, Patton and Carlin. A rubber to asphalt, acidic vision of a changing society with kindness and tenderness. A deep dive into the twisted and overworked mind of a city transit worker. A zest of a Bukowsky's post office on a city transit vehicle . A story of love, life, regrets, strange encounters but hope. Hope of an enlighten world by Jazz music. Because.

At the end of the day: Meet Orwell on wheels.

AFTERWORD

Langley hall Student Residence. Concordia U. Sherbrooke St. West. STM route 105

Floating somewhere in time in the mid-1980's.

Wake up, Adele ! Your cousin, Joey, the testa di menghia, is coming to pick you up.

What time is it?

It's 5 AM, but you have 12 hours driving to York, Penna.

-You dreamt about that book again. What is it all about? Is it one of those weird stand-up routines or one of your Mannix thing deals?

No, Adele, it's about closure.

At the end of the day, All books will be closed. Another strange dream.

The Formative Years !

Take me to your leader! I said, in this very imperative Jimmy Stewart National Geographic comedy tone of voice.

-It's nowhere to be found, she said ! She snapped de facto as she felt that I nor my friend belonged to this exquisite party. To this crowd. Those no formal invitation not dressed for the event, bums. Those public school system guys. The military mustache, crew cut and attitude guy. One has stiff jeans that make him look like a toaster, and the other with the Levis checkered shirt seem to wear a picnic cloth rather than a proper shirt. It's a sexy act here. You don't belong here.

Thanks a lot.

You stiff catholic private school Bitch, we thought. We did not say it. In fact, a few months after this rejection slip a at private party I ended up meeting this hostess and dating her for a summer. I was not the one looking like a toaster. Private school girls did not hang around guys looking like a toaster. So were the rules.

Genevieve, her name was Genevieve. Private College, blonde, classy short hairdo and deep green eyes. She styled those very trendy witches pointy shoe as they were fashionable in the 1980s. Beautiful, although a bit boyish occasionally. She went to Medical School as I went... nowhere as usual. Money, prestige and Kaopectate. I also got rid of the mustache and the crew cut somewhere too. I kept the Levis cowboy shirt for a while.

Nope!

We could not get to that private pool party at the Concorde Hotel, So, we went for the traditional Saturday night bar hop routine.

The guys. We met in High School. Became barracks, parade square and foxhole army buddies as our parents, or did we do it voluntarily, enlisted us into the Royal Canadian Army, Cadet corps? We have been buddies since then. Ages ago and still are. Me, Andre known as Touch Turtle and Jean Marc nicknamed Duck.

And, as per the tradition, we ended up at the local A&W. I had the Teen Burger trio, Duck the Mama Burger and Touch Turtle the fried chicken basket.(The Chubby Chicken special It's summer, it's 2 AM'ish and Chuck Mangione—Feel so good playing on the table Jukebox. These are the late 1970s.

The smell of coffee, the rumor of the crowd, the table Jukebox. A world of innocence and easy living on stainless steel and arborite counter. The 2 AM crowd.

Remember guys when the waitresses here were serving on Roller Skates?

No answers. The boys were absorbed by their plates. This regular convo about kids already talking about the good old days as if they were old or watched too many movie or TV series. Einstein's theory of relativity in progress with a tipsier bar hop touch and technical specs on napkins.

In those days A&W waitresses had this bizarre beige and brown and orange god knows what fabric uniform coming with a Mini skirt, a cap and a mascot. The A&W bear. An offbeat mascot walking and bouncing to the sound of a trombone. Creative and rebellious publicity statement.

Damn, we may have had a better chance for that party had we warn those Pith Helmets. Next time.

So, who's got the invitation to that Jungle Jim Party?

Me, It was not a Jungle Jim, it's Sheba Queen of the Jungle pool party

This, Queen of the Jungle, Sheba, wanted us to wear a safari suit and a Pit Helmet to attend her pool party. Her rules' brother. After all, she is the Queen of her jungle.

I never had the proper paper invitation. I think it's Jenny from the Jeans Boutique who told me about it.

Fact is that, safari dress or pith helmet or what, nobody stayed dressed for very long at Sheba's party. It did not exactly matter, but such was the: entrance ticket. Those parties usually ended up in hotel suites upstairs if you had the right connections. I did not.

So, how do you get such invitations to the sexiest party's in town?

I know Sheba, the leopard bikini clad goddess as she is also a friend of Jennifer the sales person at the L'Exode Levis Jeans shop. Sheba was a good friend of mine in High School.

I helped her with the history exams. I am the one who introduced the Bertonian position that Canada day should be celebrated of April 17th not on July 1st. We both failed in the specific question. In fact, numerous people who copied me failed too on this simple question but I felt victorious on this issue. I made my point. Fighting spirit 1 – Pencil pushers 0. I felt like a victorious Sir Arthur Currie after his victory at the Ridge.

So, you mean that you are friends with Jennifer and those fabulous-looking women?

Yes, I seem to attract them. I guess it has to do with my charisma, good look and wit. It has always been that way.

And you attract those beautiful chicks to go for a moped ride? (never underestimate the sexiness of an Italian machine). Even the red and rusty ones. Could these two bonehead challenge my ability to seduce beautiful women?

I don't know, but I seem to attract beautiful girls as much as you seem to attract our still life of local idiots. You guys are always around Ben No, Kawa and Snow at the mall eatery court. I moped around and met beauties. You play snooker with losers.

I could not expect any other answer but the traditional, Ha, fuck you!!

Let's hit the road as Touch grabbed his Kawasaki KZ 650, duck his Beige Chevette and I took my old red Lambretta that I had to kick-start once more. They had full time steady jobs, me, I was freelance or under contracts. This traditional parking scene.

We all went our way. Maybe one of the last time we met that summer. Warm summer wind. Starry night in the suburbs.

I have this vampire nervous system. I have to get to sleep before the sunrise. Unless I end up with a bad case of migraine that last a few days. Night shift are almost an impossible issue for me. I remember wild parties that ended up at the crack of dawn but I tried to avoid as per it has always been worse than a hangover.

For years, I had been able to bribe my way in events, giving wads of Italian lira. I loved playing the Austrian aristocrat visiting the country giving away thousands of lira as tip to buy easier accesses. It worked for a while until local caught up that I was not from Austria and a 1000 lira worth about 1 dollar.

In the days before the internet or the early computer version, (the Commodore 64 or the Vic 20) the car and the 10,000 watts stereo were the status symbols. Fun was always on the agenda. Academic or financial achievement, possibly later, for now there are party, women, beer, and music, All types of music.

Most guys in the neighborhood had those muscle machine or suicide bike. It was the trend. The V8 era. Cragars, the 4 barrels Holley car. The unsafe at any speed times. Big Daddies tire, Hooker Headers, but for me. I was still on the student's wheels. I was too broke for these, and even my first 1974 Mustang II wasn't much of a machine. Most of the cars I ever owned were part of the list of the worst cars sold in America, besides the Pontiac Aztec. I did not go for that one. They would have been labeled on the Dealer's Choice board game as junk, I guess. They also had this expression in this Milton Bradley board game: Fly-by-night popcorn!

Machines, freedom, less regulation. Nowadays, kids have the tech, we had the imagination and the freedom. We tinkered a lot. The discipline of freedom, let's say. Disobedience is the big block of liberty. The historical GM W-Serie. As Henry Ford introduced the V8, Chevrolet created the Big Block engine. The rest is automotive history.

Youth had to be lived and celebrated. Maybe a way that we kept from death, drama, and accident was by being stupid campers. Not always happy, but our two feet firmly in the stupid land. Potentially, there is a certain heavenly protection for simple minds.

School. Yes, the compulsory education. We learned a lot of stuff but not the stuff we should have learned namely:

personal finances, economy, workplace, real estate and other meaningful matter. The necessary stuff. The stuff you need to understand for personal growth within society.

They taught us that Canada was born on July 1st 1867 as we all know that it was the battle of the Vimy Ridge in April 1917 that defined the country. Canada was born in the blood and the mud of Northern France, and not at a stupid 3 days drunkard party in Charlottetown in 1867. That's the political take on history. Furthermore, John Cabot was not English. He was Italian and hired by the English. His real name was Giovanni Caboto.

No, that was not in the curricular but, hell were we good at fixing the toaster, doing woodwork as we all learned how to make a spice rack, bookshelf, and sheet metal work. Sheet metal work, we made a toolbox. Girls on their side had family economy class.

Family economy classes.

They learned to cook, balance as budget, make muffins, basic catholic (heterosexual) sexuality and how to invest penny stocks, bet on ponies and play the stock shorts. Classes were given by catholic nuns. Nuns are investment pros and the Vatican is a very wealthy state. The whole system had in mind that the man should go work at the shop with his homemade toolbox. It did not have to be a shop in itself, but any form of blue-collar work would do the trick. The bailout option was of buying a plastic Snoopy Lunch box or one of those massive thermos with fishing fly on a Scottish tartan. Sometimes mistaken for something else in sex shops. He will be married to the girl that would make the lunch, the muffins, the budget, play the ponies and the stock exchange. Life would go on under the grace and good eye of the parish priest, God, and the Diocese. Damn, we guys undeniably got short-changed on this deal.

By the end of the High School drill came a new generation of teachers wearing turtle-necks, long hair and fat glasses. They did not look like our clean cut, tie wearing parents, nor did they speak the same language. They looked like, damn, Planet of the Apes. Those peaces and love niks wanted us all to go to College and University to earn a degree and become an—ologist—or an eer -. They called that the emergent new leisure society. A society based on the 4 days week work and personal growth through leisure, art, and sports.

Like the Minotaur from Greek mythology class or a few classic horror movies, we all heard about it but never actually seen it. The very elusive Leisure society thing. David Vincent saw them.

So much for the leisure society. All that we learned was that meteorological thing that the called a depression that had been in and out every three years or so and that never seems to go away. An everlasting economical headache as a form of David Jansen deal hovering over your bank account, career, and car payment. As Jay Leno once said: David Jansen, the man looks like a headache.

Perhaps the systems as our parents wanted to spare us. Spare us of the ever so apparent inefficiencies of a dysfunctional system that would eventually eat us alive. Maybe they abided by this motto that education was like alcohol, too much of it is not good. Potentially, they relied on the Jacques DuTronc tune stating that: the more you learn, the less you actually know.

Perchance that they wanted us to have just enough tool to fill in the tin box they taught us to assemble. A hammer, a few screwdrivers, pliers and a metal saw. Common will or lack of budget or good plain wisdom. Don't ask too many questions. Live and learn. Would I be a rich aristocrat or an intellectual, I would have called this chapter: The formative years?

Potentially, the system figured out or presumed that we were all too dumb to get the basic rules of economics and finance.

We were an institutionally dysfunctional generation, but what a blast.

So, the 1970s leisure society, the 1989 Helsinki Summit Peace Dividends, the Yeti, and the Loc Ness Monster, the Belgian autobahn rest area Milfoy: same deal. But for the Milfoy, it did materialize.

But we did not care. We did not care because we did not know. There could not be a plan because we did not know such things existed. A life plans. A take, a gimmick, a strategy.

We all dreamt of Farrah Fawcett and the Coca-Cola Ford Econoline denim machine, or both. Taking a trip, driving the Denim Machine with Farrah Fawcett. We had the leisure and time to dream. As we all sang: Heaven, must be missing an angel. Tavares on 8 track cartridge tape.

Days of slower processes. We took time to enjoy every sip of coffee and every bite of a hamburger, while sometimes having a peek at the day's paper. Nobody does any more and even more alarming, many drink coffee in office mugs or find it natural to drink coffee in a cardboard cup with a plastic lid.

As an H.S. Biology teacher once told : as humanity mutates, the mouth will shrink and disappear, making place for an orifice just as small as, you know what. We will feed on pills, eat protein purée food type. Just like these astronauts on T.V. Seeing our today's youth, I would extrapolate that eventually female genital may be replaced by a USB port and male by a USB cable. They would download kids and orgasm depending on the download program and the twisted mind with play with the headset jack or play multitask.

As the introduction of low floor city transit buses many years ago, once could presume that the next generation of transit user will have shorter legs or that our society became socially handicapped to make space for an unnecessary borderline useless concept base on the Keynesian Beauty contest routine. Almost a comedy routine. The Planet of the Apes teachers. They looked weird, talk strange stuff and dressed funny. A for teacher, the old buses did the job perfectly, but as you will discover: this is a personal issue.

Those were the days of: No more, no less. All stocks were listed once a day in the daily paper. Banks closed a 3 PM except on payday, and there were no automatic tellers. Cash, cash, cash, and credit cards were slid on this, I think the term was a guillotine, and once a week, merchants were given a list of disabled card. One could surf a week to a month on a stolen or disabled card.

> *"Progress is not an illusion, it happens, but it is slow and invariably disappointing. There is always a new tyrant waiting to take over from the old—generally not quite so bad, but still a tyrant"*
>
> Georges Orwell.

Progress may have become a dictatorship or something tyrannical, which takes it to the level of the Marxist alienation. Groucho, I guess. That probably makes me a disenchanted, as per the Great Disenchantment theory of Karl Weber. Yet, one could be disenchanted and still happy. It's a mere observation on the state of the world that make one smirk. It is a way of life.

It's always been an integral part of me. This constant questioning about this strange universe surrounding me. This type of ever going freak show I get submitted to since my birth.

Early in life, I had noticed that no event is ever correctly reported in a newspaper. Georges Orwell. The narrative. The official tale. The machine.

The fast this, the fast that. Why fast. Why are we in a perpetual hurry? Hurry to wait, as they said in the army. We are always hooked on something. Where and what happened to quality work? Quality over time. Every 5 years or so, I have to go underneath the kitchen counter to hook up a new dishwasher. They don't even last as long as a Government in Italy. No matter how much dough you fork out. Five or 6 years. The other appliances. Eight year and you can't even fix them. No spare parts.

There is that YouTube clip of YouTube of the 1959 dishwasher that still runs. I look at the clip and this is getting almost erotic to think that with one of those suckers, I wouldn't have to spend another day shopping for a dishwasher and to install one. Appliances porn, I'd say. XXX with a rubber hose.

I would have this special request on the reintroduction on the market of this 1959 Hobart or Kitchen Aid KD 12, dishwasher for as long as some lasted over 60 years as the modern one lasts as long as a Government in Italy. Yet, Israel change more government than the Italian these days.

And I tried as much work as I could to learn a little more about life. I had a few girlfriends, a few cars, a few jobs and no clue about career, life and, or settling down and came this love of my life: woman. Some into money, some into career, power and so on. Me, I love women and easy life.

Then came!

I decided to get higher education after a work stage in the Forces. I have never been able to follow the right order of things. So that dream of Pazzaz and the Italian beauty with a temper came through.

She was all of that!

Adele was like me, questioning but bitching. Adele had those puns on how to call a man with no arm and no leg. A man with no arm and no leg hook on a wall would be named Art. As, a woman with no arm and no leg hanging from the ceiling would be named Tiffany, and there were a few of those.

She was the London scene type. The London new wave look, this Madness type mixed with the Gogo's thing's beat and a Laura Brannigan look. She was the 80s. She came from a town in Penna, on the line with Maryland. There are major differences between MD and Penna as per in the one state, upon merging on a highway one has to stop as in the other one has to floor it. Confusing and dangerous. The other is that in Maryland one expects 4 meatballs in a meatball spaghetti as in Pa, well, they served 3. But somehow, the 3 meatballs are from real Italian as in Md, it's dry WASP factory meat -a – ball. Her dad and all uncles had Pizza shops in the state or around. They all worked hard, ran good food restaurant and while overworked knew how to celebrate life. When regular folks in my family brought sandwiches to picnic, those guys made BBQ with a whole pork. They knew how to throw a picnic. They mastered the art of life. That was very impressive. How do they get this, je ne sais quoi? Traditions?

She came to work with pizza dough one day and made it spin and fly as they do in Italy. She was a Pizza Master. Damn, that was almost erotic.

She had all figured out as I was clueless. She was in this Go for it business mindset, as I feared this very cruel thing and violent thing in life: routine. Routine and hope are very violent things. Sales, entrepreneurship: Go for it. She had a thing for Pat Benatar as she never seemed to hit the right man and I lived according to this karma. Maybe repeating the lyrics of a sad love song brings you the same destiny. Perhaps this is simply how life gets programmed.

That was love, but lousy timing. We were both too young, and you know, ending up with a divorce with kids is not exactly the best start in life. I loved her deeply but, like many men, possibly it's myself that I did not love properly. It did not work out. I had to make another round of walkabout. Matter of a few years, I guess. In retrospect, you argue, love, exchange, bicker and try and unfortunately this is how you learn to love and live.

She was Madness, I was OMD, The Clash, Nina Hagen and the B52s but always remained through all those fads a Woody Hermann, John Coltrane type of person. I always find answers in life in a Duke Ellington's tune or a Julie London song. A few souvenir stays from that relationship as men always leave a part of their DNA to their partner are a few expressions said in deep low husky voice with an American Sicilian accent:

1. Yeah, Right! (are you taking me for an idiot)
2. Fine and dandy (bis)
3. Ain't too shabby, Mother F. (Cool)
4. I pity the foo (her Mr. Tee impersonation)

A quote from Liquid Sky. An avant-garde movie.

"I was taught that my prince would come, and I would have his children... and on the weekends we would barbecue... and all the other princes and their princesses would come, and they would say "delicious...delicious "Oh how boring ..."

We were both artsies in soul, but caught up in a mechanical world fuelled by expectation. But art will never deceive. It never deceives. Art takes you somewhere else. It tools us some places else.

Maybe I should cut on this stuff a bit.

Caffeine.

Yes caffeine, Caffeine takes me to bizarre places and I always end having coffee stains on my uniform shirt.

There were many more women of my life. Many more on this quest for love and stability. Quest to find the light. That too did not happen. Well, it did but took sort of a miracle and miracles are announced by angels. Angel, yes they exist, but many aren't of their classical known form as much as divine intervention may seem to differ from their biblical narrative. They are those encounter that state how could they have known that: beats me!

I am a kid of the 1960'. Early 60s, the square 60s. The: My Favorite Martian years. The crew cut days.

So, I had to evolve from Vinyl days or liquid sky.

I grew up in the days of vinyl records. There was music, taste, appreciation, and a lot of Peer Pressure. Peer pressure is what made that Black Sabbath, Uriah Heap, Gentle Giants actually sold records. It was all vile noise and later on in life came the heavy metal bands but as long as an influence leader said, hey listen, this is good, it had to be good. AM radio stations, payola, and the regular media overkill and bashing sold records. Band that looked like Minotaur and friends. Lead singers with the eyes on the side of the head type. And the kids flocked to the record store and purchased those vinyls for $6.99. As an encyclopedia many years before, they were there to fill in space. Never exactly listened to side A and B as so many books never opened. In fact, it's something like 90%.

The age of the Flavorio radio at Radio Shack (they came in 12 different colors) and the battery club. (Pistachio was the top seller) We all loved this Radio Shack catalog. It was all in there. I wanted that AM radio in a Pepsi can, as my old man wanted the weather report cube. He got his cube, but as in the catalog picture, it looked like something big. It was, in fact, minuscule. Major deception.

Yes, I had a soft spot for the Pistachio Flavorio Radio, but never got one. They were always back order. It still haunts me today. This unfulfilled dream thing deal. The same league as the Rob Gilbert, New York Rangers O'Pee Chee hockey card.

Came those existential questions of the day. Has Rod Taylor finally banged Yvette Mimieux at the end of the Time Machine. I saw that movie on a rainy Sunday PM at the local school gymnasium. The projected the movie on a white sheet. I had something for Rod Taylor, as he was this improbable hero. Charly Gordon in Charlie and an RAF Squadron commander flying DeHavilland Mosquitoes in Squadron 633. Until these days, I am still wondering if Archie ever had it with Betty, or has Jug head been faster than him on this deal. Never estimate the power of wit on seduction or a red Lambretta.

The old Lambretta has been replaced 40 years later, but a fuel injection Vespa deal. Red and shiny and I got to admit: even for a bus driver, those scooters are a blast. Yes, they are still Chick's Magnet.

Time flies and decades pass. It has to do with the hygienic concentric rotation paper roll (R-r) 2* pi syndrome. The closer you get to the core, the faster it spins, and with age comes the wisdom to start giving less attention to petty details of life, to slow down the speed by which it revolves around the time axel. Don't sweat petty thing or pet.

The 1980s were around the corner. As the music changed, so did the general mood. Hard Rock to Punk Rock to New Wave to a new form of disco. Yet jazz took a new form too. Pop fusion, smooth jazz and damn, Kenny Gee. Three letters opened a new way into music and entertainment. MTV. The syncopators were back with their saxophones and the world went, one step beyond. By the end of the decade, Pat Benatar had not found real love. A band from Atlanta, Georgia was still driving a car as big as a whale, 15 miles from the Love Shack, but without a founding member of the band. Rickie Wilson died in October 1985.

Original call from Sugg! Madness.

Hey you, don't watch that
Watch this
This is the heavy, heavy monster sound
The nuttiest sound around
So, if you come on off the street
And you're beginning to feel the heat
Well, listen buster
You better start to move your feet
To the rockiest, rock steady beat
Of Madness.
One step beyond

Comes the existential question!

Could there be a way to earn an honest living wandering aimlessly around all day. That's the question? This or later on in life. Redoing the kitchen or spending a month, or two, in Roma is also the question. It depends on the size of the kitchen. Roma has been fairly stable or static. Could there be a way to stay One Step Beyond. Roma is also the answer.

Travelling and wandering around was a living for me for many years. A cultivated bum gathering knowledge, images, and emotions. Scientist, read the letters T & E as trial and error. I figured early in life they mean Travel and Entertainment. As a Tour guide, tour director, charter driver and many others. As I loved working as the guide, I also loved playing the tourist. The Michelin guide became my favorite reading.

Travelling, yes, but also discovering new places for myself. Discovering and enjoying as well. Tourism is also a land of poetic, fast cash, seasonal gimmicks. The Polaroid thing was in. The Polaroid deal or recording a 45rpm single or having your mug on a popular magazine cover montage. I have one left in a box of me, as Gail dressed in camo with camo stick for a fake issue of Soldiers of Fortune. A classic. Gail ended up working for a symphonic orchestra. Not exactly the Soldier of Fortune look. Yet, she looked good. Even the dark green and black camo stick did not alter her beauty. She was this gorgeous, long-haired blonde. I will introduce you to Gail later on in the novel. Rumor had it that she once was contestant into the Miss America contest for New Jersey.

Having a Polaroid picture taken with a cardboard personality was a common attraction in the 1980s. I collected them as a tour guide, but did not keep many. My favorite on the scene picture is of me, Georges Bush and Mikael Gorbachev in a 1989 Helsinki conference setting. We are sitting in front of a Russian samovar. The conference that should have ended the Cold War. There I am, in the middle of the picture. I kept the one with this life-size cardboard silhouette of Fawn Hall for obvious different reasons. Thy were the in thing in the 1980s, DC tourism sites. Ollie and Fawn Hall.

Helsinki was the event that was supposed to change the world. The end of the Cold War and this emerging everlasting peace. Peace, peace dividends and high-speed trains everywhere. It did not. It did not change much in facts. We got hoaxed.

I have boxes of stuff gathered through ages. Treasure trove. Name tags from different tour brokers I worked for, guide badges, piggy banks, a few old books, Yuppie Handbook, Real Men don't eat Quiché or Real E.T, s don't phone home. A wicked collection of old Russian military komandirskie watches of many historical themes: a T34, Laika the space dog, and others. Occasionally, I like to dive in old memories like everyone else, I guess.

This everlasting rebellious bum spirit, This Orwellian perpetual questioning. Explore now, pay later type of freedom. It had to start somewhere.

In my earliest childhood recollection, I remember my big sister Diane taking me out for Sunday's discovery of the city bus ride. That's how she could escape home on Sunday and meet her numerous boyfriends, as I was the involuntary chaperon. A chaperon that could be bribed with a hot chocolate or candies. We caught those old GM New Look buses, or were they Canadian Cartage Brill's. In 1959, GM introduced this panoramic window urban bus named the New look. GM made them locally with a panoramic glass windshield that could remind of the nose of the NASA space shuttle. They have been on the road until the mid-1980s. Keanu Reeves drives one in Speed or is it Sandra Bullock.

Yes, the bus. Those great GM New Look buses. The revolutionary General Motor GM Design for transit vehicle. The world's most produced urban bus.

I remember the smell, the warmth, the way they handled the hills of old Quebec City. The padded and thick leather like covering type seats. Dark green or gray. My sister brought me tobogganing on the Plains of Abraham, to the art museum and to that Café on Couillard st. This is where I heard for the first time the sound of a Cappuccino machine, the exquisite perfume of espresso coffee and heard this divine sound arrangement. Rare occurrence in the 1960s to see an Espresso machine. Jazz Music. It all made sense. That was what life should feel like, and I made choices accordingly. A harmonic, a life, a beat, a pace.

Psychologist will argue that your experience before the age of 6 shapes your actual personality. I cannot argue with that. It is early exposures to such and such that makes, of you, who you are. You can also be Orwellian and not bitter about existence.

I became that person. A bus, jazz, coffee, women, dogs, and an atmosphere and moment person. To live for that moment and create the necessary atmosphere to make it happen. Nothing else matters.

A career is a job that has gone on too long.
Jeff MacNelly.

And where you are not learning anything new anymore. It becomes a reflex, as reflection is no more on the program.

Meanwhile, back at the ranch.

Through bizarre twists of faith, I became an urban bus driver. I had a late vocation call. I tried as many jobs as I could, but there was this little extra thing in city transit that made me go for it. Being able to nap in the middle of the day and getting a financial bonus for it. It was a natural fit as per this commandment stating: There could be zillions of good reasons to be late but none for being too early. I lived what I had to live for as long as I could learn something from other businesses, but this temporary experience became a permanent thing. There is nothing more permanent than temporary. Job security and the pay fairy her magic wand were also part of the decision to get into that.

Heading Downtown, Laura Brown !

I am working tonight. 165 South Bound. Reality check. Buses! Buses are a wonderful invention because they physically carry multitudinous personal universes in space and time and dispatch them in definite places. I guess you never saw it this way. Driving them is a bit like DeeJaying. As the driver, you are leading the dance.

It is summer. It is Friday and this has the reputation of being a party city. A sin city. A jazzy place.

Hazy lazy Friday evening driving a city bus down the Cote de Neiges hill, towards downtown Montreal. The Grand Prix weekend. Guy, Guy, Concordia Metro station. Asian restaurant, Concordia U crowd, Ste-Catherine st West, The John Molson school of business, city park, pigeon, regular hobos, high rises' apartment building and in the shade underneath a few mature trees a monument dedicated to Norman Bethune. It is called the Norman Bethune square. Land of The Miserable, as per Victor Hugo novel and later on Broadways, are all there as it is their summer predilection ground. Lousy little urban park, way below what one should expect for the grandeur of Norman Bethune, but there has been a controversy about Norman. As Norman went to fight in the 1936's Spanish Civil, the Mac Pap Brigade, war with most intellectual and thinkers of the day, namely Ernest Hemingway. He also developed field hospital surgery technique while working as a field surgeon for the Chinese Revolutionary army. Early in his career, as a humanitarian and person of conscience, he has been labelled: Communist. I believe he was.

Yet Bethune as many unknown heroes, maverick finished off in lousy park or street corner as per obeying pencil pusher and other Lackey finish off having luxuriant park named after them highway or subways stations. Those that kept following the small rules to break the big one, The moral ones.

Norman Bethune obeyed one master. His conscience and, well, the bottle. So, there is this park in front of the Guy Metro station. This park catering to a strange fauna. A poetic crowd to say the least.

My brother John was sometimes hanging with this poetic crowd. He was a brilliant stockbroker who, under pressure, fell into hard drugs. The easy way out. He also had a tendency to drink as per a form of family tradition and also had a lousy temper. I have the souvenir of him as a proud Army officer at the Military base. Maybe spending too much time at the officer's mess indeed. John and his wife Susan being young and happy, but none of this could last. Susan cut louse as he was spending more and more time drinking. The first of many divorces. The man was cut for the military, and civilian life did not exactly suit him well. He settled for this first paying job that he could get: a stockbroker. Young and ambitious. He was good at it, but he hated it. As the old man he tried many business ventures to get out of it but had not found the mother lode.

For the last month of his miserable existence, my brother John spent part of his day at the central library or as a Wi-Fi parasite at the local Second Cup on St-Denis st. I met him there as I drove the Slinky bus back to the garage after my morning shift and stopped for a coffee. There was a bus stop next to the Café, which made my life easy. In fact, I always loved abusing this perk of the trade of being to park prime land downtown, no questions asked, a vehicle as big as 10 cars. Yes, I get a kick out of it.

The man was emaciated, weak, broken and looked sick, but he kept lying to himself that he was, in fact, an ignored business shark on the out of luck mode. Waiting for the last voyage, I guess. Cancer, lung as it attacked the spine, he could not walk straight, but he was unable to talk about it. He wanted to avoid mentioning the fact that he was dying.

He had been playing the sick comedy for 40 years, which is a long time for being out of luck indeed. We talked silly. Women and booze story. Soldier tales.

We escaped our routine by small talk about travel and vacation. We both wanted to visit St-Petersburg, RU. St-Petersburg, Sevastopol, Odessa type of trip. He read books, saw pictures and had the time to go. The awake dream of going somewhere fundamentally different.

I did not nor would I be able to drag my wife for a trip to Russia for that matter. As our parents died, we've inherited some money. Nothing big but enough to take a trip there or a black sea cruise deal.

I asked: Why aren't you going to St-Petersburg (obviously before you buy the big farm or return your keys or cash in your chips)

I can't!

Why's that?

Because I am alone. I am always alone. He had never made peace with himself nor with his only daughter that he had not seen for 15 years or so. I don't know. Matter of pride or shame, but I never cornered him with the questions. Matter of never being up to the stature his old man had wished for him. Matter of chosen this lifestyle as a happy-go-lucky single camper that never grew up. So he thought.

(I think he may have inherited a criminal record for white-collar crimes somewhere and could not have a Passport, but I never asked)

I hated the fact that he kept lying to himself. I hated the fact that he should have tried to make up with his only daughter under the pretext that he once gave her $800 to go on a vacation to Cuba, and she never called him back to thank him. Maybe she did, but he does not remember.

Shit, you left the kid there she was 12, what the fuck do you expect? I give everything I can for my daughter and our father did his best for us, and we were that thankful. No, I guess because we were too young to realize how precious and fragile existence is. Damn! The man who could logically feel that he is on his last miles could not even make the wise man first move.

Younger, we used to beat one another. He was older, but I got bigger and faster. We never held grudges about it. We were from a Catholic environment. In a good catholic family, there has to be a priest and a gangster. I had a problem figuring out where I would stand on this particular issue.

When was the last time you spoke to Marie Sophie? (his only daughter).

Must have been 15 years ago

I never reacted to that one. It was too late for anything. Just too late.

If a man does his best, what else is there? (General Patton)

You should forgive a man that consistently and under any circumstance did his best, but that was not the case here. My old man had some mishaps towards me, but he amended and made up. He did his best with the life baggage he had. This should be plenty.

So, I finished my morning shift on the bus. Pulled in the north end bus division. Never easy, never simple, but lively. Reflect. Yes, it sometimes happens to me. Above all, I am not alone. I will go back to this war zone house and dysfunctional family but I am not alone in life. Yes, I will go to St-Petersburg, RU. I will do this trip for me and in his memory.

My older brother died as the 1970s died too... The decade took him away in its time spin. It took him 4 decades to realize that he was dead inside.

And I will walk out of this hospital room, or a morgue for all I know, reciting the words of this song from the Doobie Brothers. He ain't heavy, he is my brother.

It is not the disease that may kill you. It's this permanent state of stress and unhappiness that will open the way for that disease to kill you. Unhappiness kills more than anything else.

He pulled the plug while I was fully enjoying life in a pool bar in Riviera Maya, Mexico. Unclear, but he may have taken all the painkiller, anti-depressor and all shit to make a rhum and vodka final cocktail. The coroner did not tell us this much, nor has he to use ice in the blender either?

There will be this funeral moment. There was that funeral moment. You'll stand there clueless with a coffee, Chinet paper plate in hand, a crustless sandwich and some salad. Surrounded and chatted with people you know but not really know. You'll nod, smile and check your watch or your phone discreetly wondering what the hell you are doing there and why aren't there more marriages or christening instead. Damn, these Chinet sure look like real dishes, but don't have the same feel or texture. It beats the old Dixy paper plates. Something, as usual, is missing out.

It still is Friday evening. I am still physically behind the wheel of this huge Slinky type city bus, but as the soap bubbles from the Lawrence Welk show. My mind floats around freely. It goes in and out travelling in concepts and time in the erratic, a chronological mode. A place, a name, a smell, an address takes it always from this closed material universe to go hiking in somewhere else land. The bus knows the road. It has been there so many times. Let's operate on the scan and react mode.

The higher a monkey climbs, the more you see of It's behind.
Gen Joe Stilwell

Floating somewhere in the 1980s, broke but happy.

How could that have happened? I had to find a job. Something where I could drive around. Something quiet.

I had to find a job.

Get a job!
What for?
Shut up, I've got to think.
On this caffeine buzz, I was on. Deadbeat Club. The B52's

Little do we know, those guys at the Federal placement agency really work. Occasionally. Damn! I loved lazing around on the Unemployment insurance. The Pogue. Nope. It could have waited a few more months. Spring was nice. I could have spring ski a little more. They had to find me a job. Something that would fit my profile and all requirements.

27B stroke 6 forms (Terry Gillian, Brazil) for the Pogue or UB 40 in GB and well every week you had to fill in a questionnaire on a computer card with those answers, yes, yes, yes, yes, yes, no, yes. It had to be done with a sharp pencil.

The Federal unemployed placement service had the generosity to find me this job. Not that I did look too hard to find something, but it was their job. It was their idea. Early 80s there was a recession as there is one every 3 years or so- and-so in fact I have never heard anyone in the media saying:

life is good, everything is fine. This thing about finances and economics they did not teach us at school, again.

That was my first or almost first job in the big city. Big city, bright light, and this search light from I don't know where in town searching Montreal's sky all night long. Impressed. I felt it was my universe. The job now: on the road representative for a specialized bank. Bank America Private brands. (Private brand inventories) The Finance company who hired me had an office in this old office building, torn down since and then replaced by what became the Concordia U EV building. Familiar city block in my recent family history. It was right in front of the Bethune park. They needed a naive, inexperienced kid (preferably with zits) to put a lot of mileage on a company car. I loved to drive around then, I was the perfect match. They fudged the offer, I fudged my interest. We both got fudged. The Federal Government guys were happy, they could show justification for their jobs.

They had one less person on the unemployment insurance program. Rejoice. We found one job for 2.5M unemployed. Lousy lottery, you tell me!

The job sums up like this quote from Apocalypse Now.

 You're an errand boy, sent by grocery clerks, to collect a bill."
 Colonel Kurtz, 'Apocalypse Now' or
 The horror, the horror.
 The main office was where now stands Concordia U, EV building. Above Guy Metro station.
 As I spent most of my days driving to the place, doing the inventory part, sometimes in barns or unreachable building, was not the easy part. There were different types of clients and financed inventories: appliances, electronics, furniture, boats, motorcycles but mainly electronics. Some furniture stores kept their inventory in a far away barn, not accessible by car. Merchant had to take me there by tractor or VTT. Upon visiting the motorcycle store, we had to make sure that the new models were still in crates, as uncrated merchandise became demos and demos worth 20% less on inventory. I turned a blind eye to those practices as per I was the first one to say; Hey!let's take that Yamaha YZ for a spin in the mud. YZ's were a blast to ride.

 The territory that had to be covered was as big as Texas and once or twice a week, I had an encounter with a moose, a deer, or a family of bears on the road. As most customers were courteous, some others just disliked the bank kid sent from the big city and made it difficult to deal. The rates of interest went as high as 19% per annum. I had to close many businesses. It is never a nice experience. Some people had invested their life into their mom-and-pop boutique, and the finance people had the last word on what was to become of their livelihood. The where they would end up in the food chain.

As many of us, hostage of an economic climate on which we are all powerless. Unless, in those days, you had the foresight of selling Japanese products. Sony. All Sony stuff sold like crazy.

I saw what I could refer to as indecent business practice. Overloading inventories for the sake of non-achievable sales quota. Pushing small commerce into technical bankruptcy. Pushing sales to the limits of human decency. Tales of sales fiction. Screwing the system to achieve what? A promotion. The job at the office tower in downtown Toronto at the 89th floor with a enclosed office and a panoramic window ? A garage house in Orillia by the 401 connector. Vacation with the kids on a Disney Cruise. Golf Tournament to become the 19th hole. A land of corporate idiots, secretaries in tight leather skirts and intellectual emptiness. A form of business porn that, as the real XXX thing, is purely fictional. The round of extramarital affairs between neighbors that would invariably lead to the divorcees lifestyle and its workaholic compensation life. Lawnmower or garden hose talk and the such. They call it the corporate ladder, or is the social scaffold taking you to this unavoidable hanging as many go for it.

Where is that God given to man's decency?

I heard a lot about it at church, in school, and in movies. I read about it. Had lived much life episode in which I believe I got taken for a ride, but this time, in this job : that was real. Some business practices, although legal and rubber-stamped by the law, were just indecent. Now what's decency? There it is.

Let me tell you what justice is. Justice is the law, and the law is man's feeble attempt to set down the principles of decency. Decency! And decency is not a deal. It isn't an angle, or a contract, or a hustle! Decency... decency is what your grandmother taught you. It's in your bones! Now you go home. Go home and be decent people. Be decent

Judge White. The bonfire of vanities.

I drove around. Met customers, Collected check, Made inventories. Try to make this gig enjoyable, but I could not lie to myself for too long. There is always a reason why one is getting paid for a task. The first one is that it is never enjoyable. It's labor, (lavoro) which is, in Italian, a word derived of the word torture. There could be no job without aggravation. That's a rule of life.

I got what I wanted and needed out of the job for the time it lasted. After all, employer exchange your time on earth for probable time somewhere else, namely money. Money is time as time is money, and slavery has never exactly been abolished. It has been improved, and the debts replaces the whip and the new slave is not only more volunteer but act as if happy about the whole scheme. They want the Disney deal. They want this XXX movie professional sexual fantasy deal but it is cruel and costly. Happy, so, they think. Until comes the doubts, the questioning and the tiny white pills. The smaller the white pills are, the more potent they are.

I could not live the life of the indecent. There is just a limit at what money could buy, and the coffee was lousy. I did not fit it. I was unable to dream Toronto. I am Montreal.

Selling your soul to the devil in exchange for a routine life of cheap suits, motel life, diluted coffee served in styrofoam cup with small sacks of coffee mate and Splenda. Splendid !

So much for the caffeine buzz!

And so, I toured the province, or at least half of it. The boring half.

I still had no intention of climbing the corporate ladder to get more stuff. In fact, I always wanted less stuff. More time but less stuff and God know what those monkeys climbing expose. Now does that make of me a communist, an artsy or a philosopher, I don't know, but it certainly made of me an oddball at companies meeting. The buzzword of the day was customer's need. Fulfill the customer's requirement while trying to keep your underwear on. Underwear, dignity or universal decency. 99% of sales meeting are useless and going nowhere, but are part of a more sinister ritual, Company culture. Bacterial culture. Office towers like yogurt container, full of bacterial activities.

Gratefully, we were still in the pre cellular phone era. I love the call at the office, I am on the road today, I'll get back to you in two days. Ciao.

Freedom is slavery, and men were free in the days that telephone were anchored on a wall by a wire. Freedom, there is an app for that? Georges Orwell meets Alexander Graham Bell.

Some days were nice. The splendid scenery of the Laurentian wildlife reservation I had to cross twice a week, dodging big over speeding lumber trucks. Driving along the St-Lawrence river and well, looking for a restaurant in a North mining town on a late spring day afternoon. I found one on the main st where young Innus girls were rope jumping among stray dog or wolves. It was a lunch counter where the menu was manually typed off a sheet of paper in an acetate sheet. The kids were laughing, the dogs playing. It was a beautiful sunny spring day. Snow was thawing and everyone played on what was the main street. There was a cute little note at the bottom of the snack counter menu stating: We had soup on the menu yesterday, but we wiped it out. Cute. The innocence of a mining town at the end of no where.

As per this Tony Bennett song.

The frozen mountain dreams
Of April's melting streams
How crystal clear it seems
You must believe in Spring

That was on the last northernmost leg of my sales territory. The Chibougamau Chapais region. It was not on the official Province of Quebec road paper map in the 1980s. There was a verso square section with the region. In case, as in the days that the earth was flat and on the back of 3 giant turtles, a motorist would drive over the limit of the map and still find his way. Every so often, they were elephants. Cultural matter, I guess.

Chapais. Small town in the Chibougamau area. The place was made famous by a horrific drama on New Year eve 1979-80. It made international news on New Year's Eve forecast on jan 1st 1980. All over North America. I remember seeing it on T.V. in the living room at home. As most of the people of the village gathered at a temporary community center type to celebrate the passing of the year. Someone intoxicated has lit the Christmas tree on fire, as is the old age of the candles in the trees. That tree was synthetic fibers, as was most of the prefab building used as the social club. The porch in front of the building was in forged iron, and the smoke emanating from the burning building was in all sorts of chemical components. If you think the smoke of a cigarette is bad; try a sofa. As the first women worked their way out, the high heel and stiletto heels got caught in the entrance porch steel grid and in blocked the only exits, among other causes of 44 deaths. The stampede stopped right there, at the exit. Most families had lost someone in some families as a whole just disappeared. It was hard to go to Chapais with that image in mind.

Shit happens.

Seventy-seven people died in the fire of the Blue Bird Café in Montreal. Was it on Labor Day evening or about at the Wagon Wheel country Club, Don, Curly and the Dude were playing their usual routine. End of summer and beginning of class and autumn. Life went on. A few private events and a bachelorette party. . A chained door fire escape exit did as much damage as a fire in the staircases ignited and gasoline doused by highly disturbed individuals. The Wagon Wheel was on the second floor, and it went up in smoke very fast. Maybe as fast as the Chapais Opemiska social club.

The Bachelorette party was their last one. They all perished from smoke inhalation that night.

The site became a parking lot. It had been purchased by a developer lately, and it will become another condo housing land. I would not live there, as I would go 3 streets down with a bus to avoid Union st. This place is doomed.

As for Chapais. I had a customer at the entrance of the village in Chapais who owned a furniture store. I guess he could spend a day without seeing one single customers, but so is country life. He had electronic inventories, but small one. A dozen Hitachi TV sets, 20 turntables and a few amplifiers. All of his Hitachi's inventories were paid for, so there was no need to rush anything or play the serial numbers. I kind of dropped by to do PR and social. Expense account.

Broken man. He had lost many friends and family in the fire. His store was quiet but paid for. Sometime after the business was done, we went for lunch at the McCloud Brasserie next door in the village, and he told me about those people he lost in the fire. After this last store, I had to hit the road for 6 hours to go home. Total silence. Sometimes sporadic country radio music broadcasts local stuff and fills in special song requests, but I immersed myself in the beauty of nature, meditating that death could come to you when you least expect it. Even in the middle of a party with family and friends. Even on New Year's Eve. Even at a bachelorette party in a country bar on Labor Day.

What do we know! Yet, you must believe in spring.

Museum, stories, anecdotes, tales of memories are monuments dedicated to the living. Cemeteries, just as Versailles, do not have running water. Unfortunate indeed.

Parks and museums, of all types. Places where art, objects, and people can share. Share experience, stories, witnessing and good anecdotes.

In the land of anecdotes! There could be no anecdote without breaking so established rules or the freedom instilled instinct to dare to challenge preconceived ideas. Here is a story. Here is a statement. Here is a : hear me, I've got something to tell about who I am and what I have lived.

Paradoxically speaking: The worst thing that could ever happen to you is nothing. Nothing ever happened to you. Things happen if you dare to make them happen. Some never have stories to tell, anecdotes, things. They have this thingless existence. This, I don't know life. They came, they saw, they did shit.

As I heard many anecdotes in my life. Many defining moments from simple individuals that have a good story. Some are good, others are so far out that their effects last for decades. Ross Wilson, WWII Royal Canadian Signal Corps veteran at the Liberation of Paris.

Ross Wilson, Carole's father, claims to have touched the nose of the Mona Lisa at the Louvres Museum as he was in Paris on the day of the Liberation and the Louvres was wide open. No security personnel, they were all out celebrating. So as he wandered around, he took time to sit in Josephine's tub and touch Mona Lisa's nose. The problem with Canadian soldiers has always been the same. Once off-duty, they tend to do silly stuff. OK, On or off-duty, acting like goofs, was the norm. It's a way to cope with what the system asks them to perform. For that generation, escaping death a day or even an hour at the time may have been an incentive for being elated.

Ross was supposed to go to the movie theater somewhere in France in the days preceding the Liberation de Paris party. As he was to show up to the marquise and purchase his billet, some Nazi Collaborator or sympathizer decided to bomb the theater and killed many people, mainly allied soldiers, in the theater. He was right there, tickets in hands, at the marquise when the thing blew up. As he saw the crowd in the streets of Paris, he got worried. Some Nazi sympathizers could attempt to bomb the crowd. He got nervous and figured that the museum. This empty museum could be a safer place after all.

Carole was a Vargas girl type. This May 1942 model as per Vargas could only imagine his Calendar girls. Imagination, he had, She was a colleague tour guide in Old Quebec city and I showed her a few tricks of the trade here and there. The things only native from the city know. Nooks and crannies. Ghost stories. The shortcuts. We spent a summer as good friends. We were both walking out of a messy relationship and voluntarily kept it in this infamous friend zone, but it worked well but somehow, love takes over. She was a looker, and being seen with a looker is good for one's image. One thing about the exquisite Miss Wilson, Carol Ann, for friends is that thing for ice Coffee before it even had hit the market. I remember her ordering one in a greasy spoon on Davenport or Dupont in Toronto. Ice Coffee, please. Thirty years before those things got mainstream. Thirty years before Starbucks.

As the short—order cook with a tattooed anchor on his forearm grabbed a coffee silex of tar looking stuff off the back burner of that Bunns coffee maker. Poured a cup on a popped 3 ice cubes saying, it should be cold in a few minutes. Well, that was it, an Ice Coffee. So, Miss Wilson, in her habitual elegance, took a small sack of sweet and low, a cup of cream and there she had iced coffee. No matter what, that woman had sex appeal. Vargas, May 1942 calendar girl. Go check this out. Ice coffee was a simple thing. We made is complicated and time-consuming. As for everything else.

Silly to think that whenever the image of Miss Wilson comes to my mind, this old English song from Vickie Lynn comes to my mind. I sometimes spent a few days with her while she was at Queen's University in Kingston. It may have a bit of a Chita Riviera song as well.

A Lovely Weekend.

I haven't said thanks for that lovely weekend
Those two days of heaven you helped me spend
The thrill of your kiss as you stepped off the train
The smile in your eyes like the sun after rain

And so. We always laughed at Ross's story until he popped out a BW picture of a Canadian Signals Corp soldier in his wool short coat battle dress with black boots sitting in a fancy porcelain tub. Yes, he did slip into Josephine's tub at the Louvre Museum. Just as this GI who stole Adolph's photo album at his Eagle's nest retreat or this uncle who snatched a Union Jack flag, Trafalgar square in London. Trophies of youth, bravery, courage, silliness but freedom. Small chunks of eternity.

Could have been something more. Could have been another story. I had more walkabout to do as she did. We met many years later in Toronto. Life had been good to her. Life was good for me. Mixed emotion, but no regrets, just happy memories.

Is your old man, Ross, still doing silly things?

A little less, He is growing too old for that, but once in a while he still does silly. He does miss his flower house and the florist trade.

Do you still have this Simon Garfunkel wrapped in newspaper. Still dancing on the: The Cars?

Um ! Do you remember that?

Carolle Ann ?

Who's gonna drive you home, tonight !

Who's gonna pick you up
When you fall?
Who's gonna hang it up
When you call?
Who's gonna pay attention
To your dreams?
Who's gonna plug their ears
When you scream?

She loved The Cars.

Small chucks of eternity.

Some say museums are an organized display of dead, static art. I believe they are in fact very lively. Static art in plastic life. It's the visitor that gives life to them.

I have always been a museum buff. All types of museum, but museum. There are many types and in some sense antique shops can also become a form of museum. A museum is a collection of objects, physically spaced and arranged in a manner that they can tell a story.

For me, I could spend a long time observing a masterpiece at every possible angle. Posing, reflecting, absorbing as my wife and my daughter are already at the Museum boutique. To each its priorities.

I once heard that line. My Great Grand Mother posed for Toulouse Lautrec at the Belle Époque. That was Camille. She dropped it as we entered the National Gallery of art in Washington, D.C. That was a powerful statement as we know the history of Lautrec, where he artistically evolved. Here is an anecdote. Hell of an anecdote. The Moulin Rouge, Paris Red light and the city's Brothels. That young person never talked about anything else but her sex life. Seems that it was well fulfilled, so to speak. I am fine with that. I think it was one of the reasons she had been sent on tour for a few weeks in North America. Keep her out of trouble. It's business. On every tour, there was a special request. Could you please take me to that store, the museum, this Jazz bar? I have to find a? Can you babysit the kid while we, you know? Among others.

When Camille, in her 20s gorgeous, traveling with an uncle and an aunt on this east coast North American tour, asked me to take her to the National Gallery while in Washington. Redhead with freckles and green eyes. Let's say I was a bit puzzled. Her aunt was popping anti depressor like it's out of style and her uncle looked and talked like Cannon, Walter Conrad and had to have a Queen bed in every hotel. I remember having to negotiate that, when possible, to all hotels. I had never offered the couple to take the niece to my bedroom to liberate a bed and make life easier for them. It's very risky to gauge people sense of humor with the sex topic.

Sure, I could take you there and while at the D.C. mall we can also see Dorothy's (wizard of oz) red shoes and Fonzie's leather jacket at the museum of American History.

Even if I was Stoic for most of my Tour guide years, Some customer shared personal stuff to you that changed your vision and the way you interacted with them. My wife died 6 months ago. A top-notch woman Swiss banker relaxed and sitting at a pub table in front of a beer and a plate of smoked salmon dropped the: I had to authorize the last morphine treatment for my cancer ridden father as she dropped a tear. Let's have another serving of smoked salmon, life is short. That did the trick. The power of the smoked salmon plate.

Many sad stories resurfaced while those people were relaxing on vacation. Not exactly easy to deal with those sagas. Every time, it squeezed my heart and tried to make the best of their trip under my care. Those people are on vacation, sometimes to change their mind as in the case of Mr. Picard, 92 years old, from Paris. He wanted to see a part of America before he died, I guess. I showed this French gentleman all that I could, but it is a parcel of all that this person who lived in Paris from 1889 on taught me as a witness of history and final wisdom. He knew it, guessed it, felt it and could communicate it. I felt that he needed to share his life experience with younger people one last time. I was all ears. Furthermore, I benefited a lot from my encounter with this person.

As I toured the National Gallery in DC, Camille contemplating some abstract art also dropped about her Grand Father who had been forced into Nazis labor camp, salt mines. I discovered a new person, A deeper persona that afternoon as we talked about Nouvel Art, Belle Époque, impressionism as I showed her my American favorite realist sketches from Wyeth to Hopper.

Labor camp. Here are some that we could not exactly grasp here in Canada. Something was happening. A type of connection on aesthetics, art, history, but it went against the rules I wrote with a black marker on the refrigerator at home. Don't get involved with customers, or try to. (unless purely sexual) Long distances relationship hurt. They really hurt. Don't do that unless you love hitting your thumbs with a hammer for the hell of it. They are bad because they ultimately lead nowhere. Nowhere IS the gates of conscience hell.

The brain pauses. You stop. The camera rolls in the brain.

It brought my mind back home. A mental picture of home. Home as the family I heard about but never met in person. Those parents I saw in those BW picture albums, Those albums with black cardboard sheets and small fancy triangular sticks on corners to hold pictures in place. They had those family album pictures in some Blondie's cartoon captions. My family. A placid country for centuries. My parents and ancestry never had it easy, but the concept of a military invasion and occupation is something that dates from, what, the 1760s for the last time. So, I have these mental pictures of both my Grand Father. One rubbing elbows with the organized crime trading illegal alcohol and tobacco on an Indian Scout with a sidecar (the prohibition days). My other Grandfather, (a bit more disciplined and law-abiding, but this unconditional Bing Crosby fan). Same era, 1920s to 1940s) pushing a Milwaukee F7s steam locomotive to its technical limits to be on time for the Christmas mass at the Joliette Cathedral. In both cases, I can only imagine them at twilight time under a full moon for whatever romantic reasons. The doomed motorcycle or the train to hell. I could not imagine them otherwise but free. Free, as much as a family man could have been then. This lasting image of responsible family men in another era. A poetic one.

As we finished off the tour, at the habitual museum souvenir shop, she grabbed a book at the museum Boutique about the Belle Époque and through the page stopped at this picture with a tall red head. Look, this is my great Grand Mother. That thing I was feeling got even stronger. This little freckled face got to be so appealing. The staff at the Smithsonian was astonished, and they call the Conservator of the Museum for a Press picture. Little did we know, the somewhat anodyne story became important.

We talked about the realist. Namely, Hopper. I've once had the occasion to follow two people in a Hopper exhibit in Boston that had known him personally and were exchanging on the subject while touring his exhibit. I stayed behind and listened.

Hopper was almost deaf, it partly explains the stillness, tranquility and perceptible silence of most of his painting. Hopper seized the magic of a somewhat very still setting, Very ordinary to their respective period places, but he made them magic. He made them interrogative. They tell a beautiful story of everyday enchantment.

He would have loved driving a city bus in the wee hours of the morning, listening to Gregorian or Russian Orthodox religious chants. He was also a cheapskate and slept in his car while on the road, painting to avoid hotel fees. Some of his most known masterpieces were sketched in the cheapest Chop Suey's restaurants of NYC. Those that bought cheap square wrought iron teapots. I could also give an impressive lecture on Wyeth: Christina's world as she was paralyzed by polio. Wyeth took inspiration for this painting from farmland in Maine. An outstanding display of yellow, brown, and gray with this notch of pink that gives away the clues to the meaning of the painting.

I am on the road and all those souvenirs come vividly to my mind tonight. We had sparked them. I don't know. They are in the air and I am catching them back.

Meeting are event where notes are kept in minutes and time lost by hours.
                                          Gen Joseph Stilwell.

I am back on Guy st. Guy, between Ste-Catherine and De Maisonneuve. Not an interesting part of Montreal. In fact, this section sucks. As my mind, memory and imagination take me back decades behind, as my body is on that bus. Driving it would ultimately take me down to that place where I got my first job in the big city. Corner Guy st and De Maisonneuve Boul, The Guy Concordia sector.

This finance representation gig was 35 something years ago. Occasionally, when I leave the bus idling on Guy st in the Metro drop zone. I go to the Java U. Espresso shop located in front of the Bethune park. A few minutes to look at those people chasing dreams or evading regrets, like those kids chasing butterflies with a thin net or soap bubbles coming from toy shops around the block. Bubbles floating free in the summer air. Life leaking like soap bubbles from a TV set. They have this commodity that escapes to many of us; dreams or time to dream.

We've all been there. Why not quit it all and go butterfly chasing with the marginals of our society? Sell the house, sell the car, sell the kids, I am not coming home as per Colonel Walter Kurtz to his wife, discovering the meaning of life and death in the jungles of Southeast Asia; namely Vietnam. A recurring thought these days for many of us, I presume. Christopher Wool made a famous word painting of those tantalizing words as how they could be rooted in our collective unconscious.

I remember those days.

As Rodney Dangerfield had no respect, many small pamphlet books emerged. A social revolution emerged from the Yuppie Handbook pamphlet book. This $6.95 book that portrayed a new trend as Faith Popcorn invented 20 years earlier the concept of Cocoonism and Xaviera Hollander, mastered the sex writing. The Yuppie Handbook. The epitome of a material status era, underlined by a line from a Stock Market movie, Greed is good. Or later on in the same decade, the take the pain also became a society cry. I have always been more a Sgt Barnes than a Stephen Geeko.

The cell phones were not in yet, but we found the freedom of the answering machine. That electronic device that could take phone calls for you. The time of sitting by the phone expecting a call was over. Some machine answered the call for you. Magic. Later, there came a way to check your message at a distance. Wow. That was brilliant.

Rotary phone and the answering machine. The gizmo made the popular ELO song, telephone line, quite obsolete or meaningless, but it relates to many of my generation and to me for sure. A bit like this It must be his song, a bit more dramatic and jazz, written by my Vicky Carr. It's about expecting, waiting or avoiding making a phone call. The stress of the ring or the rolling dial. A phone call that may have made your whole life different that did not happen, or you missed or worse, did not do.

The song went like this.

Let it please be him, oh dear God
It must be him or I shall die
Or I shall die
Oh hello, hello my dear God
It must be him, but it's not him
And then I die
That's when I die

Nowadays, kids are nervously scrolling on their phone to check for messages. These kids, they are missing an entire universe, and they'll never know about it. Reminds me that there were calls that I should have made, but I also had the tendency to lose those little pieces of paper where I wrote important numbers. The Post it fad.

Friday. Thank God it's Friday.

It's been a traffic crazy early June Friday. Scorching hot today, as most summers have been getting since the last ten years. No AC on those Slinky models, so I sometimes drive with the door open to catch some fresh air and feel the beat of the city. Against all security rules, but weren't rules meant to be broken. A primary school teacher did that at the beginning of the school year to demonstrate grammar rules. She took a cheap wooden ruler and snapped it in front of the class, stating the three tenses. Break, Breaking, Broken. Once she saw the light in the kid's eyes, she looked at us with a satisfied smile and sat at the desk. Damn, that person would not know how she influenced the rest of my life. Mrs. O'Early. Kathleen O'Early. Kathleen, you made a rebel out of me.

On Fridays, clients are nice and laid back. The CBC Jazz radio program is at its best. The old TGIF magic is in the air. They always keep the best tracks for Friday evening. It's time to push the seat back, relax and reminisce. As the sun sets, you let the jazz sink into you like the caffeine of a double Espresso kicking in. Memories are always your best company on the job. Yet, If you don't have your marbles in line, your mind may become your worst enemy on the job. Got to keep your thoughts and doubts in structured order to last in the trade.

Radio time!

Every driver in the business create his route atmosphere. From talk radio to sport radio to whatever, we all create our riding universe. A bus route is a living thing. Someday she is nice, someday she is pissed. She will let you play your role or make your life miserable. She is as capricious as all the curves, hills, tight corner and bizarre passengers she will throw at you. The ambiance represents the state of mind of the driver. Mine is classical in the morning and Jazzy after 6 PM.

Stan or Emilie Claire or the flying nun tonight? Stan (100.7 FM) has this wall-to-wall jazz program on the CBC that smells of coffee and smoke. Stan takes you to recording in 1966 or 1972, jazz, big band, singers. He is the voice of Bessie Smith, Ella Fitzgerald, he turns your bus into a Jazz Club. Stan tells you who was there. Who was working with whom. He is a genuinely laid-back jazz encyclopedia and lives by the blue note life code. Stan takes you there. His music sets the city beat. Just as he was there when it happened and probably could tell you about the license plate number of the cars on the street parked in front of the studio and who got a parking ticket. I can imagine Stan with the record sleeve in his hand reading the credits behind the microphone.

Stan, let me see this record sleeve, is it a Verve?

There we go

It's almost like being next to him in the studio.

Yes, it's a Verve.

Take me to your record!

As per Emilie Claire, (99.5 FM) she is the négligée boudoir type. It is a sexy, sassy sax. Her playlist is always romantic and her comment with a low tone husky voice and a sexy accent takes you to her place. Her living room. She is there, talking, singing and showing you her record collection. Sexy and light with a zest. She calls her show Between the Jazz and the Java. Emily broadcasts for a private radio network, but has the exclusivity of the Jazz evenings. Whether it's Stan, Emilie Claire or the catholic nuns at Radio VM (91.3 FM) spinning classic jazz 78 rpm vinyls from labels and artists unheard of before, they take you there. Nuns devoid their life to God, she does dedicate it to God and Jazz and is very intense about it. Away from the wheel, away in time, feeling, and space, floating 4 ft above asphalt. You will be doing the same movement as the generation of drivers before you, perhaps listening to the same music on the same physical street corner with a new twist. Music transcends time.

For those that gravitated to the tight-knit Montreal's Jazz city scene, we know that Emilie Claire wears a jean and a T-shirt when she does her radio show. She pushes the boudoir atmosphere, but it never gets heavy or cliché. It is the concept of the show. I have been introduced to Emily Claire by my saxophone teacher, who sometimes does gigs for her. Beautiful, talented and easy going. Stan rarely drinks coffee and does not smoke. It's also a cliché. But, the Catholic nun spinning ancient 78 rpm vinyl, yes she does LSD. She plays all those Bluebirds, Decca, Odeon, Okeh, Crown records. All of them with the knowledge to introduce the music diligently with the special effects proper to those old plates. On the other hand, Emilie has a collection of 60s french music and has a signature on those Parapluie de Cherbourg or Un homme et une femme type music too. All that is to keep the jazz mythic going. Jazz is the signature of this city. A place of all rackets and liberties, a place to grow, live and imagine. A Sin City.

Before these guys was the Jazz ballroom dance broadcast live from The Jupiter Room. Always loved this evocative name for an optimistic futuristic space era, the 1950s. All evocation of a Jackie Gleason or Lawrence Welk format. Very Jetson's, George Pal or Rocket XL V inclined indeed. Local FM stations broadcasted Saturday evening live, the dance and big band star-studded evening from the notorious Jupiter Room and the Dorval Hilton. Those were the radio days.

Dorval airport was a stop to the North Atlantic Ferry route in the 1940s. It became an International class airport in the 1950s. The Dorval Airport Hilton, a modern 1960s hotel, was so close to the end of an airstrip that the radio audience could almost hear the noise of a Connie taking off, figuratively speaking, of course. Big bands. Singers, live audience, live music, Life in a glamorous setting. The Jupiter Room was, on Saturday evening, the place to be in Montreal and then, this generation slowly disappeared. A sort of blast from the past deal. The Evening at the Jupiter was phased out, while all those famous Steakhouse also disappeared, taking with them baked potatoes with sour cream and chives. As I miss this radio show, perhaps an era too, as I miss those old-fashioned Steak Houses with sturdy wood furniture and red leather seats.

Came that other radio show: Lovers and other strangers. One or two hours of crooner time.

Today. There are 37 radio stations in this city. 3 that plays music. 3 that talks about sport and nonsense. The rest of them play mostly disembodied voice stuff, so-called music. The same so-called family of music you can hear in trendy malls. The Muzak 2.0. Just like those IT program patches we ordered to fix programs in India or Pakistan, those new music pieces are like data patches to address the anxiety of those who cannot deal with noise absence. The white noise concept.

It calms their anxiety, but it is all far from being nor music nor art as art edifies the soul, this stuff does not. If you are patient, sometimes you could catch the news from Radio Vatican at the catholic Radio VM. They interview philosophers and scientists. They always have a different take on world events, presented with this slight Vatican Italian accent and upper politeness that smells like Aqua Velva or other cheap aftershave from their side of the world to ours. They remind me of those Priest Sermons in my youth or the perfume of the priest at the communion.

When the radio scanner starts, acting as a mega Ouija board, it picks up more extra terrestrial music. Stuff customized and made for a network or a few private stations. It sounds as if the station dictates everything, from the Lyrics to the rhythm. Standard. Standardized to fit the commercial perception of a customer need. Needs as per the committee decides what the auditor loves or condition them. Just as the mice in a Skinner box. A few keywords, a message of virtual love, a diluted beat, musical food pellets, a maze, and you are this rat. Shine bright as a diamond.

Simply put, the Keynesian beauty pageant rule.

A beauty contest where judges are rewarded for selecting the most popular faces among all judges, rather than those they may personally find the most attractive.

A universe of music and communication led by the very Keynesian rule of the beauty pageant. Misunderstood that this Keynesian rule was a parabolic joke on how market works, underlining structural deficiencies. Not a rule to abide by. A cynical joke. As an old stockbroker once told me. See how the market gets a boner out of a ticker/stock with no specific reasons, and how they speculate on it. No fundamentals, just pure speculation. Everything is a Ponzi, more or less. The profit is in the movement. My father was this old stockbroker.

As Maynard Keynes made a humorist statement about the state of our society almost a century ago, management school caught upon the concept as an approach to market rule. What began as a metaphor or an educated initiate joke became a certified rule.

There are some ideas so wrong that only a very intelligent person could believe in them.(Georges Orwell).

Since humans think they are more intelligent in a group, as it has often been historically proven otherwise, the modern era gave birth to the committee and the quintessential meeting. A nice way of sharing collective failure and have no one ever being directly blamed. Now, if your scientific spirit wants to see the utmost group stupidity possible, I would suggest the observation of a High School Basketball team going to a tournament in a city bus. Heading to McDonald's is where you can observe them the best in their natural habitat. Let's keep a scientific spirit here, please.

Now we've assisted in the birth of Snookerism. In snookerism, human resources are moving side wards to front ward, but never upward. Upward mobility does not exist anymore. You seem to be moving, but in fact you're not. You are not moving at all.

Yes, you work there but work is not what you are, just what you do, to be. A good job is less than a dog, as the dog will always love you back, Mattie. (Moonlighting). I clearly remember that line from a young Bruce Willis to Cybil Shepherd in a memorable sitcom, as only the 1980s produced them. I think it was the episode where Chris Brinkley was a guest appearance. Mattie !

Yet, there are those rubber meets asphalt that defines your vision of business and ethics.

One of my childhood friends made it big. Great financial career. Luc ended up in charge of Asian accounts for a large investment holding. He chose not to become a -eer- or a -ologist—but a -ian -. He managed billions but spent his life in planes and as he said: going to Asia in a private jet looks good, but it's as comfortable as driving all day in a subcompact. Those things are just not large enough for ocean crossing. So, there, for the life of the rich and famous. All about the impression it leaves. A holding has to look rich to instill confidence to its investor, and it's all about it, the look. The person always stayed down to earth, lively and funny, and he had a very upscale office not far from my cubicle, three office towers down the street in downtown Montreal. Here is a good demonstration on how the business world works, and it is funny. Seen from bottom-liners view.

From this lunch for this presentation to this coffee comes this: Does anyone know anyone investing in China? I raised my hand and said yes. Yes, but it has to be solid, and I will strictly introduce it here. It's a referral.

Looked at the prospectus. Research. Referral, credit, lingo, and OK lets see if this could be plugged in somewhere.

So, I had an angle to that technology that would ensure full combustion for coal. Zero emission. Proven. Couple of mad scientist entrepreneurs I knew. University studies to back it up. Subsidies and the whole Govt scheme to back it up. We saved the world from Godzilla, Gorgo and all those Ultraman monsters, but it needed market dev money with no ROI in sight. Not an easy sale. China was THE most interesting market and well, I could test the concept with a man who knows China upside down. My childhood buddy, Luc.

Here is the scene. Meets with Luc by the Roman fountain at the World Trade Center (the replica of the Roman fountain where people throw pennies).

Yo bro!

Listen, I got this business venture that may be of interest to you and the holding in Asia. It's a process that ensures 100% combustion of coal and cuts emission and CO'2 and pollution and comes in packs of 6 or 12 like the Hot Dog breads. Makes the poets, the medias and the politicians happy, so they can gather and Frolic as happy frolicking peasants

Sounds cool but, how many kids you got Bert, you still have one.

Yeap, I have a daughter and that's it

Imagine, the top dog The Great Helmsman in China has 1.4 billion mouths to feed every morning, and he worries about it. Unless it can pull 3 times more energy from a piece of coal, China will not be interested. Now imagine you have 16 kids to feed.

OK, 16, on a lousy job.

On a lousy job, do you think that I could show up at your place to sell you a gizmo that would cut the emission of your fireplace for an arm and a leg, only to please your neighbor? Dinner time, unsolicited. Those Goddamn consultants. Show me your watch, I'll tell you what time it is.

No, of course, and do I hate peddlers?

OK, now that you got your answer, the real question here is Smoke Meat. Ben's or Schwartz?

Bottom-liner never beat around the bush. They go straight to the jugular vein. Snap. Time is money, and they command a lot of time and money, so they figure out things fast, never negotiate and make a final decision. Next!

Smoked meat became the order of the day and desert, the varia.

Ben's held shop corners of de Maisonneuve and Cathcart or around. An example of Art Deco—modern streamline decor. The place was filled with BW pictures or entertainment people who made the fame of the wild night of Montreal as per many were dead for a good while as this Uncle Tom Auburn, The Uncle Tom magic show. Tom had his mug at the entrance of this non-heated restaurant, relying strictly on the heat of the kitchen. Cold, damp, but always full. The place looked like this Edward Hopper night owl restaurant with a large window pane, tile, and terrazzo floor. Cafeteria line. Chrome tubing. Turnstile and the old man on a stool wearing a black french beret at the cash. Terrazzo floor. In its 1960s heyday, Ben's would help 8000 customers a day.

Terrazzo was used for public buildings, namely school, hospitals, banks, and many barber shops. Interesting material if you are into floor and shoes, I guess. Always thought that a classy man's look involved Dacs or McPherson wingtips shoes, pants with outside cuffs on a terrazzo floor. Terrazzo was an expensive material, but it lasted for ages. Italians were the terrazzo specialists here. You had a tile or a terrazzo job to get done. Bang! The Italians were there. Now, Ben's has been part of Montreal for decades and did not age very well.

One day, someone (a real estate developer that disliked Smoke Meat) wanted the land for a high-rise tower without fashion flair, intricate architectural details, gingerbread or a common garden. Housing. Housing units. Man builds homes, banks housing units.

Another soulless place. All units painted in Greige, as narrow minds cannot afford the abstraction of colors. It comes with an elevator to share with these other condo people you would rather not see. Condo people and condo people don't like other Condo people, so be it. They are a scene of high-end prostitute, drug dealers, speculator, greedy liberal of the law profession, member of the medical scene and former glory sportscaster, entertainment people or financial gurus. This is no place to raise a kid. A place to wear gloves in the elevator. It's another form of physical or socioeconomic ghetto, or a demonstration that the ultimate scheme of natural justice works. Those that deserve one another tend to congregate in space and proper environment to their evolution.

Housing as a square box to fit components. You were a human, a person, and now you became a component and nobody told you about this change of regime. They will never be home. No matter the money you sink to make it feel homey. A few antique pieces of furniture with authentic patina, as per the one piled up on street corners at moving week and even a dog or the other beast I am not exactly fond of, will never make it a home. It is housing. Not homing.

OK, I said it. I hate cats. My book has no cats. I am allergic to cats. Be it.

Man builds home. Banks produce housing unit.

Since our world is based on the : just in time, fast to assemble and living or history of objects is somehow irrelevant, there is a gigantic market for so-called antique with a living. Objects that would have withstood the test of time and bear the scars of life. Antique traders call it Patina, as the layman would name it wear and tear, but there is a market for that. On that matter, I have always been wondering if Martians or other species are collecting old or vintage flying saucers as mankind collects old cars. Still.

So, sir, you saw that UFO landing in your field last night.

Yes sir, gentlemen of the NASA or the US Air Force

Did it have distinctive signs

Yes, it was an older model with a bit of rust and patina.

So to speak.

Patina, I could do patina. Given a frozen hockey puck, a stick, and a driveway and I could do spectacular patina. Even on a UFO. If you drive by those huge apartment buildings downtown or in the suburbs, you can notice piles of furniture once a week. Many are old with patina, and they are for free, just as those treadmills and stationary bicycles. 3 Months after Christmas, one could pick up enough stuff to start a gym, and it is free. So, there are three types of piles.

1. People who left during the night without paying the rent: Triangular. Heavy furniture at the bottom. Mattress on the side. No electronics.

2. People that died in the place but expected and supervised by the family: Square pile, mattress off the side

but wrapped. Neatly stacked heavy furniture. No electronics. Microwave missing.

3. People that died of violent death. Triangular, but wrapped in special biohazard stickered bags. (Yellow or dark blue) The whole stuff is there, clothes, records, electronics, treadmills. The mattress and sofas are missing in case there's bodily fluid or blood stains and the Microwave oven is on the top just like the cherry on the top of a Dairy Queen sundae.

* The final destination of the striped ironing board is also revealing. Right side, left side or crowning the pile... Were you contemplating having a gym at home? Wait 3 month after Christmas, all the gym hardware will be there, for you, ready to pick up free.

You can keep inventories of dangerous places or the rate of occupancy. Keeps the brain working.

So, there comes Ben's.

The promoter wanted to destroy Ben's. Stories circulated that the promoter would build around the landmark commerce. Then integrate the restaurant in a new complex of condos or. In fact, none of this happened. One morning, the wrecking ball showed up, and the comedy was over. Screw you Magic, Tom. No magic today Houuuuu dini !

As per all those demonstrations outside the city hall to preserve this otherwise ugly duckling building for the sakes of good memories or stories of hangovers that finished at Ben's in front of a Smoke Meat sandwich, a pickle and a cherry coke. No magic cure for a hangover there.

Let's do Schwartz on the main. We are closer. We were standing at the WTC building at Square
Victoria.

At Schwartz but they throw the plates at you and insult you in Yiddish. You are waited for with a stop watch and there's no parking on the strip. Somehow, traffic, tourists, staff or not, they still serve the best Smoke Meat in Montreal. It still is the best and well, you can always cross the street and go to The Main Deli. Schwartz also has a terrazzo floor and cherry coke. Just as good.

I remember meeting Celine Dion on the main street. I was driving the route 55 up North and blocking the entrance at a private celebration when her late husband bought Schwartz for roughly 40 times the value its yearly business figure. Her husband, once a young penniless YeYe singer, declared in front of a crowd that he would, one day, own a Smoke Meat restaurant. He made that statement in a booth at the Roi du Smoke Meat on St-Hubert st. My mother-in-law was at the booth next to his, but she knew him as a local bum. She hung around with those bums.

So back to the reopening of this Main st Institution. Vegas Style old Schwarz became the New Schwarz, although it still is the same old place but with a Take-Out annex and, of course, new marketization and mass distribution of the world known Smoke Meat in large surfaces. Big Deal. Unless you have a terrazzo floor at home, love to be squeezed with a loud neighbor and have your waiter raising hell to you in Yiddish, you missed the Schwartz general ambiance. It's a cheap emotionless substitute, just as watching a movie on a home theater. A fake orgasm. Too safe for comfort. There were days when everyone smoked at their table and upon at exiting Schwartz you also smelled like Smoke Meat, yet that was not unique to Schwartz. Yet, that, I could do without.

Traffic jam and local Press people. The Happy go lucky usual freeloaders. Like teenagers, always the muzzle in the trough. TV crews and the city bus blocking everyone. 55 St-Laurent North. Me, driving the 55 North that morning. She approached me with her big Jackie-O glass and by my window sang a little song to me. So, the words of her song were: Can you move your F…n bus, you are blocking the way to our VIP guest? Coming from her, it sounded heavenly, and so I did move my F…n bus because one F…n journalist moved his G. damn mobile van in the way. I and showbiz people. A love story. Pissed people lose their charisma instantly. Such is human nature, I guess. She has a Charlemagne French accent, let me tell you. You can take someone out of Charlemagne, but not Charlemagne out of a person. Honestly, it is just a funny encounter to me.

-o, Bert, you still dream of saving the planet?

Yet, I still wanted to save the planet, or more like save my ass on the planet, by helping the world's biggest polluter cut out on its carbon emission. Naive, juvenile, and silly, isn't it?

To come back to the topic of this possible human race saving technology on coal emission there it goes and remembers, it is not that a part of humanity does not want to save the planet it's more like the planet that does not want to be saved. Maybe as this abused person, that doesn't want to press charges against the abuser as it believes it's a misunderstood form of love.

OK, I know, I talk a lot or think too much.

So, whichever way you face it, *Sam Wong in China is not there to save the world. He knows it's going to be there tomorrow morning with its 1.4 billion mouths to feed. Before investing millions in a technology, they should check if there is a market, just like you check if there is water before diving into a pool. Right,

* There was one Asian family in my hometown. I know it is cliché but they held the Chinese restaurant (the one with number menu) and of course the laundry. Laundering as per the historical meaning of the term.

That was a part of the neighborhood, So let's go back to the Business scheme here

What do you think of business intelligence, The stocks are performing well? Any good to you.

The way I see it!

B.I. or B.S. you cannot spin valuable ratios at comparing apple to oranges. Fad, Fad as the Pepsi shoes or the bowling lanes. B.S. to me. There went my Cognos portfolio.

You can't push a system that could, comparing expense account and schedule and other, within the same enterprise, determining who has an affair with who and who's paying the lunch for a boss that fucks the payroll himself. As they all do.

No ROI on this one. In the corporate structure, the big boss hires people to block stuff that he is not supposed to know and doesn't want to be exposed to. You want to bypass this wall of suits and go counter culture with the execs?

I always had problems grasping the Corporate culture, as it is never clear-cut of rubber to asphalt.

Of my few unfortunate years in the IT business.

In the heydays of Montreal's IT business, when subsidies for whatever business scheme were like a fountain, sales team reps inviting each other to a fine restaurant or gentleman's lunch buffet all week as per one picked up the tab for the guys, and the next day another one and by cluster or trade show or... always on the holy expense account. The IT planet was full of those little extras, and it did last a long time before the controller on wheel figured it out. How many of those IT companies survived over 1 year? 4% maybe 5%. Not many. Why? The technology moved too fast to follow. The specialist acted like divas. The girls at those gentlemen's clubs were really good-looking and Montreal has amazing restaurant tables, but most IT companies were doomed right from the beginning. The IT company wanted to help a prospective customer's problem not by devising a proprietary technology that could be licensed and resold but by getting cash for the prospective customer and buying time, the time to find if the solution is done anywhere else in the world and be imported and adapted. They were from the Vic 20 or the Commodore 64 school. The nerds with dough. The rich pimple poppers.

Pay for a Jaguar and have a disguised Ford Taurus delivered as per this Eastern Europe rip-off. Fake it until you can make it. If you can make it, in fact. If it fails, the sales would look like a charlatan while the IT core would dissolve and start again pulling the same prank under a new name and company mission.

In the early internet days, no one or almost no one could answer a simple question: What's the difference between paying 5000 or, 50000 for a webpage. NOBODY. If some had customers like L'Oréal, I wished I could have had the Aubade account, some were dealing with more rubber to asphalt types of businesses. The less funky one. I ended up being a rep or business interface between a traditional catalog and business flyers printer and a happy lost in space IT firm with a skyrocketing stock, a sexy ticker but as hollow as a shell. It was not a happy marriage. The guys from Vignette in Texas putted on the most amazing show to get resellers.

And so, I had a few IT customers

There was this old printing tycoon who had most North American retail catalog contracts but wanted to upgrade to e-catalogue. Not that he wanted. Social and commercial and shareholders progress pushed him into that direction, and so were the stockbrokers. Some business could evolve into something else, but printers as per their tradition were doomed.

We affectionately called him uncle Charlie, and HE was not a happy camper. He was the last of the real boss. Mr. Dithers in Blondie comic strips. Charlie was a mix of Grumpy, Oscar the grouch and had this huge red alcoholic nose He saw a lot, knew a lot and loved to talk about politics and history. Personally, I liked that person. Now, unless you could entertain Charly with military history as the walls of his private office were ornate with pics or General Isaac Brock at the battle of Queenston Height or the Detroit Bluff or Passchendaele you would take a piece of his mind that lasted a few hours. He served whiskey on the rocks of those square crystal bottles from the moment he got to appreciate what you are. A bit of Blake Carrington.

For a brief moment, the man was on the top of the world's largest printer company. He loved the feeling of riding this dying wave.

Were you to avoid his eyes or start bending or being apologetic, you were dead meat. He wanted to talk to people of spine and character without hesitation. Now, I could entertain Charlie for quite a few whiskeys on ice worth of time about military history since my family has been to most of them, but at the end of the day, I had to deliver the goodies and my IT whiz did not deliver.

From the rumors on the street or at the Gentleman Club (Paree) it was clear that the IT firm I was working for was for sale. All the stippers were playing the ponies', penny stocks and the market. They all had a broker. We exchanged information between two sets of dance. The price of the stock was too high, so the short my stock game became an option. To take it down, the direction voluntarily made a bad decision over another, as it came naturally for them. Remember, Shaggy in Scoobie Doo was their professional model.

Those kids were throwing rocks at trains, made websites in the basement, watched Star Trek became top entrepreneurs in a matter of months. Their knowledge had gained instantaneous high value, and there were not many of them. They got rich, but stupid rich on options that eventually became worthless as they could never keep up nor deliver company growth. They surrounded themselves with alike, but not the right alike, I guess.

The Europeans were to buy us out. (The French.) Pilfer our accounts. Make the: We Come in Peace speech as per there would be no job cuts... (lol) It's a cookbook. Time horizon: 12 weeks. 12 weeks to settle the score with the IT whiz living on billable hours. Party was over. Reality struck. These overconfident, condescending, arrogant, Game Boy generation geeks with plenty of skills, imagination but no spine nor common sense were done. Cooked. Remember, It's a Cook Book. (Twilight Zone Classic)

Let's open a parenthesis about the speeches a new boss or supervisor or commanding officer would officially throw at you as being your boss was the job of his or her dream and yours and its presence is part of your nightmare. They dream of this moment. They all dreamt of being there, in this lousy structure. This lousy Army unit. This lousy universe. They were born to accomplish greatness and fulfill their divine mission by becoming your boss or friend or business associates. Dreaming of a job. Dreaming of a Minivan, Dreaming of a kitchen, some people really lack imagination. Dreaming of someday having a real dream or something a little more exciting.

The new guys in the field wanted to look like Bono. Bono?

Came the Bono lifestyle and look in the sales field. The Bono executive wannabe look. An attitude fueled by a former PM of Canada: Paul Martin. I once met Paul in an elevator after a meeting at the exec level of the National bank. Genuine and accessible and well, I must admit, the man was funny. Martin loved Bono for what he represented. Bono loved Martin, as he was a visionary Premier of a progressive country. Make no mistakes, for the most of us, that meant no pro bono, alright.

So, one day as I received an urgent email from the office of Charlie asking: how to remedy the situation about a Sears e-catalogue that was about to be 6 months late. I took time to be very creative. I did not feel like buying time, or being the stuff in the sandwich between the skilled unionized manpower and the direction. This gig had 3 months left in it. ¼ of a fuel tank. As the rule of the thumb. In an ailing company, if you play by your rules and proudly deliver even against the will of the corporate you'll last 3 months and if you suck up to their stupid plans and crawl your way, be a yes-man to work the stupid plan, every morning. You may gain an extra 2 to 3 weeks. I believe that it is dearly paid to act subhuman for 3 months and 3 weeks to cash in on 3 more weeks of lousy life. If I remember well, the main line of my reply were like that:

Fed up, was I, I wrote this wicked e-mail reply.

I would strongly suggest a harbor cruise for my whole IT team working on this catalog project. We could have the boat torpedoed and watch them sink and none of those turkeys will have the common sense to swim to shore, and many of them have big and fat heads. So, they sink head first. Outsource somewhere else.

Always tell the truth, George, It is the easiest thing to remember.

Glengarry, Glenn, Ross.

Evasive action! Man's ultimate mission in life is to evade from his human condition and live closer to his dream state. The separation between the real and the unreal. The exciting and the boring.

We were both U boat Stories fans. They eventually got torpedoed, but in another manner.

So, I got that emergency call from that London Schools of economics graduate, whom also happened to be my boss. Damn !!! She was displeased to say the least. I handled the largest but most despised customer. Fact of the matter is that the only time she appeared somehow alive, human and, well, sexy, was when she was pissed. She had been looking for a good reason to liquidate me, my circle of idiot friends, my out of the world business scheme and those hefty expenses accounts; I gave her a helluva good one. Had she listened to some of my delirious project concept, she would have been on the head of PayPal before PayPal existed.

Diann Clother disappeared from the scene after the acquisition too. Her absolute faith in the system had saved her 3 weeks. I must admit, she was sexy in her tight skirts. I will miss her for that but, nonetheless, party or not, she would not have danced do the hustle with me anyway.

Ho dear! Am I to be dead in the IT world? I hope so.

That brought an emergency meeting with Dr. Strangelove. The new finance controller. He looked and acted like (Peter Sellers) Dr. Strangelove. Upper management rolled him out of his Mercedes handicapped van every morning and booted him to a broom cupboard, crunching numbers all day. Workaholic and sadistic with expenses. At the end of the meeting, I informed him that his boss's car was at the war museum in Ottawa.

Diagnostic. An OK severance package. My ego was satisfied. A great story to tell. Upon reading my reply, uncle Charly smiled and laughed because he disliked this new e-catalogue era idea. He was a Yellow Pages man. A Christmas catalog person. Maybe he even bought the Mr. Snow toy out of the Christmas Sears catalog for his kids. He loved the weight, the smell, the color of those bulky books. The smile that those catalogs brought to families. Catalog and other magazines, namely those with centerfold pages. He thought that he could, in his own way, bring a form of happiness to homes and that was his mission. His credo.

His existence. The ink, the sweat, the 8, 12, 16 color process and the Scotch on the Rocks. He, like me, hated those new processes. He, like me, loved his boys: the printers. The workers, the blue collars, the skilled men. The pool hall folks. Sometimes the decent man wins for his kind. He becomes a champion. A champion of a good laugh at work. The light of the Doers in this so abstract thinker world.

A champion.

A champion of light vs. the corporate darkness. In a dog-eat-dog world, upon leaving a company, especially a dying one, don't burn bridges. Blow them to smithereens and with confidence. There is no salvation there. Make a turning back impossible, forward will be the only way up and out. You may take some flak, but the salvation is ahead. Those White Cliffs of Dover. Life is too short to suck on back at a losing enterprise You owe them shit. They bought your time, You sold them your time.

On this specific deal, I could say. Sales 10 IT team 0. Tony Randall 0 too.

Eventually, we have lost the material war, but we are still fighting the spiritual one.

On the last merry meeting with Charly we had this argument of leadership as per one of my favorite

No good decision was ever made in a swivel chair. Gen George Patton.

But all concepts don't sell. On a windy day, even a turkey can fly. Not every day is windy.

And I am back with my childhood friend on the holy quest for the ultimate Montreal's Smoke Meat sandwich.

Got that one right, Bert. Some things sell, but not all for obvious reasons.

We had this War of the World routine act in high school as I was showing Luc, martian blood on a handkerchief as per the 1953 movie. The: look Helen, Martian blood and after a 1.2.3. Cue, Helen, as women did in the 1950 horror movie, went hysterical. There was that other movie where people in a village became slaves of martian whom control their thought while they were sleeping to have them to fix their spacecraft crashed in the desert. It came from Outer Space. Only one man did not fall for it because he had a metal plate in his head and could not be controlled by, whoever the fuck. Maybe he was wired differently, too.

Sometimes I wonder how I get this metal plate in my head. Nothing seems to get through it. We also had that Village of the Damned family on the street. The 4 boys were blonde and looked evil possessed. The nickname stuck to these guys as the police were often at that place, and you could hear the policemen saying, these damn... Now, if you really want deep thought 50s Sci FI, I would recommend Forbidden Planet. Very beatnik approach to Freudian psychology and esthetic. Starring Leslie Nielsen in a serious to death role. I am confident that Martha would be proud of this description.

We grew up together. Remember, it is our meeting here. I may have lost you a few pages ago, but it is still our meeting. The meeting is a mental memory because, at this very moment, I am also driving a bus in a tight area on a Friday evening and damn it is hot tonight. Do you think this is laborious reading? Try Umberto Eco.

As teenagers, we both worked on weekend evenings washing dishes at the Ramada Hotel up the street. Keen motivated teenagers dreaming of business school and a Enduro motorcycle or such, but we were ready to work for it. Luc ended up with a Kawasaki 125 as I have always been on the scooter side of things. The Italian flair. The Lambretta, the Vespa, the Italian girls with their Sophia Loren look. PAZAZZ. Motions were setted and Espresso already kicked in.

Luc was a neighbor, an old friend and his father like mine was a WWII vet. Army. He was a Canadian Army PT instructor in England, as they were all athletes in that family. We went to primary school, HS and attended the same Catholic Church. He did all the right move and kept all the appropriate connections. I did all the bizarre moves and did not make many connections. He had faith in progress and the system. I perpetually questioned faith and the system. He loved answers, I preferred questions. He loved answers and facts. I appreciated questions and theories.

We were both into the grooves of Ramsey Lewis or Herbie Hancock. He had a twin sister, Andrea, on whom he liked to pull wicked pranks. Just like rattling her bed frame hiding underneath a few nights after, scared like all of us, she sneaked out to see the movie The Exorcist. Not a good idea.

Cancer took Andrea many years ago. Another sobering moment we could have done without.

We were from a 60s suburban mall city type. The dream was of the Evil Knievel pinball machine at the arcade. The guys in sleeveless leather vest shooting pool. Jennifer with her good look, flat blonde hair, blue eyes and this cute scarf tied on her neck as she was pushing Red Tab jeans at the Exode Jeans shop. A 70s angel in the centerfold as per the song.

So, we both worked at the restaurant hotel up the street by the Laurier Boulevard, the bridge entrance to the city. They were the first brand hotel on the strip going to the old city and catered to countless bus tours. This place was rolling. Bus tours. Plenty of tour buses.

The restaurant had 2 stories and there were two dishwashers on duty. Seafood downstairs, French classy upstairs. We often picked up that shift. We were 16 and I had a moped. The motobecane deal. There was this extra source of revenue. Empty beer bottles from the bar left by the garbage container. You could get $4 a case at the grocery store so, on the way back home, we grabbed one, two, and then the last time 6. So, last time we pulled that trick, at midnight, once all work was over we stacked the 6 cases of beer, me and Luke on the moped and that was a lot of weight. We got greedy! The Moped of fools.

On the way down home because it was hilly, the moped, already at 25MPH,(no helmet) went out of control as we ended up slipping on the side emptying 144 bottles of beer on a clean, quiet, upper middle-class cozy city street. We had to pick up all those bottles before someone called the cop. We ended up with had a few bruises, torn jeans. We laughed our head off. That was so funny. Not safe, but funny. What's a few stitches, bruises and torn jeans for a good clean fun. Now the guys manages billions.

A clean fun that you will never forget. You can talk about that to a person who is on many International company boards and known as a serious bottom-line person. In that story, his eyes will light up, and he will smile. But only two people know about that one, me and him.

We drove to Schwartz and found a parking spot. That is a story by itself.

Let's do Schwartz. They are a pain in the ass. So is life. What we lived in the 1970s. Not always safe, but so lively.

Do you remember our buddy Malloy?

Yeap, dying at 16 years old, damn shame.

At that moment, discussion sober up a bit. We were both somehow grateful of being on the short list of those who made it to our age, with no illusion as per we could be recalled to the factory up there instantly or on short notice. On the other hand, we lived the fullest of what we could live without asking or telling too much to our parents. We lived.

We went to Schwartz and at the sight of the tourist line up at the door we decided to cross the street to go to The Main Deli. The Main does not have the Cherry Coke, but has the rice pudding desert or the Jello included in the lunch deal. As in the High School days, we played talking Jello as inspired by a movie that marked our youth, The Blob. Men grow old and act like men, serious, responsible and the whole gimmick, but at the end of the day, we are all overgrown kids.

No matter what they say, we are all in this alone!

Are you taking that pickle?

Shit! Just asking.

You can't attack me with a fork, dude. This is dangerous!

Men are only as good as their technical development allows them to be. George Orwell.

Yet, it is a very optimistic view of the world

Safety, security, and the new El Dorado of those who cannot produce anything useful for their fellow man. The useless folks. Nothing ever happened to them, so they want to make sure that they will not be left alone. An highly evolved form of underlying creeping jealousy. Jealousy, which is also a Capital sin. We are led by sinners. Sinners or loser, your pick. Have you ever had any doubts? People Left… on the margins of society. The Left over. OK, The nerds.

We all worked relentlessly and took all types of risks to make our place under the sun. Physical, health, financial, emotional. We played a lot. Sometimes we win, sometimes we lose. We kept at it, living one day at the time. While we were too busy working, paying our mortgage, putting the kids to school and making a living, the world got paranoid and had to become safe. Sneaky little bastard. Safety, the new holy grail. Results of deep thinking from a leftist clueless generation. In Italian, the Left is named Sinistro. Any clue here. If the right could create a whole interstate road system, the left will configure the toll booth, rest area and bathroom pictograms.

So much of left-wing thought is a kind of playing with fire by people who don't even know that fire is hot. Georges Orwell.

The left is like this person: pants down to the knees, stuck in argyle mud and peeing against the wind pretending life is good. That's my personal take.

Just like the cats to me.

Rejoice people it is safe. Safe but, oh, so boring !

I kept hearing my mom, in her last years of life, repeating she was happy in her residence because she was safe. They also fed her with a lot of small white pills to prevent her from realizing that the place sucks too. What's safe? Nothing could happen to you. Sad. Safe of any emotion. Safe from that walk in the April rain, enjoying the cold water running on your face and the sweet perfume of spring after a long winter. Safety is a dry place. Dry, without flavor, taste, color, bubbled paper wrapped. The safeitude state shares that with the internet Porn, it leaves no space for imagination. At least the porn stuff releases some hormones. Safeitude, non, zero. Hormonal type lobotomy.

How about this new safe? The counterproductive safe. A sclerotic society. This safe that sucks up energy aimlessly, the safe that creates confusion, stress, aggravation, insomnia, violence. This idling machine. This safe that sends people into the health care system on a wide variety of psychological pathologies and creates social problems. The safe of the 2nd floor Skinner boxes at Ikea that ends up being an important cause of argument, couple dislocation and divorce. Food pellets replaced by cinnamon buns and the perfume of pine wood, humid double wall cardboard and cinnamon. The safe that will drive you nuts.

This same safe that makes traffic intersections so complex that pedestrians, motorists or else lose patience and someone gets hurt. This safe that is reproduced millions of times in our society that no one questions its productive degree. This safe makes you run through a pair of brake pads in 2 years because of this permanent overbid of traffic signs and regulation. Cooking show safe and the safest way to make a souffle. Do you know how many thousands of people died and got maimed preparing or eating a souffle? Would Martha Stewart be, in fact, a black widow?

Safe and inclusive. The day government around the world have decided to introduce the Low Floor system buses on urban service; they made us all socially handicapped. City bus became orthopedic vehicle and let's face it, the access to the bus stop on a wheelchair are for many are still almost impossible. Physical of the street, signalization, curd access ramps. Notwithstanding the meteorological thing phenomenon called the seasons, among which stand winter. Arise this good old argument between driver and customer. I may repeat myself on this one but it is a matter of pride. Bus driver used to drive buses around. Now we are more into the orthopedic thing on wheels.

You should wait for me, I have mobility problems !

You should leave your place earlier to get to the bus stop, You have mobility concerns.

For 100 years, and for zillions of mechanical considerations buses had to have two steps to climb on to In a city known for its outside iron spiral staircase, the two steps were just a normal step. What's 2 steps after walking 2 hours in a shopping mall where there are also steps. Many steps, Same height, same steps, but ours are different because we carry a public service and has to be liquified or level down to get to the Keynesian Committee perception of the clientele.

Commons sense should bridge contradictory positions but it has disappeared from the radars, something like, 25 years ago. There it goes again. The decency issues. I always think of elder at bus stop as if they were my mother. Would my mother be running after a bus ? No, she was always a few minutes early at bus stop. Would she want to get in the bus with 10 bags of groceries and 3 kids? No, we had a Station Wagon for that. Bread came from the bread man, and so did from a Milkman. A man's world, I guess.

In this watertight safe environment there are no more space to move, grow and express oneself unless one is it fits the format.

Music, art, and jazz were at the roots of my rebellion.

At High School I was already the outcast listening to the pre-Head Hunter album : Herbie Hancock, a jazz era Jimi Hendrix, Woody Herman or Weather Report. Nobody in this Pepsi shoe, US Top Bell bottom jeans and Levis shirt listened to that, but me. Me, carrying my vinyls under my arm, riding a Motobecane moped and dating a girl from catholic private school living on the other side of town. From an appreciation of art over technique, I got to question the holy rules of the rationale upon which our society is based. This rigid, uncompromising rationale.

The rational that never accounts the concept and power or love. It believes blindly in the power of the magical hand of the market and the science that pulls the rabbit out of a hat, often. Contradictory indeed.

A world under so much stress that it fuels on performance and feeds on accidents.

Eddy once ran over a cyclist on the route 30 North. Or is it the other way around, as the cyclist ran under Eddy's bus. Eddy is a former Greyhound guy that was on the Montreal—NYC line. I met Eddy in another setting and professional life in one of those NY State service centers, Ramapo or New Baltimore, there are a few, but they all look the same. Small artificial communities lost in the Adirondack. Staffed by people from small towns you never suspected even existed. Relic ate of the pre-Ike Eisenhower era and the famous interstate system that permits one to cross the continent from ocean to ocean without seeing anything. As I once mentioned, the right made the Interstate road system as the left designed the bathroom's male, female pictograms,

As Eddy was taking his route no 31 last Friday PM trip down Viger st, a cyclist slipped underneath his bus. As if that person stole a base in a baseball game. There were no baseball diamonds in the vicinity. I could give you all technical and gory details, but it revolves around the fact that after a torrential rain, for a minute or so, pavement get very slippery as water pearls on the pavement oil before being absorbed. Accidents are always simple. They are like the Chekhov's pistols.

Statistically speaking, one has more opportunities to see road accidents and social misery spending 7 hours a day on the road than taking a private car at a private garage to drive it to the office tower garage and go to your office to do shit all day. There is that perpetual exchange of the Miserable going on between, the transit system, police, paramedic, hospitals and there it goes again. The misery cycles. We are an active part of that cycle. In fact, we do harvest misery or are we brokering it. Matter of angle here.

I had seen numerous accidents in the past few weeks. More than usual, More gory and violent than usual. Too many in a short delay. The last one was on the corner of the Metropolitan and St-Laurent st. A tractor trailer stopped. Blue tarps around the back wheel of the trailer. A cop and a truck driver in obvious deep shock sitting crying on the curb and the twisted mangled remains of this kid's bicycle on training wheels with anniversary gift bows and plastic flowers. Pink. A pink kid's bicycle. The tale was easy to figure out. The parking of the video club there looks flat. It is not. Hardly visible to the naked eye, there is a subtle but dangerous dip. I could see the accident unfold. A classic of the back pedal brakes. A kid in panic state. A mother in shock. Mom, I want to try my new bicycle! As all the traffic had been rerouted to the side street, we had the—privilege – to go around the accident scene for efficiency purposes. Thank you… These images and the sounds have been haunting me ever since.

I drove to the division. Paused. Took a shower and had a special thought for all of those like the Cop, the Paramedic and even all the drivers on the road who wake up every morning. Go to work, punch in, do their work and shut up for somehow menial life conditions. It hit close to home, physically and mentally as those childhood friends who are among those folks, Duck: fireman, became a cop and Touch Turtle, Search and Rescue tech and paramedic as special investigator for war crime on UN mandates. Unearthing mass graves and identifying the remains. The dirtywork people.

I have been lucky as per I drive easy and cool. Take my sweet time on the routes. Every ice storm or icy rain morning, I get nervous. Nervous and worry that a kid I never saw would run on the side of the bus on one of the 10,000 dead angles and slip underneath. It is my only fear. It does exist. That risk exists.

The Video Club parking had been redone and put to level as per the coronaries' recommendation. 10 years after the event. 10 years too late. For the parents on the scene, there will never be closure.

Seeing so much death is such short time worried me. What if it means that I am next on this list. So far in life, for as much as I smiled back at death as it smiled to me. I got afraid that it would make me a sign from the index. I had to get out of the cycle, Cut loose a few days or a week. Change work shift. Do something about it.

I had to find someway to beat the system once more. Matter of life or death. I had to break the cycle by which I happened to be on accident scenes more often than statistically acceptable. I had to find a way not to cross the grim reaper on its way back from the job. I had to invoke old native beliefs and get away with it. It requires a few native songs, telling some legends and wearing a pair of moccasins on the job once in a while and it does the trick.

Transit society strive for performance for as long as it implies the blue collars. The management can be lazy and stupid and always on sick leave, we can't. It is a type of Peter's principle meets P.T. Barnum. H.R. pretends that the postulate to mid-management position have to go through a rigorous selection process, namely psychometrics test as administered by the NASA. That's it. We now have extra terrestrial management. Space Cadets.

Damn, I saw this flying saucer before! It's a vintage model. Nice patina.

They work with strict rules and codes according to the work collective agreement. It takes time, but one has to learn to beat the SAP system. SAP is more than an ERP, it is a religion with its, priest, followers, and dogmas. You have to be clever and know how to plug the absentees codes in the right orders. I had a union delegate friend named Stuart. Stewie, knew all the ropes. He was a union delegate, and we often sat along in the union office to invent new codes named with profanities. We added those codes to the official list manually with their new meanings. That was a way to relax. The code 60 was our favorite. At the age of 60 you can legally retire with full benefits. We dreamt about waking up the morning of our respective 60th Birthday to call a code 60. I am out of here.

Stewie died of Pancreas cancer in his 40s. Even in death, he had ways to remind us of his sense of humor.

Stewie damn !

One day, you show up and Stewie is not at the Union office. In large organizations, things don't happen. People just disappear. A union representative once vanished from his office, leaving half a cup of coffee, an open file and the computer open for 3 days. Had the Martians kidnapped him would not have made things any stranger or clearer, dependent on personal beliefs. The cops came to pick him up one morning. He had won an orange one-piece suit with stainless-steel jewelry and all expenses paid sejour at the all-inclusive Bordeaux sur la Gouin club.(The jail) Pedophilia and production of child porn. I never liked the person. I could not figure out why but, there was something that always told me, this MF is up to no good. I was right.

What happened to my friend Stewie was another deal altogether. You inquire, talk, get information and wham! He is home. He is on long-term sick leave, but why. Damn, he is not pregnant for all we know! Cancer. Re damn. Liver or pancreas. Those that don't forgive. It certainly puts life back into perspective. So, we did our best to keep the Stewie's morale. Physically, he was not doing any better. Sad and ironic. Stewie had just started a new life, with a new girlfriend; another driver. A new house, new kids, a new bike, a new, all that it takes. The guys went for a beer at his place, shot some pool, went to a pub, There was that thing missing in his life. He missed this rubber to asphalt deal. The bus. We had to do something for a dying colleague and friend. However unsafe and illegal, it might be. Rules? What rules.

On a full moon autumn night, we, a few drivers, borrowed a bus in the museum lane of the garage and took it for a spin in the suburbs. The brown 1964 GM New Look and took it for a ride for Stewie. A New Look is the ultimate city bus ride. He thought driving it could cure him as if stepping back in time deal. We obliged. So, Stu drove around under tight supervision. A bus ride under a full harvest moon carrying a bunch of joking drivers reenacting Voyage at the Bottom of the Sea or Ultraman routine in a rolling bus. A rolling party to honor a friend going out of our part of reality. A rolling bus, someways traveling back into time and memories. A bus of fools. We got nailed by the employer on this one but man, slap me on the wrist if it pleases you, what we had done was honorable and right. Be it.

One morning there was this loss of an employee's notice at the window by the punch. The newspaper type, Photocopied and posted by the union personnel. Damn. It came as no surprise. We sure hate to louse one of ours.

The Chinet moment, A funeral celebration. A picture of Stewie and an address, A funeral parlor in St-Jerome. North end. Cheapskate city. The fuel is always cheaper around there. Whichever way you face it, those Chinet sure beat the old Dixy paper plates.

And what had to happen, happened, and the guys gathered on a fall evening at the funeral parlor in St-Jerome. There stood Stu, sitting as the guest of honor in a cookie jar. What a party. Many people from former lives. Trucker, Chef, Mechanic, all trade, all types of people and a speech by a celebrant that did not make much sense. A drunk Dean Martin could have done a better job, but as I said earlier, mediocrity is the new rule. The new standard. After the service, after a few crustless sandwiches and the round one. A little coffee in paper cups, a few work anecdotes, the service was over. Matter to matter, dust to dust.

It's fall, it's dark. A moonless night.

Funeral 101: The usual paper Chinet plate ritual as everyone looks at their shoe tips while talking to you. Year after year, funeral after funeral, it seems to me that the quality of the graphics on those plates is improving. Way to go, Chinet. With all those funerals one has to attend, there must have been a type of fidelity reward program I missed somewhere. The Chinet point system.

23:15 hrs. I have to go back to Montreal. I start at 28:20 tomorrow, or in five hours. Now, for some bizarre tax regulations, the gas is always cheaper in St-Jerome than in Montreal. Around $0.10 a liter, which is around $3 in your pocket for the detour. So, I went to the Petro Can to fill in. Filled in the VW, went inside to the cash and slid my point card and waited. $35. OK, $35. Pull the bank card, Slide it in. System error.

OK System error. Cancel the transaction. Let's do it again.

OK, error message. So, I tell the clerk,

listen, if it works for you, I can pull a Credit Card, but I don't get it. It worked somewhere else a hour ago. My card is good. Maybe it's the mag stripe?

A nervous kid calls a supervisor who goes through the POS system and the main station computer and bangs, on a monochrome green screen, there it is. Error code. Code 60!

So, the clerk and his 17 years old supervisor were stunned. What, Code 60. What's code 60? Never saw this before. I'll call Toronto, something is wrong.

Calm down guys. It's only a farewell from the other side from a dear friend. I'll pay cash, I have $40 here. Thanks. Man, the kids were so nervous that I could see pimples popping on their foreheads.

For many, or some, it's in death (or depth) that their lives may be worth being celebrated.

By the way. Don't call Toronto, your call will end up in Sri Lanka.

Supernatural moment, unlike sex, happen without a hint. They are there and make you live it. Sex, on the other hand, has a predictable evolution. There is an exchange of words, gestures, change of voice, vocabulary, and topics of conversation. Then there is that feeling of estrogen in the air, and it starts. Supernatural stuff, like a trap, you walk right into it. Realize it and, like sex, take the time to enjoy every second of it.

Once in a while I get those supernatural moments. At the beginning, it scared me. Ignorance scares people, but once you sit into the moment and enjoy it, they become more frequent.

Strive and enjoy the bizarre. It's worthwhile.

I say, let's do Einstein On the Beach.

Metro Jean Talon.

On my way to driver reliefs to the Snowdon Metro. In our business, a driver could pick up the job anywhere on the transit system. They call it to relieve a driver. A change of shift in the system. I hate going to Snowdon because it's a moron's nest. The worst moron in the city congregate at, whether Snowdon or Atwater metro station. The worst specimens are hanging at Snowdon. They participate in some sort of mass or ritual dedicated to human stupidity. Their Church is there, Snowdon Metro station, as the holy land is at Atwater Metro.

Somehow I agreed to relieve a driver on the 160 at Snowdon and was on my way by the blue line. Jean Talon Metro. There is a way to transfer from the Orange to Blue line at Jean Talon, but it is as efficient and convenient as driving into an industrial sector. Many detours, dead ends and bridges.

At Jean Talon, one could walk over 1 km just in escalators, corridors, hallways, and other. There I am. Pack sack on the back, trying to figure out why the hell did I accept this run. I mean: you really have to be in financial trouble to go grab this assignment. Hell, I did. So, there I am, after the 3rd ramps, surrounded by the rush hour crowd in motion, bang, I am alone on the top of a bridge over a Metro ramp. Alone. Everyone had just disappeared.

Alone? It's rush hour, yet it feels like 2 AM. It feels like a closed station. Over there, on the dock downstairs, there is that young blonde woman dressed in white playing harp. It is amplified, it is a modern instrument. It is a harp. She plays to perfection some Philip Glass repertory. I think, damn, Philip Glass on harp in a Metro station. This outfit is getting classy. I turned around and noticed again, I am alone. Alone and I have this private heavenly concert and there is no one else. I stood there for how long? If felt like I had the whole Philips Glass repertory here. Can't tell, but time stood still, just like in this 1950s Martian movie. Am I dead or what? It did not see that one coming.

Now, had I been riding my scooter around, I might have been suspicious of a road accident because I ride this thing in a very dangerous fashion, but no. No, I was walking to work on a subway bridge. The angellike blonde figure looked up, smiled at me and went back to play. I felt no stress nor rush of being late. A sample of heaven. She was there for me. I floated in her music as she played it. Immersed in joy for while it lasted. How could that be, I thought. It was a live rendition of this popular avant-garde movie of the 80s: Koyaanisqatsi. Life in disbalance.

I believe that this free concert could have been a gift card from heaven. A specific gift. Not many of us like or liked Phillip Glass. Glass you love or you hate. Makes me wonder. Who could have made me such a gift. I know I once gave 4 winter tires for the hell of it, but a full concert?

Then came the wind and the piston effect from this metro coming into the station. Warm air with the sesame oil smell familiar to transit users. It sounded the end of the concert. Even before the train got into the station, the harpist waved at me, picked up her instrument and left. Highly unusual as the only money that can be done is with the commuter leaving the upcoming train. No. The concert was exclusive. A private event. An exclusive performance just for me. I did not get it so, once again, I inquired with the guys. We know the best performers per station. I have a guitarist friend toting a purple beret playing jazz guitar at Jarry Station. We all know him and he is great. A violinist at Joliette Station, a bit disturbed, but excellent. I once heard a saxophonist at Berri transit hub who was exceptional. Nobody ever heard about this classical harpist anywhere in the network. No one. I had a private performance. Gift from heaven and no Johnny Cash effect this time around.

To come back to our colleague and friend Eddy, a brush with death.

So, Eddy had been cleared of any blame. He did his job properly, and he has been sent home to absorb the shock for a few months. PTSD. Few months became a year, and his wife has equipped him with plenty of power tools. As he explained to me once, you should never marry an Haitian woman… Eddy's wife always wanted a house like the ones in the house magazine, so she thought that Eddy could recuperate a trauma with power tools and remodel the house for the time he is idling doing nothing. Eddy is no construction guy, and he called the colleagues often to learn how to fix things as he was slowly destroying everything he touched.

As he explained :it's not because you are on sick leave that the employer gave you a $20,000 buying card at Home Depot to buy hardware to fix your house. So, staying home was taking him down and running his bank account dry on construction supplies too, and he had absolutely no talent for renovations. Demolition was more in his cords than construction. A new vocation.

He called the psychologist to have an early return to duties, to no avail. He had to be home for PTSD as he was really destroying everything and was on the verge of a divorce. Eventually, he took his car to visit his brothers in upstate NY and stayed there a few months. It did the trick. The New Baltimore connection.

Friends come and go as enemies accumulate (as tools in fact) but Eddy was of this breed of drivers that stayed on the road with us. To mention that, tools could end up in a fat red metal box for warehousing or disposal. Enemies too, but it may not be legal. He didn't go to have the full-frontal lobotomy, handed a stiff supervisor cap and walkie-talkies to become mid-management. He did not feel like going for the Gerry Anderson's supermarionettaion look. Nor did he require going underneath to supervise a booth or a metro station or even operate a Metro line. No, Eddy, as Sgt Barnes once said in Platoon; Took the pain and got back behind the wheel because it is who we are and this is our trade. A driver

So as the crew sometimes gathered at the Urban Grange Pizzeria in Laval, Eddy came, smiled a bit and nervously cracked a few jokes. We've had not seen him lately. He was there, but his spirit was elsewhere and not at Home Depot. By the end of the evening when Pizzas turned into Tiramisu and wine into Espresso, and we hit the dogoravilis moment when all that had to be said had been said, he used to do his Bo Diddley impersonations as I replied to him doing my Malala speech at the U.N... A ritual that always makes everyone laugh to the closing argument of the owner of the Pizzeria. But, last time, Eddy did not do Bo Diddley nor as he insisted on staying after the Espresso and barely finished off the Tiramisu. Something in his soul had been broken. Nothing of a professional fault, nothing he could prevent, nothing but, the death of the cyclist broke apart his spirit. This damn Catholic guilt we are carrying with us since we got baptized by this old man of questionable sexual orientation smelling Hai Karate cologne. He still is a happy going driver. A bit more reserved these days. Death is always something hard to deal with. Even if a person you never met and tried to steal a base underneath a city bus.

You are the promised kiss of springtime
That makes the lonely winter seem long.
You are the breathless hush of evening
That trembles on the brink of a lovely song.
You are the angel glow that lights a star,

It is not part of the detour. Yet, I can see it from the road. This is where I met my Mamzelle, Jeanne. Jo, my wife.

The 666 Sherbrooke West tower. I used to pick up tours contracts and packages as a freelance tour guide from the 666. Not only was I working at the 666 the original office was on the 13th floor. This is where I met my wife. She worked part-time at the tour agency for which I took tour director (or Guide) mandates. Every two week or so from May to the end of October I had to go there and pick up the fat envelope. Bus, list of passengers, itinerary, program, budget, vouchers, luggage tags, the work. I had been at it for 5 years and that was a living. I had to get other contracts in spring and sometimes part-time jobs in fall and winter. Overall, it was an offbeat living.

I loved it for a while because of numerous perks. Someday it strikes you, it goes nowhere and nowhere fast. I felt like one of those Kerouac On the Road type of belated beatnik. I stretched the fun year after year because I was excellent at it and the money was OK. For a that moment, you wake up in the middle of the night to check the frame on the wall of the hotel room and think: Flowers pot, relax, you are in Boston. Boston is nice. I dreamt of that steady job with social benefit and a bit of stability, but was I ever wrong...

One day, as I entered the 13th floor office, I noticed this new receptionist. I was returning from a trip and had some business to do with the tour consolidator or the strega. She had a cute little face and long flat red hair. Cher with redhead in style and offbeat jewelry. As I inquired about this beauty to my supervisor and her status, her answer was unequivocal:

Her name is Giovanna. (nicknamed Jo)" She is my friend. She just ditched someone at the altar a month ago. I guess she is not ready to meet someone new yet. I also know about your reputation, speaking to many hotel sales directors that seem to appreciate your company just a bit too much. Charisma, wit and good look, but no Lambretta those days. I don't think you could be a candidate, and in fact I would not give you her phone number.

In those days, those were the 10 magic numbers. I needed an intro date or a phone number. I've always preferred the intro date because it is easier to pilot and not let it slip. All of that reminded me of a conversation I had a year before with a fortune reader from another plane of existence about my future. I thought, so, be it, but I won't give up on that one. Given that most of my colleagues were gays, I did not worry much that one of my colleagues would swipe her off her feet. She is the one announced by the Fortune reader on the boardwalk. This is for real. I am a speaker!

Some are thunderstruck, some get speechless. For me, the thing that came to my mind were the lyrics of that song; Ella Fitz or Helen Forest. Helen Forest, Artie Shaw and a languorous clarinet intro. Walking on clouds. Yes.

I often hear this song in my mind. On that occasion not only did I hear the complete song plus, hold on, the full Artie Shaw 3 minutes intro. Smooth, glossy, classy. What you are !

I started dreaming again. Love and stability and a station wagon with fake wood paneling and perhaps a Fox Terrier.

That was it. A steady job. A retirement fund. A house in the city. A station wagon, a fox terrier and a life filled on Tupperware, Chinet point, a few exciting trips and a family. A daughter whom, like my side of the family, would think outside the box and on turbo.

I know I may go over some logical steps here but bare with me, I'll explain it all to you but for now, I have to concentrate on the road. I am riding a train of thought here, It is achronological.

The next chapter of my life could be named 2 angels and a mechanic. Yeap, 2 angels and a mechanics. Foremost, the birth of my daughter has been, just like in the New

Testament, announced by what I would refer to as angels. Unlike the Victoria's secret's model.

Once at the cardboard box factory where I worked as a Customer Sales Rep.: I was back from my refused inventory on the shop floor and on the way to the office. Top of the stair stands that woman that I know as my colleague Louise's girlfriend. She does not work here, and she may be lost in the shop. I walk by her as she steps right in front of me and voluntarily blocked my way. She takes the whole space. She was in a form of a trance and like the warlock from the Ye Old Brunswick seems to speak without exactly moving her lips or anything. Words, declaration, strange disembodied voice but as she looked at me, the thing was clear.

You. You will have one daughter. Only one. She will be very intelligent.

And snap. She snapped out of her trance. Shook her head, looked at me a walked away. Nothing had happened. Whew, that was weird. That printing ink is something !

Okay!

Louise. Your girlfriend is weird.

No, she has the gift.

Life went on.

Got a call at home from an old, aging catholic nun from my hometown. Sister X. Sister X had this reputation for being a miracle worker. People waited years to get an audit with sister X, but she called me home. The message was clear. I have a message for you from God, I am expecting you this afternoon at 1 PM. Be there or be damned. Her residence was of a 3-hour drive from Montreal. Be it. Let's take the VW Fox for a spin.

I show up to her nun's residence. A small woman. 4.5 ft. There I am. Got to hand it to the Catholic Church, they, the Military and cemeteries always pick the best real estate spots. They are good at it.

Kneel young man!

OK, I will, sister. I felt very humbled and polite. So, I did.

Here is the message from God, as she touched both my shoulder with her hands.

The request you made to the Eternal had been granted. You will not feel it now, but will within the next few hours. Be it. Join me in a few prayers.

I hate to kneel because I am Huguenot, but I'll shut up. Her boss was bigger than mine.

I went through this whole prayer drill, but I felt good about it. I felt relieved. I had been touched by something I could not explain. A light penetrated me. Loved it. More kick than a double espresso.

I returned home. My wife was puzzled.

What is it all about?

I can't tell ? You have ordered something from God that I should know. Just like in the Sears Catalog.

Nothing special, just the regular grocery list.

Well, hold on, it's on its way. Certified, tracking number included. It's in Latin.

That was the month of May. Beautiful and sunny May. Over the weekend, we went sailing with my sister in Magog. We had the best day at the lake. Life was good and back home we got very romantic. We had tried to procreate for the last 5 years to the extent to go to a fertility clinic by bus, in the middle of a bad winter storm, tooting a test tube of semen. That weekend, that was it. The ladder was on the game board of life for us. A pregnancy test. The test was positive. One daughter, Only one but very intelligent, but what a lousy character. It was my wife's request to God, me, I had always been in more superficial things. She won.

Now you wonder where the mechanics comes from. A few hours before Jo gave birth, Late icy rain February, someone rings the bell of the apartment. This mechanic guys show up to my place.

Rings the bell!

Hi, I am a so-and-so from the Cobra Garage at the end of the street, and we have a promotion.

He had in hand a blue carton with this offer, 2 oil changes and tire rotation for $40.

So, there it goes. $40 prepaid. 2 oil changes and tire rotation and... Lots of stuff. He was selling those coupons. They brain switched on into the Snap On mode. That's a bargain. Where is the catch?

So as I was looking for 40 bucks and was trying to get a few extras, when my wife started screaming! I was poor and did not have much cash around. Life got stupid !

It is not the time to bargain car stuff, I have to go, It's an emergency.

Hum. I still had bought the coupons but as we crossed the door frame me, Jo and the Mechanic, the Mechanics turned around and made the same announce

Don't worry, mam, she will be fine. She will be your only one, but she will be brilliant. Always the same message as if it had been recorded somewhere ages ago and played on a 8 track tape.

I went to Cobra Garage few times but never crossed again the Mechanic. Sometimes they hire professional peddlers to do this type of promo. The catch is, once they have your car on the lift, they always find something else. I should have known, I had been in that business before.

Catch 22. The problem with kids is that they may be: just like you! It may be a form of justice for what you made your parents endure years ago. I was a problem kid. Too creative for this life.

Now I have what I looked for: family life. It comes with new surprises. I used to have calls from authorities about my daughter's creative rebellion. They were rebellious acts that irritated people without being destructive nor violent, or that violence that forces one to, for once in his life, think critically. In that respect, for people of less intellectual means or imagination it is violent. Wonder where she gets that from.

Among her live art display.

The manager of a local McDonald's restaurant complained to the cops that my daughter and a few friends jammed a Drive Thru line while disguised as a yellow Honda Civic made from movers boxes. A protest stemming from the fact that customers at Drive Thru had faster and better service than customers inside the restaurant. Now, had it been a VW she may have achieved her point, but a Honda. Fat chances. They were p...off that the kids jammed the Drive Thru but on the other hand, the fast food chain never treated those High School kids as clientele but more like paying animals coming to eat this so-called food on parent's hard-earned lunch money. The basketball team going on a tournament.

But this artistic protest urge did not stop there. In fact, it has never stopped. She is also condemned for being a Box People, just like her old man and grand old man. It has to be genetic.

On a cold winter Friday morning rush hour, some car driver, too fast, too icy, too distraught or too dead with remarkable baggage of bad karma plugged in the back of an eastbound bus 69 routes. The Slinky type and well, as it usually makes superficial damages and injuries and is taken lightly but superficial accident report and paperwork. Seems that the car driver died of a heart attack before hitting the bus that morning. Once you have a dead body in the equation, it becomes way more tedious and complicated. The coroner guys have to show up and freeze the accident scene for as long as there is overtime budget for the day at the police precinct.

Death requires a lot of coffee and donut to figure out.

Nothing of a rare occurrence here, but my daughter was in that bus. It had to be frozen on the spot until the coroner could come and check the scene and make precious recommendations, as per, never drive while dead. In those days, the transit authority had publicity panels on the back of the bus above the bumper stating, this bus is 70 cars less on the road. That morning, that was too tempting and too easy.

Thanks to a fat black felt marker (she was a fashion and design student) the 70 became a 71 to the amusement of a bunch of rowdy late for school college kids that made a viral clip of the event and that day she affirmed her right to live, to live and create and by a simple art gesture poked a hole in this shield of false righteousness and obtuse morality that imprisoned thoughts.

Freedom is the right to tell people what they don't want to hear. George Orwell.

Yet, the object of such freedom could only be coming from outside the box. Truth may be out there, outside the box. Art is the polite rebellious way to express it.

For the ecologist and the Greens, yes, that morning, this bus potentially represented 71 fewer cars on the road. No one can argue against that, but this ugly truth had something shocking about it. It was a raw truth. A tragic one, I agree, but a statistical truth and truth is something slippery and dangerous to expose. A French song from Guy Beart, 1966, exposes that: Thee who says the first person that says the truth shall be executed. Le premier qui dit la vérité, on devra l'exécuter. The first that says the truth shall be executed.

She was not supposed to do it! Who am I to tell. The man who, among some other thing, scrounged a few gallons of top secret flat black NATO armored vehicle paint to fix his car, or who became proxenete for a day for a regiment party? Given that she had been announced by 2 angels : one part-time, one professional and an apprentice one, I believe that she is part of a plan and would not argue anymore.

The doctor can bury his mistakes, but an architect can only advise his client to plant vines. Frank Llyod Wright

Transit worker are on the field on a 24/7 basis. We see and feel where the city planning is doing. Where it goes wrong or sometimes does a good job. We are the ultimate tester or witness of the city beat. To observe is what we are doing all day long. Observe, analyze and criticize. We see movement, decay, trends, and movement. Movement is after all our bread and butter.

Let's now introduce the concept of cynicism above the determinism theory for city transit as per adding an extra coat.

No matter how cynical you get, it is very hard to keep up. Don't look for the meaning of life, as there is none. Enjoy it and your karma officer will be happy. P is for Park, D is for Drive and R for Reverse. Remember what the 2 pedals are all about. Try to look and smile at customers when they enter, but never get caught staring insistently at a female customer's boobs. You have the largest big screen on the market in front of you, this is where the action movie happens and don't worry, there will be plenty of it. Don't expect anything but a paycheck Wednesday at midnight and drinking coffee while driving from that job because you will be deceived. It will never be a nice job, but it will be there every morning for you, so it is a good job. We don't mind you sporting a baseball cap. The Maori warrior tattoo on your face of the tears tattoo, it's a NO. We won't go for it, nor the Santa's tuque. You will not get fired. You may end up in the little box selling tickets at the Metro station with the other nuts. You can always be late at a checkpoint on your run, but never early. Easy enough. Ahead of schedule, you stop and that's it.

Accident there will be. You may also as the Pac Mac be chased by ghoul figures type all day as you eat yellow line dots.

Note on accidents: Sergei Prokofiev was ignored by the world press, as he died the same day as Josef Stalin. World's attention went to Stalin. They were not exactly good friends either. The same thing happened as Farrah Fawcett died the same day as the King of Pop, Michael Jackson. Her disappearance went under the radar. Under the radar but for me and a cute Boutique corner of St-Laurent and Bernard. Tikkun Olam Boutique. I had never been a big fan of Michael Jackson. Sorry.

This store made a temporary window display.

They made a special window display with Farrah Fawcett dressed as a mannequin with a marquise stating remembering Farrah. The dress, the smile, and her signature hairdo. It was right back to the 1970s. I was touched. The disappearance of Farrah Fawcett was a blow to my teenage memories. A perk dodging traffic on the famous 55 North. Sometimes life gives you a break. My mind was back at the wheel of the famous Coca-Cola Denim Machine. Tavares was in the air. *Heaven must be missing an angel.*

A Tikkun Olam is a spirit with this important mission to repair the worlds or mend the world. As it will never be fixed, the spirit would spend eternity trying to fix the flaws of the universe, which is the ultimate patience exercise. On that day, the owner, or the display designer, of that boutique fixed a world. Mine. Maybe the harpist I met months ago works there?

Radio call from Marseille. It is TF1, No! Back to reality. Like an astronaut, I went to the end of imagination string and I am pulled back to earth.

One more time today, here's a radioed detour on line 165 South. Besides the known one. The predictable one. The ones that are drawn, supervised and pinned on a bulletin board. Old drivers like me never rely on the board because it is never up-to-date. Yeap, I could have felt it. It's the Grand Prix Weekend. I could tell you the left and right, given that it's a seasonal one. Guess the new guys will panic and try to scribble it on a bus transfer or an old napkin while driving. When Charlotte from the radio control center calls a detour with the usual transit codes and lingo, she does it with her southern France accent. You can feel the warmth, just as if she were to invite you to an apero somewhere in the port of Marseille. You can close your eyes and imagine the scene while taking a visual note of what's to come.

We all make this mental picture of where the bus goes, as some turns may be tighter than usual to maneuver. Maneuvering the big thing into tight spaces to customer's utter satisfaction may be our motto yet no one will scream OMG orgasm if you destroy their car's left front end. My wife always questioned the size of the big thing, as she never noticed that what I am driving has a accordion type mid-section. Hence, the nickname; A slinky.

As they say: Someday, we will look back at those moments and plow into a parked car.

Upon training, a new driver, is taught never to rely on street name signs to guide its way around town. Nice, but after a snow storm, they are covered in snow. We all learned from that mistake. The best reference point, those lit a night and open 24 hrs a day are mainly gas stations, convenience stores and in the poor suburbs, strip clubs. You make mental notes as, turn left at Super Sex, then right at The Goddesses, straight line for 1 mile, right again at the Amazons and on.

You get to learn the location of all strip club and Sex shops.

I was comfortable with downtown routes until they knocked off my favorite spot to make place for those shinning new, Dubai type, empty hotels. No one can afford to stay there

Fixed fortifications are a monument to man's stupidity (Gen Patton)

or it is not gray it is not beige, housing world is now Greige.

I had not been here for a while. Damn, they destroyed it!

There was that area in the Bleury—Jeanne Mance / Rene Levesques district where a restaurant stood in the middle of a wasteland. A piece of chaos in the rigid urbanity. A refreshing oasis for the eye. World's renowned Latini restaurant was like a throne in the middle of this urban wild patch. A wild patch of probably downed old houses to make place for, beats me. Most likely one of those 1970s megalomania projects that hit a legal block or a financial one. It was out of the concrete zone and this restaurant inhabited on an old 3 stories red brick dwelling with a rooftop Terrassa and a patio. Nothing special in the St-Patrick's church area besides those few trees in the wild, strings of light and Chinese lanterns illuminating the place at night. That patch of land was a relief. A cool place in the sweltering heat of the city in the summer. A poetic oasis. A mistake maybe, or someone holding their ground for a higher price, but this was a comforting area. A lively place. A hybrid place between the bank sector, the limits of Chinatown and old Montreal. A pocket of greenery. A zesty bite of chaos in an over structured world. I used to open the front door while driving by this patch on hot summer days in the city. A breath of fresh air in many ways.

But a sinister plot came from the real estate martian from the Globalization Market. The one with a stiff pinky finger. Probably the same guys from It came from outer space. They never got this vintage flying saucer fixed, alright. Those guys working on night shift aren't as good as the day shift one. Those old vintage flying saucer or spacecraft: nice but never as reliable as the new one, and I know. Those new things, well, they are like the girls at Marina Rinaldi's party. They don't screw.

That was a beautiful spot.

One day, we saw the tractors moving in. In a snap of three months, it was all gone. It made place for progress in the form of 2 Marriott Brand hotels. Highly expensive hotel that are usually empty and do not render much of a service to the humankind. Two more in a saturated market. These old restaurants in the wasteland were, in their humble manner, one of those things that attracted local or national tourism, gave a break to downtown workers and were a patch of color and anarchy. A few curves among the straight lines. Some color in the gray. That wasteland as many old buildings brought way more to the service of the humankind than those high towers but maybe, again, to serve humans is genuinely a Cookbook. To fully grasp the Cookbook analogy, one has to see the corresponding episode of the original Twilight Zone. Season 3, episode 24.

A classic.

So, we navigate in this sordid environment all day and could, only, notice the decline of our society. It is part of the job, and a share of your paycheck, Being subjected to.

The hand of the market has decided otherwise. The hand of the market planed those 2 hotels on the site that will never make their quotas, depreciate every year, lose value, be an eyesore but will bring city taxes and obey to the ultimate order of the system: Make the average Joe's life miserable. The hand of the market is in fact Hamburger Helper and has a finger missing. Some deals with the Japanese Yakuza went wrong, I guess.

I told you about that movie, it came from outer space: Synopsis in 30 seconds. An alien spacecraft makes an emergency landing somewhere in Arizona. OK now, just like David Vincent 15 years later, they are spotted. Now, they made extensive damage to the craft, they needed cheap labor to fix it on the night shift. Night shift only. So, since they were on a human Wi-Fi deal, they were able to recruit all the people from a nearby village, in their sleep, to work on the craft by night, no bonus nor special pay, and return them home in the morning. It looked like a massive case of somnambulism. Fact is, these Aliens, they looked like Croc sandals, had only one eye and disliked Arizona at all. Too dry for their reptile skin, I guess. They wanted to leave, but one man, a union leader, found out about the cheap labor.

It is a nice story with a lot of dhemerine solos. At the end of the movie, the Alien had gathered enough Air Miles doing groceries here and there, the craft was fixed. They took off. Those 50s Sci FI movies are great if you enjoy seeing those well-dressed good-looking women hugging huge car steering wheels with chrome trimming. What car originally looked. How cars should look.

OK now, 75 years later the village became a suburb made of monster houses. The inhabitants (the new villagers) don't go out or socialize because they have the Internet and stream video, so they are vulnerable suckers. In the original movie, people of the village used to gather at the local watering hole, or bar. Now, they don't gather any longer except for football games and while the men are at the game, the women have their type of football giver, receiver games. They also found a way to take advantage of world events.

The geographical spot where the Alien, or Martians or talking Crocs with one eye, found to hide the wrecked craft and hold a shop is now a power mail. A large parking lot, a few big box stores, a huge 24/7 large surface. Now, using the app systems, the new age Martian are using the new device namely the intelligent phone to mesmerize people in their sleep to go slave at their store during the night. So, exhausted people leave their monster house during the night, take their cars. Not with the wide steering wheel and the chromed half moon car honk on the steering, but more like a video game on wheel and go at the store half awake in the middle of the night. Women don't sport sexy scarves and cats eyes shade any longer, either. So, in the 1950s movie, people were pulled out of their bed to go moonlighting at Spacecraft body shop and now, the same people are pulled out of bed to go moonlighting at Wally's World and God knows how the people hanging at Wally's World during the night are very close cousins to the talking Crocs.

As I drive all day in this ever and faster evolving world, I feel like this character in the; It Came from Outer Space movie. Unreachable from those that controls the society and yet witness of this highly evolved type of merchandised somnambulism that could be qualified as a permanent freak show. Once discovered, this form of uniqueness could be very rewarding, as it teaches you to see life differently.

Martians 1, Modern man 0. Technological slavery 1. Ok, there are too many players for a normal game, but remember, I am driving a bus right now. Nothing for Tony Randall.

No point for Johnny Cash on that one either.

Am I to kill this page for a few lines? It looks like it !

One more time. Feel this emptiness !

Something so absurd that only intellectuals could believe it is the proper way. (George Orwell)

I dedicate that one to my brother-in-law, flight simulator engineer.

And we were busy with our jobs, our kids, and a certain career. Trying to find constructive leisure, Teaches good value to kids and changes the dishwasher every 5 years or so as the car's every 4 years, distraught by the media, and it happened. As with the invasion of the Body Snatchers, the Reptiles replaced the human in the control of society and have this new agenda. They push the law of the lowest denominator. Martian plot? Maybe!

Got to admit it. We all entered the days of the lowest common denominator. This lowest common denominator in whatever field of endeavor becomes a standard. This standard takes the shape of lack of intellectual integrity, poor taste, moral integrity or banking on fellow man's gullibility or simple stupidity. When some authority does something noticeably stupid, everyone has to imitate. It becomes a model. A template.

There is not much opposing anarchism to libertarianism as masochist vs. sadists. Same pain, different approach. The libertarian is selective about rules he is willing to abide as he wants liberty to fully enjoy his spin on this planet as the anarchist has no clue why he is on this planet. In fact, the anarchist doesn't have a clue on much. Anarchist of the world, unite!

Even the Catholic Church joined the bandwagon. After the Council, Vatican II. Decades ago. I always had doubts about those guys. Here was a decisive demonstration.

Signs of time.

I have a good story about churches. Churches always had a steeple for bells. Bells ringing have always been a part of the Christianity movement. It is a sound, a vibration, an appeal. It makes a church. So, there I was at negotiating a funeral rite for my defunct mother. As I mentioned, she went to that church for 40 years (and hated it because it had a modern look of a Tupperware cake bell) and asked about the bells. Just like the song: The Browns, the 3 Bells. Would they ring the bells? The French version of the same song by Edith Piaf is way better as it focuses on the importance of the bell in the rites and not the other way around.

You have to buy mass services for these extra bells.

Say what?

You have to buy an extra service but as you know, this church as no bells. It is a recording.

It is cheaper than the regular bells, I argued.

No, in fact, for churches built after 1950... as per Vatican order, there were to be no bells anymore but a record. It has to be written somewhere in latin, I guess. A lousy record with outside cheap tin speakers. How about the soothing vibration of the bell? How about honesty here? No. There were no bells. They had that system of recording hooked on the telephone of the church, linked to a Telefunken tape machine. The recording of where? The Vatican, Paris, St-Peter. Not that I mind old bells, just like an old musical instrument, those made before they dropped the last A Bomb always sound better. There is a molecular alteration theory on this. So, I didn't mind the age of the bell, I wanted a fresh sound. Fresh sound from an old bell. Brilliant isn't it. The French say that the best soup is made in old pots. A very Martha Steward statement indeed. . There is something sexual about the statement to favor sexuality with elder women. There we go again, Sex. Sex is leading the world. Money and power are cheap form or transpositions, after all.

There were bell ringing but feel like I have been deprived of this clear sound of a soul traveling back to the creator on a brisk, crisp and sunny autumn sky. I had to settle for something that sounded like a Snoopy xylophone or Schroeder's piano.

No bells. Funeral celebrant with little or no knowledge of the deceased. Man, that happens to you only once in a lifetime, Maybe they should pay a little more attention.

No Chinet this time, Cheap plastic plates. I hate those plastic shinny plates. The potato's salad slips from the plate, and so is the vinegar from the Cole slaw. They are messy.

It brings me to my friend Jeff funerals. Jeff died of cancer at the age of 46. The man had all the healthy habits in the world. He was, somehow, an annoyance for us, the party crowd. Jeff never came with the boys to Ponderosa or the Olive Garden type of place because of hormones in meat and MSG and God knows what. We did not even get this guys for a 2 A.M. bites at the local A&W. Cancer took his old man away 2 years before him, and it may, in his case, became a contagious deal as sadness and the departure of a loved one could actually kill you.

We had that dinner at a sidewalk café on Laurier st a few weeks before he has passed away. The place: La Petite Ardoise, had an excellent coffee blend. A great Espresso. As Jeff guzzled his cup, I asked:

Jeff, aren't you taking the time to savor this great coffee.

He smiled and replied:

Time, well, I haven't much of it left and with the chemo therapy, I do not taste it anymore.

Predictable. As summer turned into autumn.l he was gone.

Chinet to Chinet, dust to dust.

And the guys gathered to listen to the celebrant enlightening speech about eternal life and the fact that once dead, well, your mortgage is finally paid for. And he went on and open his statement with:

I have three questions for you? The parable of the 3 questions. Hold on, kids!

Duck and Gianni were there and whispered: What's in it for us if we answer the question right?

Yea. What's in it for me?

Stoically, Duck who had a lot of Chinet point on his fidelity card pointed out a display of urns for sale of all types of shapes and color and replied Gianni:

If you answer properly the three questions, you win one of those, as he pointed out a window display of funeral urns. You can pick it and go home with it. You will walk out of here with a brown doggy bag and a urn.

We laughed. A nervous laugh, but it broke the monotony of the event.

The guys gathered a few days after Jeff's funeral. We went to Ponderosa or was it Bonanza to send Jeff a message to the other side. It is not that stuff that kills. It's the lack of sex. It's something else…

It's all statistical, it's all predictable. We all know. It always comes as a surprise.

It's crazy how those Chinet points pile up so fast. Yet, the rewards aren't there.

My old man died in a hospital bed. Veterans home. Alzheimer took him. There was not much left on the old man after Alzheimer or those tons of medication given to treat the illness. Makes you wonder about the efficiency and those treatments or this simple fringe medicine concept as used in Scandinavian countries would be better. Villages of Alzheimer patient and citizens where they could still live and evolve being forgetful, confused and a bit nuts. It must be a lively place indeed. Must be complicated to manage but cost-effective except for Big Pharma, I guess.

It was not on his will, but the man clearly deserved military honor as he was, among the handful a RCAF bombers, the first to bomb Berlin and make Goering look like a idiot. The first allied bomber to hit Berlin was a RCAF bomber that ended up being a dentist in Riviere Du Loup, Quebec, Canada.

From this gentleman on and a handful of really crazy Canucks they started calling Herman; Meyer in Nazi Germany and he hated it.

No enemy bomber could reach the Ruhr. If one reaches the Ruhr my name is not Goering, You may call me Meyer. Herman Goering.

We also intercepted the fat man fleeing in his boss car, sprayed it with bullets and kept the Mercedes at our Ottawa's war museum. Never underestimate the strength, determination, and force of a bunch of pissed off beavers. At Nuremberg, once he heard that Canadians were to be there, Goering swallowed cyanide. End of the story.

The car is in Ottawa and makes the envy of this former financial controller of mine, whom I could easily imagine wearing a SS Uniform and a Swastika. Another Mercedes-Benz man.

I had to call the Legion to get someone to play the Last Post at the service. It was not part of his will, again, but I knew I had a mission to do this last honor. I made the official request. F/O j19722Z DFC, DSO, 425th and the spill to be answered that the legion did not send musicians anymore but a record. Budget restrictions, A lousy CD record. What, I am supposed to pull a Ghetto Blaster here to play the CD. Are we to dress like MC Hammer here? That CD of yours, does it come with a Kenny Gee CD for ambiance music at the lunch following the service? Time to eat those crustless sandwiches and the potato salad.

Man, is humanity taking a beating here.

No bell, no horn. Fortunately, some people in the Force still believe in honor and tradition and the Squadron. The 425th had played it in honor and tradition, as they sent a clairone player to their fly boy funeral. Old soldiers never die and deserve more than a CD and a Kenny Gee tune for their last voyage.

Time has changed and well, this sucker revolves fast. Remember the hygienic paper parable. The closer you get to the end of a roll, the faster it spins. It's like if every little dotted square of paper was equivalent to a month worth of life. Gee, the first one take a long time. Here is another example.

Once upon a time, not a century ago, the guys met at a hamburger place and enjoyed a bit between friends and family. That was quality time and quality food. I say hamburger, but it could be breakfast or club sandwich if it pleases you. Fast but quality. Now, look at the faces of people in fast food places. Any hours of the day. Nobody seems to enjoy it anymore. Nobody. Maybe it's like everything else: they enjoy it but virtually or is it another case of the league of orgasm on the mute mode or the brotherhood of the: You've been placed on this earth to look like shit, suffer and shut up. They had just punched in this joint and needed a food pellet as the rats in the Skinner box.

Remember this 1970s McDonald's commercial where a family of five dropped in a drive thru in a country squire deal station wagon. Picked up a meal and pulled a $5 bill. $5, meal for 5 and some loose change back. What can you get for $5 today?

Once before a surgery, an anesthetist told me: remember, a glass of wine or a beer have always been the best anti depressor. In these days and age, I would recommend it regularly. A good glass of wine. One. Then, he putted the mask on a gassed me to Morpheus land.

With a glass or two of a good Cabernet or a Zinfandel, you could get someone to tell you a good story. Merlot stories are usually sad. So, let's go for a Cabernet here. Merlot people are as boring as the coffee addicts hooked on over roasted Robusta. Toxic people. Now.

I had a customer on a tour who had been an international architecture mogul. A kingpin. He drank a lot but once in a while, sober, he was or could be half a decent man. He worked on most architectural projects in Paris, Dubai, London and NY, so he said. People talk a lot, but I believed he walked the walk too. Comes to this discussion about Louis XIV and Versailles.

Here was his take on the project.

The Romans had baths, the Greeks aqueduct, and there was enough water in the Versailles area for an innovative sewage system. Proof of that and technical mastery of water distribution are all the fountains on the site and all the beautiful gardens. Hygiene was not in the priorities of the

Royals, nor of the court of France, in the pre-revolutionary days. They'd rather defecate or urinate in pots than have sanitaries infra. Perfumes over baths. No sanitaries, the court was a nest of disease, VD's, viruses, bacteria and all sickness. You know why? Because they were idiots.

They were inbred, fucken idiots with the only intent in mind of having a lavish garden to fuck and cheat one another. That's how France carried foreign affairs. Now, if you wonder why they ended up at the guillotine, you have an explanation. They were idiots and when they got their heads cut off and as they fell and rolled on the ground, they made a hollow sound because they were empty. A kind of pop!

Now, today's city is like an obese man choked by too many belts and suspenders. They choke. So, let's say that our modern-day office tower could be on the same concept of Versailles, but they have running water. Same purpose, same aim yet more hygienic. Slightly !

This other customer goes tourism to Romania, Late 70 early 80s. He drives this french Renault 15 car deal. Small but comfy. So, he drives around scenic Romania, knowing that Dacia, (Romania) produces the same vehicle under license and there are part available in case the car breakdown. It is precisely what happened, Once on a country road, he busts a muffler and has to stop to get the car fixed. Therefore, be it, he stops at a city garage to have the beast fixed to be told that they don't have the part available but will fix the one on the automobile. Remember this is Romania but it once happened to me in Virginia. They have the specs and the metal sheet and will do a new one. They did not have them in Virginia.

Nothing extraordinary here. I once stopped a Midas to have a muffler changed, but Midas had a new one in inventory. So, where is the punch here. The mechanic tells the man to, he and his wife got have breakfast at a local café and come back in 3 hours. They went. A few croissants, cheese, jam, coffee, the regular stuff. All of that dirt cheap, A handful of Romanian lei in change.

They go to the mechanic's shop. The man has spent 3 hours on the muffler. He did a new one. Fixed it on. Metal art work. Tested it, Handicraft but of even better quality that the original. So, OK, nice, what about the final bill? It costed the same as the croissants at the Café. A handful of change. Here is a new way to figure out economics.

Few friends, colleagues, pleasant setting, a glass of wine or a beer and as people unwind, in most cases, the good stories are getting out.

Have we lost track of the fact that humans are gregaire instinct creatures? Men have to gather and exchange. Man has been exchanging in front of alcoholic beverages from the beginning of time. Now.

Here is the ultimate new chapter statement:

Man is ultimately hostage of sunrise because as the sun rises, man has to face a new day. No escape possible.

Joy into work was the old man's motto. The old man would have wanted it written on the entrance mat of the house. Some have a :home sweet home or home where the heart is in an embroidered frame at the entrance of the home. Not him. Work was this very essential thing. A form of workism. He had those discussions with his friends and business peers, as who is the one who hadn't taken a vacation for the longest time.

Me! I have not taken a day off for the last 10 years.

A kind of this insane bet on the craziest of them all. I heard that one often as I also met those guys visiting people at the hospital after heart surgeries or transplant. A generation of people that stayed on their feet on mere coffee guzzling or chain-smoking. Work as a religion. Now, what is it you work for? You work to live or live to work, or have you painted yourself in an emotional or financial corner because of something stupid done at the Christmas party.

Nowadays, the gesture of doing your work properly, no more, no less, becomes an act of poetry, art, defiance, or even rebellion. Never, since the age of light, has critical or paused thinking been attacked, ostracized and designated as revolutionary or even violent.

Do More Than Is Required of You." Georges Patton.

But don't over do it.

You thought you live in a house. In fact, no.! You now live in a vehicle. You live in a financial vehicle because the hand of the market has decided so. Because you live in a vehicle.

The value of the vehicle is of the Keynesian principle. This would have investors pricing shares not based on what they think an asset's fundamental value is, or even on what investors think other investors believe about the asset's value, but on what they think other investors believe is the average opinion about the value of the asset, or even higher-order assessments.

And they would live the retirement with a freedom and leisure schedule so hectic that the former working day could have looked like a break. So in the search for freedom, one becomes leisure anxious or freedom anxious at mere look at the clock ticking and becomes a prisoner of his freedom. So, retirement freedom has the value of what, society as a whole, believes in the average opinion about the value of this option, or even more hectic life assessment. All fueled by the marketing folks and the media.

I think it's Marx, Groucho, that called it an alienation. Alienation as becoming slave of something created to serve you, and there are zillions of example of that. Now, to take society in its entirety to the stand for alienating its constituents.

A simple exercise here:

If we were to describe a day at the ski hill in a job description as per, the candidate will have dressed like the Michelin man and at temperature way below zero to shod heavy fiberglass or such boots, climb on the top of a mountain in the wind on aluminum patio chair type hooked on a cable. Once at the top, the candidate would have to affix and bind slippery plank of fiberglass and aluminum alloys to ski down hill, assuming all risks and injuries. Seen that way, I am not certain that your newly retired friends would call you at work to tell you that they are skiing while you are at work.

Ski combines outdoor fun with knocking down tree with your face. Dave Barry

If I were to devise a job description for a world-class event, I would require the help of the Kratt brother and the wisdom of the Zoboomafoo to find the right conceptualization. Chances are that the Kratt would require of me to wear a Pith Helmet before engaging into meaningful discussion. Pith helmet. An essential, as Martha Stewart would say.

At retirement, many find out that the house they live in but never noticed could be in dire need of a new kitchen. One never notices because we all spend half of our existence at work. So. Now, because retirement gives you more time to kill, you may eventually spend more time at Ikea to discover that you actually live in a dump and had been doing so for ages, and you require a new kitchen.

Early in January. Every January. Forbes or other divulges the salaries and benefit of the top CEO's in the country. At that moment, you don't think of a new kitchen but more like quitting it all or change job. They do invent figures to keep you on your toes, but will never do anything about it. They do it to poop your day, period. Now, the fact of the matter is that all contracts are rigorously confidential. Whether it's a sport star, a movie star, a porn star, a financial star, an atomic gas or an old fart, you will never know what IS in the contract. It is all about speculation, entertainment and keeping the upper hand on the working class. It is a form of violence too, but we are used to it. Rumor has it that there is an office somewhere with a team of young professional WASP, sniffing coke, creating figures all day long as much as news agencies are creating news.

News is stories. Countless people are earning scandalous living but twisting them into tales.

And comes this homeowner existential question: To Kitchen or not to kitchen, that's the questien. As you know, with that kind of money, you could pay yourself an escape to Roma a week or two or even three that you'll remember all your life long, so let's rephrase here. To kitchen or to Cuccina is the questione ! Pick Roma.

In the land of ding a ding. Yes, it does exist.

Hell, where did that cyclist pop out from. Damn. Almost under the bus? I don't know what Giro did that fat cyclist in yellow spandex suit thinks he is competing at, but by his size, it must have been the Giro Pita. They all dress like Mr. Tour de France to take the bike around the block. I don't know. Could there be a Tour of the Muffin Top ?

Yes, the land of the ding a ding.

It's a movie called Black Robe, set in early New France exploration, a group of native are sitting in front of an early model clock on a mantelpiece. They are sitting Indian style. We are talking about the mid-1600. Tadoussac harbor, St-Lawrence river. Those natives are in a Jesuit house and are quite puzzled by the machine. The leader of the group addressed the other members of the tribe and says:

This is the white man's boss. It doesn't speak but gives orders in Ding, Ding, Ding!

All the natives had a hearty laugh! They were 4 centuries in advance of the age of the apps.

The answer to that is to live a bit of your retirement while you work, work a bit while retired and never forget that the Media IS the message and cable channel are mainly sponsored by pharmaceutical companies. You don't feel sick. Check all of that you are missing.

Gee! The house again ?

So, your house or condo or property is now worth what other investors believe about the asset's value as the average opinion about the value of the asset or even a higher order assessment. This is called speculation and in the years following the French Revolution, speculation was a crime punishable by the death penalty. The Guillotine is nicknamed the Rasoir National. If you look at the evaluation of certain stocks and assets these days, it is clearer than ever that reincarnation exists, and many speculators came back to this world but headless.

Risky tie in here between financial speculation, history and thought control, I know. Remember, we all live in a freak show, but at the end, it all makes senses. It all ties in. Think about it while driving. Keep your eyes on the road. There may be another Tweety Bird of wheels in the vicinity or a delivery boy on a scooter.

> Bless me of an enameled
> Ferrari red brake caliper.
> Fulfill my desire;
> Please light me and make me
> A Chariot of Fire

For professional drivers. Those who earn a pay from the road. A Grand Prix weekend would be like working in a dangerous environment workshop like a wood shop or machine shop and having to guess a rowdy kindergarten group, juvenile delinquent. They are all F1 drivers for a day, but God knows, maybe they can't ski.

They are excited, wreckless, dangerous and do stupid thing. It doesn't make life any easier. They could be like kids playing with razor blades or probing the live toasters with a kitchen knife.

One more time. Racing weekend. I don't mind the Pit Lane girls and their parties on Crescent st, but the drivers' wannabe. Forget it.

It's early June, and it's the F1 Racing weekend. The Fast and the Furious, but mainly the Furious fest. For a period of 3 days, a so-called world-class Jet Set selected clientele will go on a cheating spree with anything that wears a skirt, male or female on this all-you-can-eat life excess buffet. It's not an event, it's a land or a state. It's 3 days navigating in the land of the unsubstantiated. A land of pure projection of being. The Peel Pub's sport equivalent of the daily 6.99 meat spaghetti special, without meat ball. So-called world events are also the only place where you can see people, men and women, wearing visors. Let's all join to celebrate the worst of the humankind. All of this mise en scène to titillate some's pituitary gland at an awful expense of energy and material resource. This good old fashionable gonadotropin party.

"It was possible, no doubt, to imagine a society in which wealth, in the sense of personal possessions and luxuries, should be evenly distributed, while power remained in the hands of a small privileged caste. But in practice, such a society could not long remain stable. For if leisure and security were enjoyed by all alike, the great mass of human beings who are normally stupefied by poverty would become literate and would learn to think for themselves; and when once they had done this, they would, eventually, realize that the privileged minority had no function, and they would sweep it away. In the long run, a hierarchical society was only possible on a basis of poverty and ignorance." Voila !
George Orwell, 1984

I know, it may get to be annoying, but: I loved the Peel Pub. The original one on Ste-Catherine. The one that was at the basement.

I have nothing about car racing. See how people gather and celebrate in tailgate parties at any NASCAR event. See how NASCAR with its minimalist rules is for the people by the people. See how the spirit of 1776 is there, is his Stars and Stripes color. But, this circus or freak show is in town.

F1 job description! If I had to create a job description to offer attendance (even free tickets) to a F1 Grand Prix race, it would start by this:

Good Morning, Mr. Phelps! Should you decide to accept it should you or any of your IM Force be caught or killed, the Secretary will disavow any knowledge of your actions. This tape/disc will self-destruct in five/ten seconds.

Good luck, Dan/Jim.

This recorder will auto-destroy within the next 11 seconds. (from Mission Impossible)

There seems to be something of a fundamental difference between a F1 Circuit race and a NASCAR. As you probably would have guessed, I am a NASCAR person.
.
As the NASCAR celebrates an alliance between freedom, brute force, people, octane, testosterone and hard work sanctified on the same red clay road where the stock car tradition began, the F1 circuits seems to be this passage obligatoire to the school of tyrants and the socially disliked. American vs. European traditions. Remember the Mayflower and the Alamo later.

As they all dream of taking a spin on the F1 Circuit, I did, with a 750k state-of-the-art (let's say) turbo machine surrounded by Grand Prix beauties, on taxpayer's tab too. I did.

The Grand Prix is usually followed by the Italia fest. Puccini in the park on penne rigate sauce Puscanese with anchovies. The fans are in for the race, but not for the race itself. It's a bizarre relation as they want the octane, the chicks, and the event's testosterone but couldn't care less about the show itself. A bit like fishing, many go fishing but don't exactly care for the fish either, it's a thing. We love things. Man fears emptiness. Man needs things. Physical or psychological things. For decades, man purchased giant Encyclopedias to fill in empty bookshelves without ever opening one of the books. We could probably hold the race thing event without doing the actual race, have the podium thing, and get away with it. Then we'll go straight into Penne Rigates week, extra Puscanese week. Careful, the plates are hot.

Delicious... Delicious!

Detour or not. Italiafest, you are going to love it.

Ital fest. Italiafest for Dummies. The city blocks the main for 4 blocks of the main South North artery of the city. St-Laurent st also known as: The main. Local shop owners empty their last year's inventory on the street. The Pirate with a parrot on his shoulder sits there with his buddy, Elvis Italiano, charging for pictures. There are pony rides, little electric motorcycles, espresso machine demos, Italian sausage on the grill, and the guys from Vespa Ducati have a stand. The only interesting one, in fact. There is the habitual Fiat Topolino 500, the originals, in parade. Almost everyone has roots in Campobasso. If you are Italian from the North, you are not welcome. These Italians are more Italian than Italians in Italy. The main discussion topic, who gave their gold to Mussolini and who had it stolen by Mussolini. There is also the common discussion among Italian women about that woman who had a cyst the size of a pea that became as big as a grapefruit. Fortunately, it has been removed before it grew to the size of a Citrulo. I heard that story hundreds of times. It looks as if it's a national obsession. Probably that Berlusconi would have tried to squeeze the grapefruit.

My wife grew up in this neighborhood. Piccola Italia. Rent was cheap, apartments were large, but insulation was bad and every so often, they ended up with ice on the wall in the cold months of winter. That was a miserable place that became trendy. Ring any bells to you? The same story goes for almost anything built before the 1980s as far as insulation is concerned. Wonder why most families had cats in that part of town. Because of mice and rats, those house Gato were fat. Nowadays, it is all gentrified as the 2nd and 3rd generation moved to new housing in the suburbs. They come to the Fest for a coffee, a manicot and once it's done, they surely take off to their AC's house with a garden and a pool in the burbs or to the parent's triplex in St-Leonard. Or this place called Mafia road.

Most but Elvis Italiano, the Pirate and the Barber of Seville and other Piccola Italia Fellini's type characters haunting the neighborhood leave after the feast. The best and most Italian cafés are still on this section of St-Laurent boulevard. My wife goes, and she takes me to the fest every year for as long as I have known her. She is of Italian descent, but did not marry Italian to be caught going to a wedding every weekend for the next 50 years and living above the in-laws in a Plex. Do the math to realize that If you can mortgage your house under 2.89% for 5 years, you are better off fending for yourself right off the bat after your wedding than stepping into the Ponzi Italian marriage scheme. Starting in life with money is nice. There is an ultimate price tag attached to it. There may be free wedding cakes in life, but no free lunch.

My ancestor immigrated to Canada before it became Canada or even North America for that matter, but listening to contemporary tales of immigration makes you realize that maybe your family had it good for the past 3 centuries or so. They got lost chasing a hockey puck on ice and ended up here, Here on this perpetual snow bank.

My wife's grandfather and his brothers fled Mussolini's Italy because they were educated or communist and landed everywhere across the world. Argentina, Corsica, Canada. The story goes that while the kids were in exile, the family farm got occupied by a German Nazi armored division that had mined the surrounding area, vineyard, and olive trees. The area of Prato is a gorgeous place. I would have picked it too as a Panzer commander, I guess. Many of these guys were from German Aristocracy and could appreciate the finer things in life, and Tuscany is among them.

The father who was still to earn a living on the farm as all of his sons were in exile and went to the field to stepped on a landmine. Game over. Swept off his feet as it could be said. Italy being what it is, I believe the succession settlement happened a few years ago, I mean 75 years later. My wife's aunt, titina, sends us letters every 5 years to ask her to surrender her rights to the property. For little rights she still has after 3 generations. So are the stories going on in the Piccola's Italia.

A mountain side in Tuscany with olive trees and vineyards, stating that she had to maintain the place, and it has been horrendous, not to mention that she lives there, and it's one of the world's nicest places. Damn, I would trade a job coming with a Bentley in Montreal for one on a moped in Tuscany because over there they master something we don't. I would go as far as going for a VeloSolex. The art of life. PAZAZZ.

I was having an evening walk on the main site of the Festival. Piccola Italia. Me, my wife and my daughter and as I walked to the only kiosk of interest to me: Ducati, Vespa. Next to CafeItalia, I hear someone screaming my name.

Bert, vieni qui! (Come here)

As I recognized my colleague from the transit system, Gianni. Yes, Gianni is the official troublemaker of the transit system. He has a low tone, almost husky voice like Adele. Gianni used to be a union delegate for the Teamsters when he was at UPS or other. Troublemaker for sure, but, well, he is a blast. He was there at the Italian sausage on charcoal cooking with someone else. I think it's Dominic from the Café next door. I know Dominic from the days I lived in Piccola Italia. I am always pleased to hear my name in foreign language, it has something profoundly international.

SI, sarò lì presto. (I am on my way)

Ciao Gianni! Che cosa succede! (what's up). I can also walk Italian and do hand gestures. Gianni was cooking hot dogs (hot sausage) at this stand with his uncle Dominic. Dominic, from what I gathered, is his uncle, but he was not aware that Gianni had broken his forearm falling from a tree in the old country while Peeping at the local brothel.

I am working with my uncle here, Dominic. We are selling Italian sausages Hot-Dogs here. Do you want one?

No Grazie, we are just out of The Napolitana on Dante. She is with the fortune reader over there. The old Strega.

So, uncle Dominic steps him the conversation: So, you did not flip over the kayakist!

Well, you know. Not that we did not feel like it … It was daytime, plenty of witnesses, we'd have to take off our shoes and as we grew older, we became less violent I'd say.

But Gianni wanted to flip him over and beat him up.

No, not that I did not feel like it, but not that this pazzo did not deserve it, but, you know, these days. It is getting complicated. You know, It is all political these days. Humor. Humor is sometimes misunderstood. It's an art, you know.

So, Gianni stepped in and said: We should have flipped him over. This pazzo is a bad example for our kids. Imagine if all the kids start doing that, dressing like a man crossing the ocean in solitaire but waddle in a foot of water. A drag queen on a pond. Disgrazia !!! What a shame.

Sure, you don't want those 2 Hot Dogs? Your wife, is she Campobasso?

Nah! Mezze. Campobasso and Firenze. That's why she has a redhead. It's from Firenze.

Take those. For you and your wife. Mangiare, Mangiare. !

Grazie.

So, guys? Who's got the best Tiramisu in Montreal? The goons hanging by the Solid Gold club confirm San Marco. Does San Marco have the best Tiramisu, or is it Allati on Jean Talon?

San Marco, and San Genaro for Pizza.

As far as food is concerned, you can also rely on Goon talk. They know the spots.

I am uncertain whether they were serious or pulling my leg. As I know these guys, it could be a type of ritual comedy thing. A cheap form of Commedia dell'arte. Did they really think we should have drowned this beginner kayakist? I'm not certain. Those little things that keep the workers going and keep the community spirit alive.

My wife: You shouldn't hang around with those Sicilians, they are nuts. Reasons more to do it.

On a lighter note. Gianni shows up to work in a late model Ferrari. He is like us. Driving buses.
Yes, he is still a bus driver.

Say Paisano, you won the lottery?

No, it's not mine. A friend of mine gave it to me for a few years. Well, until he gets out of jail!

Jail

Yes. He got nabbed for drug trafficking. So, he'll be in the can for a while. Rather than having his car seized by the police, he surrendered me the paper, countersigned. A gift, but, a temporary one. It is a nice ride, yet it sucks a lot of gas. Expensive to drive around.

And once he is out on the streets again.

I'll sign them back !

One more tale of the Piccola, There are thousands of them.

But, what the hell are you looking at !

Bert?

Yeap.

Do you think you could cover for me Friday night?

I don't know, what's in the tin.

Simple, 4 Casino loser ride and 2 spookies to Pointe St-Charles.

Why do you want off ?

Halloween party. Singles crowd. Organized event, It's a sexy Jungle Jim extravaganza party.

It's not Jungle Jim, It's Sheba, queen of the jungle ?

Yes. Yes, How do you know?

It's a long story. Make sure you get to wear the safari jacket and the pith helmet. Now, I could not trade off one of my day assignation for one of your stew. Casino runs and 57 Spookies, no shit. Here is the deal. You call sick around 19:00 hrs. I leave an emergency pickup note at the desk around 18:45 stating that I would have a preference for the Casino run and the Spookies. I'll get the part at times and a half. You go to your party and I'll owe you a lunch at let's say: The Peel Pub.

OK, let's do it. My routes will be covered. I'll go to my private party and, but, forget about the Peel Pub. It sucks. Nobody likes the Peel Pub anymore, It is from another era.

I have never done the 57 Pointe St-Charles route. Someway, a supervisor will have to help me out on this one. I'll manage. Casino shuttle is a piece of cake.

There it goes !

The Casino shuttle or gambling 101 by a master of the trade. Vegas Harry.

Odds.

Odd put Vegas Harry on my route to teach me about the gambling business. This industry based on deceit but someway so exciting. This lifestyle built on beating the odds. The odds of life or this honest day at work is for chumps.

One of the worst things that can happen in life is to win a bet of a horse at an early age.
Danny McGoorty.

Harry led the good life as so he pretended. He has this waterfront Dorval's condo. A vintage Ferrari and surrounds himself with hot mature women. He has been throwing the dice of life for the last 40 years or so. It's a living. Sometimes dangerous, but still a living. He caught the buses to go to the Fairview mall almost every day to get out of the house and share his knowledge with us. Harry always had good stories for drivers. Story has it that he has no more points on his driver's license that are now suspended.

So, the story goes like that.

A regular conversation, usually started by such a statement.

Man, you know those government pencil necks have been at screwing since you were born. Which is a very libertarian statement indeed.

Sure Harry, but we do have some stuff in return, like services

Those are cheap, low end, low-quality service that could be supplied by the private enterprise at way lower cost

OK, they are not very competitive, but at least it extends the population with a social safety net.

It is not a safety net, Bert. It's a catching net. It's a trap. They have the same safety net in Lobster trap at the bottom of the ocean. You are getting trapped by these guys and to keep you quiet, whether they buy your silence with a Welfare check or the illusion they may let you gain your absolute freedom betting against the odds.

Like the Lotto game, I presume

Exactly, you schmuck! The lotto games. They get you to bet every week and raise a gigantic stake. The bigger the stake, the more people buy. Now, they have that computer that is programmed to spin any combination that had not been played until all the possible combination are actually played. Statistically impossible, following me?

But sometimes people win Jackpots

Not on this side of the borders, they don't. Go figure, those guys are more vicious than the Mafia. They are the law or have it on their side. They are at cashing in without giving, just like the insurance company, Are you still there.

I am, but traffic is getting thick here, so go slower. I have to grasp all that.

They have this gigantic stake they've built up. A computer program that will minimize any gains across the country. Do you really think that they would let out a winning combination for a Jackpot and give one of us, taxpayers slaves, a few millions of bucks? In your wet dream, brother. They will never do that.

How about those people who claim the Jackpot and are given those massive checks on TeeVee?

Those are actors. They represent a profile. They are for the gullible that still wish upon a fucken star to break free from the ever oppressive machine. They want to keep you here. Here under the false pretense that it is the greatest country in the world. Here because you are happy to belong to what. They are not for real. The only way to win a lottery is to have those numbers written on a official statement, namely a ticket, and have the Lottery making the draw in public with those number ball machines. Those machines are like a deck of card, they are the safest way to play for everyone. They draw the balls, you have your numbers in hand and there is this social contract between you and the state, and you may, there, have a shot at the odds. It's Jean Jacques Rousseau 101 Brother.

Never thought about it. Thanks for the tip.

And I never played lotto here anymore but sometime purchase tickets online in place where they still have live drawing.

On Harry's planet... If you want to play, go to Atlantic City or Vegas, but never in a state-owned Casino. The theory is that if you sit down in front of a slot machine and play for 18hrs in a row without leaving the machine and the end of the ordeal, you would have gained the equivalent of minimum wage for 18 hrs. State Casinos are stingy. Some states consider players as a form of entrepreneurship and likewise, the state insures, thanks to the Casinos, that someone who spends 18 hours in a row spinning slot machine wheels, deserves some sort of retribution financed by those who are just playing small sums here and there. Those on whom they make a profit and eventually taxes. Lotteries are getting somewhat political these days as only ultimate jackpots are ever won as if the lottery computer could not find anymore a combination that had not been played and when it gives out, if it gives out to a large group of poor people in a sinister area.

As the old balls pulling determined a winner, the state computer is programmed to find a way not to give the lot or a few millions losers. Just like playing blackjack against a computer. Or is it God? Harry had only one religion; the dice. The dice as one of the commandments of this religion is that God plays with dice. That's all there is to life. Odds and beating the odds. There is a certain mathematical as well as philosophical depth in this philosophy.

So there, I have been doing a few happy camper's trips to the casino and forth and have been waiting for the supervisor to bring me the 57 Pointe St-Charles – Griffintown layout or Carjours they call it. The average slot machine addicts or plain loser trying to sneak in the casino for a free drink, maybe a meal or feel a bit of Monaco glitz

So, this homogenous group of well-dressed, young professionals that did not exactly frame the Casino slot machine crowd, walks out of the Metro Station. There were about 40 to 50 people and those kids. Looking sharp, impeccably dressed, the little black dress or the sports blazer. All balanced to perfection. Nor too heavy or too light. All in professional balance, they must have had formation from professionals of look. They were a group from the prestigious HEC MBA level business school and fitted the reputation of the school.

So, the leader of the group, (it also sounds like a martian or jimmy jungle movie type, take me to your leader) comes to me and ask: (hence the eternal pith helmet requirement)

Are you the bus that goes to the F1 racetrack paddock?

I know that I go to the Casino, I am filling in, but the Racetrack, I don't think so. It's fall.

He said: according to this paper schedule, you pass by the paddock lodge. He showed me the plan. We are having a private party at the F1 Lodge, the school has rented the place and tended me the summer schedule of the Casino Shuttle. The HEC Halloween extravaganza.

I looked at the schedule and, as I thought, that was summer months, we were late October. I felt terrible at breaking their party and being the lousy civil servant spoiling a great evening for regulation consideration. Some love this power, The sheer power of being a party pooper, or a killjoy. Not me. This is just not me.

But

I said, Listen, as far as that schedule and layout are concerned I am supposed to go strictly to the Casino. You got a summer schedule in your hand, and it changes after Labor Day. It's fall. At first glance, looks like it could be detoured, if the track is opened, which it should, or else I can take you to the Casino, you call 10 cabs, and they take you 4 × 4 to the lodge. I could bend the rules for you, but I got to know if I can access the track, for one and for two, it will be a faked mistake; you'll have to play with me on that one. The famous O'Early rule.

So, the group leader said, OK, We'll play the game.

In 5 minutes, supervisors will come to meet me with an envelope. I'll get my information on the gates but for all that we are all concerned, you guys go to the Casino and play the part, 5 minutes.

I wanted to avoid getting stuck with a filled bus on a desert gravel road in the dark, just as David Vincent in the 60s sci-fi series, The Invaders. The narrative intro states:

The Invaders—alien beings from a dying planet. Their destination, the Earth. Their purpose: to make it THEIR world. David Vincent has seen them. For him, it began one lost night on a lonely country road, looking for a shortcut that he never found. It began with a closed, deserted diner, and a man too long without sleep to continue his journey. It began with the landing of a craft from another galaxy. Now, David Vincent knows that the invaders are here; that they have taken human form. Somehow, he must convince a disbelieving world that the nightmare has already begun."

It looks and sounds just like a regular day at the office for a bus driver.

Fortunately, David Vincent saw them!

I have an old friend in Paris, the real Paris. He is CEO in a large pharma company and every 3 years or so, I pop in Paris as he invites me over for dinner in a traditional Brasserie. He knows the best places. It has been a ritual for the last 30 years or so. At the time of the digestive, he throws in this comedy spin. He recites the Invaders' intro with all the drama and intonation. Word by word to the end and puts the emphasis on the David Vincent has seen them.

Hey, the man has seen them. Case closed. What do we have to worry about? Circulez, il n'y as rien a voir. David Vincent saw them. There are millions of David Vincent in this world saving humanity every day. Let's order one cognac before we hit the road.

A toast here! A toast to David Vincent.

There is magic in the art of crossing humor degrees with people that understands where it is all going, but almost to have dinner with close friend in Paris. Because Paris is a magical place.

My turn! A toast to Paris l'eternelle and to friendship.

To friendship!

So comes the Encounter of the supervisor kind!

The supervisor showed up. Martine, an old friend of mine from the beginning of my employment at the Transit commission. She had decided to join the forces of darkness and become supervisor. She disliked it all. Cute little blonde with a square haircut and a bob. She pulled in by the bus in her Jeep, toting an envelope of stuff for me, and walks in the bus entrance.

She said: Hum, nice crowd here, beautiful men. Think I could join in. (you Cougar)

She could read me as I could read her. One of those things. Can't explain. As she mentioned, the attractiveness of the young crowd, I could have felt a bit of nostalgia there. A bit of : I have been in that crowd before. The crowd of the dressed office party. The professionals and those who could carry an upbeat conversation on different topics. The Martini glass crowd. It must have been somewhere in her curriculum of, as she mentioned, it to me before. She knew that I once belonged to that crowd too, and her eyes sparkled.

She knew damn well that I was playing the lost driver game and was just about to short circuit all the transit rules to help a group of young people that were there to enjoy what is escaping us these days, life. Was she to intervene and save the day and make sure that the world abides by: No?

She could read in my eyes that in fact if we should both shortcut the system. Take her mobile Jeep on flashing light for a spin to open the way for a bus filled with a crowd of people on a party. Youth and ambitions. Dreams. To disappear momentarily to this private party. Slip into another mode or dimension. Maybe we could disappear off the radar, cut the GPS, hook the Walkies Talkie, the time of a drink or two with the in crowd. Time for a dance. Time to Do the Hustle. (Van McCoy) In fact, we both dreamt of that escape. We both should have had this discussion with Thomas Jefferson on freedom. Disobedience is the cornerstone of liberty. Now, there are many types of disobedience. Social, material, philosophical. In the case of a supervisor disappearing with its mobile unit, accompanied, by a bus full of party goers, a few hours. Yet, it did crossed our mind in full synchronicity. We may have gotten into trouble. It could have been worth the risk. It could have ended up into something more substantial, romantic or even erotic. We skipped on this opp. Too risky. Nonetheless, I have once disappeared from the grid for 3 hours and no one noticed. Maybe we could have pushed our luck.

Do the hustle. A disco theme song. Very innocent flute tempo but at once, a Cuban trumpet kicks in and makes this routine so sexy. Time for sparkles, sexy.

In fact, we dreamt for a moment of small black dress and pleated pants for a change. Rich wool suits, silk, leather, no synthetic, blazer with fancy liners handstitched and maybe a boa. Dressed opulent and free. Style, elegance and PAZAZZ, (You wear those shoes and I will wear that dress) Those parties that last until sunrise. This escape of our routine reality. More than those Politically Correct family feast celebrated by a dollar store gift distribution to the kids and the inflatable toys on gas engine compressor that smells like puke or the McDonald play land. All served with some BBQ food on Chinet plates. I know, I mentioned Chinet plate as nobody is dead nor overseeing the party from a cookie jar sitting at the master's table but still, it resembles cerebral death. Those utilities party (the essential workers of the society) where no one knows about the Edison's house, Bretton Woods, a few Winston Churchill citations or was Ste-Catherine actually Hypatia of Alexandria. The fate reserved to the essential service workers by this ungrateful social system of ours.

Gasp! Somewhere we traded that sporadic life a bit more exciting and challenging for this employment security, this pay fairy and her deposit wand dropping by your bank account on Wednesday at midnight and this job security. This paid bungalow, this Hyundai or Nissan and this nice paycheck until my taxman moths it in half. We all have those Thomas Jefferson moments. Me, Martine, all as the citation from Jefferson. If you are willing to sacrifice a bit of your freedom for some security, we will lose both. This is the poetic position. The punk group The Clash summed it up differently: Should I stay or should I go ! In periods of doubts, I listen to that tune.

I guess we both missed those party days of an age we still had a life, reasons to celebrate and a soul that could be bartered or bar tendered. Yet, it appears to me that we both could relate to something we lived before as many in the trade have no clue of what these experiences are all about so will never miss it. They live for the system and will never miss this 11:00 PM diner in Roma as per, they never went there. They have a Pickup truck, but never Did the Hustle.

So, as we were both on the same page and somehow wavelength, we played the overlapping 3 degrees humor scheme. We may have gauged each other on that play.

They are going to the Celine Dion concert, I exclaimed!

Celine is in Vegas. You've got to be kidding, she's in Vegas!

Damn, you are sure about that, I'd hate to break the bad news to them but since you are a supervisor, let's say that it would be your job.

No, your show, they are yours, they are behind the yellow line.

By the way, would you know if the racing circuit is open? In case, I may have to go through there to get to the Casino.

Yes, it is. The story is that there are many private parties there and there is only one access. It's 250M to your left. There is no lighting in case one would get lost there by distraction or simple inadvertence. Please leave me 1 minute before you leave. I will not notice that you made a mistake on your way to the Casino.

It could happen, you know, I am just filling in here tonight. The regular driver would not make such a simple mistake.

At the very moment she mentioned that the road was open, one of the passengers, who was supposedly going to the Casino and was this Greer Garson lookalike dropped a Yesssss!!! The return of Mrs. Miniver.

The plan was uncovered. LOL. Yet, we could not get a derogation nor a detour from the company within the next minutes, see hours, days, or months.

She left and waved, Happy Motoring.

And there I was. A brand-new vehicle with a Detroit Diesel Turbo Charged. A nice crowd to drive at a party and a F1 Circuit to try on a racetrack this beast. I had this MP3 Blasting. Ramsey Lewis with Earth Wind and Fire, Sun Goddess. Through the road, to the oups, left, Circuit entrance and right on the concrete. Slick, no streetlamps, no holes, no police and the Charter sign lighted in case I would get caught by a security camera. No Invaders... Freedom at last. And so, I really pushed the machine to the point I felt the turbo kicking in and with 60 some passengers it hugged the road. Buses are engineered to be a smooth ride when full. , The frames are bent and straighten up with the weight of the clientele. Straight line, we are going to the party in style, followed by a full moon in the sky. It had the doomed vessel mystic here. Loved it. There is a German word that describes being one with the machine, as she becomes an extension of your mind and body. There I was.

There I was until someone started mentioning: Slow down, slow down, the wall.

Wall, what wall?

Incidentally, there is a hairpin curve that only one that knows the circuit could foresee. I am a NASCAR man. I did not expect that one, but we managed to make this magisterial entrance in dust and smoke, just like the Fast and Furious.

Everyone enjoyed it. It started their party and as the group leader approached me to thank me for the break and a personalized service he mentioned to me:

Would you accept a tip for your service?

No, I can't, I am a City Worker, and it's against all rules. The kid had a wad of $20 in his hand.

Business school kids know how to maneuver around regulation.(Leadership but natural charisma type) So, he nodded, looked at me, and dropped the wad beside me, saying. This is not a tip, this is money you found.

My pleasure sir.

And I thought, kid, nothing you will ever learn in those specialized MBA's school will ever prepare you for the chaos you will face every day in the business sector. Nothing. Keep your dignity, decency, and enthusiasm, and you may get through life. In case you get to the end of your rope, we are hiring. I'll teach you the ropes. One more time.

Ok, I may have bent the rules a bit but in the end, Haven't I put a publicly owned vehicle at the disposal and service of a city's institution, the very notable HEC. Haven't I helped keep the spirit and reputation of the City as a great place to work, study, and party alive? Haven't I given the right service for an employee of a Sin City to the benefit of all taxpayers?

Whenever you break the rules, you have to mentally prepare an excuse speech in your mind for 2 people, the mayor, or God. The excuses for the Mayor may be a little more complex, as far as God is concerned, he will understand as per the parable of the talents.

And yet, I finish off with a great story and $100 cash.

This story always remind of Martine.

Her name was Martine. As in those children books made in the 60s to educate kids in France. Martine at the Beach, Martine at the store, Martine at…. Cute stories, great quality, amazing illustration. Those Martine books were gems and introduced children to a certain level of etiquette.

So, at one of those upper management transit meetings where the big cheeses, the top dog and the honcho put a white shirt on, roll the sleeves and to do the usual city hall meeting or preacher pep talk. She was there. That specific year we had more accidents than usual as we faced way more snow storms than the usual winter. No passengers injuries, tough. We canned more cars and sent more buses to the garage than usual. At the first snow storm the company introduced the slinky double bus, 80% got damaged or stuck in snow as Park ave looked like the battlefield of Stalingrad.

On that year, the management went out of the way to meet the 5000 drivers, paid us 2 hours to attend the meeting and displayed this remarkable cold buffet of hard crust sandwiches and delicacies. Real plates. Hot and cold, Espresso Machine and no Chinet. 5 stars hotel buffet.

At the question period I intervened grabbing the mike on the topic of accidents as per, with a great drawing, someone could just fill in the text description with one word. Bang. (Sh happens). Yes, Bang is a 4-letter word, as Love is too and there, work. I had standing ovation on that one, and it did not stay unnoticed. Mike Drop !!!

After the meeting, sticking by the Espresso machine with the Italian goons. I am always sticking around with, whether the Italian crew or the Ruskie, Martine comes to meet the crew.

(as a supervisor)

That was funny. Remember me, we started together at St-Love many years ago. I remembered you from the Casino shuttle. So? Did you get those kids to the private party at the racetrack?

Yeap. Couldn't help it. You should never be an obstacle to a great party.

I knew it. (but she had that light in her blue eyes that said, how about a coffee, the two of us out of this setting). Maybe her career or couple or just life in general was going through a rough spot. The daily life of public services workers.

Guys were joking, the party was on, the Italian winked at me, the Ruskie made suggestive remarks. They have the Russian expression for making love all night in 2 words. This is how you learn a new language or culture. That was neither the place nor the moment to engage in anything. It may have been weak or completely improvised, but the only reply that came back to me was the simple one.

Years ago, this company hired the best. Here is my badge number, you can always know (as a matter of facts) where to find me.

Our path never crossed again. Maybe it's better that way. Maybe it's like the Olimpico Café in the Mile End.

You get better paychecks, work more and frankly get greedy before life teaches you that sleep and rest are important too.

The Tuesday evening school special on Cote des Neiges. 23 minutes work, 3 hours pay. A sinch.

As I once told you, my daughter is creative but also has a short fuse. That's got to come from her mother's genetics.

To avoid screaming matches between my wife and my daughter, I often took her with me on the bus. Mainly evening overtime extras or the wildlife bar closing special. I get this run frequently. The 165 N special. You take the bus out of the garage, position the vehicle idle, stand by in front of a Gov't run nursing school and pick up the student at 22:12. Once the load is in, you go up the hill to the Metro Station. On the way, two, three stops max (Van Horne, Cote Ste Catherine) and you unload the last ones at CDN Metro station Blue Line at 22:27. Usually, you go downhill downtown to Concordia station empty or almost since there are 8 minutes service on that line. Easy to do. You are back home by 23:10, and it provides the opportunity to go for a Downtown dip and back. I always loved to see the street life around Concordia Station on Friday night. It's like The Petula Clark song, Downtown.

The ride also gave me the occasion to take my daughter Downtown and stop for her $10 tea macha coffee at the Second Cup Café and to talk. Talk about work, life, talk father and daughter. Dad's job. That dad job that my father didn't really have time to fulfill when I was young as he was traveling Europe for work. The good old Swiss tax haven connection and a handful of very wealthy clients that did not feel the necessity of chipping in for taxes once in a while. They were flying him on the Concorde plane and had those fancy Europeans, namely Austrian or German aristocrats clients. Business felt fine until that day that the RCMP agents knocked on the door to investigate some paperwork. Or was it. We were kids, we'll never know. He was getting involved with the wrong crowd. Looks like there is no age for that.

This is where he changed his line of business. I may have changed mine too for the same reasons, Being a decent man and an example for my kid.

Different times, different generations and different types of dad. The beauty and quietness of the evening work. It always calmed her anxieties and she got to understand the transit culture, becoming one of the boys. I would not wish for her to join the transit society. I wish she has a different life than mine.

One September night, there was a group of University students on an initiation Party outing. They were waiting for that first 165 N to show. Regular or special, the first one. I was the chosen one. I love those trips that take you out of the comfort bubble or the comfort zone. Let's get creative, the bus is empty.

And so, they got in, invaded the back section of the bus and started singing led by that 20 something years old French woman, party organizer and group leader, who knew many french traditional songs that were a bit modified to make them, to put it mildly, a bit grivoise. OK, I could live with this, but my daughter was a bit scandalized. She takes that from her mother too. Some songs went a bit overboard and were on the verge of scandalous. It reminded me of those Army walking songs. She had a song with all the slang expression used in France to describe a sexual practice. All of them. Frolicking peasants 101. Hay, well, donkeys, wine, the whole renaissance era was there.

There were tens of them. They were all enjoying, and I learned some I never heard about. It was an answering song, and all the kids knew all the answers. Life, youth, fun, whom I am opposed to this paid overtime rate but, if a regular customer walks in and complains, I may get in trouble. Remember, if it is behind the yellow line, it is your ultimate responsibility. So said Padre Pio. Another one of my regular customers. Yes, Padre Pio is a regular.

Trouble could come fast as a passenger that would not appreciate the sexual content, the noise, find it demeaning or sexist, or strictly that his or her religion forbids music and even fun. Like the TV disclaimer, but with a bus. Just to remind that a full bus empties itself in one stop when someone walks in with a service dog, blind or other. Many people are just scared of dogs and for many religions, the fat retriever or Labrador is the devil. It is always touchy and many blind or low vision people joke about it saying, man, don't worry, they'll leave me a place to sit.

So, I checked if I had a regular service bus behind me and turned the bus signs in front of 165 N to Special Day camp. I sent my daughter to the back of the bus to ask where the group was heading, so I could take them directly there. One of the passengers told us, We are going to the 3 Amigos on St-Catherine st. From that point on, it became 3 Amigos Express, Non Stop.

Once you take a creative initiative with city equipment you've got to think of the simple rule: Had I had to explain it to the mayor, would it make it smile and make it feel, eh, this is good for the image and the spirit of the community? Always is. Ask Padre Pio?

It reminded me of this expression I learned in Belgium, bouffer du millefeuilles, or se faire une demitasse au café des deux colonnes, It all seemed very innocent in its first degree as it points out to a flaky French multilayer pastry filled with cream as the two columns point out at women's legs. Now, you see the where it leads. I must have missed the French "me" in the statement. As in, "me" Bouffer le Mille Feuille. Bouffer or Broutter are slang word for eat and are from old argot or peasant language.

Given that the 3 Amigos restaurant and party spot happens to me on the loop where I do the turnaround to go back to the garage, I have been delighted to extend this, so researched by the management smile and service and dropped them right at the door. They serve food at the 3 Amigos. Honestly, people are going there more for the Margaritas than anything else. Once again, I saved the day and the reputation of this town.

Bouffer du millefeuilles! Delicious, Delicious... Yes, Adele !

To come back to the pastries and café, my mind had to go back to a business trip in Belgium decades ago. I was there in a panicky business move for a new Tour Operator trying to push its services on the European market and ended up with this senior Hotel Sales representative, in her Audi from Brussels to Antwerp at 180 KMH. She represented a large chain of hotel and knew the market inside out. We've been connected by the Govt of Canada commercial delegation in Brussels. She had those outstanding legs. She offered me a ride from Brussels to Antwerp, as she had an appointment in that city that same day. We synchronized our agendas accordingly. I was young and naive but I looked like this man doing a TeeVee kids show in Europe and it sexually aroused many. Maybe I was just good-looking.

We had met a few days before the appointment and had time to exchange on everything happening in Europe in a Brussels Brasserie. From the Glasnost, the Perestroika, and the imminent fall of the Berlin Wall. The late '80s were a very exciting time. Optimism and the legend of a better world and peace dividend added to the atmosphere. How naive were we to believe that those peace dividends were to mean a tax break and better living conditions for most of us? The assertive business-driven type but, as I said, she had legs. Again. The way a person drives tells a lot about personality. She was fast, focused and steady. Career woman in her early 40s. Sit down, kid, and take notes.

Europe has something that hits the eyes and the soul when you are North American. It appears that you have been deprived of such beauty, aesthetic for so long that it is hard to grasp how this sudden discovery affects your soul and how. It has something of a revelation moment.

So, here I was in her German Berline Audi or top of the line BMW gliding at 180 KMH on as smooth as silk road. No pothole, no bump, no nothing. Those lanes of road are or were all light 24/7 and people are driving fast. Fast but well. No incivilities. People open the way if you flash. No slow vehicle in the right lane. A driver's dream. I looked at the names of cities on the road, and it's all history books that come back to me, WW1 trenches, battles, and all those, but as my mind wandered, the sight of those small villages was also breathtaking. As I landed in Brussels a few days ago, I noticed the way that land was divided into small square lots, as those BW pictures of WWII bombing missions my father kept in a trunk. Now here I am. Well sunk on an upscale leather seat, hearing that overkilled music on the radio. Enya. Life is good. For generations people from Canada came to this part of the world in a green wool uniform with putties to kill or get killed and bang, here I am playing business tourism.

We had small talk, weather, life, economy and how life is in North America. Tourism, sales, a nervous laugh. I was there mentally, but wasn't. So, among that exchange of words and thought came this: Ca te plairait de me bouffer le Mille Feuille. It was a very direct sexual proposal under a polite slang word disguise. It meant what it meant. It is meant as per you can answer no, I am dieting or not into sugar or can decline politely. But why decline. I did not know but it was: The high tea time of cunnilingus.

It could have been an invitation to stop at a pastry shop on the road and stop for a coffee and a local delicatessen. Remember, I am still Canadian here. Well, in fact, it was a local delicatessen but more in the alive model. Now, the thing is that my brain doesn't seem to work like everyone else's. I presume by life experience. Someone should have told me about it, but science did not figure it out, nor medicine when I was born. I blame it on a motorcycle or a ski accident or maybe I am extra terrestrial after all. So !

It appears that I assimilate words one by one and store them by their emotive wavelength to store them in memory before retrieving them, to assemble them and make sense of the statement. It takes time but, being a nice person, I usually, by default, answer, yes, of course. It took a while, but in my recompilation process I spotted the term Mille Feuille, so it must have involved a pastry in a cardboard box. Fairly innocent indeed. My mother bought those pastries at the Steinbergs grocery store when I was a kid, but it was not exactly what was the intended subject of discussion but more something that was multilayered, could be sweet and served with crème patissiere depending on the existing societal structure. I guess my mind is wired like Martha Stewart's.

At the very moment I abided by the offer with an enthusiastic affirmative answer, the topic of conversation became more personal and intimate. The tone of voice changed a bit. The adrenaline seems to have booted in, and the sex moment is coming with the feeling of hormones in the air. Yes, I could feel it. As I went to the memory bank to make sense of the words and put an image on them, I finally figured out that I signed in for something I was not exactly sure of, but I looked again at that woman I thought: it has to be sexual. Shortly after these bits and bites of conversation as she sped up to a service center rest area exit, we ended up in this beautiful, strange place.

She found a parking place among other top of the line luxury sedans with steamed windows. Turned off the engine, kept the music on, unfastened her seat belt and pulled the skirt up. Silk, lace, black stockings. Just like in movies. The best thing about it. I am on the job: paid for that.

At the end we were the three of us in a discretely secluded area probably known to the extra marital or the quickie crowd. Me, her, and the very elusive Mille Feuille.

Maybe a local tradition like they have in Hawaii, the Lei tradition but with a pastry twist.

Life is full of surprises, and some are better than others.

From a North American standpoint: Ok, they eat better, have smaller cars and appliance. They seem to enjoy life a little more than we do and work less. They also had this tendency to bash each other's skulls with cannons every 30 years or so, but, looks like it's been quiet lately. Their TeeVee is as stupid as ours. Kids appear to have more vocabulary here than adults in North America.

The ride was over. I had dropped my group at the 3 Amigos. They loved their private city limo ride. Ste-Catherine st is lively. It's early autumn. Sidewalk terrasse are filled. The air is fresh and people enjoy a nice fall evening. Job's done. Aced it once again. Let's fulfill my share of the deal to my daughter and take her to the Second Cup for her $10 coffee. Damn, life used to be so much cheaper and less complicated.

As I walked to the Second Cup Café on Ste-Catherine street for the promised Macha Late that was to bring peace to the house and open a conversation with my daughter, she pointed out to me the evening specials. After a certain hour, the Café liquidate the pastries of the day before having to throw them away.

Dad. You seem to enjoy that French song about the Mille Feuille, maybe you could grab one with your coffee. They have some for sale.

No, thanks, It's not the pastry that made me smiled but the way my mind related to it.

If everybody is thinking alike, then somebody is not thinking.
George Patton

I was on a business trip. Building a business relationship with a European company takes time. They may try you and your services for a petty thing, but it takes years to talk about real business. Something that can't be done at a few months notice.

Air travel. Nice, but someone is not thinking properly here.

Just like in those kid illustrated encyclopedia of the 1950. Cruise ship. Cross the ocean on a cruise ship. New-York, Le Havre in less than 4 days. 4 days in heaven of 12 hours of hell ?

Made me think that those luxury liners up to the 1950s. Those ships were taking 4 days to cross the Atlantic. Life was on pause in transat chairs, bars and dining rooms. Not a bad concept after all given if it only takes 8 hours to cross over the ocean by plane your brain is badly damaged by jet lag cabin pressure and airport procedures for a 4-day recovery period. Notwithstanding what, you really breathe for 8 hours in the air. Body and soul meet after 4 days later. The body could do plenty of stupid things before it get reunited with the soul. On a cruise ship, they travel together. Healthier after all.

Before the era of air travel, people crossed the ocean in style on the Cathedral of the sea's liner. Those cathedral cruises across the ocean at 32 knots to take you across the world in class and style. Now those Shopping malls of the seas cruise around the tourism area, max speed, wading at a ridiculous 8 knots and sometimes to be served at high cost by Mickey Mouse, Goofy or else. It is worrisome, but who are we to worry. We may just be collectively brain-dead after all.

I took many cruises and love those ships. I love the good life of cruise.

I love cruises because it gives the impression to splurge. A few day diving in a world where nothing makes sense any longer. Technical sense. Financial sense. Some place where this so Canadian guilt and rationale can be put aside in room safe with the passport. Someplace where the cold is not the conversation topic. Someplace where living can be fully unapologetic. A full place. That place away from a land where the motto should be: Ad mare usque ad wimps or OMG we are so sorry. Sorry about events happening in times and places before the nation was even born. Government event kept in the secrecy. A cruise gives you the opportunity to momentarily live out of this Canadiana guilt trip narrative. The narrative by which everyone subconsciously abides by and fed by the ever omnipresent in our lives medias. The life traps. The CBC

I was on one of those cruise ships leaving Viletta, Malta. On the top of the biggest, latest and most marvelous MSC marvel of the sea. Viletta is a beautiful place, but I felt somehow embarrassed by all the opulence and luxury of those overstaffed ships. The good old Catholicism guilt reflex that kicks in once again, but should not. On that evening, while dressing to dine, I noticed in the cabin mirror that my eyes were green. They are usually muddy brown, but once in a while they are green. It reflects a state of mind. That evening I put on a white shirt with cuffs, a navy-blue blazer and dressed as a person of the world. My wife dressed a bit sexier than usual for all those photographs, taking pictures on the grand stairs. Every evening, the heart of the ship grand staircase looks like a Glamour photo shoot. Later, on the deck under a starry sky, I heard the definite sound of jazz music. A clear vibraphone solo. Again this Lionel Hampton tune emanating from a deck bar. One of many, but there was the Jazz lounge. The real deal. The lounge lizard type of place. As I grow older, I seem to fit better in this type of setting. Sat at the bar and ordered a Canadian Club on ice. No guilt. My Premier and the other Teletubbies of his Cabinet would be so ashamed of this so reckless behavior. Imagine, alcohol on a ship!

A floating Jazz bar on the Mediterranean sea.

The music was great, the mood brilliant. I was a happy man in a happy place, and I believe that I deserved it. I work hard, do an honest man's job. Take care of my family. Do the utmost I could do for my fellow man and my job. I believe I could enjoy this moment in its fullness. Now, is this whole model of leisure, steel, energy, business model, invasion by many cruise ships simultaneously on the same port city, over tourism and all defying all logic and moral. Of course yes. How do they make money? Beats me! Lousy for the planet.

Perhaps lousy for the planet as many things in facts. The system is very selective at pointing guilt on environment issues and created a new breed of people: the envirohypocrites. The Quakers of smog.

The planet could perfectly live without the human race on its back. In fact, I believe that just like a dog scratching its fleas in some zones when it's too much, the planet throws us a local catastrophe to remind us that, she is the boss, the top Dog. Allow it a few hundred years to get rid of our infrastructures and a few more to reestablish the animal kingdom balance and bang it back in business as if nothing happened. The integrity of the whole human experience could be composted within, more or less, a few hundred of years. Mortimer, we are back in business!

Think about it, as Patton would have said.

We need this planet more than she needs us, so saving our asses on the planet should be the motto, and not saving the planet. This is a very sufficient homo centered concept. Saving the planet has something so noble yet those who are claiming to do it are very arrogant about it, They are beholders of their truth and would love us all to abide in their creed and religious madness. It may, in fact, be happier for a while as those that borrow or pilfer into its resources account with no decency nor reserve forget that they'll have to pay back the loans and compounded interest. Looking at the state of the world right now, I believe our collective account is into collection mode. There is something in the Bible about the concept of man and dominion over nature, but this whole thing is not without minimal responsibilities for those who dominate nature.

It has the overall feeling of borrowing the old man's car for a date. You could not care less about the machine, but require its benefits. You are not scared about the scratch or the dent on it as of the reaction, wrath, of the old man on the issue. So, you are careful. Careful as we should always be careful for the same reasons. Now, given that I never had access to the family car, I can go guilt free to cruise. Given that, I never had access to the family Ford LTD Brougham. The Ford LTD with the retractable light beams. The one driven by Farrah Fawcett.

Putted this way: I have no intention whatsoever of saving the planet. I will not go to marches or else, but will not waste anything because I may just be cheap. I always drive small cars because I love the way they handle and, hell, it is just a car. So, I am cheap. I always drive the same model and brand because I hate car shopping and new thing because I am neo Luddite. I will not buy a property far from my workplace because I have to sleep more than the average, having to limit all commuting: a form of laziness, I guess. I ride a scooter around 6 months of years because I hate looking for parking spots and will not go for motorcycle because it involves changing gears, so I am cheap, lazy but Jazzy. In my line of work, I save society time and pollution and energy. This is my ultimate share.

Vacation ends and you are back to the grinder. I love the smell of diesel in the morning.

Back at the workplace, in this grandiose employee multi function room, I am talking vacation and transit with some colleagues. We develop an eye for that as mere reflex, as per for many it is a passion. City transit.

So, me and a few drivers at work were discussing Metro and bus systems in Europe. Madrid to London, to Paris. Bus system and rush hours in Roma and the subway in Barcelona and all the guys popped pictures of their iPhone and well we are transit professionals and many of us are passionate about it. It is a universe. We were arguing about soil, speed, efficiency, cleanliness as per I was the only one who saw the Moscow subway. At this one point, from a table, next to ours at the employee lounge, a driver addressed us with this accusative assertion.

I guess that you guys don't have a Pickup truck

We all shrug.

No, actually we all have small cars. Little import jobs.

If you guys had a Pickup truck, you would not travel this much.

Maybe there is a societal divide here over the financial angle, as Pick Up owners are in fact content with the sole usage of the vehicle. Perhaps the satisfaction created by driving the Pickup by far surpasses the satisfaction of traveling or discovering. Potentially, somehow, all the discoveries were done and cataloged and whatever fills in the trunk or cab or box (the load) or I don't know makes life complete. They are fulfilled with the snowmobile or seadoo they fit in the box. They are into their toys and those are expensive. I am puzzled, but it is possible. That would be great to answer my wife's suggestion:

Honey, I would love to go Island hopping in Greece this spring!

When a conversation starts by the word honey, I know it will be expensive.

Let's take a ride in the Pickup. It will go away. We could drop in by the Peel Pub ? But it won't work. Not with mine, for sure.

We all had a good laugh.

Why is my mind still on the Brussels mode?

Brussels. Land of Stella Artoise, the Falstaff, chicons au gratin and the millefeuilles. Yes, I am back to Brussels. I had to make a detour by the cruises to explain the body and the mind traveling at different speed also known as the jet lag effect. I think it is a way too simplistic explanation since it is purely material. I am stretching on the string of Mishio Kaku string's theory here.

As I landed in Brussels. My brain had already been severely attacked by a movie on board. A version of Crocodile Dundee II in Flemish. Jet lag and all those people asking for autographs, sometimes on their boobs or butts with fat black felt markers, and this Quiz Show. Seemed that I was mistaken for a very popular comedian doing a kid show that was not exactly and always meant for kids. Yet, it was labeled as a kid show on the TV grid, and I was mistaken everywhere as Uncle Jackie. It had its benefits, I guess.

I was also puzzled by this German quiz show on TV where at the end of the Quiz, all contestants had to trust a rat out of a Skinner Box to select the winner. The name of the show was 4 against Willie. Willie was the rat. It all relates to the concept that whatever you do and how good you are at doing such and such, in society, the rat has the final word. The rat fills in for the committee. Screw meritocracy. Screw the fairness of the system. It's the rat. No matter how you excel in the rat race. At the end of the day, you are still a rat.

So, I had that unforgettable ride to Antwerp to meet potential clients.

First travel agency in Antwerp. A small office with a lot of dusty naturalized heads of all types of antlers or others. The agency once specialized in selling hunting trips to Africa. Very 1950s or 1960s. This market was going down. Very Pith Helmet once again. As I walked in the place, the owner asked me. A dusty place full of paraphernalia of former travel days.

Man, what happened to you, have you been struggling with a bear, you look beaten.

No, in fact, it was more like a beaver.

So, he suggested, how about you tell me about your agency at the bar next door, while having a beer. You look as if you should have one. In fact, we've had a few indeed.

And, we went there. Had those magical laughs. We talked about everything. Same page on everything to conclude at the end. We both thought that the Perestroika would bring peace to Europe and peace financial dividends. Were we ever fucken naive? One more time.

Listen, I like you a lot, but I have no tour business for Canada as is, but I know a few people who would require a tour guide with culture, intelligence and a good sense of humor for the U.S. East Coast on private tours. This I would help you with. And so he did.

I have been on maybe 10 of those private tours contracts and had a great time and the money was good. There were perfect fits with the tour agenda, the clients, and the Tour Guide. I guess the story about the beaver is where I made my closing argument. Man should always trust what the beaver say and never turn its back to the totem with the turtle. Old native saying.

I made as many visits and sales pitch as I could, but it never seemed to work my way. Business relation takes time, and we did not have that luxury. Every night I walked back to the hotel from a restaurant, a subway station, a train station. Always carrying a huge brown peddler briefcase filled with heavy and humid brochures.

Lodging at the WTC Sheraton in Brussels, I had to walk through the Red-Light district to get to the Hotel. Let's say that women in the display window were always pleased to see their childhood hero from TV sneaking in by the Red lite after midnight. They had a special way to greet me every night. Inviting indeed, but I was numbed by jet lag and a dramatic change in life pace. 50 years ago, I would have taken a cruise liner.

On the last night of this exhausting sales tour.

Brussels, World Trade Center area also conveniently the Red Light. Prostitutes of all walks of life, unite !

I was on the way back to the hotel dragging this massive peddler's case after an exhausting day on the road meeting travel agents, brokers and other agencies. 11:00 PM. As everybody I met seemed to enjoy life in Brussels, I was the lousy unshaven salesperson with a trench coat, a tie and a lousy look. Yet, even beaten, I still resemble this man on TeeVee. I looked like those kids from the church of J.C, and the latter-day Saints traveling around in impeccable white shirts and ties. All that I had missing was the black name tag. The same white on black engraved name tags we wore on Army uniforms. As I walked by the whore house or close house or Brothel or whatever, walked out this beautiful girl from the window display that had been trying to seduce me every night for more than a week.

Her duty shift was over and to my dismay, well, she didn't live where she sells her charms, although the place looked homey to me. It had this Ikea ambiance look from the outside. Europe is a strange place. So, she walks out of work, crosses the door and sees me and waved.

Eh you, Uncle Jackie TeeVee guys. Uncle Jackie. Take me out for a drink !

The scene was so damn unreal that it could not be deceiving. How about that?

I was not sure about anything, but hell, a cold beer with someone would not hurt, and I had that fat wad of Belgian Francs in my pocket, so why not. Belgian Francs as Italian lira worth less than the paper it is printed on but it is a blast to hold fat piles of it and give it by thousands as tips. She seemed to be like me, Off-Duty and from peddler to peddler I am sure we could have a great discussion. Aren't we in the same business, selling dreams and leisure, after all? Aren't we all prostituting ourselves somehow to barely get by? Professional speaking, I am the person that dresses the table, and she serves the meal so to speak. Very Freudian indeed.

So, I snapped, OK, let's go for a beer, but I am not a TeeVee personality, I am a Canadian business person on a business trip. Let's go for that drink.

Has it ever crossed my mind?

Sex. It crossed my mind. No, Too tired, too exhausted, too Europe struck, too disillusioned about life and hell, too fucken catholic to seize this opportunity, Too stupidly Canadian to seize an opportunity too. Imagine the scene at the Commons if my Premier and the Teletubbies Cabinet ever learn that a Canadian citizen would have engaged into sexual activities with a sex worker in Belgium. Man, I would have the CBC on my tail for months.

You get to think where is it all going, as if there should be only one direction to go in life. A rigid model to follow, a holy path that would take you home like the fairy tale about the kid who left bread crumbs on his way to find his way back home. Comes the question, where is home, and what is home?

There were no wives, fiancée, bambinis, kids bicycles in the driveway, white picket fence or rows of fluo painted Clorox plastic can whirl wind in a driveway. Home was aging parents that I loved and always pushed me to travel and discover myself by myself as I was a lousy learner at school and as my old man said, younger you were a smart ass, now you are a playboy. Damn! But at that moment I also realized that millions of men would quit everything of their rational emotionless boredom routine to take my place. You are having a drink, a no strings attached thing with a very attractive person.

A prostitute ! At least she is honest about it. Some are lobbyists, journalists, and never mention it. It's Brussels, it's Europe, you are young, it is all inviting and this tourist zone has its charm. Like in the movie, someone plays a jazz accordion, What a sweet sound. Enjoy every second of it, eventually reality will kick its lousy face in. It is offbeat, and I love the offbeat.

There would be millions of people willing to trade a boring, routine life in for an instant. To take my place having a cold Stella Artois with a ballerina that became sex worker and who told me the story of her native Ukraine and the life in Eastern Europe with derision, laughs, and humor. Land of restricted material offering but boundless optimism and love. I explained mine, life of love, opportunities in a self-centered society.

We closed the place. I extended her a wad of Belgian francs, she smiled, went to her purse and gave me a handful of local change and wished me Good Luck in Ukrainian as Nadia Commaneci, Romanian gymnast wished the best to my friend Malloy at the 76 Olympics. There is something highly appealing in those Slavic languages. I fell under the spell, just as my old friend Malloy fell maybe a decade ago.

In the constant battle between Eros and Thanatos, Eros won one more round, and I was the brilliant knight in shining armor with a white shirt, a tie, a trench coat but no name tag.

A beautiful soul and a wonderful body to vehicle it around. Back to the airport. I hate taking the plane. I hate Crocodile Dundee movies.

This is not a knife. That's !!! A knife.

And I am back behind the wheel of this slinky bus. It is still that Friday evening. It is still hot, humid. It is still the Grand Prix weekend. Still on this detour.

Here we go, a new message from Charlotte from the Control Base. Ok, Gas Leak on St-Mathieu st between, Ste-Catherine and Rene Levesque. The street is closed to all traffic. Consider an alternate route. The polite way to tell you, we have no clue how to get you out of the mess, so, at the salary we pay you, we are all consenting adults here, figure it out by yourself. We picked you because you had an HS diploma here. Time to figure out all options here. Adaptation is the name of the game.

We got to adapt here. This is a large part of your wage. Adapt and shut up. This system will never improve simply because there is no political will to do so and it also attracts low mindset management (upper and middle) to comply with the political orders. Garbage, sewage, overall sanitation, road work are on the same foot here. They are essential to keep the business running. We pay well and on every Wednesdays at midnight the pay fairy takes her magic wand to deposit your after taxes paycheck and that's it, that's all. We carry people, but it has to add to their daily misery of life. I asked friends in the Police forces, and they confirmed that it is even worse and over and above, the daily drama is played on a 24/7 basis. At least, we have minimal operation during the night in the transit system.

Notes on the vague concept of adaptability.

Adaptation and flexibility. I was the youngest of the boys and my brothers were somewhat very reserved, almost shy catholic boys. I could not exactly rely on them for any type of sexual education, and my father was too busy or clumsy to introduce the subject. Once again, I would have to learn the hard way. For my brothers, all sang at church service or married their first love. In my old man's book, not talking about a problem may make it disappear.

Fortunately, a client of mine, paper route (beautiful divorced woman in her 30s but bored I guess) paper route to paper route and snow shoveling to paper route, and slow shoveling and mowing the grass and, paint and on, and on, took some of her precious and valuable time to teach me a little more about the THING. A rescue type of deal.

Great opportunity for a young entrepreneur like me. From a glass of lemonade on a hot summer day to. Or was it Tang, for those who can remember what a glass of Tang was all about. To this: every time I showed up to her place, she had fewer clothes on. Figures.

As she often called on the phone for many services, (remember, there was one telephone in a house, or sometime two, and the phone were anchored on the wall and sometime had an optional longer wire, so whoever picked up the phone could take the message) my father got suspicious about her sensuous voice and that I could have been seduced and having this torrid affair with an older woman while minor. It never left the place where it happened. I believe I have been lucky on this issue because I could not have relied on anyone else. I have been lucky in that sense. The old man figured it out, I know.

The paper route and other gigs became a part-time cook job at KFC, it became a part-time Army Reserve job, and it all disappeared. I once was with my old man at the local Credit Union. Remember the day you had to go to the cashier to cash in your paycheck? As we walked out from the Credit Union where my father acted as a volunteer loan officer, we came upon her. As gorgeous as ever. I was in full Army dressed uniform. I looked good in a uniform. She glanced at me smiled as she recognized a young promising man that had matured a bit (not a lot) As my father asked me who that person is, I just answered, Mrs. X from the paper route, the lady where I did all those chores a few years ago. I could see that he was impressed. As we turned away to the glass door entrance of the bank, she looked at me and winked. The complice winks. Closure, I guess. That was the last time I saw her.

Gianni, my Italian colleague, had the intro straight from a professional. In the Sicilian village he came from, a small place, there was a brothel. His old man was not a great communicator nor was he a patient person, so he cut the chase. A man of his generation, I guess.

At the age of 16, he took his son, Gianni, to see a prostitute and get the initiation. Done deal. The old man thought that it was all fine and dandy until the lady told that Gianni was often seen in the tree next to the brothel, peeping into the place until he fell from the tree. Yes, Gianni fell from the tree and broke his forearm. He told his old man it was a bicycle accident. He took a beating that day.

Gianni was cool, colorful, and sometimes unpredictably funny. I was once at the end of the line pause on the Marie Victorin campus in Montreal North. Easy June day. School is over, The terminal is in front of the gym. 25 minutes to kill, do a Sudoku, email or snooze. I sat on the curb and watched this person kayaking in the pond in front of the main entrance of the College. A pond. A duck pond, 3 feet deep, maybe 12 × 10 feet and there is this individual all equipped in a sea kayak, wetsuit, floating belt, helmet in this ridiculous pond. A ridiculous scene, but some have their ways. Indeed.

So out of the blue comes Gianni.

Man, have you seen this pazzo in the kayak? Where the hell does he think he is? The ocean? This is ridiculous.

I know, but he must have grown up with Sesame Street while we watched Popeye. You can see this guy is fucken insecure. Beats me.

This is so ridiculous, we should go to the pond, flip him upside down and give him a beating!

Nah, Gianni, we can't do that. There are cameras all over. Our buses are right there and damn, we are both in uniform. We may get in trouble. Somehow, my brain made a risk assessment of what could be acceptable. Not acceptable, but funny. Or plain stupid, funny but risky. Hence, came the term may.... I admit, it did cross my mind. A 3 Stooges moment to cut on boredom.

Good point, we may get in troubles but, man, does this guy deserve a beating. What a pazzo, Now what, is he kayaking in his tub too. It's because of guys like that, that we the real guys are losing credibility. Because of guys like that, women expect us to be nice, soft, protective, and gentle. That guy is trouble. He definitely deserves a beating. He is a traitor to the gender. His gender theory had costed him a few divorces too, but, nobody's perfect.

Sure, Gianni, but not today. Yet, I agree, we should flip him over to see if he could get out of the kayak while upside down. That's the name of the game, isn't it.

Gianni started walking towards the pond, cursing in Sicilian as calling the Kayakist Testa di menghia and others. I am familiar with those expressions.

I yelled, Gianni, don't do that as he turned around and started laughing saying: You really thought I was going to drown this Mother F

He went back to his bus, still cursing in Italian. He got me alright. I was sure he was to flip the kayak guy over, but he pulled that type of stunt often.

Whatever job you have, you could always go the extra mile. Doesn't cost much, and satisfaction has value. Flipping a kayakist in a patch of mud is in no way part of our job description. Maybe General Patton would have agreed.

From Greed is Good to Take the Pain.

WASP, big dough and the B movie. The Toronto years.

I spent part of College Years touring repertory theater and hanging with Movie Buff in search for the meaning of life. The one besides the number 42. B movies, Ed Wood's, Thor Johnson became part of this Nickelodeon $2 a movie ($1 on Tuesday) lifestyle trying to assimilate Edward G Robinson lingo or Betty Davis seductive woman's line or this $30,000 mansions on the hill of Beverly Hills. (Double Jeopardy)

The revelation came to me from a line from the Third Man. There it is. An Orson Well movie about order vs. anarchy, structures vs. chaos and well politics. I loved this line so much that I concluded an essay in Philosophy on the social contract, Jean Jacques Rousseau and David Hume by this famous line from Harry Lime. Switzerland ! .

On the top ten of the Film Noire reply:

Harry Lime: In Italy for thirty years under the Borgia's, they had warfare, terror, murder, bloodshed. They produced Michelangelo, da Vinci, and the Renaissance. In Switzerland, they had brotherly love, five hundred years of democracy and peace, and what did they produce? The cuckoo clock.

The ultimate Libertarian scream. Damn, I am one of them. I am a Libertarian.

Could we say more about Switzerland ! Shall way say more about an oppressive left ?

I am on tour. Working. That's my full-time job. That was my career. That was it.

Every 2 weeks or so, from April to late October, I picked up tour groups at one airport or another. Pick at one airport, dropped at another, or finish off in a parking lot or a rest area. Every season has different clientele. September always carried the best groups. Every so often, I had to drive and guide. Other times, I had a designated bus or a group of buses. All contracts and tours were different.

My clients were exclusively European. Europeans coming to see Canada and America. Some companies had it all figured out, others left the guide the program and Hotels Voucher, some meals, but mainly it was to figure it out. With a small group, I loved to drop in by public market or on the road, sometimes, truck stops. The daily life of America besides the official tour attraction, the monument of General X and the cannons in the park. Life off the tourism Skinner box. Truck stops are a good show for European, and they play it well. You are always welcome. The food is usually good.

They have this unique American imprint. Every time I stopped by one of those Truck Stops (small groups only) I had customers, men mainly buying everything at the boutiques from Stickers, T-Shirt, Caps, and even trucker Boots or 8 track tape. Trucker boots were in as I had to transpose what's a 42 EU in US Sizes and help the shop owner with this influx of customers. Everyone was in heaven. Money was just no objects, I saw so many shoe boxes with this famous number 42 all my life.

They wanted to see this flip side of America, they had it live and in color. As I walked out of the place, the manager typically gave me a $40 or $50 cut of sales that I graciously left as a tip to the waitress who was also part of that show. A show dedicated to the simple man, earning an honest living, on the road. Folded bill underneath a coffee cup saucer. To Insure Proper Service, TIPS. I bet you did not know what it means.

East coast tours: 14 days loop, 5000 km, 6 cities, 2 National parks. In those days, you had to read a lot of those Michelin guides and history books to be up to the task, but in some ways, I learned more from some of my customers than I may have taught them. Yesssss, Marathon tourism.

I had this couple of clients in their late 30s or early 40s traveling with their 7 years old son. Everyone knows that once you travel with a kid, kiss it goodbye sex life ... You are a parent, you are a machine. Libido disappears, and life as you once knew it.

On group dynamics. Name may change, but structurally it stays the same.

In a French group, there are always Marcel, Rene, and Lucien. Marcel is the leader and has a funny wife who gets along with most pranks. Lucien knows all the scheme and has abused everything life has to offer, yet his wife is always on edge and complaining, so Lucien is happy to stick around with Marcel because he has a good time there, for a change. I am pretty Lucien as far as my life travel companion is concerned. (Lucien always likes to be called by a nickname that rhymes with his name, like, Lucien, poil de chien). At the end of the trio, there is Rene. Rene is the thoughtful and calculating one. Rene has a more professional background than the two-other one. He is also a bit chickenshit, so he relies on the 2 other ones to initiate the fun stuff. Rene cares about consequences. The two other don't give a damn.

A bit like Freud's theory of personality as per the ID, the Ego and the Superego or the 3 Stooges, Larry, Moe and Curly. The father, the son and the holy ghost. You know that Sigmund Freud and Karl Jung once had a fist fight in a train in Switzerland, but this is irrelevant to this story. Cool line for a cocktail party. It's a cocktail party line. It had to do with the impregnability of the collective unconscious and had nothing to do with hooligan soccer type of deal. A form of firewall deal.

To pass any deal with a French group you have to address Marcel with a slap in the back and a drink but say: I have talked to Rene about it, he was with Lucien. It always worked, but you have to keep Lucien's wife astray.

But all construction workers are called Marcel ?

In the 1930s to 1960s France, they called most construction workers Marcel for one simple reason. They all wore camisoles on construction sites from that brand. Marcel. The name was visible on the label so when a contractor wanted to call someone whom he was not aware of the name he just pointed out the workers and said. Marcel, come here. The addition of a mild curse before the name makes it also more casual as: Putain Marcel !

I stopped on the way from D.C to NYC at the trucker stop at Havre de Grace, MD. Beautiful to cross the Chesapeake in the mist and see beautiful farms on the other side. Not every trip could stop there. Only small or middle size groups. We were off rush hour and I called ahead and managed for one bus. The other one had to stop somewhere else. European tourists loved this incursion in real life Americana. We ate there. Took time for coffee as my clients wandered around, engaged in conversation and took pictures of the big trucks. Always a hit.

So, there I was on top of things having Breakfast in America with the guys stretching my legs on a restaurant booth, writing instructions on napkins about American boot size in US sizes while planning the by night instructions for a NYC tour. All was in control. It is always perfect in this place.

That was on one of those small private tours booked by my Belgian friend in Antwerp. The guy with all those naturalized animal heads peeking at him in his travel agency. The Beaver man.

The Swiss guy comes running all excited. I am not sure of his name, Christopher I think, telling me to come and see that. Chris traveled with his wife, Monique, and a kid. They were, the perfect Swiss family. In their 30s with an 7-year-old son and were, obviously career oriented people. Always nice, smiling and polite, but the 3 people shack up every night seemed to get them a bit edgy. Swiss they were. It's a sex thing, I guess. So, here we go.

Chris drags me by the bathroom door. (A common bathroom) all excited with a few voyeurs listening at a moaning couple obviously making it, loudly, in a toilet stall. Yes, they were loud. He was stunned, as it was a revelation that the thing could be done in public in America. So, I told him that if he had to use the washroom, he could use one of the 2 other stalls. Personally, I would pick the farthest one. The last one on the right side.

Normal, no. Unusual? I've observed that, or did it before. Listen, it's a truck stop. It's a way of life. They have their ways and rituals. Maybe his partner or her husband is sleeping in the cab right now, and there was an offer on the table. As Chris wife's joined the group it was easy to tell that she may have felt like taking an extra stall and doing it according to the local rite and customs but. In Rome, do as the Roman. There were too many witnesses, running out of time and well, they were too Swiss for that type of peasantry. From frolicking to.

I acted cool and told them to warn me when it's over, I still have hot coffee on the table. It made me smile to see them both ambiguous as were they scandalized or sexual aroused see horny to death. I thought, Swiss, always the same. Helvetica hides the dough of the most despicable human on earth, when shit hits the fans stay neutral, give remonstrance on human rights and democracy and yet can't create anything over a Swatch or pocket knives. Now, there are also sexually prudes. Damn. The Cuckoo Clock, folks.

As we approached the hotel in NYC, I could only notice how restless my adorable couple was behaving as per, time to settle the score on their sexuality schedule came and the demo at the truck stop actually turned them on but, the kid was in the way. Now who else could take care of the kid while they were performing the thing that could be available and trusted and well, I knew they were about to ask me a favor. Not that I minded. There was a block of a few hours off, but I knew I held them: by the balls so to speak, and I thought it would be funny to abuse it. I told Marcel and Rene about it, to their amusement. A : check it out guys, I bet Chris will come to see me after check out to ask me to babysit. Will that be expensive, guys?

The guys laughed and said: Man, he is Swiss, it's payback time for all the money laundering they handle. European inside joke.

As predicted, as the hotel check in was done, instruction given, the time off, the break in NYC, a shy Christopher came to see me. He looked like a teenager trying to borrow the old man's car for a spin.

Can I talk to you for a sec?

Sure, (I knew it) what can I do for you?

Do you think you could babysit for us for 1 hour ? We need some rest to recuperate from the jet lag and with the kid, he would rather not sleep, and you know. TV. Barney and all the entertainment parents have to do. Jet lag, sure ! As I smirked and raised an eyebrow.

Jet lag, Eh Moe !!! Nyuk, Nyuk, Nyuk !

Yeap, no problems! A few hours. Sure. But it will be expensive. As I sunk my right hand in my pants pocket as if I were looking for money.

In the back of the room were the guys, Marcel, Lucien, and Rene, raising eyebrows and laughing.

Sure, I will pay for this. As he was also nervously looking deep in his pocket to get as much money as he could and fast.

The joke was over, and I have always been a decent Tour Guide, so I said.

Listen, keep your money. We are in Hell's Kitchen here. I'll take the kid for a walk at Time Square, kill some time and take him for a Checker Cab ride to Battery Park, and we'll walk back. That should give you plenty of time to… rest.

I always have the same tariff, you owe me a beer upon arrival. He will remember all his life the Checker ride. In those days, they still had many Checkers, but you had to wait at the right corner or wave to the right cabby, but it was all worth it. We had the ride of our lives. I could bet, the kid now in his 40s still remembers the cab ride. There is just no money to buy such satisfaction from a job well done.

Sometimes you can do your job properly and sometimes hit the mastery of Magics.

Marcel talked to Lucien who turned around to Pierre who had talked to Lucien's wife and there we had the request.

We are not familiar with NYC. It seems intimidating, and not many of us speak the language. Do you think you could organize a dinner excursion?

They noticed that once you enter Manhattan by the Holland tunnel and drive by 42nd street, NYC doesn't look like in the Gene Kelly, Rock Hudson and Doris Day movies. I may have changed a bit since the 1950s. A bit. It's a shock. We always work the itinerary on purpose.

It's Saturday afternoon here. It will be difficult to manage a dinner for 96 people at a 3-hour notice. Let me make a few calls, and I'll get back to you. That was a group of independent hardware store owners from southern France. They did not mind forking a few dollars for a nice evening. They were fine, pleasant people in holiday. Be it.

I had a mental plan. I knew where I was going, but for those people I wanted to surpass myself. I wanted to create magic. The real deal.

Magic. Yes magic, (here is the definition) once in a while you can line up everything for you and create one event that is so perfect that it can be called Magic. Magic is the one thing that makes time or money an accessory. Magic fulfills the soul in its entirety.

The power of apparently influencing the course of events by using mysterious or supernatural forces.

Magic doesn't have a time limit, but once it's over It cannot be repeated nor replicated. The coincidence can take you to magic, and magic takes you to that first slow dance or the kiss under the rain. After life takes over and takes you to routine and from routine, you'll desperately look for a new coincidence to start the cycle again.

Magic, that day, was this last-minute group dinner at a NYC restaurant club. The place was called Adam's Apple. It closed a few years ago. It also had a resident Jazz singer and on the very night my group showed up to that place they also guested a Graduation dinner for a High School from Manhattan that evening. Adam's apple had a type of inside orchard decor. It was surprising as well as refreshing. Graduations are always impressive. Kids look good. On their best behavior mode for a short while, and it was something my clients never saw before. Graduations are full of light and hope. The decor, the atmosphere were perfect. The evening was perfect. As I was eating with other tour directors and drivers, we could only hear this magical music of the dishes being served in perfect coordination. No dishes drop, just like a utensil symphony. Positive sound waves for serving after serving. Food is good, Great service. Amazing scenery, Good

Jazz and live entertainment from Blossom Dearie. We were in control. We achieved perfection. Given nice weather conditions and a short line up at the Empire State at night with its remarkable art deco entrance, we were to make the perfect score and be back at the hotel for midnight. Smooth as silk. We made this by night to perfection and made a few extra $.

As we returned to the hotel at around midnight on that perfect late summer night. As the last customer, enchanted and thankful for this wonderful so American out of program excursion, the staff gathered to share the loot. The Lucien, Marcel, and Pierre's of the world were satisfied and happy. There was good money in there. On that night, as we all gathered on the curb by the hotel entrance to share the loot. Nobody wanted to discuss money as if it were to tarnish the moment we all lived. We made, or I made, magic. Money and time became accessories.

We savored the moment of seizing perfection and the enchantment. We lived something else, We lived magic and satisfaction.

Radio noise from the control center. Damn, it's the other Cannon of the control center. Charlotte must be out for a coffee. Reminds me of this sergeant in the army who had that routine. He called you on the phone and the first question he asked was:

Corporal, are you at attention when you talk to me on the phone !

The obvious answer was to drop the phone because you cannot be at attention and hold the phone at the same time. He was ironic.

In city transit. Every one of your passengers has a story to tell. They tell it by the way they approach the bus, wait for it, run, walk, pay, dress, talk, address you, and you have 6 seconds to make a call whether he joins the voyage of the damned or not. They haven't said a word but already had spoken to you, and they read you as you read them. It's a constant flow of energy, and you are Dee Jay ing it. Rather than having a plate on a turntable, you have a steering wheel that you spin.

This young GQ exec looks man shows up at the bus stop. He is presumably dropping his son to some work kindergarten before hitting the office. It is the downtown bound 80 Park South. It is cold as hell, and hell must be an icy place indeed. Sharply dressed, laptop case in hand and the look of the guy who won child custody in court but has no clue whatsoever of how to take care of a 7 years old boy. The consultant. The new sales and IT plague. This: Ok, kid your lawyer must have been better than hers, but I guess she was a better parent. She knew how to dress the kid for winter. Yes, you screamed victory and yelled, she won't have a cent from me in front of those boneheads at work that you call the friend. Those same guys who get you in trouble but will never be there to help pick up the pieces of your shattered, dysfunctional life. I saw that dumb movie times and times before in their wildlife environment: the downtown office tower. As he was walking tall from a fashion or GQ magazine, the kid looked like out of a zombie movie. Are you dressing this guy with stuff fished out of a recycling bin or given by the local church, I thought? Damn, it's winter.

There is no shame at being poor or not well off for a while. No shame at waiting for a commission or monthly bonus check. Many of us have been through it but fiercely fighting to avoid alimony or pension for a kid, all backed by a bunch or rowdy office tower idiot has no excuses. Unless Versailles, today's office tower do have running water but are inhabited by the same type of narrow mind or greedy SOB's. Colleagues are colleagues and are seldom friends. They keep their cards close to their chest and will ill advise you as if your life were their game.

Yet, being a careless idiot and a bad example is in the land of shameful.

I looked at the kid, tried to figure out size and weight, and put a verbal add at the employee room for a clothing collect. All you have to do is to talk about it at lunch and the wave starts. You get messages, email, all of it. It takes one or two days at most.

Anyone would have some extra winter clothes for a little boy in need here? Sport, dressed, whatever, I know I can trust you. Leave the pile by the clerk's office. I remember what the note I left on the bulletin board: Kid, son of an idiot in need. Require winter clothing.

The morning after, I had to pick up, 3 large bags of sports and dressed clothing for the kid. The beauty is in the spontaneity of the gesture here. A total detachment. Someone requires help, we give help. A kid they never saw, knew or heard about before. A kid in need. Some of those clothes still had price tags on them. Winter coats, hats, boots, a bicycle, mitts, and glove. As I pulled in to the Bernard and Park bus stop that cold winter morning, they were there. There waiting for the usual routine. Drop the kid at the kindergarten and after go to work. I stopped the young man saying:

I believe this could give you a break, You and your son. Showed him a bag of nearly new clothing at the taste of the day. The seasonal look, color, and tendance. The look all the kids in the city have.

He looked at it. Surprised but moved. Moved that someone actually had an intention to help. Some people who would not be on the thugs of legal war, but would help with simple things 'til the paycheck gets in. Some people he never met but would not judge. A break from a city worker usually minding his own business driving and listening to the radio. Something way out of the office tower's dog eats dog attitude. This: greed is good M.F.s

He took the bags, smiling, comforted and happy that he was not alone in these challenging time. For the next few weeks, I received a few more bags. Toys, games, books, a skateboard, and other gizmos for the kid. This kid that a division (a garage) had adopted without knowing, He was part of the family. A kid that several transit workers already loved without knowing. A kid and a situation that made me proud of my work, my mission, and my colleagues. There is just no money to pay for such a feeling.

And they showed up one morning. Well-dressed, happy, smiling with the question: How can we pay you back?

Pay it forward ! If you ever hear that we, bus drivers, are to negotiate social or financial benefits, call the mayor's office and tell the mayor how wonderful the drivers are.

Anything else ?

Maybe you should consider the full meaning of the word, maybe!

The existential question would be: why do you do it for people you hardly know? As per my answer would: why don't we do it more often. It's so fulfilling to bring hope and joy.

The violin kids.

One kid voluntarily left or forgot an expensive violin in the bus every afternoon, thinking that, once lost, his music lesson may be over. Wishful thinking. Not on my watch. He did that to me every day, but it had his name and address on the instrument case. Every day, I took the instrument to the garage office and the clerks called the parents. It went on for a while. He thought that we did not figure out his little mind game and that he would eventually get rid of the instrument. So, I locked the back door and had him to exit the bus by the front door. I could check that he walks out with his violin. He was getting annoyed. Immigrant's kid, (first generation) I know his parents forked a lot of money for his education and were hoping that he would get it.

I talked to supervisors about it. They talked to the parents. Just informally exchanging on this. Parents to parents. Musician to supervisor to parent. Opening communication channels. Nothing official. Nothing of our work contract, Nothing of our mission. A mere suggestion. Maybe he'll never dig violin. Maybe a guitar or a clarinet would be better. Maybe the system never asked him what he thought about it. Maybe he has never been gauged by a professional for his instrument pick. Maybe all that he wants is to be happy. Maybe if you put too much pressure on the kid, he will snap. Maybe you should inquire about suicide among teenagers. Maybe he also has the curse to be a Jazz person in this impossible world.

Maybe, maybe not. Perhaps. Yes, no, I don't know, Can you repeat the question?

A week later, I pick up the kid at the bus stop in front of the highly selective college. He is excited, smiling, carrying a Clarinet case. He is a Benny Goodman, not a Stephane Grappelli. Cool. He never left his instrument case in the bus again.

Maybe talking about it could make a difference in this world. Maybe we had a real chance for peace in 1989 after Helsinki, yet some found a way to blew it on purposes. Maybe we could have fixed part of the mistakes we made in Versailles in 1919, 70 years later.

On human dignity. For many, what's left of it !

I am not always nice. There is that Saint-Exupéry – Night Flight—novel, experience that often takes over me as I am somewhat possessed of since I had to read the novel in College. Everyone knows St-Ex as per the : dessines moi un mouton—could you draw me a sheep please—Le Petit Prince novel? Cute indeed. St-Ex had a darker side as he presents one of his boss in a South-American airmail stories taking place in the 1930s. A film noir theme. A love triangle story about a heartless boss, rough flying and work conditions, desire for the wife of a pilot employee and Simone, the seductive woman femme fatale wife. All the explosive element to make Martha Stewart scream, this is so french, Bravo ! I would bet that Simone has a low husky sexy voice smokes cigarettes and wear sexy hats.

The point of interest here is that me and Riviere; Fabien's boss have this reflex in common. Riviere has something for Simone, but as he accomplished anything with Simone. I'm not certain. I haven't finished the novel. I do remember that Riviere despised weakness and sickness. He was not picky, He hated all type of spineless people. So, as I said, Fabien and I hate people who are not walking tall. He is fictional, I am driving buses.

Reality strikes again. Metro breakdown !

Comes this man in my already overcrowded bus! A Garfield crowded as of the stuffed animal sticking on by suctions cups on the window pane that would inspire many in the transit system. This bus was full. Overloaded as per, the Metro system broke down and people chose to try to do the same route above ground. It doesn't work that way. We make sure that it cannot work that way. So, this man, in a state of panic, is obviously taking a beating on his cell phone. He was taking a massive load of ... but kept apologizing to the; Mom, wife, boss, probation officer, or boyfriend with a female voice. Not Simone. I called her to check. No, it was not Simone.

This horrible thing (of the female gender, obviously) on the other side of the conversation was ballistic as the poor man tried to explain that he was to be late and it is because the Metro train broke down. He went on and on, on how the transit workers are overpaid bums and the system is lousy but he kept on licking. She was about to kill him. I would have too. A little more respect for the transit workers, please. They are my family, after all. Some are bums, OK, but no one escapes that. Bums, they are everywhere. We have the dignity of the uniform here.

He was next to me, taking a beating and babbling against my employer and my colleague from the Metro system, but above all, he was weak. He was in my work operational bubble. Beyond the holy yellow line. I hate having passengers babbling on the phone within my work bubble. Weak as unable to say: listen, I am late, I am sorry. I'll turn off the phone, there is a tunnel and if you keep quiet, I may take you to the Peel Pub tonight and bang you a few times after. No, he did not. He kept on with his apologetic narrative, and this is bad for all of us, men. I thought, what a sorry mother F, and well, this thing is almost sitting on my lap. Damn, I have a bus to drive here.

As for anything else in life, there could be no freedom if you are sticking to the narrative. The narrative is this ultimate invisible chain.

Here came this Riviere moment ! Riviere or Snap On or Tzatziki or Eureka. Pick one ! I would pick Riviere personally, but feel free.

As he was standing next to me on the phone, I went on with this tavern waiter routine loud enough for whom it may concern on the other side of the conversation (or monologue) to hear very well and may drop one of the tentacles holding the phone.

So, guys? Another round here. What will it be for you? Another Dos Equis! How about you guys? The same. Let's see ? Two Coronas. One Pabst. Stick around, guys, the next girl on the stage is Cassandra. She is something.

I heard the drill before. I could repeat it to perfection.

I heard the tone raised on the phone. Medusa, damn, she could speak too. Could not hear the exact words, but the volume went higher. The man became all white. Ghostly white, I mean. And he was there trying to explain that he was not in a bar (or a place of perdition so to speak) but caught in a bus as the Metro broke down. He could not be believed nor trusted as he did not sound any credible. Weak person, weak voice, weak argument, weak. It sounded like he did not convince anyone here. Just as he mentioned that he was in a bus, a few Greek passengers that had caught on to the prank started laughing.

This man, he thinks this is a bus. Ouaa, too cool !

He turned even paler and left the bus in a hurry at the next stop. He was running for his life.

Sometimes, I think that I should not have pulled that stunt. What would Riviere have done at my place? Comprehension and empathy. No, those value don't work in a rush hour environment. We have no time for that. Try another time window or another route if you feel like being weak.
Weak or undignified. For crissake, take that whatever life throws at you with some dignity. Dignity is not strictly for the dead people. Live in decency and dignity. Simone .

That deeper existential question remained unanswered: Pabst ? Are there any other type of Pabst than the Blue Ribbon? Just asking here Like what, Pabst yellow ribbon ? I should inquire about that.

As individual sense of dignity seem to dwindle or getting gradually diluted in a sea of individualist false material Gods and strange value narrative, the universal one ain't doing any better. Universal dignity has been misappropriated by an establishment class, using it to serve its enslavement purpose, as per holding the top of the moral moat. They've autoproclaimed, in pompous manner, this ultimate power of dignity attributing titles to members of this elitist society as per, master, honorable, councilor, right honorable as per to hide an illicit moral or even intellectual deficit.

Happy parody of a cynical attempt of democracy of red velvet or rye bread. They carry out this political freak show as genuine as a cheap porn shot in an opulent setting. The red velvet concept. They push for the appearance of justice, and we know it has more to do with a parody. It has been working since what? The beheading of Oliver Cromwell.

Hey! Knowledge is power. Once you dig the game, you can carry on your life with fewer illusions. It is very healthy.

At 5:20 AM on a bus stop in the middle of the winter, there are no dishonest people. Were they to be slightly dishonest, they would not wait for a bus to show up in the dark and bitter cold.

I have always suspected that I pick up an impressive number of dead people. You know the drill. They died unexpectedly and suddenly or were never exactly alive and their spirit and image keeps going as if nothing happened because even while alive nothing really ever happened to them. And this never happened is a state of emotional, intellectual, affective, physical death. They have their routine but never notice that nobody ever pays attention to them because even while alive, they were just soooo fucken boring. Sometimes I stop one to touch it if he is for real. It surprises them, but I have to make sure they pay the right fare. Those I have in doubts, I asked them if they had walked to the light lately. Could you walk to the light, please ?

This huge tin can that you are handling moves around. Your life could be summed up by a sequence of right turn and left turn synchronized by a clock. A thing that talks in digits or dings. Some stay distracted by following the movement of the thing on a GPS. Interaction is usually minimal. For every question in the universe, there are 2 possible answers: Yes or No. Sometimes you just don't feel like getting involved. This Tuesday morning looks like a Monday morning but, yesterday it snowed, today it rains. The sound of the wipers take your mind somewhere else. The radio is your only friend, and it talks to you. Low monocord sound. You are somehow absent or not totally in contact with the asphalt. Somehow you are happy. Happy of this routine. Happy of that route and schedule you have selected for 3 months. You cross another bus in the opposite direction and wave. It is a big family after all, and we all have a signature wave depending on the instant humor. You are the accomplice of all those people you are moving around for whatever purpose there will be. Sit in the city beat and deliver the ride.

Are you happy ? Genuinely happy, or just too tired to inquire about your state of mind. Does it really matter? The city need vehicle to move the lifeblood in its arteries and this in what you do, day in, day out. There is a certain nobility in being the people mover. The knight in the shinning tin can or the urban farmer on his holy tractor...

And, with time and wisdom, your work becomes your daily prayer to urbanity and I envy all the Pizzaiolas of the world who can also raise their arms while working because ours have to stay in a boring emotionless angle. You drive this machine, and this machine becomes you and follows your thought. Sei der Wagen is the term. That gives its whole meaning to the concept of driving and makes the concept of a strictly reactive mode of driving an announced failure.

As per a psychology teacher's advice at University on a row of traffic lights, just as in life, observe the farthest one and factual reality will adjust itself. He also gave me an A + on my analysis of Jean Jacques Rousseau social contract and how too organized societies kill the push for creativity. Unless for tax evasion or other forms of creative finances...

Technology is a way of organizing the universe so that man doesn't have to experience it. Max Frisch

For years, this building was Montreal's heart beat. The Forum. This old Forum that had been moved to become a Telus center as the old one is now home of an anonymous megaplex deal showing mainly movie of superhero as if, the average Joe supporting a family and not snapping under societal pressure these days is not one. A superhero. The Marvel franchise sells and honestly the days of a good and inspiring movie at the theater as over. Have adult regressed so bad that the only to entertain them is to dig deep into this improbable youth they may have entertained? When I was a kid, those comic strips were already for nerd as we mostly dig the Chevy Camaro or the Ford Mustang glossy promotional brochure or where we to get our hands on a Playboy or Penthouse issue. Are we led by a generation of green nerds? Yes, I guess.

Namor, was the superhero's nobody dug because he looked like a sissy in Speedo bathing suit. Nobody wanted to be Namor. Sorry ! Namor the submariner...

As far as the new Forum, now Telus or I have loss track of the name center, it is in one of those inhospitable parts of the city. A place where only idiot would build and started a housing project that fits the jock and goons hockey team lifestyle. They sold all units, but no one actually lives there or if they do, they don't turn the light on often.

They use this new amphitheater for various shows but it has no soul. The ghost of the Forum did not move as it is bigger and hi tech and modern and all the mentioned above, it will never exactly replace the old Forum. There has been too many embedded emotion in the old place to move in this new, whatsits name Amphitheater. Parking around, forget it. The new thing is well located in a section nobody would ever go unless for business or paid for.

So, here I am parked on hazard light waiting for my wife, daughter, and her aunt Carole stepping out of this Disney on Ice show. I did not go. I worked night shift and was exhausted. I was a fall rainy day. Lots of traffic and people running. Parents pulling or dragging kids by the forearm. No one seemed to be relaxed. They punched in on this extracurricular work activity, Disney on Ice. It is supposed to be nice but, at the look of the families walking out of this huge concrete block, it did not seem to be much fun. There I see my daughter, Nini, dressed as a princess holding this huge Magic Wand. She seemed to have been enjoying it. She was happy. My wife and aunt Carole looked pissed but, hell, it is her party. It is her Birthday gift. Nice. One and only time I went to the whatsits name Amphitheater downtown next to the Jockstrap city luxury condos. This place where you should wear gloves to take the elevator.

The girls were pissed because they had to buy this Disney On Ice magic wand that costed an arm and a leg. Yet, it was a impressive magic wand with a star and sound effect to the extent that I took it to work in my briefcase to the office and namely and sales meeting. Whenever sales quotas or objectives were mentioned, I took the magic wand out and granted wishes as a flaky fairly sales person. It has been a blast for a while but it also got me into troubles. Some people lack this essential thing in life. A sense of humor.

Via De Maisonneuve Boul, left Atwater and left again on Ste-Catherine St. by the infamous Atwater Metro terminal. Also known as Cabot square or the gate of hell.

Driving by the old Forum brings back souvenirs. Of course all the shows and events in town were happening there as it has been home of the old Hockey Team, but above all else I remember a childhood friend. John or Malloy. Malloy had been volunteering at the Forum in the 1976 Olympic game. He was a volunteer gymnast. They had some competitions there, namely the one where a Romanian gymnast had scored, for the first time in the history of the Olympics, a perfect 10. That event was held at the Forum. It is a perfect story of joy, hope, and a kid promised to a bright future.

This is where the story gets tragic.

He died young. Was he 16 or 17 years old? We called him Malloy after the Adams 12 guys, Reid and Malloy. I was Reid. He was that 16 years old Adidas Tobacco totting kid, enjoying Happy Days and Adams 12 and progressive Rock Music. It progressively bored me to death as I was already, in those strange days, a Jazz man. He was Gentle Giant, I was Herb Albert and the Tijuana brass band, yet we could meet on Weather report and Herbie Hancock, but Mike Oldfield, forget it.

We gathered in his basement to watch TV. He had cable TV with a Jerold box with 32 channels. In those days, cable companies were already talking about pay TV. The joke was where we would insert the dollars bills on the TV. They found a way !

Old American reruns. From Happy Days, to Adam 12, Voyage at the Bottom of the Sea, Dream of Jinny and well Star Trek. On the offbeat side: The Prisoner, Men from Uncle, The Champions, and Mission Impossible. I am not a number, I am a free man !

That was just about all that was available on the cable and on the Jerrold Box. This big brown plastic box with 32 buttons hooked by a wire to the TeeVee set.

With his athletic club, he worked as a volunteer at the 76 Olympics. He met Nadya Commanecci and Olga Korbut, and loved the way the perfect 10 Nadya said the name of her hometown in Romanian: Bratislava. (Sounds good in Russia as the B is pronounced as a V) Well, he was really Olympic Star Struck when he came back to hometown from the games and went double time back to the gym for his double or triple Salto routine relentlessly to catch the 1980 games in Moscow. The games that never happened. Nothing new, but on Sunday evening, the installed gymnasium's floor cushions weren't thick enough to prevent injuries upon a fall. There were one or two floor mats missing. Thickness made the difference. Sunday nights, Sunday night and are more Sunday in the summer. Lack of staff.

Bratislava (pronounced Vratis...) it the brotherhood of all Slavic people.

He missed on an easy routine, fell on his neck, severed his spine and died. He tried to cling to life for an extra hours or so, but he really snapped his spinal cord. Hitting the Tubular bells, that tune he loved so much for its end, as I always hated progressive Rock. It is a generic way for me to designate death, like cashing in your chips, buying the big farm, eating dandelions by the roots or Hitting the tubular bells.

Here is the death lingo: Buying the big farm, Cashing on your chip, Eating Dandelion by the roots, the Big Chill, Hitting the Tubular Bells and the new one. Royal Chinet Party.

It happened on a Sunday night while I was at the Army Base summer Bootcamp. We had met the day before at the park when he expressed how impressed he was by the games. How exciting life was. Big dreams, Big city, Good life. Yet, the day after, I was back at the Army barracks shining boots spitting on them or starching Korean war uniforms. Yep. Army Cadet, family rule. I and my 3 brothers all went to the drill. I felt that Sunday night that something wrong had happened. I had this eerie feeling, but I could not relate to anything.

We had permission from the camp on Friday PM. Perm document properly typed and had to show it up at the gate to exit or return to the camp. This thing was pretty damn serious. At the military base entrance gate was a check point. They had those part-time retired military, the Nazis type, inspecting with zeal all the paperwork. It infuriated my old man every time, who had trust to the military institution but had been to action and hated being questioned by those pencil pushers in uniform. Sometimes he dropped a 4 letters word and that was not Love. It was his army, his air force and his Victory.

So, on a Friday (a week after Malloy's fatal accident) evening, my father pulled in at the gate of the military base in his light blue 66 Strato Pontiac Chief Station Wagon. He always wore a beige gabardine jacket with his DFC ribbon and RCAF wings on it, cigarette and sunglasses on. His civilian life uniform.

The man was a person of little words, not that I guess he didn't have feelings to express, but the outlet to process them was somewhat clogged by some contradictory emotion, or he just didn't feel the need to express them. The concept of fun seemed to be something he had no need nor intention to grasp. Our journey on this earth is no punishment but a reward and the learning that is acquired can be fun too.

The man was, as most men of his generation were, a Darwinian, without knowing it.

Darwinian, Damn Darwinian, they'll never get over it. Nothing on the car radio on the way back home except, when weather permitted it, some opera. The Military base was in a remote, cold, and full of flies and pine area. Military bases create jobs in areas where nobody wants to go because of the size of the flies. Military bases and their location are strictly political. Nothing to do with any strategic location. I must admit that the Navy has always been better at finding the best real estate spot compared to the Army or even the Air Force.

He once told me that during the war, as a Bomber pilot, once the night mission was over at the early hours of the morning, they listened to the BBC, classical or jazz, this is where he got the kick for classical music. When the boys could see the White Cliffs of Dover, they felt safe. (I grew up with those Vicky Lynn, well, Lady Vicky Lynn music) I believe we share that taste for beautiful music and flying at night.

He was dealing with PTSD and could not sleep at night, which made part of my youth interesting. Could not exactly sneak in at 4:00 AM unnoticed, he was awake or having a nightmare. 60 years without a restful night.

The man was always awake and the hardwood floor, the squeaky plank, betraying me every single time. I've once cut the car engine on the hill home to avoid noise and wake up dad, but the steering column and the power brake also jammed. I've had better ideas.

Story has it. Tale confirmed by the curator of the Bomber Command Museum in Edmonton, Canada.

On that Sept 25th, 1944 at his 31st mission over occupied Europe my old man and the crew of G13, KWG went to bomb Calais because the Gerry's had massive anti-aircraft power at that strategic point. All allies Air Force was crossing the Channel at Calais, and there was an obvious high concentration of Flak at Calais. They did a lot of bombing runs lately as Le Havre and Calais became the flavor of the week. He's got hit flaked bad and had to go back to Yorkshire on 3 than 2 engines and, yep, no hydraulic, so he bellies landed his beloved Hallie. (A Handley Page Halifax, 4 engine British Bombers) He had it new from the factory, and it was his baby. It had been wrecked (decommissioned) for parts 2 weeks after his last mission. 2nd Crash in 18 months. First a Wimpie (Wellington) and now a Hallie's (Halifax). On both occasion, he and his crew managed to came back unscathed.

As most of the pilots would have taken a few days off to digest this, nope, he asked the crew if they remembered where the flak battery that had hit them could approximately be and if they were ready to go back and settle the score. Those guys were all nuts and went for it. Leadership the man was a born leader. They were all on their last points mission and could not wait to finish it off.

He went back to Calais. Settled the score with Adolph and this anti-aircraft battery. He came back victorious to Tholthorpe RAF base. He had it his way.

He gathered enough point. Victory points.

The tour of duty was over, but he left some belongings in the plane that he had not had time to recuperate. Yet, he took the time to steal a Union Jack and a RCAF flag. He kept this St-Christopher (or is it St-Judes) medallion on the dashboard of the Hallie, as some kept a pink stuffed rabbit called Vicky. It's a tin embossed medallion. 40 years after the war, upon a visit in England at the Tholtorpe RAF base, his former bomb aimer and friends gave it back to him in a proper frame. It sits on duty above my home door.

He had the stories on how they bombed over and over again the Lorient sub base in France with no results, how they sunk the Tirpitz in Norway and the VW plant in Wolfsburg. An offer to join the Dam Busters, the 617th. At some point, the allies forgot about bombing L'Orient Submarine base as the bombs from above did not really damage the place, so they putted a sentry at the exit of the port and had tank busters plane on stand by, Tiffie the Typhoon or P51 to hit the subs when they were at the most vulnerable.

They went to bomb Wolfsburg on the Ruhr over and over again to the extent that an unexploded bomb, a British one, kept Ford motors from taking over the plan, the brand and destroying the factories. Faith saved it in the form of a REMI British engineer who believed so much in the VW Beetle car that he took the bet of clearing the unexploded bomb and bringing back the line of product to life. Major Ivan Hirst. Uplifting story here of forgiveness, beliefs, and instincts. Yet, not many people know about that story.

He has been the Prime Minister of Canada staff pilot for a few occasions, as the Premier's plane was used more or less as a decoy. Story taught us that McKenzie King was afraid of flying and always caught the train to go to post-war conferences in Washington, DC. So, he secretly took a private train but to preserve the modern image of the new era of air travel, he sent his DC3 empty with some political assistant. He was never there in person. In those days, the DC's obelisk was the beacon for air travel as it approached Washington. He loved going to D.C. as much as I did, many years after.

He had this thing for DC, as I got one too, decades later. Many for the same reasons.

The war was officially over for him, as he had enough points to complete his tour of duty. He spent the next 55 years fighting his demons. Let's say that he passed it onto the next generation, as per the theory. Ours. It sorts of enters one DNA. The intergenerational epigenetic change theory.

We learned all that because of the TV interviews. He did not share much. He maintained for a while this poetic unapologetic version of the war as of the WWI Edwardian prose: the young and the braves did not die on the field of honor, but fell into grace. He had a particular affection for the memorial monument at Windsor train station, where God is holding in his arms the body of a dead soldier. They've inaugurated this monument dedicated to WWI a year or two before we've got hit with the sequel. Blame it on Versailles, 1919.

As he grew older, the toned down speech got a little more acid as this question on those military objective he bombed:

For Chr... sakes, we indiscriminately smashed 75% of all of Europe's industrial might. That bought us 30 years of uncompetitive peace, being able to dump lower quality stuff on the European market in the time they'll pick up and figure it out. We lost thousands of plane on non-military objective or mission destroying industrial non-military might. Post-war period, even the Limey found a way to sell their lousy automotive. A cute note for my uncle Andrew, holding an Anglia car dealership in Canada.

Concentration camps. Some Air Marshals had been approached by Winston Churchill to bomb gas chambers at concentration camps in Poland. Neutralize their killing capacity momentarily Yes, we were all well aware these things existed, but we could not drop a bomb in a pickle barrel in those days. We knew about it. The scale of the tragedy escaped us. It escaped us as it because goes beyond the real of human reason. We were still at human reasoning level.

Would you do it again, ask the CBC reporter at home ?

Hell yes !

I'd like to see the government out of war altogether and leave the whole field to industry. Joseph Heller.

I heard that anecdote of the post-war France from a distinguished countess and fashion icon in Paris. A simple person who had this capacity to imitate the French actress Arletti to perfection. She repeated some line from Hotel du Nord movie to everyone's great amusement. As it goes: for years after 1945, all lingerie came from the US. There were giant bras made more like horse harness to us than provocative garment. We had to modify, remodel and adapt them to the European market. It did last for about 10 years.

It crossed my mind that I never saw the old man actually smiling. He was always tense. Only a few glasses of gin could loosen him up. He was still on guard. A WD-40 loosening effect. I may have been too young to understand why but, maybe, me and my brothers (or just me) had him worried. In the summer of; 80 something, he had a heart surgery.

I guess that the sum of all the instant coffee, cigarette, blue cheese dressing, Coffee mate, many bottle of Beefeaters, a job on the stock market and 6 kids may have contributed to his heart conditions. Pork roast and gold potatoes. Not to mention, those Pontiac cars did never start in the winter. Yet, better than any Anglia sold by the official brother-in-law.

Like most men of his generation, he had been a chain-smoking workaholic, and the heart suffered a lot. Notwithstanding eating habits and midnight refrigerator raids. They did not do the coronary angioplasty technique back then. They had to open. So, there he was after surgery in his hospital bed, in a nice PJay my mother purchased him. A cool PJ with watermelons. Sound asleep, the man was smiling like a baby. I looked again because I never saw him smiling. I just had this wild urge to buy a Teddy Bear and put it in his arms. And all that peace and harmony struck me. Probably the first time of quality sleep in over 60 years. The man was in peace with himself. He was knocked down but serene. It came to my mind: Be a better son, the man worries about you. Stop chasing happiness where you won't find it. Cut being a womanizer idiot, here is a second chance for you. I had to pause a moment on this and absorb all that. Maybe next week. !

Coffee Mate is made of powder scrapped from the walls of nuclear reactor. A silent killer, alright.

On summer time boot camp routine.

My mom usually drove us back to the Military base on Sunday night. I remember my mom, listening to Sidney Bechet, Gilbert Becaud and her favorite song, this ever beautiful and so sad Honey from Bobby Goldsboro. (Goldsboro sold millions of records on that song) See the tree, how big it has grown. Mom, a beautiful soft-spoken red haired, drove us to the military base on Sunday nights with the family dog: Kenny the Collies. In those days of the Station Wagon movement, long before the seatbelt was invented, the kids and the dog crawled around in the vehicle, jumped seats and stuck their head out of the window and namely the big bay window in the tailgate door. Mom had been raised on a farm by a tall, very progressive mother raised by the sea in Massachusetts and a father not too gifted with agricultural skills but roaming the county for all kinds of illicit or bookies trade on his Sears Roebuck side carted Indian Scout. Once a week, he loaded the 4 girls onto the bike and took them to the Catholic convent for education. The nuns were not exactly fond of him, nor of my very progressive grandmother. I lived a live version of the Green Acres as my father wanted to be a Gentleman Farmer and my Mom, having been there and hated it, was very Suburban indeed. Grandfather's family had a high-ranking member of the clergy, as it is a historical fact that one of his uncles sent Wilfrid Laurier to the seminary, as he later became Canada's Premier in 1900. Her family was somewhat untouchable in the county. My mother got away with a lot of misbehavior at the convent.

My mom was the type or person who loved running with countless kids in a field to have a 69 cents kites flying on a string. Spending times with us picking 4 leafs clovers in a bunch, preparing Kool-Aid for all the kids in the neighborhood, flooding the house all summer. Loading a beige 1958 Mercury Meteor with tons of comfort food and Christmas basket to drive to lower town, distribute to the less fortunate of our society. She left me with a simple rule of life: Be Good. Her name was Marguerite: Daisy. She was a flower.

I often have compliment from passengers on how I showed humanity and help to lost travelers or other transit users. I do help for as much as I can. Doesn't cost much yet I have this already prepared answer to those who come forward to tell me how they appreciate how I handle things: Thank and tell my mom about it, she is the one that raised me that way.

My parents met on a nowhere bus event. 1948 and got married after a few months dating. The concept of the nowhere bus disappeared and the main street look alike contest where mom won the Bette Davis look alike prize. They dated for occasional coffee at Beauties on Mont Royal street as Beauties is still there and as of a few years ago they had the same narrow dinner booth. Narrow. Men were smaller and slimmer than. I like those old restaurants as most booth or decor are still intact and tell stories, Stories of love, drama, life. All you have to do is to sit down, observe and listen. The place will tell you it's story.

My father: some days he was a millionaire, some others he was broken, but never lost faith in life. Beautiful wife, 6 children, a Lassie, and home and a farm land a Station Wagon. Wartime England thought him of composting, recycling, recuperate. Those values were not very 1960s, and he was always ahead of its time. He had business ventures in that field that did not work as expected until he found a way to trade defective paper rolls out from the mills, the 20 to 40 tons type and find them an alternate use besides high speed 4 color process printing. He was back in business. Place mats, table cloths and Bingo cards. He has been able to surf onto that market for 20 years until paper mills updated on their quality process and implanted the ISO norms. Damn, there goes the neighborhood.

So, the old man pull the Pontiac in the driveway. Put's it in Park, cuts the engine and bang.

Bert! One of your friends died. The guy you called Malloy. Your buddy, Luc, came to tell us. (Sir yes sir, sir no sir)

You could have told me Dad... How did that happen

A gym accident last Sunday. He fell from the anneaux routine and broke his neck, He died at the hospital. He was to be paralyzed from the head down all his life. Bottom line. Death 1, Malloy 0. Sorry about your pal, kid.

The funeral and stuff were last week and well, we doubted that it was worthwhile
to tell you and get you out of the Camp for that.

I don't know, would have been nice to have a break from hours of drill in the sun wearing a WW1 wool uniform with putties, but as they say,

- Putties were strips of wool to be wrapped around the ankle over the top of the boot to keep mud and sand away from entering the shoe. Old British military tradition. It is said that the Scot wore them around their C... to keep them warm in winter, and they wore kilts.

I Could only Imagine, this good, clean, athletic kid Olympic hope dies off at a Gym accident at a University Gym while me and my Boot Camp friends jumping from rope bridges, ramping in mud, play with explosive, ride a APC, play with FNC 1 assault weapons and hand grenade and yet, make it home alive and kicking. I guess it's those damn tubular bells that would eventually kill you. We learn life on motorcycle wheelie or picnic under the old bridge at the time and yet, Malloy, you didn't miss the 1980 Games, they did not happen.

Karma, I guess.

The old man was from Survival for the Fittest school. A devoted catholic but a Darwinist. I always thought that you could not be Darwinian and catholic nor Christian at the same time, since the Bible tells us:

The word dominion means "rule or power over." God has sovereign power over His creation and has delegated the authority to mankind to have dominion over the animals. David reinforces this truth: "You made [mankind] rulers over the works of your hands; you put everything under their feet" Humanity was to "subdue" the earth —we were to hold a position of command over it; we were placed in a superior role and were to exercise control over the earth and its flora and fauna. Mankind was set up as the ruler of this world. All else was subjugated to him.

Yet, this position does not come without a form or responsibility to insure proper use of the dominion. Dominion or family car as I've once mentioned. This is where the human soul is still searching. Mankind cannot abide by the same rules as the subdued animals because God is part of humankind as humankind part of God. Theoretically speaking, what distinguishes mankind from the animal kingdom? Intelligence. So, they say, but as I grow older, I have my moments of doubt about human intelligence.

A spiritual light drives this intelligence. A belief in something bigger, brighter and better. A state and condition above the animal kingdom or this plane of existence limited by physical laws and limited physical perception. Men's creations, yes. Finances, Government, Industries, but not the man's soul. Beyond Darwinism comes other values, such as moral, duties, work, values.

For as long as the story is concerned because, as you remember, I am still operating a city bus on a summer night, I will cut to the chase by showing an image. Yeap an image.

I have this image in mind about this generation that preceded mine. It's a simple image capture. A few minutes seized in time. An image.

On June 6th, 1944, my Grandmother, Annett Geoffroy, had her 3 eldest sons under the flags. She had those 3 stars on her window to display at the family house. They were all in harms way. She also had 10 other kids to oversee.

Faith is what saved them, or was it fate. Faith in what exactly. I could not tell.

On a Philco cathedral radio in a humble flat in Joliette, Quebec played her song: Vera Lynn (VIcky Lynn).

My Son.

For heaven blessed
And with great joy rewarded me
For I can look
And see my own beloved son
My son, my son
Just do the best you can
Then in my heart I'm sure
You'll face life like a man

Vicky Lynn, the voice of the allied, was 16 or 17 as she started her singing career. Singing, love and light in the gloomy days of England's WWII. What did she know about all those emotions and drama? Nothing I guess but she knew how to render it. Another Mrs. Miniver.

I checked if I could get the local weather on that day of 1944in the village of Joliette, Quebec. I could not find it. Was she in the kitchen managing a still considerable family, helping the war effort at the Acme Glove company or having a coffee on the porch of the house. I don't know.

And come those Chinet moments. Royal Chinet. Sorry.

At 80 years old, the old man wished he could have slipped slowly to the other side of life in his beloved armchair surrounded by family, an old faithful dog, a sheep, farm animals on a rainy night. It is said that thunder and lightning could take a soul back to heaven. To go to the light in peace, to the White Cliffs of Dover, but he passed away in a hospital bed. Hooked on many machines. Surrounded and in a clean sheet, but not home. The veteran house that he hated so much has transferred him to the hospital for pneumonia, but Alzheimer also took its toll. He went back to his family.

Upon the last visit at the Vet's home, as he moved his electric wheelchair in the tight door frame of his room, he squeezed his hand between the arm of the wheelchair and the door frame. The man who flew 4 engine propeller airplanes in the thick of the night and drove a truck could not operate a wheelchair.

He looked at me like a 3 years old kid that did not understand why it hurt, but the pain he did not feel. I felt it a thousand-fold, and it went straight to my heart. A mix of despair, sadness, and rage. I hated this veteran house, but the rationale of our society has no place for an Alzheimer patient in the open. On all accounts, this rationale does not only work, and shortens the life of valuable old warriors. Thanks for your services 75 years ago, but some pencils necks, not even born in 1944 nor even Canadian as of 5 years ago have decided that you cost too much to the system and have decided to over drug you and place you in a medical drawer, so you could kick it faster.

After all, this money they will save for civil services and politicians, will be at better use at the Canadian Embassy at the Vatican to throw useless cocktails for the Pope and a handful of millionaires Cardinals or anywhere else in this plethora of Government waste missions made to provide official duties to the entitled and their families. Even if the country sometimes looks and feels like a shitshow, it has to keep a positive smiley image in other foreign lands to attract more immigration due to cheap labor once here. A country that never fulfills its promise. Bang. I think that we should not pay taxes to live here, and it should be the other way around. Being paid to live here. Is this land going to the dogs? I would not wish it on a man's best friend. Is decency part of curricula somewhere. Do lawyers have a mother?

Political language.... Is designed to make lies sound truthful and murder respectable, and to give as appearance of solidity to pure wind. George Orwell.

The 19 years old kid, working as a clerk for the Royal Bank, decided to enlist as he saw a movie. James Cagney in Captain of the Cloud. The movie played at the Yorx on Ste-Catherine st. Conveniently locate in front of Montreal's main recruiting office. I married after seeing Moonstruck, at the Yorx, too. The power of inspiration, I'd say. The St-Catherine-Bishop area, A place of strange, sometimes paranormal encounters.

And I am driving by Cabot square.

Now ! Cabot square. The old Forum and Montreal's hospital for sick children, since the healthy one usually don't go to hospital.

In front of the Cabot square stood the old Forum and that peculiar triangular-shaped building with 3 wide round windows. A McDonald, the 4000th one. The side is shaped like a 4. Nice, avant-garde, and spiffy. Before events. 1970's and 80s the place was filled with people lining up at the granite ordering counter, where there were lined up 12 cashiers and order takers with new space-age flat cash registers. That was impressive. It was a flagship store and the place was lively. Lively before events, lively after events all until they move the amphitheater somewhere else downtown, relabelled it and this section of town has lost its soul.

There was an aura of benevolence over this land, maybe because most of us believed in something or held some kind of faith in the fate of humanity that fueled this aura. As we questioned the relation between mind and matter 30 years ago, nowadays, it's the mind vs. profit that is investigated. It's gone. You can see the vacuum of direction in the way people stare or dress.

Driving by, I could still hear and feel, Donna Summer's synthesizers when she sang I feel Love, see the Boston's flying saucer, Pat Benatar's hard love life or Cyndi Lauper electronics Bags and Pipes. Cindy, took many of us forward all through the night. For 80 years they all came here at the

Forum. The flagship McDonald's franchise has moved across the street and a larger mall space, and the 4000 building is now a spa type place where they sell Mexican Terra Cotta stuff. The Cabot square is now a squalid zone inhabited by some homeless tribes where stand proudly facing the wind of the seas, Giovanni Cabotto. John Cabot. Gift from the Italian community to the City of Montreal, 1931.

Prosperity. The city felt prosperous. We all worked. Everything was made in Canada. Furniture, clothes, toys, tools, electronics, automotive. Everything but, low-end toys or elastic wasted jeans. Sneakers. Yes, sneakers, We had North Stars sneakers made in Montreal or some got those Adidas Rom imported. Snobs. Until someday someone questioned the system as: Man, I don't know! I thought about buying myself a AMC Pacer or a Pinto but those new imports, Honda Civic or the boxy thing from VW, the Rabbit may be a better deal. Betrayed by the maybe, the Detroit Bees and the wannabes. They drive better in snow… They are front-wheel drive like those Austin Mini or the Fiat 128, but more reliable.

And there you had it. Detroit had been failing us for decades, and time for sweet revenge rang. Blame it on Detroit. You look at one of those Vega, Astre or Firenza and you can actually see them rusting. We have been falling down ever since. Ultimately, the beginning of North American decline can be blamed on Motown. The Big Three are ultimately guilty of the downfall.

I will, as the detour mentioned, as if we follow all those instructions, make a left at Ste-Cats and pass by the old Toe Blake's tavern. Toe has been a prolific hockey coach for the CH, and the tavern was all about hockey. Hockey was a religion before it became street gangs on ice, (the days of Bobby Clark, Moose Dupont, Schultz) and then the Ruskie came and showed us a different faster and more sophisticated, disciplined to play the game

The 1972 series Canada vs. Russia changed the scope of the sport as a Russian Military team made of amateur players who were, as the Russian propaganda stated then, in Canada to learn how to play the game. They gave us a lesson in humility and showed us a new way to play the holy game, faster, more precise and less robust. The days of the dinosaurs were over. The same series opened the cult of the missing O'Pee Chee collectible Hockey Card. Rod Gilbert. NY Rangers. Rod was for team Canada and was the card missing to most collections, and it drove mad many kids. Those kids have grown old and have repressed this subconscious thought in their lives as this card is missing and they replaced the card with companies as they buy companies and collect them to become monstrous edge funds managers. Rod Gilbert or is it O" PeeChee created, hence, a generation of monsters. All this suffering and exploitation in our society for a missing Hockey Card, imagine. Helsinki 1989 !

We've adapted and it did to the game what the seat belt and the oil crises did to the car industry but then came the Disney guys and since then, kiss it goodbye pro sport and family outings it is now Entertainment. So, we have evolved from the 1972 Dodge Challenger to the 1982 Reliant K...and now we are at the top of the Volvo line, safe and expensive. Entertainment is expensive. Period.

A comedy became a cult movie here. Slapshot. In Slapshot, Paul Newman played Reggie Dunlop: a disabused hockey team captain from, somewhere, Pennsylvania. Reggie had remarkable comeback lines. Lines that would be deemed socially unacceptable by today's standards but we thought they were so funny in the 1970s. Comments that would make political correctness cringe, but so were the day. Funny in some violent way, I must admit. Maybe we were somehow violent as we had been raised by Lee Marvin, Popeye or the 3 Stooges. Pulling teeth with pliers or poking eyeballs had something of a slapstick act in the day of the depression years short movie. We had unrestricted access to all of that.

A classic routine. Reggie meets the owner of his hockey team. A woman !

You know, your son looks like a fag to me

There was that one about Hanrahan's girlfriend but it could not be published in these days and ages.

Hanrahan. Your girlfriend is a lesbian !

Say what?

30 years later. High School friend, former hockey player Erick T, now President of a steel groups, greets me in his posh office and breaks the ice with that line: Hanrahan, your girlfriend is a lesbian. It took us both back to High School day. This will be a tough sale!

Ouff! Blast from the past. Yet, business is business. Where did I land? Bizarre landscape here. Posh office in redneck city.

I raised an eyebrow on this one as I did not personally know Hanrahan nor his girlfriend but from what I gathered, she also slept with Reggie Dunlop. It must have been at some companies Christmas party, I guess.

Those unpolitical correctness or incorrect political line endured the test of time. Are they just funny because they are so damn improper, preposterous and provocative? What funny. Are they just a violent catharsis mode response to an elite class from over controlled worker or citizen? Is it just the spectacle of the scandalized reaction to such line? A form of, you want to make our lives miserable with all your rules, hear our answer. Your girlfriend is a … It maybe is like those 3 Stooges routine, a guy thing, or is it strictly generational. God knows but they always bring a chuckle or a slap that sleeps within's most unconscious that has to get out. This Reggie Dunlop that once in a while get out of the closet and let it all out. May explain why Sigmund Freud gave a beating to Karl Jung on this train in Switzerland. Sigmund, your girlfriend is a lesbian. Beats me. History doesn't tell us who got the top on this argument.

At Toe Blakes on Ste-Catherine st west, as in all Taverns, waiters were all dressed with black pants and a white shirt, they all carried cash in black leather aprons at the belt. Taverns were men only place until I, can't remember exactly. Smokers. Everybody smoked then. That was normal. Minimalist decor, oak tables and chairs, a clock and mainly terrazzo floor. Rudimentary men only bathroom and quite convenient when you were plastered.

We got to remember that there was an age where not everyone had a phone at home and the crews, trains, construction, and others were hanging out at Taverns and when employers needed the guys, they sent a kid to get them. Part of the land's DNA. Beer was not a luxury it was a commodity as per Gin was used to cure a cold before it was prescribed by the veterans affairs for PTSD. Beer was delivered by pint as much as milk was. Beer was the only safe thing to drink in springtime, when sewage and aqueducts were flooded by contaminated snow thawing waters.

Everything could be traded at the tavern. Curb traders sold stocks on tables at the tavern. Train crews were waiting for the call at the tavern. Construction men and cops finished their workday there. Horse betting, Irish sweepstakes, illegal lotteries all schemes and combines were available from there. Boxes that fell from the truck were traded at the tavern, as much as anything could be bought at those taverns by the port. All that you had to do was to inquire with the waiter.

This whole worker, blue collars or low-level white-collar workers were hanging out at the tavern. Almost a catholic institution, there were more men showing there than at Sunday's mass service. Many local jokes feature Jesus Christ walking into a tavern and addressing workers issues. They were all bathing in tobacco smoke and this odor of stale beer. Some places advertised sanitized glasses as it was known that the city water was not safe to drink in spring or after torrential rain Sanitized glasses advertised in neon or frozen mugs were a hit.

. All those taverns in the Belle Province of Quebec were male only places as of the early 1980s and had to have glass blocks windows as the spectacle of drunken men in the inside could have a disturbing negative impact on women or children by passer. The image of good societal manner had to be preserved for the public and the clergy. A scandal arose in the 1960s about a brewer, the Dow brewing company, that spiked their beer with Cobalt salt to increase the foam collar on their beer serving. Some people loved this 1 inch collar on the top of the glass. 48 people were sent to the hospital because of that commercial process, and many died.

Curb traders traded stocks on the curb. Hence, the name Curb Traders and they wore Curb shoes as a Derby with thicker leather sole. Today, bailiff wear sneakers to deliver their bad news. Curb trade were also made at the taverns.

When the business was good, the traders went to celebrate at the Gaiety Burlesque Club down the street by City Councilor st and when the market was slow, they also went to the Gaiety. The Gaiety had a win-win situation. The place became legendary as it offered the first Strip tease show, as it was the home of Lily St-Cyr. Montreal's very first stripper. My uncle John dated Lily a few times. He was not a gangster but knew them all very well as he supplied them with a precious commodity. Telephone line and confidential anonymous telephone numbers and equipment to operate all schemes. Those tavern and their stories and legends are part of all of us who grew up with those intertwined in our DNA as it became a part of us.

So of those place became Jazz Club. Montreal was a part of the international Jazz scene.

Many became Jazz clubs, as the name of Oscar Peterson and other little Burgundy kids became famous jazz people. Even Miles Davis had his circle of French Canadian friends. Rock heads' paradise was this top-notch club down on De la Montagne, 3 stories of Jazz. The owner stayed by the entrance door, handing a flower to every woman customer entering the Club. Ellah Fitzgerald made her Montreal's day view appearance at Rock head's.

Most of the clubs are gone. The Discos replaced them in the 1970s.

Driving on Ste-Catherine West in the 1970s.

They were all lined up on Ste-Catherine West st VW Beetles, Datsun 510, Ford LTD Brougham and Pintos. All those cars were different in shape, color scheme and had a personality. There was a love relationship with cars. I tried all afternoon driving the bus trying to find an analogy to new automotive: They are nice but they don't screw. Seems to me that the early 80s became the coitus interupted of Detroit's creativity, and the withdrawal has been messy. They lack these personality traits. They all look alike. This aura freedom they've once procured. The sexiness.

The Mustang horse or this Pinto Pony running in the wind. Not to mention Farrah Fawcett stretching her legs on the front seat of the brand-new design 1970 Ford Ltd. Redesigned with a leaner dashboard and those retractable headlights. Maybe it was the Mercury Marquis, so stable that a group of German jeweler could precisely cut a diamond on a company road circuit. I can only remember Farrah's legs anyway.

Today's car remind me of those parties with Marina Rinaldi. Marina was always surrounded by many cousins but you could not exactly approach any of them. They are nice. Is this a car or a video game you're driving? I'm not sure anymore. There was always that overkilled song in the air. Jerry Rafferty, Baker st. 1978, 1979 I guess. In those days, the GM car had a plate in the door with a Brougham. Body by Fisher. Now it's dashboard by Fisher Price.

But in all that came good news. Coffee.

The good news is for coffee lovers. Damn. 30 years ago, you could not get a cup of decent coffee anywhere unless you knew the handful of Italian cafés that had an Espresso machine, a Barista and did not keep the Espresso grounded in a Tupperware in the freezer. There was coffee in paper cups of a strange ancient Greece design. At the first lesson a driving school, the teacher gave you on the road was how to use a car key to make a spout out of the plastic lid. GM keys had teeth on both sides. Ford only the upside and well, Dodge of the downside. Ford was on 302 or 351 and Chrysler 318 or 340. Easy. From that angle, the world has progressed. Occasionally, we win.

Occasionally, the mind takes you to strange place. It is important to let it go. Drive around the bus on the scanner mode and it will all be fine. Operate without thinking and answer the 2 basic if asked anything, Yes or No.

There is a perpetual war between good and evil, and restful souls are given a rec and leisure break on earth as this physical life should be something of a reward. A cruise or an all-inclusive trip but could also be formative in the enterprise stage.

I'll pick the cruise.

It doesn't take a rocket to travel in outer space. A good radio frequency, too many hours on the road and bizarre work schedule. There you have it. The minds leave the body sporadically and takes you to this bizarre place. The strange land of Lorie Brown.

The signal. Lorie Brown, space odyssey radio show.

Quote from Lorie Brown in her (or almost) The Signal broadcast. CBC Night radio. An eclectic night radio show that introduces live jazz performance, metaphysical thoughts, new age music and the familiar sound of the magic wand. Live or almost from seaside, Nova Scotia, for what I gathered. Wee, hours of the morning in daze behind the wheel, parked by this publicity panel. Pause before the last trip. 362 night bus. Half a trip.

Snoozing a few minutes before catching the Night Shift people going to the fruits and vegetable brokers, taking the last Metro. They start at 3:00 AM. The last Metro is called the broom. If the broom is late, you have to wait for the broom to show up to the station before leaving for the trip. As per many drivers will say out loud, take your broom by the stick and shove it, time for the garage. As you close your eyes for a few minutes, all you can see are those yellow lines in your mind. You'll get home, watch 45 minutes of T.V. Grab a bowl of cereal or pick up fresh hot croissants at the gas station and you'll see them again. Yellow line. The yellow lines, or the snowflakes, Depend on the season. Croissants are ready at 02:40 next to the division or 26:40 in transit language.

And there is that huge publicity post by which you park the bus for the last trip. You will be parking on the same spot every night for 3 months. A semester or what they call in the business; a list.

My Indian Village, 100% Good Food, In God We Trust. I and many drivers all questioned the claim about the 100% Good Food and figured that we should all show up one day and challenge that ludicrous claim as per my fellow Red.

Red usually knocked on my bus door by 26:50 hrs. Red has a long scar from an eye to the cheek, farming equipment accident when he was a teenager. Yet, it makes this gentle mannered guy like a Russian Mob hitman.

Every time the discussion hits the same beginning.

- Yo Bert. This guy over there, the Indian, The Indian Jardin or Village man. He pretends that all his food. 100% is good, but what do we know? Think he is B.S, ing us. What do we know about his food? Do you know any good Indian Food? Is he taking us for idiots because we are not Indian?

Red, man ! I am tired, shot. It's beyond exhaustion. I was just over with Lorie Brown at the CBC but, given that we are in Park Ex district, I would believe it is good but me. Honestly, Indian food, curry, nah. But listen, we'll ask Rajeev at the Division to drop by and he'll tell us about it. He has uncles around here. They have a Sweet Shop on Jean Talon. I can tell you though that there is a great Greek Restaurant down the street corner of Jean Talon and Durocher, I think.

I heard about The Panama.

Panama is a great Greek restaurant, as the old Hermes was. Hermes had been closed a few years ago and it's an Asian nail place in an old Greece decor. Cool, isn't it. But now, Panama has this remarkable Tzatziki cream. The Greek fashion one. Not the Lebanese. One of them adds mint leaves and uses sour cream. Now, that old friend of mine Suzie Milos knew about those Indian restaurants. She could have told us if it's any good.

I always thought that people starved to death in India and Pakistan, so how about their cooking?

A classic. How about the Ethiopian cuisine? Damn you idiot.

I have a good story about the Panama.

I went to dine with Suzie Milos once in a while between 2 tours while I was a Tour Director. I left a group at the airport on Saturday lunchtime and usually picked up another one on Sunday Morning or about, So, on Saturday evening, since I was in the city. Suzie and I went to the Greek down the street. She had an apartment in NDG by Loyola campus. Bus route 105. We once had been neighbors. Not that we were attached or somehow in love but we loved going to dine on Saturday at the Greek. We had plenty of stories to tell, as we were both looking for happiness in the wrong places or had it but never realized it. No, in fact, we were getting in love but could not figure out how to approach the whole issue. Or else, we were both in love with something else, our freedom? Those joyride moments were so perfect and precious that we could neither imagine spoiling them by moments of daily life as cleaning an apartment or doing the groceries or all those scenes of the grinder of daily living. We lived those escapes, enjoyed them, and assumed the lie in all serenity. A form of highly evolved social delinquency.

Greek restaurants: Montreal's tradition, I guess. Now, Suzie was Miss restaurant as she knew them all and always said, there was something in Indian food, a spice, or something that made her extremely horny as she ate in those places. Nice to know... She always told me that as we walked out of a Greek restaurant. She grabbed my arm to walk her on the city curb. I should have caught on that extremely significative gesture but I did not. No, I was an idiot.

Not that I..., but on the other hand, Red, she was good-looking. She had the most amazing, sexy mouth. And I was young.

So ?

So, now the thing is that those Indian meals could be good, but I never dated her to a Indian place, but one evening I noticed how she attacked this dish of Tzatziki in an almost sexual demonic manner. Kind of an erotic food trance. She was eating all she could, fast, taking all the croutons and dipping them madly in the Tzatziki. One of my exes. Adele was like that before sex. Hungry, focused and determined. She had to get to the bedroom fast.

That man!

She was obsessed with it. She loved Tzatziki and raunchy Greek words. I was not in the Indian regime then but it rang a bell to me. Seeing how she would behave on a side dish of Tzatziki, and a few glasses of dry white wine. I figured, maybe if I can get to her place with a container of that stuff, we may spice things up. It comes in three sizes.

Small, medium, large, I guess.

OK, smart ass. It's almost 2 AM and we both had a long day. So OK, this was obvious.
They also had something more of the size of a bucket. Remember those KFC's family buckets? Well, that size.

Last dinner, before the end of the tour season and the summer she took off for… I don't know where. As we exited Panama, there was a take-out refrigerator type counter and some of that Tzatziki on display. Three sizes. As I was asking the cashier for a large container she looked at me, pushing a sigh or a sexy moan but something very suggestive. She had that sex shop moment as I had my Snap On tool moment. Snap On moment is when you get some kind of mystical revelation on how to handle a technical problem using the perfect tool. Eureka on a ¼ drive.

Large please ! There were just no words for this. It was, let's go to my place and open this thing up and, well, spread it to our utmost fantasies. So, we did. To the extent that I had to take a long shower to get rid of that stuff all over my body, and I smelled like garlic for three days.

As we had the full pikillia experience. Her now keratas so-called boyfriend Derek got suspicious as she really smelled garlic at every part of her body and figured out what happened as he found the Tzatziki pot in the refrigerator. She had a boyfriend, I was not aware of that detail. Well, the guy was not the sharpest pencil in the case but he figured it out. I was out of town, as usual, as he started harassing Suzie and making violent threats. She vanished working for a hotel in Toronto area lakefront place incognito. She had to hide, and even her mother could not tell me where she had gone. She may have needed this walkabout to figure out what's going on with her life. I met her once again for lunch in a food safe place, a Chinese buffet, and she settled down with a trucker who also owns tobacco fields. She now lives in your neck of the woods.

As I said, I don't know much about Indian food and Italian or Greek always did the trick for me, nonetheless I think the claims on this publicity could be viewed as fallacious.

Now, I know that Gianni would bomb the place for that, but he seems to get carried away once in a while. He'll claim that it is his Sicilian blood.

Going home after the shift, or are you going to sleep at the garage for what's left of the night...? Sleeping in the van?

Is the term vanishing a conjugation of the word Vans as I Vanish, You Vanish and so on or does it take a van to vanish or is it vanity or are vanities fitting only in van or is there a spin-off with Mini Vans? I minivanish, You minivanish or I pick up your pickup and so on. Meditate on that, It's 26:40 right now.

I have overtime starting at 29:40. I will catch a few hours sleep in the dorm room at the garage if nobody snores or you know... before the regular shift and go home after. You know, I live in l'Assomption and it is a good hour drive from Montreal.

Note that one could sleep a few hours at the dorm room for as long as the snorer of the other defectives digestive tract problems drivers are not around. That does not happen often, but many drivers sleep with CPAP. Sleep apnea is a common occurrence among professional drivers. At 28:45 the garage comes back to life as 300 buses roll out of it within 40 minutes and that makes a lot of noise. Don't set an alarm, you will not need it and if that doesn't wake you up, please go home and book sick, you are unfit to drive.

This 100% Good Food deal was still in the air. 100%, this is a gigantic claim. Nothing on the menu is bad. Hard to believe.

I am telling you. I'll check with Rajeev about the Beau Jardin, whatever India, if it is any good and if it is 100% Good Food and if it is not up to the 100% standard, we send the food inspection for false publicity. Got the message that the broom will be late tonight, are you sticking around or are they to shove it. I live 10 minutes from the garage, if you want to go, I can pick up your regulars.

OK Cool, I am dead too, I am pulling out. Could you please pick up a few lost in spaces U of Montreal kids on Jean Talon and drop them for a walk at Wilderton rd? I am cutting loose and check in at the division to get a few hours of sleep. Please remember my African friends, The shouldn't. The usual ride.

Yeap, the Africans !

They should not be people. They should not be in Canada, They should not work here, nor have an apartment, kids and all because they don't appear officially anywhere. They sneaked out or containerized their way in the country. Those guys figured out that once the bus ends its regular route, it goes to the garage and they can be dropped by the vegetable brokers firm in the industrial district by the garage. No buses go there officially but we manage to give them the ride because those guys are gems.

They are smart, intelligent, polite and share wisdom we forgot about here. They should not, but are always happy.

Yes, happy. As the invisible hand regulates the market, their invisible hand sorts, quantifies, qualifies and transports every day fruits and vegetables by night. Invisible but such a gift to our society and a privilege to meet.

Good Night Red, see you tomorrow night.

And days, after days, night after night for the time of a list. 10 to 12 weeks we had the same discussion about the Beau Jardin India thing. The pretext of an aimless discussion going nowhere but to open a late night or early morning interaction. Same routine done with the story of Colonel Whitelaw in this other circle of friends. The man who could have been at the head of NATO but declined to be a teenager's bootcamp honcho. A hearty cheap laugh. Sometimes we inquired about the menu but it became a regular stand-up comic routine. Some way to open a contact or a conversation between 2 people, caught in the middle of a strange place, a strange job at strange hours whom, even if surrounded and seeing a few hundreds' people in a day, feel the loneliness of the job and the need of human contact. The silliness that keeps us bonded and alive. Conversation between driver stopped making sense after 1 AM, as a way to keep us sane. Keep us from wondering: what the hell I am doing here, shouldn't I get a normal life?

Last thing Red?

Yeap!

Remember the Village Peoples ?

Sure, like YMCA. Thing. (doing the hand gestures)

Now, why is ii that they had no Bus Driver ? They had it all, but the Bus Driver

Good Night, Bert.

The signal.

CBC's Space Odyssey.!

Yet, this Lorie Brown show opened my mind to very specific metaphysical matters as per angel, speakers, messengers and other forms of divine interventions as this encounter with a fortune-teller many years ago. Lorie opened my mind to this other world just as Jane Robert and the Seth trilogy as well as Julie Nesrallah has been teaching me all about Classical music, 3 hours at the time, 5 days a week. Blessed is the CBC, for as long as you don't listen to their newscast or their TV.

Time lapses. The mind travel back in time.

So, I am back at the Boardwalk with the Fortune Teller. Hampton Beach, N.H. Many years ago. My camping years.

Under the umbrella, a young woman. A young woman student completing a summer gig reader palms on the boardwalk, figure. This is late in the season, after labor day. It's the weekend but she seems to enjoy herself working on a boardwalk by the sea in a stormy sky screaming tempest. It's New England. It's cool. I approached the booth and said:

Hi, time for a palm reading for a lousy tourist here

Sure, she said, what took you so long, I've been expecting you for a while now. As she looked at her watch.

In fact, we are outside the town on route 3. I was travelling with Duck on that trip.

She said, yeah, at the KOA, I know.

That started to get interesting as not only she was expecting me, or us, knew where we camped, (but that's easy) but it felt like daylight under the umbrella as if she had her personal sun. Her voice was soft and as we spoke, it seemed that some of her physical features changed, eyes color, nose, hairstyle, and hair color too. It all happened slowly. Subtly.

As she started the consultation she said; Hi I am, X and I am a messenger, and you are Bert and I have to announce to you that you are a speaker. There is no coincidence here, and I was expecting you. Metaphysical trap. Lol. I have been to the first name routine once in Mexico as everyone in Playa Del Carmen seems to know your first name since they heard someone mentions your first name as they also know what hotel you are staying at by the color of the plastic bracelet on your wrist. Easy here.

You are a warrior. You have been a warrior for ages. Your friends are also, and you guys have been crossing swords for ages. It's like an immortal club. Sometimes adversaries, sometimes on the same side, but you fought. You always did, You always will.

Listen. Not that you are into the Zoltar's confidential, but as I sport a brush cut, a khaki t-shirt with the Better dead than red logo and am in good physical shape it is easy to tell. Anyone could tell I am or was linked to the military.

What you are wearing as your body and what you wrap your body in, your clothes, are simply a manifestation of your inner soul brother. Your body is the materialization of the person you are, and you maintain it as is. So, accordingly, you picked this circle of friends that you've forever congregated with and this physical family, which had been an adventurous booking.

Your brothers and sisters or more mercantile than you are as you'll seek for an absolute truth as they could manage with a partial one or a plastic one for as long as it pays off. A purist in a pragmatic world. You are the acting black sheep of your family as you never understood who they really were and this simple fact that your parents never expected less from you than being happy. They caught up with your different take on the universe. It took that Emergency visit at the hospital to understand that you could not abide by everyone's rules, and the laws of physics definitely apply to you too. A motorcycle accident. It worried them for a while, but saw that you are taking your place in the world. Maybe your old man was right, After all, the clergy may have been a good place for you. Clergy, it once crossed my mind.

Tell me more about this Messenger vs. Speaker deal and what else do you know about me.

Speaker communicates the wisdom of the universe. As easy as that. This knowledge is inherent to you, that's why you are always in quest to understand WTH is going on with the human species. Now you know. Obviously, it does not come with the same type of maintenance manual as those lying at the bottom of the glove compartment on your average Mercury Topaz.

And you have been mandated to carry this message to me.

No, It's a summer gig here. I borrow human appearance to do the job, but Sheila here working with me is a very nice girl and she has beautiful friends.

Now, are there any fringe benefits at being a speaker besides always being one step ahead of everyone you meet.

Sure, charm, and charisma come with the job, but no salaries nor financial incentive. Live it, Be it.

Now, since I have charm and charisma, you know that you are beautiful. Maybe we could... How do you do it? You seem to change appearance as we speak.

Cut it out. I am the image of all the women in your life that you are constantly pushing to me, and so I adapt and project what you strive to see.

Can you do Carmen Electra?

Have you ever met personally Carmen Electra

No.!

Here is your answer ! This is official business here. You cannot push images that are strictly based on a superficial perception.

Is this really happening and it is an exchange of information?

Is it a pull from you or a push from me?

You are pushing information, as matter is made of information. You see outlines of physical objects, but these physical frontiers don't exactly exist. All the universe is a whole and we are simply part of it. As we speak, you're pushing unseen to the ear or the eye information that I pick up. This is my gift.

Here's what you came for. Future. Every single day of your life will be challenging as you'll try to conform. Conform to what you imagine a committee of your parents expects from you and the way you should live your life. Your life. Your life is way different from your brother who is satisfied in normalcy as in your case, normalcy will fail you every time

Every single time. You are not geared like everyone else. You see, assemble, link stuff like no one else. Striving for eccentricity and creativeness in any work environment is your only way out and way to happiness and fruitful life. Every day will be for you a leap of faith as those leaps may become routine but still, they are leaps.

Friends are friends, and friends cannot be trusted simply because they are friends. It's a form of love, but challenged too. Your freedom of thinking and spirit makes many jealous, as you seem to always find a way out of boredom and redefine yourself and find material means to do so. Friends and family are very annoyed, but will never let you know. You are sovereign of your life, but this has its cost.

Remember Berthold Brecht as a high school student: I don't trust him, we are friends.

As we spoke under this lit umbrella, the sky turned black, wind blew, the storm was brewing across the boardwalk pushing everything of its way, but our island. We were in a bubble away from physical time, space and she told me about those toys I cherished when I was young, a dog I had forgotten about that I picked in a farm for which my father paid the farmer a brown $2 bill. She knew all about me.

So at the end of the séance, she said: here is the answer to the question you would not dare to ask. Yes, you will meet her, sometimes, but not soon. She has issues to resolve for now, and you are not on her radar yet. She will be beautiful, a stunning woman. At first sight, you will know, but she'll have a distinctive sign. She wears old jewelry, Camays and brooches. Type of stuff that were hers grandmother.

Remember those Belgian comics strips of your youth, there she is. In there, in those drawings. In your mind. You'll know. I knew.

Incidentally, nice t-shirt. Better dead than red. Totally you.

Thanks, I appreciate it. This khaki green sure helps outline those yellow military letters. Very MASH indeed.

For now and before you leave, stop being so damn polite and catholic. Moreover, your pal over there. He is a bonehead.

We are all someone's else bonehead, aren't we.

Once gone, and as per our search for her stand on the boardwalk, she seemed to have disappeared or had never existed on this boardwalk, this year or that season, this lifetime. That's the beauty of life.

After this out of this world encounter, life appeared different.

So, life took another direction. I knew who I really became. What I evolved into as a person.

I am a speaker. Here is something to look forward to. Young, charismatic and finally understood. It's the good life.

Oh, the good life, full of fun seems to be the ideal
Mm, the good life lets you hide all the sadness you feel
You won't really fall in love for you can't take the chance
So please be honest with yourself, don't try to fake romance…

Avoid normality and enjoy life. The other existential question is why do men chase women. There doesn't seem to be a definite answer on the topic but I love this biblical theory.

Man chases women because God took man's rib to make the woman, and man wants to recuperate his rib. (Moonstruck). For now, I question the tool man uses to go extract the famous rib?

Johnny: but it could as well have been Gianni.

Well, there's a Bible story… God… God took a rib from Adam and made Eve. Now maybe men chase women to get the rib back. When God took the rib, he left a big hole there, where there used to be something. And the women have that. Now maybe, just maybe, a man isn't complete as a man without a woman.

I met many, loved some, but lived out with this perpetual feeling of emptiness. You can do many jobs but hardly hold one for a long time because it gets normal and normalcy will never suit you. Damn, did you ever try to fit in? Did you ever try those suits jobs? Those sales meeting as the object of the meeting are customer needs, as the image of customer needs in your mind looks like dog poop. Those power lunches where IT buzzword are on the menu. The sales quotas. Those company organigram getting liquid paper painted every week as per official pictures in the Soviet era. No, nothing exactly jibed but, let's enjoy life and see where it will take me.

Life isn't that bad, actually. Is it better for everyone else? Aren't we all searching for happiness and stability? Are all those people stuck in traffic on the highway 15 South on the way to work at 5:40 AM happy with the role in society they are about to play? I often drank a coffee on the Sherbrooke St. West overpass over the 15 and thought: how could there be such a high unemployment level in that city, as I could see all of those people heading to work. At 5:40 it is all too early to go to classes or to a professional appointment. Little did I know.

It all reminded me of the lyrics of this Gilbert O'Sullivan song. Alone again, Naturally. What do we do, What do we do ? Here is an honest question.

And came the tale of Gisele. Gisele, like Gisele Bundchen or the ballet Gisele. Gisele was that blonde nymph, acting naive girls playing the local vamp. She was hanging around with Cathy. Cathy was my roommate's girlfriend: John. John was a cinema major who had this delirious collection of B Movie and BW classics, and our apartment looked like a video club. Also in the portrait were Melanie R, Sheila, and the Iranian girls who, with Sheila, had the hots for me. Yet, I was only interested in Melanie R because she looked like Stephanie Powers. Heart-to-heart. But, for me, this was all a popcorn scene that I wanted to leave and left it every spring when the asphalt thawed and the air smelled of dog poop, mud, and fresh diesel. The tour season was back. They were not real friends. They were geographical friends. We all happened to live in the same neighborhood and that was about it.

Duck has been a friend for decades. High School, Army Camp. As I was in College, he already started a career as a fireman. We've always kept in touch. Sometimes going our way for a few months, a year, but always found some way to hook up. He loved to play Mr. Calendar boy, fireman. Working part-time, I usually ended up in a work environment with a high density of available women. It started in those moped days many years ago.

Duck's approach to life could be summed up in this line: Water is more dangerous than alcohol, as you never see Life

Guards in bars. Logical, twisted and pragmatic. He has his particular kind of spirituality. Rubber meets asphalt deal.

I introduced female colleagues and friends to Duck. Duck introduced girls to me. I always pushed better than I received so to speak, but. So, among the few who can remember referring or double dating with him were Julie, Gisele, ... and finally Celine. But Celine was a mistake. So, I think.

I introduced him to Julie, who works with me at the credit department of a woman apparel's store chain. We were, or was I, pushing fur coat financing plans. Most of my customers were sex workers or airline stewardess, smuggling cheap fur coats around the world as a sideline gig. So, Julie and Duck met at first snow so they thought of something romantic to do after making love or was it before. (the first snow always has some kind of magic attached to even more on 4 seasons tires) The good old donut in snow ritual as going to the Blockbuster's mall parking lot and doing some donuts with Duck's new Toyota. It's like doing angels in snow, but in a car. Duck loves his car and takes special care of all his stuff and toys. That kind of makes any type of close relationship uneasy, and he trades house and wives faster than he trades in cars.

As the donut making technique tells, on that night, Julie pulled the handbrake and turned the steering wheel to the left at top speed to make the car spin. This is how you do donuts. But it did really uncontrollably and in the Blockbuster windows. They busted it. Last time we saw Julie. Nonetheless, I thought he could be the right match for Gisele. She had no driver's licenses as far as I knew.

Donut are well done with propulsion cars. The front-wheel drive may react differently. Now you know.

Julie was not a donut person. She was more into the neck brace mood.

Gisele and then Celine, or Celine than Gisele. Matter of chronological order, I guess.

The story of Celine from Nice in the portrait has more of a saga than the regular story. It stretches for a few decades. This young Ivory girl's natural beauty came from one of those Mediterranean paradise cities or villages. The type of place where men spend the day at the Café, drinking Pernod, snacking on olives and playing Pétanque while wearing French berets and the obvious mariniere shirt. Not a Marcel. Somehow Celine came to this side of the ocean to learn English I guess as she lived in Dorval at Mr. Smart, the local Snapple juice distributor's place. Otherwise, she worked in the family enterprise, a fragrance factory in or by, a place where women sunbathe topless. So, they say.

So, bang. ! Celine is part of one of my 14 days tours, alone and the only person under the age of 60 years old. On that one I was, tour director, local guide and driver at the same time. She sat up front on the passenger seat of the minibus and we talked. Talked about whatever she felt like, but there was that unhappy trend in her speech. It was just as if she were born to be unhappy. She loved those strenuous tear-jerking violin solos of life and this emotion, sadness. She was the kiss of death.

At the end of the tour, the last of the 14 days. Lucien, client on the tour and a man who looked, dressed and talked like Kojak, told me:(Lucien had a fleet of limos and taxis in Paris and had lived a lot. He also looked and talked like Telly Savalas.)

Maybe, you should take La Petite out for the last evening of the tour. They called her La Petite. Looks like she may appreciate.

Sure, I'll take her out on my time. And so I did. The last evening was in my hometown, Quebec CIty and I knew all the nice places as I always loved the Café St-Malo on St-Pierre st. They knew me then, and I have always behaved according to the strict rule of etiquette of Amy Vanderbilt. Always look excited or surprised by the zest of a cherry tomato when biting into it.

We had a great dinner. It was all lively and romantic and it all went well, but that person is a sad soul. Sad souls are toxic. It is written in BW on my fridge door. You will not get involved with sad souls, avoid long-distance relationships, buy a Ford Automotive anymore or try to fix things you are not trained nor equipped to do. So, it stayed at the polite bise of the cheek and this is where it ended.

I reported to Lucien. Lucien had been an Adjutant in the French Para, so I responded to him at attention, doing my military style report with notes. She is nice but I can't take these 100 shades of gray.

I carried on with my life. She went back to France and she sent me a few letters. And she came back the next summer at Mr. Snapple and we met for a glass of wine in Lachine but she was still the kiss of death. More violin, more sadness and more prickle my brain emotion and I was not up to it. I knew that my old friend Duck was going to the dunes skiing in Tadoussac for a few days and arranged a meeting. It all clicked very well and they went to the Gulf, enjoyed each other and that was case closed. The usual exchange of service. The Fridge commandment had been respected, except for the Ford. I had leased a Mustang that fall. So, life went on and Duck visited her place in Southern France and fell in love with the person and the concept of living the dolce vita under the olive trees or at the village square, but his job was here. Here as here in gray, cold snowy and dark damn Montreal, Canada. End of the story. End of the story as Duck, – fidele a lui meme- had a few relations, one marriage, 2 boys, a few houses, many moving, his share of the small white pill and as every time he introduced his new love of his life in a new house or setting, to me and my wife.

He once betted that my marriage would not last over 1 year. He is paying his bet every year and it is costly. His ex-wife keeps benefiting from it. I remind his wife every year to cash in on that bet upon my annual wedding anniversary date.

The man was an excellent and distinguished law officer. Had a bumpy life, but aren't we all. Like many cops, I guess, he was more married to the job than with all those women, but what do we know. So he retired. He stopped a mad man totting a AK47 to do a carnage at a political rally. That was the straw that broke the camel back, A big straw.

He retired. Had many parties because the man had plenty of friends and is an estimated member of the police force. In fact, he became a National hero as he prevented what could have become a real slaughter. Later that fall, he invited me and Jo (my wife) to one of his numerous new houses, for dinner. He had great news for us and wanted to show us this bizarre bungalow with a 2-story bathroom. 2 stories bathroom link by a fireman pole type of deal. Maybe the former owner shot porn movie in there as this was used as a studio. Beats me.

So we had dinner. He cooked, we brought dessert and a bottle of red and at the Clou of the evening he announced that after all those years, he was to retire or live or what with Celine from Saint-Tropez or Nice or a place where Louis DeFunes made movies in the 1960s posing as a Gendarme surrounded by incompetent other Gendarmes, nuns with winged cornettes and Citroën 2 CV wheels. Damn, I thought. The man had preserved this relationship secret for the last 25 years. He kept this young adult fantasy on the back burner of all life.

That must have been a heavy cross to carry. This emotional way out. This pipe dreams. Does he know she is nuts? 25 years, people change a lot. What's with her, she did not find anyone on her side either. My wife, Jo, looked at me, rolled her eyes, looked at the ceiling and asked me: who the hell is Celine? She is very pragmatic. Sometimes it creates conflict in the family. As they say: From the shock of ideas gushes forth the lite ! My place is very well lit even in the dark.

I knew that could not work. I knew that person was toxic and lethal. I knew that it would crush him, as he was a bit fragile in those days. They tried. He finally discovered that she was a toxic person living multiple secret lives, not exactly honest and well from the Ivory girl he knew, she became miss silicon boobs and Botox lips hooked on her I-Phone permanently.

I still had the decency not to bet on the odds that would work. Maybe I did not have anyone to bet against ?

Lot of time to think while you are driving a city bus. The mind cuts through layers of memories that you thought vanished, and some strange emotions surface. It cuts by theme, overall feeling, a perfume, an odor, a wavelength. It cuts in erratic, unpredictable fashion.

The only reason why it came to my mind is that I felt bad for a while for having introduced these two, namely, pushing them into each other's arms. I knew years ago that she was a depression on legs, the kiss of death, a soul sucker. I knew. I should have been a better friend, and I started having regrets. Regrets for having matched him with Gisele, that was also a bit of a sexual nut job. Gisele threw a fit at him, demolished his kitchen and left a nails scar on his back and butt that caused him a rupture.

Among few others. As one ages, wisdom kicks in and life is not a sitcom. I should have known better. I should have been a better friend, but then again, aren't we all major and vaccinated. I am no priest after all either. Maybe, one of the tasks to learn on this existence is not a John Hughes comedy.

Yet. It all crosses our mind to think of a, what if scenario. What if I had engaged or married such or such. What if I had put all my stuff in a U-Haul and moved with that person, What if, and what if all to keep a scenario like that on my emotional back burner. That is insane and dangerous. This is emotional hoarding. What happened with your life?

The downside of that was that I had to explain the story of Celine and she told me once again: Your pal, Duck, he is a nice guy but he is crazy. Sure, I know, but I never saw any problems with that. Our souls have been traveling together for many centuries. I am somewhat tied with the man. Yes, he is crazy. Aren't we all?

And that happened again. The eternal quest for normality. This eternal failure.
(this is from me).

Someway, somewhere, somehow, one has to grow some skills that will bring him money. I thought I could become a good stockbroker. Not that I was mathematically inclined but I was no Hank Kimball either, still he became a county agent in Hooterville.

I tried studying finances and stock trading in Toronto. I thought I could follow the old man's footsteps that did that for years and hated it. My brother John, womanizer, and a bit alcoholic was a successful broker. My sister Diane, who does the job, loves it and became addicted to a new drug: Money. Only my love to gamble and understand newness by following the money kept me in that program, but again, it takes a lot of money to make a little money. If you don't hold a large capital, as my blue-blooded Capitalist sister would say; Pay your debt, stay afloat and shut up. So I did. I still gamble small caps, junior mines, penny stocks but it's a hobby. It keeps a bus drivers' brain active because the job does not.

I did study the structures. Got the hang of it. Could push the product. Play the Hot Shot. I could do it, as there was way more to live in the 80s Toronto scene. The Comedy Club scene was just remarkable.

My mind wandered again to the days I was in Toronto, taking classes at Ryerson and spending most of my time at the repertoire theaters. It's an erratic novel, not an erotic one.

You think I am pulling it thin but I am tired and remember; it's Friday night.

Maybe it's the music. This jazz music playing on the radio.

In the glory days of Bloor street.

I had that routine of cheap Pizza, Hungarian Goulash soup, $2 movie night at the Bloor repertory theater and the classic a beer or two or three at the Old Brunswick house. All on Bloor st. All straight line.

Ye Old Brunswick was a beer garden hall, No more, no less. With a wideband stage, it had been there forever and was reputedly haunted or a bit, or we were all too fucken drunk to see clearly. They had $30 tables. For $30 you could order 30 draft beer and fill in the round table. Very convenient indeed. Gathering there were regular U of T students, Ryerson's, workers from the area, steel guys from Hamilton (Steel city makes nails so we love to get hammered) and maritimers coming to the big city for job opportunities among others. There was a stage in the main hall that could be described as a Andrew's Sister meet Gary Larson type.

Guys and gals gather around small round table and started talking nonsense, urban tales like the one about this honest politician or others and while playing drinking games with a pack of cigarettes. The good old topic of haunted houses and flying saucers popped out. A classic. Everyone enjoys good ghost stories. Ghost stories. The maritimers were outstanding at flying saucers stories because in the maritime, not only are those UFOs' flying above the ground but they are also flying out of the ocean and it is documented. They have an extra set for Ghost Ship, mermaid and lost souls, the ocean. It's a perpetual 2 for 1. They are the masters of their tales.

We were around the table telling our most scary telltale of apparition, ghost, spooks, and encounter with UFOs and it kept going and going as it all seemed credible as to say to you can go to that old boarded up theater in the north end after midnite and see a play that happened a century ago, by ghost and well it's free. All that was known, factual, accepted and daily life stuff until the kid from St-Catherines's, Ontario pulled that one:

Many years ago I was at a strip joint in Hamilton. Hamilton is a steel city. And I saw the now known actress Stephanie Powers dancing naked on the stage.

Everyone one was in shock and disbelief. Questioned this very bizarre and questionable tale. Stephanie Powers at a strip joint in Hamilton. I mean, hey ! Ghost, spook, UFOs, werewolf, levitating friends, past life experience and others were just normal occurrences of life and given one or two more pitchers of draft beer, there could have been way more stuff but this Stephanie Power story. Hum. Not that I would not have liked to see that yet, it seemed all wrong to all of us around the table.

Damn, Stephanie Powers dancing naked in a sleazy steel city strip joint with red neon light. Scene from the movie Flash dance, flashed in my memory. What a life shattering thought. The St-Catherine man really killed a vision of beauty and purity I had entertained for ages on that actress. Here, something unbearable for one person alone. Waiter! I'll have two more X's. Molson X. All you had to do was finger work. 2 fingers for 2 glasses and the X for Molson X.

Retrospectively, I guess.

It may have started there. At the Ye Olde Brunswick. Seeing dead people. I know I come from a longline of medium but nowadays, it seems to me that I cross dead people on a daily basis. A lot of them. They take one of those many workers' bus routes to go to the shop, glasses, and headsets on, punch the bus pass and go sit in the back of the bus. Sometimes I tell them, Walk to the light. Some do, and don't show up the days after.

The Ye Old Brunswick has closed years ago and the building became like everything else a Drugstore, as much as the Bloor Theater I guess that had not been saved by a dreaming millennial who would have wished to save it from ruin, purchase it and turn the hand of time back to the days when people went out to the movie, To socialize, to date, to enjoy a film to be entertained, to live. But the kid did not win Mega Bucks, and a version of so-called progress Blobbed The Bloor too. In facts, nobody ever wins the Mega Bucks, it's a hoax as per many professional gamblers I met and the king of them all, the great Vegas Harry.

One evening, having had too much beer with the guys, upon leaving Ye Old Brunswick, one of the guys said: Someday you'll have that glass of Burgundy with Stephanie Powers, Promised. The man had the reputation of being a warlock.

Yeah, right !!!

You'll see, remember !

I made that left turn on Ste-Catherine street, passed the infamous Cabot square and drive eastward by Lambert Closse st.

Fortune Tellers and palm readers on St-Cat's west have disappeared and left their local to pawn or sex shop. The fortune-tellers have been replaced by the Misfortune teller, and the urban gangrene and its graffiti signature have slowly crept in. Paper kiosks where you could get a fresh hot copy of today's paper at 4:45 AM disappeared as did the snack counters, Gone, just gone. Gone with those papers from around the world in colors. Printed on green or pink paper. As the Woolworth snack counter, all chromed bar stools, cake bells, and the ever-present orange and grape juice fountains always pouring.

4 Winter tires for 20 Godivas chocolate and an everlasting flirt episode

There was this 3 story Sears (type) Auto Center on St-Catherine West, (I had a toy one of those when I was 5) I worked there as a grease monkey between tour seasons before I landed a Dee Jay job, graveyard shift in the many Crescent streets meat markets bars. Money and overall conditions were lousy in those auto centers but the workout of changing oil, tires, and batteries compensated for it all and the season was short, 6 to 8 weeks, the most. There are always perks for cheap auto parts when you need them. A good mechanic will never have to buy a car battery in his professional life, as a bus driver will never again have to buy an umbrella or a pair of gloves.

Somehow, every cold as hell Friday night, some nut... went around the posh Down Town neighborhood and punctured tires on the flanks. Always two on the same side. Why and with what tool, beats me, but I know that it is a lousy thing to do given that they officially can't be repaired and since the front and back were simultaneously punched and have different wear, well, all the 4 must be replaced? A tire seller's dreamboat. So, early and all days on Saturdays, the towing guys were taking frozen solid cars to the garage and were given a kickback for choosing us. Working under a thawing car must be like a Das Boot experience, as being the mechanic is a submarine engine room. Damp, humid, dark, oily greasy with water dripping all over. I learned a lot about car maintenance on that job.

Every Saturdays we had the same emergency fixing routine.

Friday evening: 19:40 or about. A last customer. My last Friday evening on this gig too.

Comes Heidi, in a state of panic. She had just discovered, searching through the mess of her glove compartment, the maintenance booklet from Ford and all those things she should have had to have never done. She drove the ugly Topaz for almost 2 years now, but had not done any maintenance. And she reads the maintenance novel in 754 inspection points, and she freaked out. The full drama was in. How could I have done such a mistake? A Maria Callas damnation moment on full drama mode. Where did I go wrong in my relationship with this Topaz? She is the person that discovers that her apartment is haunted badly and looks for a priest. She had to check it over with a mechanic, and although I was not exactly one, I could play the Mr. Good wrench part, but I was not a fully certified mechanic. A bit of this Hank Kimbol routine.

At first, glance, there was nothing wrong with the machine but the fact that the motor oil was as dark as an espresso. No cream.

Like a smoking gun, she showed me the maintenance manual for that ugly tub on wheels, signed Ford or Mercury. The 2.3 liters guys. The guys who had a seatbelt mechanism embedded in the front door. The guys who figured that a car for old folks should resemble an orthopedic fixture. The geniuses that capped wheel nuts with thin aluminum caps that stripped easily under impact drive pressure. The same guys who invented the 754 points inspection that could be summed up by 9 maintenance steps.

305

So I asked. Have you ever opened the hood or the trunk before in your life?

No

I smiled, raise an eyebrow. This is getting better and better.

Obviously no, now let's open the hood so we can demystify the beast. So, pop, here it is, the magnificent Ford 2.3 in all of its splendor. First, oil, oil dipstick to check the oil and well change it. Below there is the oil filter that I will replace. There is the battery. I will check if it is eroded. Spark plugs and cable, I'll spray WD40 or silicone. They seem humid. Now, Windshield washer, low I could see, I will add some antifreeze in this container. Lift it up, Check the grease hubs and verify if the belts have to be changed or just tightened up. If there is anything else, I'll take care of it, no sweat. Here are most of the points and remember, it's a machine, it holds no grudge against you. Still, you can take it to see road movies at the Drive In, they seem to appreciate that. Love Bug or Vanishing Point, but be careful. Try to avoid affluent shopping malls or Mercedes. They talk to one another and gang up on you after and want a garage, a block heater, frequent wash, Turtle Wax, new sets of tires more often and finally, premium unleaded only. As if they were all turbo performance imports?

There it was. Light at the end of the tunnel, The magic of empowerment. You are not alone in this thing. You understand now. You can do it all yourself. You feel good, this is at the limit of erotism. Given a piece of chocolate, it could have been as powerful as sex. Major crisis avoided. It all made sense. A bit of skills, tool and manual work and of explaining. She dropped the heavy cross she was carrying, had light in her eyes and as recommended went for a long walk and a coffee. Mr. Good wrench saved the world and the December fat snowflakes light snow may pave the way for some a little more romantic. Yes, you can hear the theme of the Love Boat here ! There are no mechanics on the Love Boat, nor are there Bus Drivers in the Village People but maybe I could invite her to the Peel Pub? The hell with the Village People.

As I started the tune up and realized that this car is the same model as those we maintained for the utility company. Gas Metro. Same year, I had an account number for Gas Met, so I ordered a few gizmos and filters and installed them on Heidi's Pro Bono. She must have been a good customer of Gas Metro. Here is a form of dividends. Since it was my last evening or about working there, well, I looked at those 4-season tires. 4-season tires cannot exist in Canada. It's a heresy. We have winters that require winter tires, and this is all there is to know and say on the matter.

Case closed. Somehow, there were 4 of them on the lift working bay next to mine. They were Pirelli's winter branded winter guard II with a Snowman pushing a plow engraved on the side. The real deal. Top hat, carrot nose, and coal buttons. 165R13. Grabbed 4 bags, Bagged the tires and put them in the trunk. I went after to the maintenance counter to see the fat Greek dude with his golden tooth and counterfeit Gucci watch, and borrowed the fat black rubber stamp. Tires in the Trunk.

Took the bill, initial it and stumped the rubber stamp. Job done and a note, should see the customer to explain maintenance. I may have pushed the concept of the, Random Act of Kindness a bit but it felt good. The joy of giving.

Heidi came 1 hour later to see me totting a box of chocolate. A smile, a wink. Thank you for helping me with the car. Godiva's. She had appreciated the way I handled her car problems and believed, by the glance, that she could see underneath the dirty overall that there could be, after a long scrub bath, an interesting naked man. A bit like that dogs that followed you home. I liked her too but I was in no position to go over small talk besides Mr. Good wrench advises type of conversation. I was looking for an angle, but could not figure one out. As she picked up her keys, I explained to her that the thing should work better, that she doesn't have to worry and that she should have winter tires installed. Just as the one in the trunk as I put my greasy thumb on the invoice and on the maintenance manual. She did not get it right away for the tires, but as for the glove compartment, she had never been to the trunk of her car either.

21:00 hrs, the garage closes, we all pick up our tools, clean them and stack them in the tool box. So guys washed the orange concrete floor with a rubber hose. It's winter, it snows angel feather flakes outside and Ste-Catherine street takes in winter postcard pose, the neon lights are dimming and out. One by one. No wind. The place is now closed and Heidi drives away in her car, liberated, smiling and waving as this older mechanics winks at me saying, I think she likes you. As I walked down the Cath's with a box of Godiva under my arm, Walkman came that Francoise Hardy tunes about, discovery, friendship, faith, and karma.

> *Beaucoup de mes amis sont venus des nuages*
> *Avec soleil et pluie comme simples bagages*
> *Ils ont fait la saison des amitiés sincères*
> *La plus belle saison des quatre de la Terre*
>
> *Francoise Hardy*

With the sun, and the rain, (and those angels' feather snow) as only luggage. I felt wholesome and satisfied.

Later on, back home further west in NDG, after a good hot shower and a coffee I opened the TeeVee to watch Late Night with David Letterman and decide to pick one of those rich and luscious Godiva chocolates. Letterman and a good old Edward G Robinson movie will be just fine to unwind. This person undeniably knows her chocolate, I thought. Besides the ribbon, nothing else held the box and lid together. No shrink wrap but, no Godiva, does not seal boxes with shrink wrap anyway.

So, I opened the box and checked the chocolate map to avoid the strawberry mousse one. On the cover of the box were handwritten and signed. Merci, pour tout, I am Heidi, Call me. Heidi and there were the magical 7 numbers. 848-xxxx.

I called. The beginning of something new.

Gas Metro absorbed the loss and an accounting computer system still try to figure out where those 4 Pirelli 165R13. You know, the one with a Snowman pushing a Plow. The
one with a pipe, a top hat, a carrot nose, a scarf, and coal buttons. The real deal. Rumor has it that they have left for Brazil.

There were some dates with Heidi but it could not work out as per I was too stupid to seize a great life opportunity. Once more. See, I am honest about it. I met her many years later as she was catching the 80 Park South on a cold, sunny February morning. Was it in Felix the cat comics that there was a professor Nutty Nut Meg. Yeap in Felix the Cat. The professor had invented a device to auto-kick his ass pulling a rope. I should have ordered one somewhere, to let such beautiful people slip away from my life.

I had just crossed Cabot square. The infamous Atwater Metro station area. Man, is this place going down. Red was there in the Ontario bus loading zone but he was sleeping. I waived hand, He was gone. Asleep, resting behind the wheel. I wanted to tell him about the Indian restaurant in Park Ex. The 100% good food. In God, we trust. It is 100% Good Food. I had to let him know.

For me, this is the last stretch of the week. Once I hit Guy Concordia station, I am off. 813, In Transit and back to the division. The day started at 6:20. It's evening and I am still on the road.

Behind the wheel for the last 7 hours, up and down the route, and coming up with memories from High School, or is it the encounter with Giovanni Caboto's Monument at Atwater square that triggered those memories, Nonetheless.

One girl in High School called me Giovanni because of Cabotto. Giovanni Cabotto. A history class hero. John Cabot. She was a special friend, let's say.

Pokey (as the name of Gumbie's horse) was this private nun ran Catholic school student who had been transferred to Public High for the last High School year. Was it her laugh or her wooden clog that justified the name of a clay horse, I can't remember but. She was good-looking, a sex Goddess body had a good twister sense of humor and I guess that her skills for the sexual thing as well and an insatiable appetite for the thing may have contributed to her trouble at her former college ran by nuns. She was this live version of Jessica Rabbit. Giovanni Cabotto. And there he stands, in the middle of Cabot square. As I once said to one of my somehow rowdy teenage female client: Is your mother dressing you exclusively at Sex Shops ?

She was also hanging out with people that we could qualify as Sugar Daddies since while we were riding motobecane mopeds, well, those guys were in Cady's and Corvettes. They all had mustache too. So be it. She was a friend. A person avoided by most at school because of a certain reputation, but me, I did not care. Every once in a while, we ditched school and had a walk to the mall. Pokey at 16 years old was wearing a twist and stiletto at school.

We went for coffee and to Sears (store cafeteria) at the mall. . Yeap Sears, Eaton's was not opened then and Simmons was in an old town. Sears Bunns coffee makers and Sterling Coffee on Muzak mall music. When I did not know what to wear or buy, she showed me stuff, Stuff that would be attractive to the other gender but I was a bit shy then. It did not last long.

And the time to hit the work market came. High School was over and I just could not see anywhere I'd go but the Army. I had to give it a try. I could hear the Desert Rats theme in my head as this safe space song or the Colonel Bogeys whistling march. I was painted khaki ! Born April the 17th.

From the time I had my first Tonka jeep I have been mesmerized by all big green vehicles, from jeep, trucks, half tracks, tanks. I had to drive those machines so I joined the Army, well, Reserve forces. They worked on 6 months contracts, which allowed me the flexibility to surf the khaki wave and leave when desired. Yet, now and then there was a be all that you can be offered on the table to join the permanent forces. I did not know what I wanted to do with my life and still, 50 years later, I still don't know. I know this is embarrassing but yet, it never exactly prevented me from doing anything. All options had always been opened and living to learn is the best school.

Note: I always envied those that knew day one what they wanted to do with their lives. Day one, as I never had a clue. I could not go onto plan B as I never actually a plan A. My mind has always been into the mode Z plan, I guess. I am from the crowd that drives on what they don't want by default filter. It makes it very hard to focus on specifics. Makes life a bit on the unsecured side.

I had been in uniform for 3 years and I ended up with a civil servant type of job but in a uniform and with bizarre traditions. Dangerous eating and drinking habits, It took me nowhere intellectually nor spiritually speaking. It felt more like the relationship Mannix held with Peggy or Dr. Marcus Welby with Consuela. Office work. Emptiness. Abysmal emptiness. Mannix was a natural hero. He carried criminal interview while Gogo dancing with hippies chicks. He had a Dark Blue fortrel blazer and drove a convertible in the swinging 60s Frisco.

He could get into bad fight to ended up with a simple band-aid of the forehead and could ask his secretary, Peggy, for a coffee without having the whole civic right movement on his asses and the EPA for throwing coffee with creamer in the sink. He was the Man X of the 1960s. Mannix became than my hero.

Mannix was the answer.

Mannix and the Jazzy show theme. Mannix, introducing Gail Fisher as Peggy. Mannix and this Piano bar solo at the end of the theme. But in those days, the musical theme honestly introduced the substance of the show. Barney Miller had the amazing Sax solo, I dream of Jinny, this Eli Fabricant bouncy tune and later, Hill street Blues a electric piano proper to the 1980s. The themes setted the audience into the mood of the show.

Yeap, Mannix was the answer ! I had evolved from Charlie Gordon, (Cliff Robertson) to Joe Mannix. Considerable step here. I had to become a Mannix.

Mannix was no military man. Damn and re damn.

As per the military mess tradition. In case of doubts or existential crisis, a beer is always the beginning of a reflection. Maybe I should, in fact, quit the Force so I went to the usual place, at the pub, the Montcalm and sat at the bar in an era before the 24hrs news channel, there was a TV and reruns of the Ronald Reagan assassination attempts. It was between the Reagan and the Lennon assassination if you want a time frame.

The event becomes a timeframe. The where anywhere happens Chronicle. Makes you wonder : where it is that in the continuum of life you started lying to yourself, and when was it that on the same vectorial line you realized it.

In the daytime, the shopping mall type pub looked like a still life of social misfits. Those, Mr. Snow, Kawa and Ben No were still there. Hanging at the bar, year after year. A bit like those billiard balls that have stayed in the middle of the table after the triangle break. The white ball hits the triangle, as most balls got displaced by destiny to karma pockets. Life then pockets you on events. Things happen. The very worst thing that could happen to you is nothing. Nothing ever happening to you as per I guess: Mr. Snow, Kawa and Ben No. They are the balls left on billiards felt of life. They got snookered by life.

Mr. Snow got his name with his pale face and dark eyes. A snowman. He looked like a granita making toy from the Christmas Sears Catalog. A snowman figure with an ice grinder to make slush. Snow looked like the toys. Many years later, he still looked like a Snowman but doesn't grind ice anymore, he sniffs it. Hence, Snow adapted. Alias Hank for the close friend as per Hank Snow. Kawa? Damn Kawa. Short, stubby man with one eyebrow. No gap between the eyes. Kawa had his name as he could scream like a racer bike passing 6 gears on a quarter mile. Impressive indeed. As far as Ben No is concerned: it is his real name. No. And his life has been a succession of No. No this, No that, No there. Nothing ever happened. As the Pub closed ages ago, I would believe it is now a drugstore and those guys who used to hang at the bar are now showing at the prescription counter for their weekly dosage of small white pills. I must presume that the prescription counter stands where the corner bar used to stand. Nothing actually moves in this universe. It all may relate to Mishio Kaku string theory.

Pokey ran into me at the pub. Being at the Military base and engaging in Tourism and Convention, I became an interesting potential sales representative for her and her portfolio. I was shopping this Mannix blue sport jacket in my mind.

She knew about my career whereabouts.

As she said, I knew you were here, I saw your, in desperate need for paint, Mercury Capri in the parking lot. The mall lot, in front of this massive Steinberg's Grocery store. For from Mannix convertible Cuda. Yes, Steinbergs, where my mom did groceries and bought those boxes of milfoys.

We crossed each other here and there in town but she always seemed to be dealing into something and we were not exactly dealing with the same crowd. She always waved, sent a kiss or a wink at me. She was still a friend, A friend in latex and stiletto, but a friend. The Montcalm, as there were many in the days, was a shopping Mall type of pub. Raving at night, but a quiet place in daytime. Business lunch. Shoppers dinners and Disco Night for 9 PM to 1 AM. A money printing machine.

She became a Madame. World's oldest trade. She was particularly gifted, I guess. If you enjoy what you are doing, you will not have worked a single day of your life. May have been true for her but she must have had her not so enjoyable spots too.

A young but proficient one, She rubbed her boobs on my shoulder plates and whispered my ear;

Do you still have intense sexual dreams about me?

Wow, Sheba queen of the jungle, How are you !

Doing great good-looking. My next them party is Mata Hari, sinful spy of sex. My Sheba Queen of the Jungle was 3 years ago. I didn't see you there !

We missed you at the Queen of the Jungle Party. We did not know about the Pith Helmet but I'll sure take a few tickets for your next event. Mata Hari, you said ?

Hence, we ended up at the A&W at Place Quatres Bourgeois,

I guess you also missed my latex night ?

I guess,

Is there anything this Sex Goddess I can do for you or to you?

Maybe, you may be able to help me on that one.

Somehow, as I mentioned that the men of the army unit trusted me to throw a party (I had connections in the convention and tour and travel crowd and knew how to spin a good one) I hated it because that always ended up the same way. No women, (but...) and everyone was getting drunk to coma or death in stupid drinking rituals and games. Every time we had to deal with a deep psychosis, a bad trip, car accident or someone smashing a car in Big Bertha. The German cannon seized in WW1, war memorial at the gate of the base at the road fork. Hospital job and explanations to the Military Police.

Then came the $100 question. Drum rolls !

Do the boys have cash available. I mean some serious money here.

Yes, they do. (once a week on Friday, the paymaster nicknamed Fitzhugh walked through the military base with a suitcase full of money. Hence, the nickname Fitzhugh- from Land of the giant)

Do you still have that ugly rusty red scooter to run around in a cloud of smoke

Nah, I had to scrap the Lambretta a few years ago to buy an ugly car.

Remember Jennifer from the Jeans store

Pokey, a dead man, would remember Jennifer from the Jeans store. Was she ever sexy. She was Penthouse sexy.

She really had the hots for you when you were riding this thing around. She thought that was so sexy that she almost had to confess her sexual impulse to a priest but you never took her for a ride. She wanted to eat you alive. You really missed on that one.

Wot !!! Again a wot moment, is more than a what moment and it comes with some Johnny Cash music.

Nice to know. Now I know that I am fucked. Once I'll show up to heaven gates, I may have very difficult question to answer as per: Why didn't you offer this lovely person a ride on your Lambretta. The answer: because I did not have a spare helmet, won't save my ass from being sent to hell or back on earth as a Kawa character. One more bad comment in my life file.

And !

She made 2 + 2 on my organized party event as she sent some of her workers to the scene to break the boredom and kick off the party. It became a memorable one at the old armory. It got me in trouble, but nobody could prove anything, The famous hearsay thing. And so, I could write on my Resume that I have been, once, Proxenete of the day. My social theory worked. It had been a very civilized party. Everyone enjoyed. Some more than others. No trauma, no psychosis, no accident and the integrity of Big Bertha has been preserved. I still wait for the Nobel Prize nomination.

You remember my motto, she said !

Let's see: hum ! Sex appeals, Give generously

Exactly it ,Good looking: Sex appeals, Give generously !

35 years later, I received a call from the unit for an anniversary gala of the actual and former members of my former unit. The centennial anniversary of the unit, which had changed name a few time since 1914. We are the unit that had sent the military sapper who, in the movie, blew up the Bridge on the Kwai river. Dirk Bogart was really pissed. They had a note as per, I knew how to organize this type of event, but the liaison officer who was not even born when I organized this last feast did not know the whole story. He asked for help. I laughed but declined the offer. There must have been a post-it on my personnel file at the unit.

Yeap, the flat black paint. My 1973 Capri, originally British Green racing on rust, suddenly became flat black. Flat black as the Camo black used to paint armored vehicle on the base as per.... Someone's order. Not only was it flat black as Mel Gibson's interceptor car in Mad Max was mine also invisible to spies satellite as it reflected waves. From space, it could be confounded for a piece of wood.

The background of this astonishing technical achievement is this.

In the late 1970s, early 80.s. The Ruskie intended to invade Europe. In those days, they were the Soviet Union. As we knew that the military of many satellite countries would give up fast the fight to become western aligned countries, we also knew that they had the Russian armored division to push them from behind. As per our Guys from Military Intelligence... Came, did speeches, showed us maps, introduced new anti tanks weapons besides the girls from the Infantry unit next door that could have killed one bare hand. Just like in the Atom ants cartoons teaser.

I was more into the femininity of Pokey, that of those weekend warriors. Not that the Armed Forces do not carry their share of fatal beauties, yes, Penthouse even made a few specials about women in the Marines, but not at the Infantry unit next door. I believe that Tourism Germany might have been behind the seasonal fall panic episode as the NATO Reforgers military exercise unfolded and brought to Germany 40,000 soldiers, young, paid and ready to party. Good money for Oktoberfest. Sure, beat a World-Class event and no, soldier won't wear Titleist visors.

On the ground level we did not take this threat exactly seriously until September 1st, 1983 when the level of threat stepped up dramatically. Someone in South Korea did not take its topography lesson seriously. Panic last a few months and it calms down.

Panic is what keeps the NATO money mill churning of a military base functioning. NATO should be like an insurance policy trying to prevent war, but no. No in fact, they are always for new business ventures. A scuffle, a conflict, a peace mission, a whatever. The Warsaw pact had no more intention of invading Europe in 1980 than it does today. Imagine, the Club Med they maintain in Europe. Peace is the threat to them, not the Ruskie. That said, I guess that even the Soviets top brass had their social club and benefits in Eastern Germany or in Hungary. The Forces have to keep young men, at their best hormonal age busy, out of trouble, show some results to the taxpayers and well art and Play Dough cannot be part of the scheme.

Every morning, the Commanding Officer of a military base has this puzzle. How do I keep 5000 soldiers busy, out of trouble and minimize the cost because the military hardware is expensive? The new tech stuff, like satellite camo, is costly.

Every morning, the great helmsman of China has to keep 1.4 billion people busy and fed. Every morning, millions of faithful are awaiting the arrival of a messiah, fearful because they know he'll be pissed by what we have done to our world. This may explain why I never liked mornings.

Military base. Infantry. The term Infantry contains the term Infants. Go figure.

At lunch hour at the men's mess hall, 2000 or so men were in line for lunch. Army and Navy cooks and few civilian workers. Cafeteria style but, as anything else, made in large quantities it never tastes delicious. It is the best quality, but cooked in vats. On Friday, during lobster season, the military offered us the Surf and Turf special. I remember the plock sound of the spud ice cream spoon hitting the plastic plate every day at the same hour as the tattooed Navy cook asked, one or two boobs. The same plock sound on the same plate that resonated on those Russian soldiers on the other side of the world. Trained to kill, as us, Kill time. As per my Moldovar friend who was for the Russian Army then. Their plates were in Lomonosov Ceramics. A better plock. A classier one.

Yet, the Soviets tanks build up was as massive as all the cars in the lot at Sears days on Saturday morning. Customers at Sears days were also in for a kill. They had them all piled up on the borders of Germany and Poland, and they had this new model with extra armor and the porcelain shell to protect from direct hit and save the crew from the shock. They had those pop out turret to save the crew from the shock or the air blast of a direct hit. Imagine, those lousy red had a special thought about saving the crew. We did not!

Eventually, Canada had to defend or hold the fort in Finland or Norway. No wonder why any other NATO nation declined this assignation. It sucked. The cold places and I hate winter warfare since the food is always cold and lousy and gives you the thing that you undeniably don't feel like handling in winter wind with hygienic paper in your hand at -35. The hygienic paper also has a NATO number. Cold is the way God tells you not to go there. Cold is a relentless enemy.

It never gives up, it jams all rolling equipment and makes maneuvers almost impossible. Cold doesn't rhyme with camping. Cold makes war impossible. It is a peace factor. Maybe this is why the term Cold War comes from.

When someone at NATO meeting said:

OK, who is volunteer to insure the defense of Norway and Finland some top brass pinhead in a dark cacciatore green uniform raise his hand and claimed!

Canada volunteers!

No, they haven't taught the pinhead at the Royal Military College that, those were cold countries and troop do not like cold countries. War doesn't like cold. Cyprus, how about Cyprus.

Why not Germany, at least you can go out? We are familiar with the place. We've been there twice and still have some military base there ? What about this army that conquered the best spots in the World? The ever so ferocious Club Median and their army in Hawaiian shirts. I believe that they are way more dangerous to our way of living than the Ruskie as they do nothing all day and they pay stuff with beads, not unlike our politicians at the everlasting all-you-can-eat buffet in Ottawa.

And came.

Sept 1st 1983. The KAL flight 007 incident over the Sakhalin island. Now to introduce that there is a bit of topography to understand as it had been taught to us at the military bootcamp in the 1970s. So, there we go. The regular pals, me, duck and touch turtle in a military tent in the middle of a field surrounded by swamps. A big tent with tables used as a classroom with chairs tables and board. Hot, humid, the stench of waxed cotton and flies. A good military base setting. I thought those were supposed to be summer vacation from class, but remember, good old Colonel Whitelaw has to keep us busy from dusk to dawn and even more with night runs. Like the great Helmsman or the commander of the base or the captain of an aircraft carrier. Like a kindergarten teacher. So, there we were!

When was the last time this country got involved into something nasty and bad? U.N. job !

Korea I guess

So, we have uniforms from the Korean war, I believe.

My mom had pictures from her brother Phil at the Korean war wearing one of those uniform. Phil became the staff sergeant of the Canadian 1st Airborne Regt and was nicknamed the Tasmania devil.

Yeap, but in the summer it beats the WWI wool battledress, I guess.

Looking pale this morning, Touch!

I and Morenz were hanging by the messhall after breakfast, smoking a cigarette and sipping coffee, as we got caught in the DDT fumes from the ¾ ton. Dodge M37 truck.

Love the smell of DDT in the Morning.

Early morning, that Korean war era truck was smoking the whole military camp. Thick, poisonous smoke. Sometimes they even ran the truck while the troop were in platoon walk, Physical Training or on the holy land of the Parade Square. I also had a teacher at primary school coming from the Asbestos mining region. She brought to school Asbestos powder in 50lbs crates. Once mixed with water it became a cheap form of deadly Play Dough or clay but we did not know it was cancerigenous. Neither did she, I guess The age of health innocence.

And we were all wondering why our parents sent us to that army summer camp rather than the one ran by the priest a few miles from here where the rich kids were sailing, golfing, swimming all day.

Rumor had it that, by night, they gathered around a camp fire, toasted Marshmallow while good-looking Christian chicks like the one in the Juicy Fruit commercial was out playing guitar and singing. Christian anthems, I guess, but at least they had the Juicy Fruit chick. For us, it was fire picket at night and keep an eye open, for the black bears spotted in the area. Later on, in life, we heard that Catholic priest dressed in black were more dangerous than black bear for teenage boys. It was not the chick from the Juicy Fruit commercial that tried to sneak into the sleeping bag at night.

We did not have that worry. Parent had to pay for the fun camps, we had a pay bonus for attending ours. Lord Strathcona's fund gave us $100 bonus for 6 weeks of toil. They played safe and saved money. As in the Johnny Cash song, a boy called Sue, our parents threw us in the strange disciplinary arena to make us tough as nails. I must admit that it worked. No hard feeling, and we eventually caught up with the Juicy Fruit girls for more than Christian anthem around a campfire under the eager eyes of priest monitor.

Yet, we have built this friendship that had last for beyond 40 years. This famous Esprit de Corps.

So, it was the topography class and how to use a compass properly. Use a compass and read a military map. The class was taught by the sergeant that spoke just like a broken AM radio, but knew his stuff. There is your standard military map. Green, gray, yellow. Red line for elevation, blue water, railways, roads, swamps and all was well indicated if you knew how to read it. Ok, guys, we are in business, but for one thing. One damn important thing. The magnetic North. Yes, the magnetic north deviates of dismal degrees every year, so! So, you have to adjust your compass to the age of the used map and it is a simple calculation but it is necessary. We did and never ended up in: A. The swamps. B. the Local turkey farms of C. The Local Hells Angels land. D. Over Russian Airspace. We were skilled. We knew our way around way before the GPS device and know how to read a paper map. Useful skill. Useful in tourism too.

As for the KAL flight 007, taken down by the Soviet Air Force on September 1st 1983, the magnetic north adjustment on the flight plan seems to have been estimated properly. We are talking about a Boeing 747 but, if not fed properly, the navigation guidance system may deviate from its course and end up, whether at the turkey farm, in Tewksbury or over Soviet secret Navy base in the middle of a cold war. It ended up oversensitive Soviet Airspace while the flight crew had over 18 hours riding this plane. They may not have been at their best, either.

The story has it that Soviet Sukhoi SU 15 interceptor trailed the plane. Then sent warning shot with tracer. Then sent an international type message as you are violating Soviet Airspace, change course or follow us escorted to the next military airport.

Story has it that the plane slowed down to make an early approach to South Korea, as it had been mistaken by the Soviet Air Command as a form of evasive action. Someone in the chain of command got upset, scared or obeyed the book and ordered it taken down. We have a family story with evasive actions indeed.

Those were the last official word of the Russian pilot on this chase. Not exactly edifying:

U menya tut net vizuala. Eto der'movoye shou. !!

It's in Russian and it does not mean have a nice day.

For decades, Military bases in Europe were in the watchful eye, business as usual mode as both camps piled up weapons without clear intentions of making a move and playing the war games on the taxpayer's tab, but in after the Sakhalin island incident, the mood changed. The days of the easy-going NATO Club Med bases were over. Party was over. At least for a few months.

"All that we had in Europe was collapsible and could be dismantled and shipped within 48 hours in case of land invasion. Bases, infra, equipment, Now the Ruskie made inventories of our forces on the ground, spying with satellites or disguised as Austrian tourists toting Leica cameras driving around Lahr and Baden in orange, old Opel cars or Trabant. Permission had been given to moon them, yet some guys could not make the difference between a VW Dasher and an Opel. The locals were not pleased"

Now, since we could not exactly oppose on the ground because that was way too massive and the idea of nuking it all seemed to be a bit stupid (but then again). Hasn't Westmoreland ever stated that they had to destroy a village to save it. Now, the brilliant plan was to make our inventory of armored and other vehicles invisible to satellites or to Trabis. The big bluff. Rumor had it that they had the Neutron bomb that killed all living things, but not the infrastructure. To that avail, the Pointer Sisters responded by the Neutron Dance. To make a story short, we started the ball with the W66 Sprint and came the Nike X and I know it sounds like the inventory of a Foot Locker sneakers shop. The Warsaw pact responded with the A-135S, the 53T6 and came the W70, the MGM52 and the W703, the WD40 and the Jig-a-loo when the nuts were stuck. In 1992, they scrapped it all, with the billions invested into the program. With that type of dough we could have built a bullet train from coast to coast and stopped being silly stupid getting caught in traffic on the ways to the airport.

The airport security, The airport mall and the airport food. History teaches that we did not have to invest into useless weaponry to impress the Ruskie. One of the reasons why the Ruskie never attempted to move on in North America is the precise fact that there were no bullet trains and as an invader, they did not feel like going through the airport routine. All that said. We had to pretend to have 10 times more equipment on the ground.

I could only guess the guys for Dupont, the DND, or Armor All came up with this idea. A paint coating that would make our equipment invisible to satellites and that would cost an arm and a leg to the taxpayers. The good old NATO gimmick. The useless but costly spec sheet.

So, they did, and all the equipment had to be painted according to a strict painting scheme with the new stuff. But a gallon of the new stuff could be traded inside for 2 cases of instant coffee, or a case of wool socks, or 3 pairs of combat boots non punched. (non punched combat boots could be traded over and over again for as long as you knew someone in the system).

Some said that waves could bounce on them, well, it could be invisible to radars. I had to try that out and well, in the Mad Max days, the concept of a flat black car was socially acceptable to those, like me, who enjoyed The Clash or the Smith or the Sex Pistols. Nowadays, kids fork a lot of money for those flat black AMG Benz as I was the original guy with a flat black European coupe and mine, mine was invisible to satellites.

Hence, the story of the Black 1973 Capri. I had this assignment at the mess hall and could reroute cases of Taster Choice coffee NATO number XYZ, in exchange for a few gallons of that black paint. So, I did.

It has been proposed that a certain hi pitch wavelength could crack the porcelain liner of the T. tank, just like the music of Captain and Tennille or Minnie Ripperton, but that has not been proven and have the duo playing keyboard in the middle of a Cartophen patch by Stuttgart, did not seem appealing nor to the Captain, nor to Tennille nor to Minnie and not to NATO. The DND doesn't like box people, withstanding that they are usually the one that wins war. My old man had the same problem with the RAF 75 years before with the extra armor on sensitive mechanism on British bombers.

Thinking outside the box is a form of evasive action, so as trying to save your ass on a daily basis. Evasive action has to become a reflex. A life reflex whether you are in the military or civilian. It has to be practiced every day.

Wars might be fought with weapons, but they are won by men. It is the spirit of the men who leads that gains the victory. (George Patton).

The land of evasive actions.

That brings me back to the evasive action story. Evasive actions as this war prisoner commandment, From day 1, as a war prisoner all that you have to do is to try to escape. I believe that the first commandment of life should be to attempt to escape. To attempt to escape age. Age that sounds like a cage. Disobey nature and time. Disobedience is the cornerstone of freedom and freedom is what all humans strive for, so one has to learn how to disobey.

My old man was an outside the box man. After a few bombing missions over occupied Europe, he found out that the beloved RAF or RCAF took all available metal sheet to fix holes in the fuselage of a plane that could still be airworthy as to make it showroom presentable and hesitate on extra armor on more sensitive parts of the plane. Engine, cockpit, hydraulics, and those places that could get a plane down as it could fly, demonstration made, with many punches in the fuselage. After all, a bombing mission was not a socialite dog show.

It has to fly by night and carry many tons of bombs, a load of fuel and a 7 men crew back and forth. The RAF did not see it that way. Fact of the matter in their book... is that if the planes were back from mission looking like spaghetti strainers it is the pilot faults, no matter, the darkness of the moonless night in fat black planes tight formation, had to apply the principle of evasive actions. Evasive action with a bomber? Employers always blame the driver or the operator for damages. Always the same blame. Evasive action as this reflex we should all have right at birth.

Tholthorpe, Yorkshire (land of God as per the British) somewhere in summer 1944.

Man, the grass is wet. We have to walk to those plane in wet grass or take a bicycle. Damn England. Food is lousy, women aren't good-looking. Check, the American pilot all have Jeeps, we have bicycles and they have two tones uniforms. Check ours?

Yes, but they fly bombing mission by days and they have the Luftwaffe on their ass, we don't.

Right, still, our shoes will be wet all day.

RAF, RCAF, 6th Bomber groups airbases. 4 engines bomber took off from the field. No paved landing or take off strip. On the grass,

It was a gray, pinkish day in the Yorkshire. Tholtorpe RAF base. Summer day but graying with shades of purple when my old man's crew had to take off for evasive action drills. The old man, then in his 20s, was not impressed. He had delivered the load at the Foret d'Eawy in France the night before, and the return had not been smooth sailing. The crew had been at it 20 sometimes and were very confident and tightly knitted group. Cocky, sure, why not. They have lost two gunners in action. Two guys, reservists, that joined the crew for a mission, did not like the ambiance on board, and chose to switch crew. Both went MIA the next mission. Maybe they should have stuck to the original plan and fly with the one the nicknamed Jock, the boomerang. There is a picture in my father's BW wartime photo album of him and the 2 gunners at parachute distribution. Last picture of this poor soul. Reminder of the life choices one make.

And so, they went on an Evasive Action drill. As if anything could be said or taught anymore. As if they could be scared. As if they had anything else in mind but getting those 12 missing points on the scorecard and going home. They flew that huge 4 engine, flat black bomber in the morning light with an AIr Marshal or a Commodore or a whatever on their tail in a state-of-the-art fighter plane.

A Spitfire MK IV or some buzzing around and twirling around, screaming on the radio: Evasive action !!! There wasn't much you could do in a gunnerless bomber against a state-of-the-art fighter. They had to play the sinister comedy of a bomber trying to escape fire from a fighter, and the guys were annoyed and cynical...

As they had watched the weather forecast before leaving for the drill, the Radio Operator noticed that there could be a massive patch of clouds at accessible or limited altitude to take cover, which was against all rules of the war games. Rules were meant to be bent, or weren't they? He also had this English lesson at primary school. Seems to be the way the system builds the rebels of society. Seems to run in the family.

And so they were. Chased by an aristocrat "Limey inbred" in his state-of-the-art Spitfire, screaming to use Evasive Action as they spotted the patch of cloud. Hum, patch of cloud ahead, tempting but too high and would require the use of the emergency Supercharger on the 4 Bristol's Hercules radial engine to get to those clouds. That was too tempting and a way to get rid of the pinhead on their tail. So, they did, Jock, (my old man) cranked up the supercharger and climbed to the cloud patch screaming on the radio, I am evading, I am evading, now try to find me. Yes, they did regain their freedom. Embarrassing, a top-level officer of the RAF. They flew carefree into the clouds. Tried the one time only using of a supercharger. They were momentarily out of that war. The plane of fools. Now, the radio telecoms system and the PA were hooked together so as they escaped to the cloud, one of the crew exclaimed: So take this limey to (used the 4-letter word in its verbative form) off.

They all won 2 weeks all-inclusive sejour at Sheffield disciplinary barracks. Yet, they would not have missed the opportunity to even the score with the top brass. I saw the same guys coming into my home, 40 years later, still laughing about it. It became a concept to me. A vision of a crew of fly boys in the prime of their youth, flying in memories for eternity. The running joke of the anecdote is that it was the only Limey of the Crew that called the other one a Limey. Jenkins, Ken Jenkins with his Cockney accent. The others were all Canadians.

There is the lesson about the freedom of disobedience and how about exploring the real meaning of leadership because, accordingly, a true leader should disobey once in a while. Leadership is an art. As every art, it could not be taught. Whether you have it or you don't, it cannot be properly instilled. There are those leadership camps or school or training but it is an art and art is a form of rebellion.

Hey Ken? (Jenkins, the only Brit in the crew)

What ?

Do Brits know that there are also good cuts of meat in a beef. Because since we are in England, all that we eat are meat pies or kidney or tripped. What happens to the good part ? They go to the American or the Royals. Milk, always and only powdered milk?

Sure thing, Gentlemen, they don't go to Sheffield!

While the old man was on tour in Tholtorpe, England, a young woman working as a mechanic visited the base and shook hand with most of the volunteer Canucks present on the base. Protocol's visit from the Royals. She was a 17 years old Princess dressed in REMI overall. Princess Elisabeth became Queen of England, The rest is history. Leadership we said.

Life has to keep going so I tried tourism for a while. A few years. It was fun. Tour guide, or tour director or gofer.

Over and above guiding all summer on European travelers to America, from April to October non-stop and there were many contracts, I toured old cities, worked on ski trips, French Immersion tours, band festivals and worked, in the winter, as a Deejay on Crescent St. Once your name is in circuit you end up being just like a sock in a dryer, bouncing.

I took a tour director contract gig for this company in Philadelphia that organized ski trips and Band Festivals. A regular contract company led by Pol who was known to wear matching color sweat suits, pants and shirt, The Golden girls experience. The concept was easy, the ski trips were designed so that skiers binged into apres ski parties so they get too hungover to hit the slopes the morning after and soo, our job was to take them out. Their profit was made on breakage. We were the ski instructors and the MC's.

Pol also had volunteer staff traveling with the group and helping us out with the paperwork and coordination on site. Tour escorts or organizers. This is how I met Zeta.

Zeta !

In the land of snow Bunnies, Hot-Dog the Movie and Wayne Wong appeared Zeta.

She often came with ski tours, but was the discrete type. She was from the Philly area and almost every two week she came with a tour. A few busloads. Every two week or so she forgot her ski equipment at the local office to come back up north to recuperate it. That was her official story. She was on a sabbatical type of leisure time between 2 PhD degrees and liked hanging around with the ski bums. She had that nostalgic early Liz Taylor look, A bit withdrawn and discrete. Andrea from Philly or Bala. One late afternoon, back from the mountain, we had a hotel lobby chat and decided to go downstairs to the bar for a coffee. Every good thing in life starts with a coffee. Witty, funny, brilliant. In the land of snow bunnies, she stood apart. A dry, dark, swift sense of humor. She was everything I was not, namely with a precise aim in life, while I was more into trying it all out until I find my way or let's see where life will take you next. Hungarian. She spoke Hungarian and this is sexy. As most Slavic languages, I'd say.

Since it was a Saturday, we were in the Grande Allee part of the city and the place was lively. We convened to meet later for a drink, a date, on the Grande Allee at this cozy bar with a glass house and a fireplace. Romantic place. Yet, I had to go home to the burbs, change, shave, dress and all by city bus and in those days, city buses alone were an adventure. So, there it is, hi mom, hi dad, let's have dinner, shower, Irish Spring, I have a date tonight, she is nice. My mom loved to see me happy and elated and always had this caring look. My dad was always puzzled at the number of dates I had but never settled down just like for the jobs but he knew that I was one of a kind and fortunately for him, his 3 other boys were more stable. Predictable as I was not.

As I walked out the door to catch the very elusive bus no 14 back to old city, he said:

You cannot go out dressed like that with a ski jacket ! Obviously, it swore on the concept or to make it simple, you can't go on a date looking like shit. Yes, it did look like.

I did dress like a gentleman for the occasion. Dressed pants, white shirt, tie, Tweed blazer. Rare occurrence, but I did. I made my research on that Esquire special issue book, The Gentleman's wardrobe, 1958. But, I did not have the dressed winter coat.

The ski jacket was the only winter coat I had and it was an ugly member only thing. It was also burgundy. I bought burgundy ski jacket at Sears, I believe? So, he went to the cloak room and extended me his wool long coat black winter coat and added, now you look like a man. " The man had been a RCAF officer, an outstanding Stock Broker and had a successful career but was out on his luck in the 1980s. He knew how to dress and address and stand. Basically, I had no taste nor dressing skills. I also got influenced by this commercial on TeeVee with an Irishman cutting a bar of soap with a buck knife. Yes, there is green Irish Green perfume right to the core of the soap.

I took time to look myself in a mirror and hell, that looked good.

Damn, he was right, this coat suited me just fine and yes, I looked good and felt good. All dressed up and one place to go. They say, look like a million on public transit. My three brothers and elder sister all had an accident with the family car so, when my turn came, he passed. Twice the family car had been totaled. No car for me, and I ended up becoming the only professional driver of the family. How ironic! I got the coat, not the car. Esquire 1, Mercury 0.

I also heard, Bert, be careful on the road, we are expecting a giant snowstorm! ... I was taking the bus. !

Yeah, right !!!

So, as convened, I met Zeta in the Hotel Lobby at 8:00 on a snowy Saturday night in the middle of this Grande Allee Saturday night spree. The hotel had a meat market disco in the basement, and chicks and dudes started their ritual to our amusement. She was wearing a classy dress, I had that long coat and had caught her eyes. Well, a man who knows how to dress. We walked out, out across the street among the waltzing snowflakes as per they were musical notes in a Lionel Hampton's tune or those famous Lawrence Welk soap bubbles. A quiet bar in a glasshouse by the hotel. A liter of house red wine, a place by the fireplace, two people in a love bubble away from a crowd exchanging, laughing and I guess in love. Time flew and Cinderella's last bus story was coming. Midnite, the last bus in this town, turns into a pumpkin. I had to go to the bus stop but she opened the window of her soul. Her dark brown eyes were twinkling like stars in the winter starry night. We walked back to the hotel. The night was beautiful. The angel feather snow was still dancing in the night as from a Lionel Hampton tune.

And we made love. Adults caught up in the magic of a snow storm. As I woke up at 4Am that night and pulled the drape from this 20 hotel floor room, naked, I saw this white-out. I mean snow storms, and I know those by experience. We had 6 buses that were supposed to leave for Philly in the morning. I had to figure a way back home, but life was good and I wanted to have an extra few hours to enjoy life. Made a few phone calls to my supervisor in the boondocks, to the boss in Phlliy who called the bus line to put the drivers on stand-by and with the help of many hotel employees who made it to work on foot for a living we had breakfast.

It was a Snowday. It carries a special spirit.

The kids found cardboard boxes and were tobogganing on the streets, making giant snowmen, snow fortresses, and snowball fights. Snow had made its magic before, becoming the motorists' nightmare. They all enjoyed these extra few hours of extraordinary freedom. As in the act of love, once the fury of passion had been unleashed comes a period of calm. As in nature keeps a bit of energy to enhance its exhibit of white, blue sky, foamy snow at freezing mark temperature. As if nature tells us, come and look at this before temperature drops and the snow get crunchy and planes whistle in the air. It's a few hours of calm, stillness white perfection window before reality strikes.

We went for a storm walk in the fortified part of the old city. Made our way to the latin district. I took her to the same Café I went with my sister as kids on Couillard st. This place where I discovered the perfume of Espresso coffee and the gurgle noise of the steam machine. The Café that had shaped my persona. It is still there after all these years.

It had been nice for a while. She eventually went to Med School as I tried my way at becoming a stockbroker. Those were lovely years. Few trips to the beach. She made it. Not me. ! Med School. One more time. All those years of study to end up working with sick people, in an hospital as we all know that hospitals are a very dangerous place to work and through osmose one may end up looking like Chad Everett after a while.

All relationship leave an imprint on you. They reflect themselves under various forms, A smirk you borrowed, an inflexion, a gesture, words that pertains to a foreign language, culture and many more. They manifest here and there without your knowledge. You have been borrowing these from former relationship, some from friendship, companionship or more intimate relation.

But on a busy Friday night, while driving a transit vehicle, it may get back to you. It may get back to you on this, how do you explain this type of scientific curiosity or how you tell off people with such hand gestures. This is this memory vein that your mind is drilling tonight. I owe some traits of character, good one, to Zeta.

Zeeta, remember that obsession about all the glass in landfill. Don't worry, glass is silicate and it is ultimately sand. Sand to sand. Dust to dust and Chinet to Chinet.

Many years later, walking down the aisle at my wedding with my old man I took the occasion as he asked me to walk straight, be decent and keep my nose clean and everything will be fine.

It came to my mind that our father and son relationship came a long way from this who breaks whose character to a more benevolent, sometimes crazy relation that may have started that evening. The peace truce had been signed. The evening when he gave me an honest advice and lent me a wool coat.

Remember that evening, you lent me your long coat?

He was a bit puzzled and said yes but I know that he clearly remembers that when I walked home late afternoon after a bizarre ride home from a motorist in an AMC Matador looking for $10 to buy gas and hit the road to Red Bridge. Red Bridge (Pont Rouge) has always been a strange place to me, largely inhabited by the militaries from a nearby army base and the strippers working on Hamel Boulevard.

Yes, I remember. You walked home with this usual grin on your face. The, I did it again look. It was of no surprises to us.

We became closer that day. Now it's a new family for me but for all those scary moments for you, I have been more scared than you.

It was the first time we shared something that made me successful, desirable and confident and I guess, I am walking back into life, with someone else. My father left this world 20 some years ago, the church where I married is still there at the terminal stop of the bus 18. It became luxury condos and this beautiful light blue at old pink disappeared. Progress cannot afford a beautiful place to meditate in silence and peace. Progress hates the introspective and the unproductive. Progress hates humanity.

Yet progress did not handle the Matador man. Many years later while on the quest to find a quiet place to keep on going on a "Schmooching" party I crossed the old Matador man on St-John st, by the gate, trying to hustle another $20 to get gas to go back to Red Bridge. Same old car, same old line, same old, same old but in a summer setting.

Take my hand, We'll make a space, And here we'll stay. Until it's time for you to go!
Buffy Ste-Marie

I would like to introduce the next line with a clip from The Wild Kingdom. The Mutual of Omaha. I would show you breathtaking nature of snow melting and dripping into a creek to join a river. On an exquisite Alexander Glazunov violin solo.

As winter turned into spring, new contracts came for spring and then from May to October I had the European tours. Canada and the US and winter, I could relax on UI and find some work as a Deejay, making Pizzas or in the garage for tire and battery season. I worked that drill for many years. A freelance man. A Free man, but something was missing.

Pol again, and The Sound of Philadelphia. TSOP. A band fest gig.

Annapolis Maryland. I always loved Maryland. Meeting in Philadelphia, in and out for synchronization of all teams.

The Band Fest gathered thousands of HS kids in a city, and they practiced their skills and competed to get a bursary or monetary reward that always disappeared before the final showdown and presentation. Someone has lost the famous financial document envelope. It happens at every single festival. Pol, the boss, loved to show many employees on the ground he could gather wearing his corporate polo and name tags, smiling and doing not much but being there. The money was not exactly there but it was all expenses covered and always a great party and yes, in those days, everybody was wearing those black (dresses...) Reebok sneakers with a Union Jack on the tongue.

That year, his big event was in Annapolis, Maryland. My first observation is that I had never seen such a concentration of good-looking people in this place. Yes, they are much alike but, all gorgeous. It had the overall feeling of that Plastic Surgeon T.V. show; The Swan. All Swans, but all looking alike. Wonder if they cage or expatriate those that don't look perfect and everyone or almost seems to have a Convertible Mustang. Spring always has a certain hormonal magic as well. Magic hates to be contradicted.

So, there stood Sue. Alone at the bar, surrounded by as many sharks as Captain Cousteau in a cage. The pro ones, those guys who know how to cruise and hit, next to those guys, I am a Boy Scout. They have positioning strategy. Work in packs like the wolves. They put a great show for those who like to study the moves. Sue is ? She's a friend of Gwen, the Lily Tomlin of the outfit, and she had to take some air from an ending relationship turning abusive and violent. She needed a walkabout, like many of us. Like most of us in the business.

Uneventful Festival, nice weather, great parties, easy pay, Fudruckers and Dos Equis. Easy money, easy time, loved every moment of it.

To make a story short. I was caught with a cheap flight deal back to Montreal with Continental from Philly, with a 3-day layover. 3 days to kill time in Philadelphia. I must have misplan this airline booking? I didn't know what to do and where to go at the time yet, Continental airline was Greyhound with wings. Snack on board? Bag or peanut or pretzels, your pick buster. I heard, well, the rumor was that Sue's group was going to Virginia Beach on an extra day to open the Beach Season and yet, somehow that information that could have been trivial to most landed on my lap by, I don't know who. Guess. She had leaked it on purpose. Women?

Until Eve arrived, this was a man's world. (unknown).

Spring time. Opening of the beach season in Virginia beach. I could not let that slip away. No siree !

Eureka ! The Snap On moment. There it was before my eyes. My plan was easy, I jump ships, (bus) switch paper, put my bags in another bus loading section and rather than ending up in Harrisburg, PA. Sue's group is making this hook detour by Virginia Beach. It could mean an extra night at the hotel. I'll rent an extra room group rate, a few more meals, maybe good company, as she looks goods and nice, and I end up two days later in Philadelphia almost in time for my flight. I always hated the last day of the trip when the bus dropped you and the group in a parking lot because it makes you feel emotionally empty and you have to figure a way out and back home. The day when a phone booth could become a good friend and it accepted only quarters. In the last year of the job, there were calling cards and faxes. That was a revolution. Cell phones in buses came in the very last years in the field, and they were expensive and attached to the vehicle.

In the bus loading zone, while Pol, the boss asked me if I was gay (because I was a bit more selective and refined than he is) I took time to switch the paperwork and, right under his nose, take my luggage and put them in Sue's bus loading zone.

Gay, Paul, hum, let me think about it, I am not certain? Could you move just a bit, I have to put my suitcase in that bus bay picking area? I'll get back to you. Paul, is that the bus that goes back to Philly?

Yes, but it goes to Virginia beach before.

Thank Paul, just asking ?

Life is often like that. Snakes and ladder board game, no dice, live. Most stories sound like a Blues Song or a 3-dimensional snakes and ladder board game. She was in this life Blues mood as I escaped the Medusa one. I was riding the ladder, she had hit a personal snake.

So, Sue, you are making a detour by Virginia Beach?

Yes, The group have an extra day on the tour.

Mind if I join in. I have a few days to kill in Philly and would not mind opening the beach.

Sure, as long as it is OK with Paul

Don't worry about Paul, I am freelance tour guide here and my contract is over. He knows about my flight.

And it went accordingly.

I joined Sue on her bus and we went for the ride. We opened the Beach at Virginia Beach that spring. We had time to exchange on the theme: how's life had been treating you so far. On a perfect day at the beach, drinking a Pabst in a bar facing the boardwalk. Profound discussion about the meaning of life. We were on the same page. The opening of a Beach season, a day of hope and joy. They were all so happy, students, teachers, chaperones. Spring. God made the moment just perfect, and I would have loved to seize it in time for a good while. Openings are always filled with light, joy, optimism, life. I always loved being at openings.

Here was the plan for me: I get to the hotel, take a room. Have dinner with her and the group, breakfast the day after, and I am well on my way to Philly to catch my flight. Hers ended up being, 9 and a half week, she was Kim Basinger and I ended up being Mickey Rourke, but the schedule had been compressed, a lot. We had to work double shift.

It ended up her way. The 9 and a half week scenario. 4 days of pure no strings, the no-nonsense pure enjoyment of the best that youth and freedom could throw at you without restraints nor limits. Just like that jazz song, *Time for you to go.*

It's always a matter of time and money. Tourism is always on a tight budget.

Upon arriving at the group, check in at the hotel.

Listen, the place has no more vacancies. I asked the management, she said.

I thought, damn, there is a Best Western on the other side of the road. Might as well line up my stuff and cross the road. Trying not to get killed crossing the highway.

If it works for you, you can shack up in my room for the night. We have 45 minutes before dinner with the group.

And so, to save of budget, she offered me to sleep in her room and have the meals with her group. I thought about something more Platonic, nice but boring. The problem with lying to yourself starts when you really get to believe your lies. Of course, the mere perspective of kissing her and holding her in my arm would have made my day, but things were what they were. I was hesitant. She was still legally married after all, but did it really matter? I was ready to sleep on the sofa and respect her intimacy and play the : I can't relate to but it may exist, loser. As we handled the room key and distribution was over, we walked to the hotel room. It had a strange feeling to it but we entered this hotel room together. The front door moment. At the very moment, I heard the click of the hotel room doorknob. The click where the rules of engagement are clearly stated, I had the reflex to let her have the first word. So they were:

You are not to get out of that room unless I am fully sexually satisfied and it has been a while.

I was to play the Platonic thing as I will sleep on the sofa and try not to peak at your nipples if your walk out of the shower, thing. Change of plan. LIfe is good.

I also had plenty of catches up to do, to be up-to-date. She took a few days off from work and I postponed the flight as we both had some sex to recoup. Screw the flight, This place is way more fun. Had we have 9 and half weeks, we would have stretched it.

I guess we broke the rules as she was still officially married I guess, but then again. Rules ? Rules were meant to be broken. Officially married, what does it mean ?

Or something like that !

> *Never let the enemy pick the site of the battle.*
>
> *George Patton*

On this slice of life: Gen Patton met Mrs. O'Early. My 1st grade school teacher, as she broke the wooden ruler in front of the class. Break, broke, broken. Rules are meant to be broken or some say bent. I bent the rules about the battle site, but let me tell you, it has been hell of a fight. We made no prisoners. No Sire ! No matter the feather display or firework a man could show, the truth is that: In this world, woman, expose, propose and dispose. They let you do the stupid little dance and choose the scenario. If you think you, as a man, have any power or control over seduction, you lie to yourself or are victim of marketing scheme. You have been for years or decade a sucker for all those false beliefs and you, they all cashed on your gullibility. So, there, exposure is the only thing one should do. It is the other way around.

I looked at the hotel king bed and figure that, for once, I'll let the enemy decide where to engage.

In a real Christian spirit here: Christ died for our sins, Dare we make his martyrdom meaningless by not committing them, is a daily existential questionnement. Jules Feiffer.

Or else: If you don't believe in anything, how can you believe in love and as far as being out of belief or a God, how can you have this ecstatic moment to scream Oh My God ?

This Joyride. Fun, freedom, pleasure and hoagies, took me to many places since she was into the separation process. There was that punk shop called Zipper head, where we bought very obnoxious T-Shirts and Dead Ken's paraphernalia. It all happened fast, but that was funny. There was Barb's Victorian house, and there, and here and one night we spent the night at a friend of hers place, a townhouse in North Philly. Her friend Barb had inherited this old Victorian house with antique furniture. A brass bed with an old fashion box spring. That had been the most erotic moment of my life. Most erotic moment of your life on the bucket list. Check ! So, I thought.

Since she had no official place to stay for a few days because of her divorce thing we had to change place every night but I thought that was part of the adventure. Our Pablo Escobar moments. Last night was spent at a friend's place. A great person. He was a childhood friend of hers, and he told me something I will remember all my life.

I have known that girl for a while. She had been down for so long that I can hardly recognize her. I don't know you how you do it. She looks happy.

Likewise, my friend, I am having the best time of my life.

Before leaving early to work on a weekday morning this man who had the great generosity to give us room, shelter, and comfort and of whose name I would have loved to remember he said: Got to leave early, we have a promotional sales meeting. The guy was selling Dodge, Chrysler products. We are having a spring promotion on the Reliant K.

I opened my eyes and said, what the Reliant, K?

He said, Yes, the Reliant K, designated car of the year as per Motor Trend magazine two years in a row. We could sense some irony in the way he said it.

There's fresh coffee on the kitchen counter.

That statement hit me like a brick wall. How could Motor Trend do that?

I may be no Xaviera Hollander to paint all the juicy details of this little getaway from it all, but I sure I am no Lee Iaccoca to pretend either that a Reliant K is a good car.

She lives in Florida and remarried this fantastic guy. We are all remarkable for a while. The challenge is to stay remarkable for a lifetime.

No, no, I have to put an additional section to this episode:

This is too brutal and emotionless here. So, there it goes. Few years after we spent this joyride and had a few more encounter, life happened. It was time for me to go. Somehow, we would have wanted for something else, but life is cruel.

Life is a bitch, so they say, but pain could be eased or stunned. Out of the blue, I receive this call from Sue. How she got my number, can't remember, but I was happy to talk to her. She was coming from Philly to Montreal for an accounting audit at a Ikea warehouse on the south shore of Montreal. In and out, 1 evening, 1 night. She went up the corporate ladder since I met her first.

We agreed to meet for one evening and have a Peel Pub beer and steak, but the meal was not it was all about. We met, dined, chatted, laughed and this young woman at a turn in her life was now a stunningly beautiful executive looking person. I was impressed by her, tailleur, blouse, high heels, new hairstyle.

She was spectacular. She had changed a lot since her day at accounting for the Fashion Bug. It had been clear right at the beginning of the evening that I was to get married soon as she met someone new that she wished to share her life with and were we just 2 persons who had lived something special that would have fixed them both.

Time was for her to hit the road, as was it for me. A train, a bus, a taxi; wheels! We walked out of the Peel, on Peel avenue and strolled a few blocks on Ste-Catherine West on a wide curb overlooking window displays from The Bay, Simmons, Eaton's, The atmosphere was relax, the evening was warm, it was summer.

As she mentioned; I like this city, I feel safe. It is clean. It is nice, It is quiet,

I could have lived here. I could have learned French, as her mother was of French origin.

We could have lived here. Sigh.

Yet, it is not how life happens

I kissed her on the cheek as per the French tradition bise to say goodbye.

Before she walked in the night she said:

 You know, when we met, you kind of save my life !

No, Sue, you are the one who gave me mine back.

It brought back this dignity that seemed to have slipped away from my life. It all came back. Yes, we are on this life to fully live it.

It was not exactly Paris. I was not exactly young.
But on a quiet night with the door locked tight
And the silence weighs a ton.
Of all the men in my life, I remember one.
Chita Riviera

And as the silence of this in this bus stranded in the middle of nowhere under a bridge on a New Year's Eve weighs a ton, Of all the women of my life, I remember a few.

The year before, the Toronto event.

Toronto, Niagara Falls. Niagara Falls to Toronto, via New York, or did I move a lot? All that I can remember is that it always finished off in a parking lot or with a pause on the way to the airport at Chazz Bar. Chazz was a bar and grill between two highways. A sort of rest area place. The place was paranormal, as Pol's certificate and bursaries always disappeared at Chazz. It had a type of Philadelphia experiment triangle or God knows what. The black hole loved sucking up checks.

There was the big flower clock in Niagara Falls. For ages, my father kept the only picture that existed from the great uncle Charles Edouard in his WWI uniform in front of the flower clock. Rumor has it that the picture was taken in Scotland. Yes, Grand uncle Chuck, who survived all the WWI battles to end up at tank school in London. So, nobody knew where the picture was taken but it was in Niagara Falls not in Edinburg, Scotland. There is a plaque by the clock stating that WWI allied soldiers camped there, as Niagara Falls was a big training camp. Little did I know. I have to go back to Chazz.

Toronto, Niagara Band fest. 20 buses, 3 instruments truck, lousy weather, the opening of Marine land, helluva lot of people but, Bubble, Gail, a beautiful young blonde violin teacher with a multi level sense of humor, uncanny ability for Sudoku and a visceral hate for the Suzuki teaching method, she also loved Twisted Sisters.

She had friends on the tour, opening the grounds and keeping someone away from her. Another teacher on the group figured that the tour was the perfect time to make his move and have her in the sack. It did not happen. Wherever I went or walked or sat, someone was dragging Gail to join me. I felt like being setted up, but it was a good plan. Remember, my parents met on one of those Nowhere Bus tours. A tea leaves readers could have told me ages ago: I see massive chunk of leaves in my tea. It must be buses.

Was it a social challenge, a game, a prank, or some sort of applied wisdom ! For all I know, were they to organize a match or one-night stand between us, it would not have been any different. It may have been a matter of ages. Must have been a form of spiritual help, for they knew that at a certain point in life you get shoeboxed. Point of no return. The party, well, the real one, is over. Life takes a new meaning, and so they saw. They saw two people they were deemed to be ships crossing in the night and decided to alter their course.

Once you know that a certain point in life, you are boxed. Marriage on one side, career on the other, mortgages and kids, bang, bye bye emotional adventure if you don't want the cover of the box, the law firm on your head. Seemingly, those real friends of hers were carrying out a social experiment were trying to tell her, "Look, you are in your 20s, gorgeous, free and spunky. Enjoy life, it won't last. Just as if they were hammering her head with 10 years of Cosmo magazine issues. Those were very thick in the 80s and were very sexually suggestive about all types of freedom and had much publicity about the contraceptive sponge. Cosmo had many contraceptive sponge publicity as Penthouse radar detector ones.

Do that thing now before you wake up in 10 years with regrets not having done so. Hope and regrets are violent things. Feeling like living something a bit wild. Go For It.

On this first day at work, it became evident that something was bound to happen. I always thought that once you had the first slow dance and the French kiss under the rain or in an elevator, things were going downhill. I know, I am a rain or snow person. I had never dated a professional musician and she had been contestant for a Miss USA pageant too. Life is short.

Somewhere along in a conversation, I pushed: if it pleases you, you can put your pillow under your arm and join me in my room. She carried her pillow everywhere.

So she did. I saw her walking toward my room with her pillow under her right arm. Oups. That was not planned but, life is full of surprise. Students, teachers, chaperones were all there witnessing this choreographic statement walk. This, you dared me to. See, who I am walking tall with a pillow under my arm to someone's room and guess what is on the program. She made that statement loud and clear. That also got me in trouble, but then again, life is too short to avoid all troubles.

I had to send my roommate of the tour to see the Blockbuster movie of the summer and fork $5. An action packed movie starring Bruce Willis. Die Hard. The original.

That was good. Then again, I am no Xaviera Hollander to depict it all but that was brilliant or as they say today, epic… Russian say Cosmos !

And so, the end of the trip came and there I was, again, dropped in the middle of a parking lot, somewhere I had never been before and had to find my way back home. I had been doing that a lot and feeling that it was not a living.

A wink, a kiss, a question.

Up to what?

I don't know, maybe go to the city, sleep at Leo's house in NYC and make a few museums or get to Newark, try to catch a standby, buy a cheap flight or a Hound at Grand Central, roll all night and grab a tuna melt at Ramapo or New Baltimore's service area. Buses stopped at either of those as the regular compulsory safety break. Drivers and tour guides often met there to exchange info, deals, business cards, and dates. The Deli at the bottom floor of the Empire State building was also, then, a meeting place for the tourism people, as many waited there while the groups were off the observation deck for night sight. Before they remodeled the entrance of the Empire State after 911, the entrance hall was breathtaking.

Honestly. I don't know.

Leo's house was a Roman Catholic boarding house on the 23rd in Manhattan. No frills, no nothing but a clean room, DT Manhattan for $27 a night. I frequently dropped by Leo's when I was stuck in Manhattan or wanted to go Museum hopping in NYC. The trendy thing to do in the 80s was to grab a Village Voice or the 20 pounds weekend edition of the NY Times and plan a getaway trip. The Guggenheim, the Frick collection, the Vanguard, or a Nina Hagen show. Nina, the dead Kens, the Cramps or else of the punk scene. As hotel rooms in Manhattan were always expensive, one way to go around that was to stay at the Leo's. Jet Set on a budget. Nice, safe, clean, quiet, the Leo's was perfect but so damn depressing. There were crucifixes over the bed in every room, and you could guess what was in Jesus' mind every time as: why aren't you at Nina Hagen's concert? You really left this beautiful blonde in a parking lot when you could have spent a Joyride with her? This girl in Philly, you love her but won't make a lasting move? You were lousy at school, why did you keep pushing? What happened to your Capri, and did Pokey ever give you a cut of the deal? Or that type of questioning.

Jennifer from the Jeans shop ?

I hated being left alone with Jesus in a room.

Normality, Being normal, Going back home. Saying no to an exquisite offer. Acting responsible. Seemed to be a statistical concept, A dangerous statistical concept since it denies beauty and the intervention of the divine. Once again, let's defy normalcy and believe in the magic of life.

Heard about those Thomas Edison Portland Cement house neighborhoods? They are in Montclair or Edison, if I remember well. One piece house in one mold. A beauty.

Historical interest she asked as a tour guide thing.

No, strictly Cocktail, if a conversation falls flat in a cocktail you could always pull that one like ever heard about this Thomas Edison one-piece molded Portland Cement house in N.J. there is a whole neighborhood of them. They look just like those little green plastic houses in the Monopoly Board game. How would you like to dance? It's Val McCoy's do the Hustle. Love the weirdness of life.

If you had a few days ahead, we could probably go to check this out.

Nobody waits for me, I am a freelancer these days. Next contract in 2 weeks, I could try to catch a flight this Tuesday but you are the one working.

No, because of the trip they gave me 2 days off, there is my car. (she had one of those Toyota Corolla, labeled Chevy Nova) right in the lot, over there.

Will you play me the violin in bed.

Yes !

That was a no-brainer.

This one was all spontaneous, there were no plans, none that could be felt or planned ahead. The fairy of Spontaneity took her wand and bling ! Magic. Yet, Magic and coincidence are not at the same metaphysical level. OK, same family of genre but, coincidences are a wink from God and Magic more to do with a temporary arrangement. No mistakes here again. Magic or the spell is to last a certain, definite time. It could not be replicated nor stretched in time. You have to live it and leave it.

And so, it went or goes.

She shared a nice white bungalow with a friend of hers. I think it's called Cape Cod style. She had her room in the den section of the house and it was all surrounded by gardens. Almost the proverbial white picket fence took place but no fence but it came with a pull start gas engine lawn mower and a garage. The 1950s style that had to be pulled with a rope with a wooden handle. They have a very specific choking sound that sounds like a certain laugh.

She went to many private lingerie sales and other sexy items. Just like Tupperware on lace, latex. A bit like the relationship a man maintains with the Snap-On tool man, but on another social plane. People giggling and getting excited, and the two meet at the Snap-On cheesecake calendar level. She took the occasion to show me her latest acquisitions to the point that I had to turn around to pinch myself to see if I was not dreaming. That was too good to be real. Yet, it was for real.

We spent the next 3 days together enjoying life and, besides a bizarre incident involving an ex, coming early on a Sunday morning to mow the lawn, this was just perfect and all sense of the word.

We were sleeping in her den in the morning sun, happy and easy, just when we heard. Well, she did, The distinctive sound of a manual garage door opening. Yep, the garage door and I thought that I was ready for one of those Ciel mon Mari moments as the traditional French Vaudeville cliché. At the moment, the lover has to flee the scene fast and naked. A classic.

No, it was her ex, Yes her ex-boyfriend or else that came to mow the lawn with this old pull start lawn mower that just did not want to start.

So I asked. Who is it

It's my ex. He comes to mow the lawn.

Does he know he is your ex or he became your ex last night

No, no, it's clear, but somehow, he insists on coming here once a week and do the lawn

He must have known that something was going on but, to my dismay, that person started the lawnmower, took 45 minutes, did the job, put the thing back in the garage and took his Reliant K and drove away.

There were no real Ciel Mon Mari (french Vaudevilleesque) moments but it shook me a bit.

And so it went. I remember the New Thai waterfront restaurant in Weehawken, walking in So-Ho, Dancing at Nirvana, Dancing at Time Square. A drink at the Vanguard. She knew the city, but preferred living in the burbs. My job took me to the city often, but Bubble was the one that made me discover it. And what goes through the mind is, this is too good to end, but it will. She had this visual artsies sister living in SoHo that knew the Big Apple inside out.

And I ended up there, In an original stainless steel-clad Dinner somewhere in N.J. Dumont, (I think it was the Crystal or something like that) not far from NYC. Most Dinners have the same name. In a booth with this amazingly beautiful blonde music teacher among the tinting of the dish, the rumor of the crowd and the perfume of coffee and bacon and eggs. At a distance, I could hear some jazz music, a Chita Rivera tune, and the world at the very moment was perfect. I believe in moments when happiness could be looking like this big fat Red Velvet cake, sitting under a cake bell at the end of that dinner counter. All that you have to do is to ask the waitress for a piece of that cake. The cake, so to speak, was right there, in front of me.

It was not exactly Paris, but for me, it was close to it.

I could have had much more faith in this story and pursued happiness yet as in any opera, it never turns out nice. And life spins so fast. I tried normal, I tried the suit and tie, I tried boring but nothing worked out and who would spend the rest of its life with boring. Normal just did not like me, and so I kept going as a Box People. Abnormal people create abnormal situation and setting to create stories that are a cut above the normality. Stories that normality cannot afford to spin. Stories that rigid framework cannot even grasp or imagine. Maybe it is a form of justice or balance for those who prefer to live their lives out of a rigid framework.

It slipped away. As many other life opportunities. It slipped away as there is no sure shot or silver bullet that tells, blue line (as in the pregnancy test) pack your gears, rent a U-Haul, she is from a world apart but you love her and that should be just plenty. You will find a way, but the odds are stacked against you. There are no ways, there never be no ways, and this is the Classic line. The love song, one. The Pat Benatar ultimate scenario. Listen to your heart because your head knows nothing. Day in and day out, those unfulfilled stories haunt you as you find a way to keep going by becoming something that you are not. An unhappy person.

Those were the aleas of the tour and travel business. Always physically and emotionally on the move. It is a living, but I also felt condemn to that living. I could never settle down with anyone because instability is my line of living. I feared growing old alone, childless and getting bald. Gee, getting bald, what a drag.

She lives in Kansas. She still teaches violin, but never with the Suzuki method. She is still a classical beauty. She has her webpage.

It's the story of the man who shows up to heaven drenched, soaked, dripping. The Saint on duty on heaven's gate asks:

So, what's with you?

I drowned: flooding in the prairies. I had been a good Christian, and so I thought that God would rescue me.

OK, so let's check. According to the file, you have been waiting 2 days on the roof of your house for help.

Yes, 2 days or more.

So, at some point we, sent you a floating massive trunk of oak that you did not grab. After, we sent an empty floating canoe you did not you seize and on an helicopter passed overhead your house and you did not respond!

Yes, I thought that God was to save me.

Those were acts of God and intervention to save you. Those weren't coincidence. Coincidences don't exist, Even the boss here sometimes plays dice. We wanted to save you but you voluntarily declined all opportunities extended to you based on some wrongful perception of how an intervention may look like. Were you waiting for the hand of God to pick you up ? Therefore, you may have to go back to earthly living as a man named: Kawa. Can you scream like a racer motorcycle passing on 6 gears on a quarter mile track?

Ultimately, I may be or have been that man waiting for those things to showed up in my life but did not decipher their meaning or presence. It is scary. Scary as the parable of the talents.

But tour and travel could be an exciting business too.

The tourism lifestyle gets addictive. Switch cities, live in Grand Hotels, meet interesting people in the vacation spirit. A fringe benefit. From a Nobel Prize to a great industrialist or a woman who admitted after a few drinks that she is a known opera singer and started singing Musetta's part in La Boheme. How could you go to normal or this vague impression of security through normality as a trader is just as good as his last trade, a guide as his last group and a bus driver, just as good as the cyclist he barely avoided on Park avenue? For everyone, security is an illusion. Just an illusion. My daughter would call it a shitshow !

If you are willing to give up some of your freedom to gain on security you will eventually lose it both but every single time, a bus leaves you at an Airport or in a parking lot or an interstate exit, the old Gilbert O'Sullivan song comes back to mind, Alone Again Naturally. What do we do?

3598 is the exact figure. Yeap 3598. I had to go back to the 666 Sherbrooke to pick up a few paychecks, the next group package and a short meeting with the Stregga. With a little luck, the cute Redhead, Mzlee Jeanne would be there and I may have a chance to meet her. The one that destiny was supposed to put in my way on Pacheco Boulevard in Brussels, as I never found the damn artery. I went astray in the red-light district and did not emerge sane out of it. Met someone there.

The office.

Here I am, little correspondence from satisfied customers. Internal memo, forecast of what's to come, but it's the weekend, so the receptionist is not there. The office is officially closed. Only me and two supervisors. So, here comes the meeting with Stregga. My supervisor. I am pushing a bit but in fact she is good-looking, dresses well but has that Degree in tourism so for her, tour director or guides are just Cowboys or asphalt junkies sniffing the yellow line on the thin line between being Tour Escort or Escorts period.

And, there we are:

Here is your stuff, next tour, paychecks and we'll be busy until mid-October. So, what's on your side?

The usual, good group, great weather, lousy vehicle but someday tourism here will rise above Third World countries business and the Novotel in Toronto had been a problem. Always fucken Toronto we get trouble, the beds are not to American standards, they are at least 6 inches smaller. I had to manage that a few times, but overall, it's been a great 14 days.

Well, in fact, Mr. Villa or I am not sure came to the office to complain about that. The beds. He came with his wife and his niece. Cute young Redhead. He complained about some hotels and a note surfaced about the guide's overall morality, but as far as your tasks were concerned, it was flawless.

Some people start a tour at zero, me, I start at minus 10 because of the small vehicles and this man was oversized and his wife on the depressed side. Novotel in Toronto has always been a problem but at least they are honest, The Bond is problematic and they steal customers, so, it's a Catch 22.

I noticed that he was pushing a bit to get a credit but as he spoke I noticed the young woman behind them rolling her eyes and looking at the ceiling as if to say, never mind, it's N' importes quoi (anything). Gets me to wonder, as I know you, did you... you know with the niece. It gave the impression that you shared a little more than a regular tour with her.

You know my generic answer on this. 3598. It's a case of 3598.

3598. You have been serving me this sequence a few times, what does that mean?

Someday I will publish a book that will reveal the secret of the 3598 but in the meantime, for the book and the rectitude of the company and even if two major and vaccinated adults could have been concerned. Nothing besides this Tour director vs. Customers relation had happened and besides I am following the very rigid rules of Amy Vanderbilt etiquette rules as per smiling of pleasure upon biting into a Cherry Tomato. The zesty little squirt that takes you by surprise every time. You can always fake it too, as anything else, I guess.

But now, since it is my book, I will reveal what really happened between me and Camille on that last evening of the tour.

We just checked in at the hotel in Quebec City, up St-John st when she said: This is your hometown, you must know a few good places. It's summer fest here, and you take me out for a drink tonight.

Obviously, I knew a few good Jazz bars and the Summer Fest made the atmosphere special. Light, happy. The happiness of those that experience the spring after a long winter, and that place has real winter. So I agreed.

Sure, Camille, I'll take you out ! I know a few good places

But the uncle, as he agreed, had sleeping problems and said, sure but be back by Midnight.

So, 21:00hrs, Military time, We join at the Hotel Lobby up on St-John st and walk downhill slowly towards a Jazz place on a second Floor on the busy part of St-John. By the St-Matthew's cemetery where people are still having Picnic or drinking wine, the Youville Square where City buses of my youth used to do the terminal stop and the St-John's gate and the fortification where I hung out as a local tour guide. That seems ages ago but it was no more than what 5 – 6 years. I moved around and went to big cities, but this quaint little town still had its charm. When Montreal is a cool place, Quebec City is not as cool but way more charming.

By 22:00hres or 10PM after a line-up we were at the Jazz Bar. The place was crowded. We were parked at the Bar and the music was good. A simple jazz quartet, but our eyes got locked in, and the music became soothing, inspiring but somehow accessory. Floating around at the bar.

The seduction game went up one step. We were a bit more than a host Guide in his City or predilection we were becoming lover or sexual partner or God knows but it was not to end quietly nor be easy because of the Midnight deadline. I said it before. The paranormal moment are instantaneous and unpredictable as the sex one have an evolution and a buildup and the needle was on the record.

In the middle of a drink, a tenor sax solo, a song, and a space of time she kissed me. Kissed but not this normal half wet lips puckered. This woman kissed with all of her soul. She unleashed all the dogs of passion, erotism in one move. She was all of it. She was the Moulin Rouge and all the Red Velvet extravaganza and passion. The beauty of the Art Nouveau, the Belle Époque. Stunning out of this world experience.

We were both engaged in something that could not be ended abruptly by an excuse or a faux fuyant. There will be no excuses, you will engage this Goddess to the bitter end so to speak or die trying. The moment had to be appropriately consumed to its fullest. It was more than breath, lips, teeth, she was pouring her soul into this smootch and she knew how to operate. As for me, it is my religion, the 3598, to take advantage of anything that would make me feel alive. Alive for all of those who had their lives interrupted for matter of honor, of duty or mere accident. I had to feel her skin, her body, her curves and they were many and advantageous but we had to get out of this bar and go somewhere a little more appropriate namely discrete. Remember it was my hometown and I knew all nooks and crannies, but time was running out and fast and I had, we had, this deadline. Once more, but I did not have to fight a snowstorm this time around.

You know what they are saying about redheads ! Well, it's a lie. She was particularly gifted.

As we were walking up the street to a more discreet place to continue this ultimate smooch session. I crossed again the snow storm man, in his red AMC Matador, trying to pull the same stunt. I need money for gas to go back to Red Bridge. No upgrade. We were already in the age of the Honda Civic, the Renault Le Car. Still at the age-old scam of abusing people's trust on a lousy survival story. Maybe he is not real after all. Perhaps he is just a mirage of some sort. Now, the charm of those old fortified cities is that they are full of discrete areas that could be called—Propice—to.

The cute note on this is that as per customer requirement, the management has been able to find a suite with a king bed for Mr. Villa and family, but the room swap had to be done after we left. Given that we did not know what room number it will be or confirmed, well, we agreed upon having the luggage moved by the hotel concierge and the: Camille, will ask for the room number once we'll be back, at midnight. A suite, they said. Yeap, the suite next to my room and with a communicating door. Would have been nice to know before we sometimes spent on my side of the communicating suite.

But for the supervisor, it was:

No, nothing happened. We went for a coffee and I took her back home before midnite.

Incidentally, is your friend, the Redhead receptionist, Jo, be somehow, someway or somewhat available. Maybe, you know, we could meet. Nothing engaging, just see if it could be done.

She may be ripe to meet someone new but she is no Peel Pub date. She doesn't go to amusement park either. I have always had a soft spot for those: Moon and June and Ferris wheel. They remind me of Jill, Jill, my soul sister from D.C. Jill has this Joni Mitchell overall presence. As per, Jo, she has extensively traveled. Goes to Italy often and she is part of the museum crowd. It is unclear to me why local women hate the Peel Pub ? Unclear !

Museum. Do you mean the Art Museum?

Yes, the Art Museum! In fact, we intended to go to this Bouguereau exhibition next Sunday. We could probably do something and double date there. I talked to her. You take it from there.

`I know Bouguereau and love his predilection theme. Women. Women of pale skin and curvy. Women and angels. Centuries before Victoria's Secret. Cultivated women. I went to the library to read a bit about the oeuvre de Bouguereau, although I will definitely live and die as an American Realist. That's my artistic rebellion. So, I went to that Museum, met the date. I spent a good 30 minutes just absorbing the energy and the beauty of l'Aurore as a real deep artsy. It went well, very well, we married 2 years later. The rest is history. In those days, I loved going to the original Peel Pub on Ste-Catherine, the one in a basement, but the Mademoiselle was too classy for that. I had to let off old college rituals. No more Peel Pub and no more Chalet BBQ.

There has never been anything wrong with the Peel Pub. In fact, it's the wildest place in town.

3598: On the morning of the 9th of April 1917, (Easter) under a Canadian Command for once in the history of the Colony. The Canucks realized that they had fought like lions for years, but were led by donkeys. The usual inbred stiff upper lip Aristocrats private lounge military that weren't very efficient and dangerous by their megalomania. They used military resources as cannonfud without strategy, knowledge nor simple discernment as they had been doing for centuries, but the men from the new worlds weren't to go for it. The thing is that there were good enough reasons why our ancestors fled Europe, and being led by inbred was one of them. Limeys !

The massacre of the New Foundlanders Regiment at Beaumont Du Hamel proved without a doubt that Canadians should be led into fight by Canadian, even as a colony. We wanted it our way. After preparation and with the utmost pride and a new warfare science, the Canadians launched the brutal assault of the Vimy Ridge (northern France). All allies have failed at the ridge also known as Hill no 150. The Canadian fought bitterly for 3 days to a full victory to become the Storm Trooper of the Empire. The colony became a Nation. Those, 3598 never made it home. So, if on a summer night, the God of Luck and Beauty offers you no strings attached the occasion of something beautiful and romantic, honor the offer and have a thought for those who made it possible. Those that gave it all for your freedom. It is a good enough reason. You owe them.

I picked The Ridge, but there are thousands of such events or battles of campaigns that should be kept in mind without leading a life. Stories of devotion, altruism, courage, sacrifice, light. It is there. If you don't know where you are from, you'll never know where you are going. It may explain why I had to become a Guide. There were no more shepherd job opened when I started working.

Live for something rather than die for nothing. Gen Patton.

I was a gifted Tour Director, Guide, could have been a great historian or a stand-up comic but I still had to learn some more and have a family. A reduced one, but a family as per those, 3598 that did not have this chance. It's a creative way to keep their spirit alive among others.

Life sent me a cascade of those floating tree trunks while I was on the roof of my employment house as the water of unemployment were rising and I then had responsibilities. I grabbed a few. I got wet, but did not drown. I was not surfing, but floating in the black ink waters of society. Most of those job were based on sales, technologies, myths of a better world though progress and the ultimate deceit. The deceit dead end. Let me drive into the light I secretly wished. Well, it could not have been any clearer. I drive and yes, it is well into the light.

And came this kid's dream and the floating canoe. The transit commission is looking for city transit drivers. Those warm and comfy buses like the ones that I took with my older sister for her Sunday's escapade. They were always in my realm of reality. It could have been a temporary thing but as most temporary thing that one became more of a permanent fixture.

The job consist of maneuvering large thing into narrow space at customer's utmost satisfaction. Heard that Pokey. Some more customers for you ! When sex appeals !

I would rather drive a bus in hell than sell for an IT firm or Financial services in heaven. When you are where rubber meets asphalt type, you can't go wrong with that. The official version is rather be free in hell than slave in heaven, or so they say.

Driving a large vehicle around is the easy part. It takes a bit of skill and a lot of practice. It's 40% of the job, the other 60% have to do with attitude, behavior and new types of skill sets
Transit is not sales, so you have to learn to cut the salesperson gimmick as per that one:

Sir, I rang before the last stop and you missed it. I will have to walk 2 blocks because of you.

The thing is that typically they rang in their head, but the hand did not actually pull the string or as a policeman once told a friend about a missed stop sign: You did the stop OK, but your car did not.

And the not to answer reflex here is:

Don't worry about it. It's in the price. It is the same price one more stop or two. The actuaries made all the calculation, and it would not be worthwhile to go after a few cents for an extra stretch.

Sometimes, I miss the point.

Could you be an urban farmer after all? Is city transit a form of farming. Maybe ?

Somehow, the original bus driver's drill reminded me of a summer on a farm.

Farmer. As the farmer harvests and exploits rurality, the transit driver exploits and harvests urbanity. They both start their day before it could be called a day. Sit in a vehicle mounted on a gigantic wheel and rolling into a tillage road for a few hours. Spends the days dealing with cows, beef, dogs, chicks. Countless chicks. Cackling chicks on cell phones. Goes to the siesta, Start the afternoon dealing with Chicks, Dogs, and vegetables. Comes the evening with the regular nuts of all types, many vegetables. Fruits, fruit flies, small fruit and bang, the shift is over. The Orwellian animal farm starts again the day after. Bang. If all animals are equal, why do some have to rely on public transit.

There are no bus driver Super Hero. Yet, we are part of this exclusive league. The league of the: You can't make up this shit. This: What's the weirdest thing you have ever seen coming after a long pause. A very long pause. Accidental chaos junkies feeding on chaos.

Imagine the only job where there could be zillions of reasons for being late but none for being ahead of schedule. A job where you could get a bonus for having a snooze at home in the middle of the day. A recession proof job for rubber meets asphalt reliable people

That's where it gets important. Figure that you'll give the responsibility of a bus to a white collar, Let's say a lawyer for instance. Foremost, it would never get to the final destination, there would be extra delays, he would bum some extra fare in the middle of the road, get lost without apologizing about anything, nor noticing and check jurisprudence in fact book to find its way around. Moreover, they would pretend that they know the judge or the mayor or the Metro operator who may stop the train for you.

Besides, all those jobs before and a lot of studying and reading took me to the conclusion that : There is no gravity. The earth sucks. Somewhat based on an inventory of statements and observation as per: Plymouth's Reliant K was 1987 Car of the Year. Where was it that I saw this wonderful vintage calendar of a Collies Dog, in 3D sitting by red roses, Is a galactoboritos an evolved Greek filo pastry based Mille feuille, If God has stopped creating ground but keep manufacturing people, why are all those people wanting to live in the same spot and pay considerable price for structures made out of brick and 2 × 4? Why is a car depreciating every year as a house appreciates every year, as if we were not wearing out the walls of a house? Why does Hamburger Helper have only 4 fingers, has he had an accident? Is he getting blackmailed by Japanese Yakuza crowd, whom have already amputated him of a finger? Reasonable people can't die as they never exactly lived, their existence fades to oblivion not leaving a speck of happy memories nor of cosmic dust. The chaste are the indecent. They came, they saw, they did shit. Things worth what people are willing to pay or even if it means paying 225K for a baseball signed by Babe Ruth as if there is no counterfeit in the market.

Could our dreams and deep memories be, in fact, intuitive access to parallel universe chronologically located on the life string as per Mishio Kaku's theory, and how can you surf multiple universe while being multitask enough to operate a large vehicle in one precise while simultaneously listening to music from another era and drinking a coffee while driving? Do we have internal memory, or are we just networking dummies? Is the theory of everything for real.

Do I drink too much coffee ?

Little things are the beauty of life.

I often cross this blonde woman driver early in the morning while coming back for the 45 route. She always seemed to have a bad case of hangover. A bit like the Lola character in the Blue Angel, who drank and partied all night. We always crossed paths at the corner of Jarry and St-Laurent streets. She goes straight and I turn right. My part is over, I am on the way to the garage, hers continues on. At first, it looks like she had one of those Gypsies East European parties all night. She wore a mariniere, bell bottom jeans, played accordion, smoked stogies and drank Vodka, grabbing the bottle by the neck. All along singing Russian sad love songs or playing entertaining polka. She seems like that woman that may have woken up at 4:30AM with a few men in her bed and a 3 feet thick headache and after a quick shower, fed the house dog, put on a uniform, a coffee and still on the alcohol vapors drove to work. She has that look, That look 5 mornings a week, or is she a Tupperware mom having to take care of a family alone and waking up before everyone else to make sandwiches for the kids.

The thing is that we know one another but never actually met. We wink, flash and wave but never had a conversation. Until one day, as I was walking in the garage to find my vehicle to start my PM shift, she crossed me and started bitching about those damn buses, always dirty, in lousy conditions. Fists in the air, she was cursing this lousy life, karma, and company. Russia, I knew it. She speaks Russian. That speech was more a violin type than an accordion one but it had all the Slavic drama in its intonations and gestures. She was intense about it, So it came to my mind that maybe, yes, it is not only my wild stereotyped imagination. She is a party animal.

Happiness can exist only in acceptance, or is it submission. Always a deep but lively discussion.
Georges Orwell

The usual Vendome Metro station 105 West meeting, or What the fuck are you looking at.

At High School, guys gathered in a circle playing Hacky Sack or having someone surrounded and playing the washing machine. The regular nerd ride. Many years later, the same guys hold impromptu union meetings at the terminal by the 105 Sherbrooke Vendome station stop. On that day, rather than bitching about work conditions and customers, they were acting up about this consumption society and the elusive theme of happiness.

They were all there. The Greek with the ancient Greece tattooed on his forearm. Athena, the acropolis and all, and it is in color too. It is all there. My Moldovar friend, This French guy who had a fruit brokerage business in Mexico. So it started.

The Greek guys started: I was working in construction back in Greece. Hot, sweaty, humid and the salary sucked but every night I went out. Sat among friends. Drank some Ouzo and was happy. I had nothing, but I was happy. Here: I got this brand-new Honda, a house in the burbs, a pool and I am working maybe half as much as I worked in Greece but yet, I don't feel anything, anymore. It's a fucken neutral state of mind. We have access to all the material stuff we need and for cheap, but the essential is missing. If I could, I would go back to Greece. So, happiness is everything.

The French guy added an extra coat. I had a fruit business in Mexico. Worked over 60 hours a week on a slow week. All my employees worked their asses off, and Mexicans are hardworking people. (Nice to hear that for a change). At the end of the day, I felt fulfilled. Here, I make twice as much. Pull my weight for 37.5 hours a week. Will have a retirement fund. Owes my asses to the bank but got myself a Tesla thing and man, I still feel hollow, empty.

Sergei from Moldavia went at his turn. In Moldavia, we had state-owned farms. We ate well, had all that we needed and the right to have 3 pants and 3 shirts a year. They were of good quality. Everybody had a gimmick or a sideline, and life was quiet and happy. We celebrated a lot, and one person in the village had a car. A Lada. Somewhere, in the late 80s, as we heard that the Berlin wall had fallen and that the market economy would finally hit Moldavia, we thought we could get rich selling our goods to Europe. Get ourselves new clothes, new shirts, maybe a Pickup truck. We thought that we'd finally made it. No, in fact, Europe had food surpluses and wanted to dump them to the former Easter Block countries. So, there ! For the dismantlement of the former Soviet Union. We gained nothing. Eastern European did not gain much but they are free. Empty promises from the west. You are free but not competitive, therefore poor.

You cannot be free and poor at the same time. It's a lie. So, he joined the Russian army and ended up being a weapon specialist attached to the champignon center in Moscow. As everyone else, he has a Dacha that he owes to the bank. 2 jobs to get money in. Top of the line Honda sedan, but not a Pickup truck. At Christmastime, as many of us, he looks at all those presents to reminisce that having an Orange from Gruzia when he was a kid was a great gift. He looks at the pile of new shirts and ties and pants and shoes in his wardrobe but it makes him perplex. As one, we have a uniform to wear 5 days a week, and where the fuck are we all looking for happiness. In big box stores. Empty and hollow as the other ones.

So, they look at me. The only guy who was actually born here. Nicknamed the pure wool here.

What's your story?

I am descendants of one of the 1000 eldest family in North America, but the title does not come with any benefits whether financial, fiscal or even spiritual. It is merely a symptom of stubbornness, resilience or the, how could you have endured that lousy weather for centuries?

My family immigrated to Canada in 1632 or was it 1642, In fact, being Huguenots, we did not have much choice to flee or finish off burned at the stake. Protestant had a raw deal in France in those days. Look at the story of St-Bertrand. Yes, there is one. We celebrate St-Bertrand on Sept. the 6th. Check how he ended and you'll get that hitting the road was a healthy choice, salt or not. Since we are on earth to work, we've decided to become sailors. All those things that had been said, I couldn't agree more. All those stories of hard work, happiness, material limitations or even deprivation. Pride and quality I heard before, but from parents. It is not the country or the place that got empty or rotten, it's the mentality of the place that makes it hardly bearable.

For generations, we picked a large family's type of life and simple work to occupy the territory. That's what the Catholic church had in mind for us. Not many of us got rich but we were somehow happy. It sucks for us too but we know it's a matter of social readjustment and not strictly of market orientation. In the meantime, thinking outside the box may be your way out.

Men can only be happy when they do not assume that the object of life is happiness. George Orwell.

So, Sergei: Those yearly 3 pants and 3 shirts, could you at least pick the color?

- No, not until 1989 !

And happiness is no material thing. Maybe it's within the service to the fellow man who comes the satisfaction and comes the ultimate happiness. Maybe this is how the world is supposed to stay in balance. A world in balance. The Koyaanisqatsii concept. As per this wonderful Philip Glass exclusive harp concerto at the Jean Talon Metro station.

Sometimes the first duty of intelligent men is the restatement of the obvious.
                                   Georges Orwell.

The narrative has taken over the factual, the virtual, the physical so as far as reality is concerned, it is dead or merely negotiable. . Just check how the kids look and dress like, we can see that there is this aura of defectiveness floating around. I see sexy and provocative all over, but not much love anymore. My mom had the same observation about those that are and were my nieces. They end up having career, kids, living with men but I don't see the love in them anymore, I had never seen them in love. They borrow on each other mechanically, I presume. I can see you in love with your wife. I can feel that there is something between you and Jo, but these kids, they worry me.

This job has the clear disadvantage that you have plenty of time to reflect, maybe too much time on your hand, you get to think of all those closures that for one reason or another you did not handle well. This physical succession of left on right or right on left turn becomes a mental one as the brain turns idle. Then comes the inventory moment or those lapse of time when, stopped at a traffic light, you wonder, where the hell you are. You also meet strange situations and have to learn how to gauge fast and react and learn a lot about human nature.

Notes on human nature ! I had to pause awhile to select this weird story among all those that my memory carries on all day.

A story related to me by the mayor of a small French city in the South of France. We were having this discussion about human nature over a Pizza in the Back Bay district of Boston, Pizza, Regina, if I remember well. After quite a few glasses of white, he said. Listen, I have a puzzling one for you.

The story is about the grave at the entrance of the village. A grave and a monument dedicated to a 20 some years old student that joined the French resistance in the last days of WWII and got killed by fleeing Nazis. Things were moving so fast and without much ceremony that villagers buried the kid at the entrance of the 1945 village and made him a temporary monument. À la gloire de la France et de la Résistance.

The makeshift wooden cross became a marble one and well, after 40 years the village grew and became a sought tourism location but, this monument and ground was in the way of real estate progress so it had been anonymously decided to relocate the grave and the monument with all due respect, politics, and ceremonial.

All precaution had been taken to unearth the body and keep the pine box or coffin in a garage by the city hall until redirected to a new site that had already been determined and with all ceremonial respect put to rest in peace to the ground this forgotten hero. This is where the bizarre happens.

As they worked at transferring the remains into a more suitable ceremonial casket, someone had noticed that the remains, the kids, had brand-new shoes. They were, looked and, even after 40 years underground, miraculously as if they were right off the box to the absolute disbelief of everyone who had seen them. And yet, to make a story short, during the night, someone had stolen the shoes. As simple as that. Anodine acts, but with much philosophical questioning here. As per one: who the hell could have done such a thing. Two, are we to replace them? Three, Where are we going to find identical shoes? Can we find the culprit and have him return them anonymously? If you are the mayor of the hamlet, what are you supposed to do besides shaking your head in disbelief?

Yet, the waiter came, asked us if we wanted coffee, an Espresso, a digestive, the mood, and the discussion shifted and I never had the answer to what happened next, but the philosophical implication of the question was puzzling enough to shake me years later.

It has been haunting me for a while. Put those thought on the back burner.

On a cold winter morning, life creates another magic moment.

I rekindled with Heidi on a winter morning on the 80 south. She was running after a bus waving on the other side of the street. The cold as hell sunny February morning. Corner Bernard and Park Southbound. Park is a wide street, 2 lanes on each side plus a parking lane and short length traffic light. On cold days when the snow does crunch, crunch and you can hear the whistling sound of the jet planes flying low, everyone wants to take the bus.

I had not seen her for decades, but there was Heidi. Waving at the other side of Park. Waving for a nice driver, warm and snug in his bus cabin, heated by sunlight reflecting in a large windshield and a foot heater. The magnifier lens effect. It feels like those ski chair lifts with the moveable smoke glass windshield. The Bubble. WIth a little imagination, you can close your eyes and imagine you are spring skiing. Shades on, coat open. Cold winter air is always pure. She had her boots untied, a strange hat, a few scarves and was carrying those artist cartons. The typical McGill Artsy, but still this cute little freckled face.

She felt lucky that morning as a brave bus driver waited for her, from the other side of the street in the middle of the morning rush hour. Was it her charisma, her charm, generosity or just pity. All of the above. She ran to the bus door to thank the wonderful driver for the break as she recognized me from decades ago and we went out a few times together. I was Deejaying on Crescent St., the famous hookup st, that winter. So, here she is in her normal disarray and disorganization and boots inverted in hurry to catch a bus.

She looks at me interrogative look:

Is that you !

That's me alright in a uniform.

My God, that must be, 20 years ago and you still look the same. Do you still seduce young, innocent women with your philosophical approach to car mechanics and a set of Winter Tires and an unbeatable price?

No, Not exactly, but you:

Do you still seduce young men with the ingénue look and sexy messages in Godiva chocolate boxes? I can't supply you with new tires, as those Pirelli with a Brazilian Snowman pushing a lawnmower, but I have an unbeatable deal if you want to go downtown for very cheap.

No, in fact, you were the last one with the Godiva Chocolate. I felt inspired that night. I will leave you at Milton. Milton, I am teaching visual arts at McGill. What happened to you? You were a Deejay, then a Tour Guide, and you left one spring morning not to ever see you again.

Life went on. Many more jobs. Many more bizarre business endeavors. Life went on and yet, now I have a city job, security, or type of, married with kids, dogs, and a station wagon. Happy, yes. Tired, yes, but I kept the circles theme. I always work with circles. See, tires, steering wheel, vinyls record, smaller steering wheels, and I am aiming for Pizza and Coffee cups.

You still hang on in jazzy Cafés and reflect upon the future of the humankind?

A little less. A decided to play jazz, learn saxophone and got myself an Espresso machine and the right type of blend.

It's Milton. I got to go, I am in a hurry. It's been nice seeing you after all those years, and I am catching the 80 often. I have my table at the Olympico Café. I am there almost every day. Ask for me if you drop by. Ciao Bello.

Heidi left at Milton st, a few steps from the McGill Campus. It's been delightful to see her. To see her with 20 years more and reminisce. Nice to see that I left a good impression. You never know. I guess she must be living in the Mile End district. Upbeat, trendy, hipster and well located. The Olympico. The Olympico and the Centropol or the St-Simeon. Love those cafés for the atmosphere and also for their mix of coffee beans. They serve this well-balanced

Espresso. Not too cooked, enough Robusta yet more arabica. The right coat of creama. The perfect music. The blend makes you feel good, relaxed, but a bit elated. The perfect mix. You can pick a word or two of Italian or Greek. They are neighborhood places.

And, I left or dropped, in the transit lingo, Heidi on that anonymous street corner. On that morning at 99.5 Radio Classique, Gregory Charles, Jazz man and radio deejay and philosopher and poet among others, pick two pieces that aren't played much or anywhere else in fact. Nothing one usually hears on main stream radio. The final of "Les parapluies de Cherbourg" is so sad, but such grandeur. The movie scene ends at a Esso gas station in Cherbourg, France, under a light snowfall. The angel feather snow. It always leaves me in awe. Absolute awe. He also played, I wish you love. I wish you love Heidi, as light snow fell on Montreal:

> I wish you shelter from the storm
> A cozy fire to keep you warm
> But most of all, when snowflakes fall
> I wish you love

I never crossed Heidi again on the road as I also changed work districts and moved to the hybrid and the electric AC'd bus. Nor have I dropped by the Olimpico Café, either. When I think about her, I can see her, in my mind, seated at the Olimpico, reading an art book or drawing something on a napkin in the superb 1940s setting. Overall, the thought is comforting. I did not mess.

As for Heidi, as for Emily Claire at the Jazz and Java show, read my mind tonight here is Moon river. Moon River by Audrey Hepburn. The theme song of Breakfast at Tiffany's that I never saw. No, I never saw the movie nor the thing of Bread and Roses, but Moon river is this perfect love song for a kiss under the rain. I know it is not safe to kiss under the rain as one could catch a cold but remember 3568 and the safe, for a French kiss under the rain I would not give a damn. Live only once.

I did not have the first slow dance with Moon river. I think it was McArthur's Park, Donna Summers or some rock ballad. So, no it was not Moon river then but I remember kissing someone under the rain listening to Moon river. I always thought the slow Dance in Born the 4th of July, Tom Cruise and Jessica Prunell is one of the most romantic moments in Cinema.

Café Olimpico. Bernard or St-Viateur st again? Definitely a Miles End job.

*Just for a moment I was back at school
And felt that old familiar pain
And as I turned to make my way back home
The snow turned into rain*

Christmas, unlike other holidays, is not precisely defined in time. It is seemingly more sketchy, abstract, as it finishes the day after the official day as a reuptake of the same pill. A Boxing day.

As December 24th unfolds, different clientele use the transit. There are those that finish work early that start showing up at noon. A few shoppers in the afternoon. By the end of the afternoon, early evening come those carrying those huge Tupperware or aluminum pans full of food to relatives or church parties. They are joyous. They are those human trees whose roots keep the soil of humanity stable. They are life. They are mostly dressed for the part and it goes up to 21:00 hrs. Atmosphere is joyous. The mood is for celebration. For those like me, listening to the radio in a sourdine mode, some offer Christmas classics or a good Christmas oratorio or Handel's or Vivaldi. Sometimes a broadcast from Radio Vatican. If you finish your shift early, there is usually a buffet at the garage of what's left of it. The social club throws a lot into that buffet and it is typically excellent. For the rest of the evening or night, it may resemble this John Fogerty song about Christmas Eve.

We've all heard the song without paying much attention. Deep but sad yet so revealing. It is about a former High School lover couple that meets by accident at a convenience store. It's December 24th, evening, and everything is closed. He tours the country as a musician, as he could be a bus driver, a tour guide, a pilot, as she got married to a professional that she doesn't exactly love anymore. Had she ever did ? Keeps her warm and dry. The discussion goes, and the souvenir reemerges of a life before life. Love and this youth insouciance. Innocence.

As destiny splits them and they both walk back to their lives, this beautiful snow that made the moment magic turned into rain. Rain: as this ugly thing punishes the beauty of life. Rain that turns dreams into nightmares.

Now, if you follow me, the clients taking a bus after 23:00 hrs are usually the ones for whom the snow turned into rain. The wetted by life. Those maybe going to work, Those with no place to go. No friends, no family, no life left. The NO crowd.

Transit is an essential service but let me tell you that if it could be stopped, every bus or train in the garage for a few hours once a year, it may save a lot of despair and depression. From 21:00 to 28:00 hrs. Just the time to celebrate with family or create one for whoever needs it in some of our locations. We could probably, at the transit society, throw a party for the left apart at a central Metro station.

Drivers seldom finish at the same hour. Small groups share the Christmas buffet. The guys (and the gals) are usually enjoying the meal in silence and reflection. Reflecting about those that did not make it to Christmas. Did not make it because of disease, accidents. Those that were celebrating with you many years ago that retired and died. The kid who got himself a brand new Triumph Bike that killed himself on the road. Three drivers died in motorcycle accidents this year.

In the ever prosperous and exciting private sector, they throw huge Christmas parties. It's a club, a society, or a ghetto in itself.

I once belonged to that club. The downtown crowd. Those of the exciting office tower jobs where the decisions are taken and you get lined up for the fast track and those Hot Wheels on those orange plastic racing circuits to be assembled.

Time passes. Tempus fugit. Priorities and realities changed.

The jobs changed, the friends changed. Kid grew and all that while you were giving your best years working. The bus crowd is now a little less festive. I am on the last leg of the trip and should pull in at the division at 22:00 hrs. I am up Park Avenue, it is well decorated. Countless souvenirs coming back to mind. The comforting humming of the engine, the slapping of the wiper and now, snow. The fat snowflakes.

As I was driving, I remembered some lyrics of John Fogerty's song. They are priceless.

The snow turned into rain.

Lousy weather, lousy time.

Time comes in, in 3 different theories or flavor. I say, Quantum Mechanic, Relativity, and Sting. They could also be seen as flavors. Flavor on which conscience and the wicked witch of introspection surfs one. The witch loves putting on her pointy hat, pointy shoe and take her flying broom to go introspect into your conscience at your most vulnerable moment. Christmas Eve of one of those, lending the flank moment of vulnerability.

Sometimes she takes along the three sisters of guilt vocal trio for the ride. As I write this, I can clearly visualize my older sister, Diane, at her desk in her law firm cabinet. Shoes, hat, broom and all the signature apparels.

But this life is on the road. The whole city is your office. You are part of the living city beat. You belong, but it has a cost.

And he said, "Son, this world is rough
And if a man's gonna make it, he's gotta be tough
And I knew I wouldn't be there to help you along
So, I give you that name, and I said goodbye
                                                     Johnny Cash

Was it on the day he died or was it just a retrospective of the career of Johnny Cash, but there was a full radio program with all of his songs with comments and anecdotes about the life of the country legend.

If I remember well, I believe it was on the day of his death. Not that I am a great fan, but some of his songs are dear to me. That evening I was working on route 17. The 17 has this thing as it follows above ground the orange metro line. As long as the Metro runs, it is gravy. If it stops: it is no gravy anymore. So, there I was working on that line on a rainy Saturday night. I don't remember when the shift started but I know it ended at 25:40. I started early in the morning and picked up that extra Overtime. I was asleep. Very much indeed.

On the second trip, I was early at Place St-Henri metro station as rain and wind shook the trees around and people had decided to stay home or take the Metro. This station is in an old neighborhood with plenty of mature trees and a dark area. Perfect to take a power nap and carry on. So I did. Pull the bus in a dark area. Turn off the engine. Put the In Transit sign on and push the seat back, pull the armrest down and unbuckle the seatbelt. I intended to leave this world for 15 minutes as I listened to the Johnny Cash retrospective. I listened to low volume, almost sourdine, but could distinctively understand the lyrics. It went on with a few jail type songs, and I slept well and profoundly. I was on cloud nine. It was all perfect. The sound of the rain on the bus roof, fresh wet air, a little summer breeze. At one point, I had a good laugh at a song about a man who named his boy:Sue. A boy called Sue, but life was good and I was still in the Morpheus arms and life was fine, and the rain was soothing.

After a while, the speaker said: and this concludes our 2 hours Johnny Cash retrospective special presentation.

At that point, my brain started to decompile this information. As it did years ago on a Belgian autobahn road, but this time around there were no pastry on the menu. Say... 2 hours. WOT??? You have been there sleeping—In Transit—for 2 hours and the panic seized me. How the hell could I have been sleeping on the job unnoticed for 2 hours? Looked at my watch. 23:10. Look at the schedule, next departure 23:20. Man. 10 minutes to pull to the stop, wake up, act natural and go back on the belt. I pulled at the stop. Nobody. Started the run and I picked up a handful of people here and there and had time to pick up a coffee on the road. Unnoticed by neither the supervisor nor the clientele as the district supervisor was stuck on an accident scene in east end, Pointe aux Trembles. I remember the panic, the damn moment, but most of all this song. A boy called Sue.

Route 15 north, service way. Summer. Corner Ferrier or by the Shell gas station. The Orange Julep sector. The street racer mecca.

On the pull in way to the garage to change a bus with a hydraulic problem. Loss of vacuum. I pulled in by this stopped at a red light vintage convertible Ferrari. Ferrari Red with this dude in Hawaiian shirt and fat glasses. Red light with radar. Nope, I will not paint it.

Vegas Harry in a red convertible Ferrari on the 15 collectors lane at Ferrier. Waved hand, salute and ! He did not B.S. me on this one, unless it's a lease or a stolen car. The man is charismatic, as all members of the happy-go-lucky tribe.

Eh Bert, what are you up to? Quit this lousy job, honest work is for chumps.

Given a few extra pounds and I could look like Minnesota Fat or Ralph Kramden here.

I'm going to Vegas, I got a couple of junkets here, Join us, I'll teach you the strings. I always loved his Minnesota fat spirit and freedom. Let's do an hustle or two.

It sounded, to me, as I remember from 1st grade, a class reenactment of the way Jesus recruited apostles as I remember clearly playing the part of St-Mark or St-Mathew as the Christ said: Drop your tool and come with me or was I the accountant. And well, it has been tempting to ditch it all. Follow me, I walk on water but it takes a lot of faith. Yet, Harry is no messiah. Nor was Mrs. O" Early for this reenactment idea, but the rules were meant to be broken on the other hand was of proverbial teaching.

Harry believes and preaches that working is for wuss and that man goes to the station of the cross every day until they eventually get crucified before going to sleep. By the end of life, someone dressed in a white coat just like Pilatus working for the health system will wash its hand, look at you and finish you off on morphine. Now, here are some of the stations of the cross. Career and work, marriage and family, kids, silent killer, work hazard and accidents, having its paycheck butchered before your eyes. Harry being Jewish makes me wonder where he got this New Testament profound knowledge, as he once mentioned: Jesus Christ is the best ever marketer of the universe.

On the same street corner the man who risks everything he owns and got lucky to go Vegas enjoy a careless life, a worker with wife, kids, dog, red fish, a mortgage, a Vespa, and a Saxophone who doesn't take many risks and is well in line for a lousy retirement watching grass growing in his backyard with his wife glued on TV and this other bum, who also risked everything and loss and is panhandling with a paper cup to bum a few bucks here and there.

But Vegas Harry is very much like my friend's day trader. (I also play the Ponies or the Penny stocks here and there) When they do a 30% scalp in 3 hours they rave about it on the net but never mention where the portfolio takes a... beating.

And why didn't Elvis end up marrying Ann Margaret. I would have.

Harry, those sunglasses.

Yeap!

They are women's glasses. Man, Harry ! You look like Jackie O on a sex change.

Harry took off in a screech on a yellow light corner of Ferrier and screamed to me, Remember Bernie, Life is a gamble, Get used to it. The damn thing is that Harry was right, and my life was somewhat put on hold the moment I stopped gambling with life.

I shook my head. Is my mind creating these outrageous archetype character like Vegas Harry and this man that pretend to be Padre Pio. How could they be so beyond any societal rules? So, one step beyond. But these guys surf through life like in a Mother Theresa's security bubble world where nothing could ever happen to them. Yet, they are solid, they occupy physical space and primordially they pay proper fare to the transit society

The detour instructions said Via Ste-Catherine. Left on Guy and Left again on R Levesques Boul, formerly known as

Dorchester Boul, and then, Left of Bishop. This area was beautiful 75 years ago, as city archives show. Not only were there large and wealthy mansions on the side of the mountain, were they as nice as the cocktail dress of those women and socialites gathering in them. Large house with terraces and porches with stained glasses and gingerbread trimmings. An era of beauty. Over there, where this anonymous glass building now stands was Her Majesty's theater, demolished to make space for progress in 1962 and on the corner a seafood restaurant: Les Jardins. Many anonymous tall apartment towers on the site where those mansions used to stand. Progress wave from a bald mayor who believed everything should be straight and square. As his sex life, I would bet. The key of progress was population density.

Les Jardins was an Art deco gray building with a vast parking lot to welcome the Duesies Packard, Ford of a distinguished clientele spending honest earn dollars for a sumptuous meal at the well known enseigne known for its beautiful neon sign. A nicely crafted neon red lobster. Well-balanced in an age of beauty. As time went by, wealthy families that owned those mansions disappeared one by one. Those beautiful home and land became abandoned land and there were no more socialites gathering on those porches nor beautiful cocktail dresses and long gloves. We did not preserve them as much as we demolished this old Ben's place and many more to make space for ugliness.

I still can see those people, or their energy shadows, going to the seafood place to dine in style and proper attire to end their evening at Her Majesty's theater in grace and beauty corner Guy and Dorchester as per this actual vision of this corner looks like a bunch of kids with torn jeans, washed colored hairs and crocs sandals skateboard their way down the street from Noodle Express to the Yellow pages building or into those condo towers

Where have we gone wrong? Where did the aesthetics of life went astray? Is this the meaning of progress, or have we started declining as per Weber Great Disenchantment theory? Maybe society's elastic has been stretched so far that it had snapped.

Oups, a red light. Numerous pedestrians around. No time to paint it.

Anyone ever had a look at Xaveria Hollander, who made a sulfurous letter in Penthouse magazine in the 1970? How did she look like this Xaviera baby? As Xaviera was into the erotic novel or letter, I chose this new concept: the erratic novel. As anyone ever told Faith Popcorn, to : get out your cocoon and get a life? What year did they retire the orange and grape Crush juice fountain on the snack bar counter? When was the last 45 rpm sold? Those too hot girls dressed in Victoria's Secret outfits in night commercials on TV, are they really spending their Fridays and Saturdays evening on the phone with strangers and having a good time? Is it all dressed up and nowhere to go? Chevy Nova. I lost track, but what was the last year they built the Nova. I remember those Corolla branded Novas, but I meant the real deal. The old coot hanging out with Babar the Elephant, riding around in his

1936 light blue Bugatti. Is she deaf, nuts, or just speechlessly oversexed? Makes you wonder about the moral of those old French children books.

Come to think of the three Georges I admire: Orwell, Carlin and Patton. They have the exact same message on the fate of humanity, but Carlin had a lighter and more Jazzy approach. Logically speaking, we are all doomed, but it should not stop you from having a good time and sleeping at night. As Adele would have said: Yeah right!

Not that it is somehow physical, but driving a large vehicle in a downtown setting takes a lot of energy as you have to be hypervigilant. It all happens between the shoulders and the head. A torso job, I guess.

And the yellow line on the roads get even thinner and when you start stopping on green light, looks at the flasher foot pedal in your personnel car and wave at bus driver on the road while you are off work. The way off moment when you are stopped at a traffic light and for a moment you really wonder, deeply, where and what you are, and looks inside the bus to find out a route number or a schedule. A clue of the where you are located in the universe. Inventory of life and equation time comes; Has Pokey ever given my cut of the deal. Was there a deal, or have I again been mesmerized by her boobs ?

I would love to hear Chuck Mangiones Feel So Good tonight. I miss home, my friend, my dead parent, Friends gone. As Francoise Hardy sang: La Maison ou j'ai grandi. Maybe the notes of that tune would bring me somehow home again. Home as this home of my youth, not this present one. Travelling through time and crossing the door of the family home, once more, seeing your mother in the kitchen cooking as if time had not past.

I was driving around with the door opened that evening. It cools the non AC bus and sometimes lets you have an ear drop at some curb discussion, namely by the goons hanging by bars and clubs. It lets you join in the rumor of the night. You become part of their secretive life. So, there I was at the end of that detour, approaching the final physical destination: Guy Concordia Metro Station.

Right there, on the corner of Ste-Cats and Bishop she stood, She must have fallen off a Vargas Calendar or a BW Femme fatale movie. She had the look, the dress, the walk and totting this huge wine glass around in tipsier or dancing steps. OK, there are a lot of pit lane babes, high-class prostitute and the normal crowd in town because of the event, but something is so damn peculiar about this wine glasses totting person that made me curious. She was walking with that nonchalant dancing step towards the intersection where I was stopped. I was trying to grasp the moment and figure out if the vehicle fits on that tight right turn. Was I just enjoying the beat of the summer in the city as I watched the PVM searchlight in the sky? Those search light that my old man feared so much.

As she walked in front of the bus, she dragged her index finger on the windshield as the hostess did in the Price is Right TV quiz game show. A local Vanna White thing. Smiling and still totting this gigantic glass of red wine. So, she approaches my wide opened driver window and said:

Hi, Good looking in a comedy tone voice. Low, sexy, husky voice.

As I am always willing to play the part in those encounters, I answered back:

Hi beautiful, what is a beautiful woman like you do in this part of town?

I am here for the race but I am just walking out of this great restaurant down the block. I had the most amazing lamb rack and a few glasses of red wine.

Damn, I thought, the Jardin has been closed so many years ago. I mean, decades here ? How strange !

Now, How would you like a glass of wine, my dear?

It is a beautiful and thoughtful offer but I work for stiffs and have to decline this wonderful offer as I am driving a city bus here and rules are strict about consuming alcohol while on duty, but yet, since it has been so graciously offer, I may have just a sip to taste it and share with you.

And so, she extended her arm to present me this glass of red wine, saying: Hold on, you never tasted such a great Merlot wine. It's heavenly. It felt like a dream but I often drive asleep so nothing to worry here. The bus knows the road.

She was right, that was or must have been the best red Merlot I had ever tasted and if I had taken the whole offered glass.

I said, Merci, Merci, it is a great attention from you and I must admit that your great beauty reminds me of an American actress of the 1980s. Stephanie?

Stephanie Powers, you mean. Yes, I know her very well ! And she said in broken French, Bonne Soirée a vous. She winked, turned her heels mounted on stiletto shoes and walked down Bishop street towards the bar and terrasse section.

I had that glass of red with Stephanie Powers, or was it the Hamilton stripper. I did have a glass of red wine with Stephanie Powers. It took 30 some years but it happened. This guy at Ye Old Brunswick was right. It did happen.

On the other side of time and the planet.

Early in the morning, on a hot day at a small village of Southern France, on the steps of La Mairie (City Hall) a cardboard shoebox of a foregone era with a pair of lost shoes, cleaned, shined and ready for a long voyage. Size 42. I wish I could supply you the sound and image special effect, as the morning would be sunny and quiet. A bit windy as I would also throw in church bells. Authentic church bells.

Time only exist as it is defined by sequences as music per the beat. There could be no creativity without memory or memories. A beat, a Jazzy beat.

As I moved the bus from Bishop to right Ste-Catherine st, I heard a trumpet or was it a bugle horn in the night. Is it Chris Botty or? No, that is the intro from Chuck Mangione's Feel so Good.

Very appropriate.

Sigh ! At the end of the day

Made in the USA
Columbia, SC
05 February 2023